Reflection

Reflection

DONNA RAHKOLA

TATE PUBLISHING
AND ENTERPRISES, LLC

Published by Tate Publishing & Enterprises, LLC
127 E. Trade Center Terrace | Mustang, Oklahoma 73064 USA
1.888.361.9473 | www.tatepublishing.com

Tate Publishing is committed to excellence in the publishing industry. The company reflects the philosophy established by the founders, based on Psalm 68:11,
"The Lord gave the word and great was the company of those who published it."

Book design copyright © 2016 by Tate Publishing, LLC. All rights reserved.
Cover design by Bill Francis Peralta
Interior design by Caypeeline Casas

Published in the United States of America

ISBN: 978-1-68352-257-7
Fiction / Romance / Historical / Medieval
16.06.09

To my Father, Jehovah, my God in whom I trust, the patience, love, grace, and forgiveness that You teach me through Your Word has truly changed my life forever! I look forward to what you have in store for my life. This is Your book and all glory and honor to You!

To my Lord and Savior, Jesus Christ, if it was not for You, I would still be that nervous, insecure person who would not step outside her comfort zone. You are the light of my life. Without You, nothing in life would be possible or worth it!

To my mom, Julie, your heart for people has always touched me. You want the best for their lives and shows. God has used you in mighty ways, and He is not finished! You are my best friend, and I will always cherish our relationship together, through the ups and downs! You are such a beautiful woman. Thank you for always encouraging me and helping me to find my way to Christ!

To my father, John, your loving heart and caring ways have always touched me. God has such a powerful testimony in your life. As you start your new journey in life, I know you are going to thrive and grow greatly in all that God has planned for you! You are such a wonderful, caring father. Thank you for helping me with everything throughout my life, for taking care of me and helping to build me up.

To my sister, Angie, you have always been and will always be close to my heart. Your innate ability to make me laugh when I am down has always lifted me. You are such a beautiful woman inside and out! I love spending time with you and enjoy your sisterly attention. You truly have a heart of gold for people, and I cannot wait to see what God has in store for you!

To my brother, Steven, your life is such a light for God. Thank you for being there to help build me back up and keep me going. You are a wonderful man of God and so very talented! I believe God is going to take your far in your own adventures and bless you in more ways than you can ever imagine!

To my sister, Karen, your heart for your family has always touched me. God has such wonderful plans for you! You have always been dear to my heart, and I greatly enjoy the times we have spent together. I cannot wait for the day when I will be able to fly to your home and see you more often. You have such a gentle and caring heart. You have always been easy to talk to and share anything without feeling judged. God has such great plans for your live, and I cannot wait to see what He has waiting just around the corner for you. You are so very talented in many different ways!

Acknowledgments

PUBLISHING HAD NEVER BEEN ON my thoughts when I started getting serious about completing my first book, *Reflection*. I want to thank my mom, Julie, who had been the first one who persisted me into allowing her to read it. The first time she read *Reflection*, it was halfway done with a lot of holes in the story, but she stuck through it and greatly encouraged me to continue working on the book so she could read it fully. She has been my push that I needed to get it completely written. She has been awesome sitting with me to proofread the edits and helping to make it flow better. I could not have done it without her. She is a blessing to my life, and I thank God for her.

I want to thank Tate Publishing for helping me to get my first book published. It has been a step of faith for me in trusting God. I look forward to what else is in store with more books to come.

I was inspired to write *Reflection* by the life of Queen Esther in the Bible, a Jewish girl who became queen at the right time to stop the killing of the Jews in the Old Testament. I tried to base the time period around what I figured the laws and life would have been somewhat like in her time. Though *Reflection* is completely fiction, Queen Esther and God (Jehovah) are very real and not fiction. Her life and faith in God stopped what could have been a horrible day for the Jews.

I want to thank Jehovah, my God, the Uncreated One. This story would have not have been finished without Your inspiration in my heart and the ideas that You would give me to help fill in the pages. Thank You for redeeming me through the blood shed by Your only begotten Son, Jesus, on the cross. Thank you for teaching me what it means to be beloved by You.

I also want to acknowledge the two horses that helped inspire the character of Mirage. To my Arabian horse Asher, his willingness and close developed bond with me helped to inspire the closeness and bond between Amore and Mirage. Asher would leave the other horses in the pasture to come and play with me. He would pick up on everything I would feel and react to it. Many times I could see the concerned look in his eyes when I would be feeling down, and then he would stick out his tongue or do one of his tricks to make me laugh. He is such an awesome blessing to my life. God, through Asher, has taught me how to be more confident in who I am. To my miniature stallion Soli, his confidence in who he is, inspired that sheer confidence in Mirage. His gentleness and tender approach with his foals inspired the relationship between Mirage and Shytoc.

Contents

Valley of Fernon

THE LAST RAYS OF SUNLIGHT sprinkled over the hillside hitting three hooded riders. A pure black horse pranced under his rider's command. Tossing his head, he chomped on the bite, demanding to be able to race ahead of his companions. Feeling the reins give a little, he bolted along with the others. Their strides trying to outpace each other, with a quick check from their riders, the horses settled into an easy lope, sending dirt flying behind their charging hooves. The rider of the black stallion slowed the excited horse to a stop as a town appeared on the horizon. The rider glanced toward the east, her eyes coming to rest on a large company of people leaving the town heading away from them. A couple of the horses stopped and whinnied making their riders look. The black stallion snorted but did not return the call.

"Good, Mirage," his rider praised softly, stroking his neck before glancing to her companions. "What do you think? I thought you said Tyron lived in a quiet town," she commented, glancing back toward the lit-up city. Music reached their ears along with the sound of laughter.

"This is the right town, Aishlin. Do you think it will be safe to arrive tonight?"

Aishlin's dark green gaze studied the party leaving the town's festival. They had captured the attention of four riders. "I think it would be best to continue on into the town, it might look suspicious if we did not. Besides, it looks like a celebration that we are arriving for, a good cover," she pointed out, looking back at the

11

older sibling, who nodded his head approvingly, his darker skin blending in with the night air.

His gaze shifted quickly to the youngest in the group. His horse danced to the side as he commanded, "Amore, ride between us." Vainer looked at Mirage's rider.

Hardening her gaze at her brother, Amore turned her stallion with a slight touch to the side, around her brother's tall bay, Mystique. Mirage tossed his head with impatience and flickered his ears back as he settled in between the two.

The town street was pack with people dancing and laughing. The horses slowly made their way through the crowd, their body pressing close together, smashing their riders' legs in. Mirage flickered his ears, drinking in the sounds and smells reminding him of their busy home.

"Vainer!" a loud voice called out from the crowd as a broad man waded his way through the people. He stopped next to Mystique. His smile was wide with joyous glee. "Welcome to my town! Let this fine young man take care of your horses and join the party!" he exclaimed, patting a young boy on the back. Amore slid down from Mirage and studied the boy. Mirage was picky about who he allowed to take care of him. Tossing his head up, the stallion reared as the young boy tried to take his reins.

"Sheza comesa!" Amore scolded the stallion, calming him quickly. Arching his neck back, he nibbled on her fingers before letting out a sigh. Taking the reins, Amore held them out to the frightened boy. "He's fine now. Here, take them." She smiled at him. The boy looked terrified but with a firm push from the governor he took the reins and began to lead the stallion away, his wide gaze continually glancing at the animal beside him.

"Your horse has quite the spirit," Governor Tyron commented, nodding his head in approval as they headed toward a large burning pile of brush.

"Yes, he likes to make sure everyone knows he's there," she teased, her eyes watching the dancing flames reach for the heavens.

"Governor Tyron, let me introduce you to my youngest sister, Amore," Vainer spoke suddenly.

Governor Tyron smiled at Amore and gripped both of her shoulders before hugging her tightly. Stepping back, he smirked and gave a quick wink. "It is good to finally meet my old friend's youngest daughter. Tell, does he talk about me often?" He whispered the last words.

Amore leaned closer to him, her curled dark brown, almost black, hair falling forward. "Only when he is not asleep." She smirked, making Tyron laugh. Offering out his arm, he looked toward cushions sitting on the ground not far away.

"Come and sit with me and tell me how your father is doing." The blazing fire warmed her skin as she took a seat next to the governor, her mind tried to think of what needed to be spoken. "He is most certainly well, Governor. He will be pleased to hear that you inquired of him." Governor Tyron raised an eyebrow as his smirk grew wider.

"Really?" he remarked. "That is well and good to hear…tell me some more," he asked, leaning closer. Amore smiled and shook her head. Her father lived a very busy life. One of the court and busy with the army. She began to tell him stories that the governor would enjoy while being mindful of those near them.

The governor could not contain his laughter as his hand slapped his large knee and he leaned backward, closing his eyes as he continued to laugh. Amore's eyes stayed hypnotized by the fire as she smiled at the fond memory of her father.

"That is wonderful! Your father was always the one to get into trouble, but he was always a popular one with officials and leaders. Very daring, unlike me." Governor Tyron winked.

Amore tilted her head slightly and studied the older man. Governor Tyron was stocky and very tall. To most he might seem daunting, but he had a very large open heart that could be filled with honey.

"I am sure that's not true, Governor Tyron. You must have had your wild adventures when you where younger!" She smiled. The man was incredibly nice. She could see why her father praised his name.

"Yes, my dear, but I did meet a certain beautiful woman that took me quickly away from all that in my early years. However, I am happy where I am. Now you should go find the other two and bring them to me." Governor Tyron patted her knee and looked around, his eyes searching the crowd.

The blaze from the fire kept her skin warm as she made her way toward the last spot she had seen her siblings. Thankfully they had already been on their way to see the governor when Amore found them.

"Governor Tyron would like to see you. I am going to check on Mirage to make sure he's settling in okay." Aishlin kept walking but Vainer stayed and leaned closer. His expression showed his discomfort and uncertainty of those around him.

"Just be careful, Amore, please," he begged, his eyes pleading before walking away, shifting through the crowd with ease and grace. Amore sighed and shook her head. Would she ever escape the continual worry of her family?

Slipping through the crowd of people, Amore made her way toward the horses. Her eyes instantly found her brother's bay that towered over most of the horses there. As she made her way closer, brushing her hand against a lean work horse, she smiled as her eyes came to rest on Mirage. She started toward him then froze as a figure shifted next to the stallion's head. Mirage gently nickered, nudging the person stepping away from the horse. Amore stood frozen, her eyes never leaving him as the dark, hooded figure placed his hand on his chest and bowed slightly before backing away, retreating from her presence. Amore raced after him, turning the sharp corner. Her hand grabbed the building, stopping her momentum. The figure galloped away on a white horse that glimmered in the moonlight. Mirage let out a high-pitched whinny in protest of her not coming to see him. Turning around, Amore glanced once more into the dark. The way that the person had moved, it had to have been a man. She was certain of it. Interest perked up inside of her as she walked back to Mirage. Nickers of greetings floated out of his nostrils, making them vibrate. Smiling, she rubbed the silky head as it bobbed up and down.

"If only you could talk, my friend," she whispered, then kissed the stallion between the eyes. Leaning up against the railing, Amore closed her eyes as a warm breeze danced around her, sending her long hair swirling around before coming to rest against her tan skin. The peacefulness of the air soaked away the cares of the day and allowed her mind to rest.

"Amore?" a worried voice called, breaking the stillness and jerking Amore from its grasp. Patting her horse on the shoulder, she started toward her sister who looked impatient. Her sister twitched as if something crawled across her skin, irritating her. "Come along, let us get back to the governor."

Taking Aishlin's arm, Amore allowed her sister to lead her back across the town square and to the men who waited, allowing Aishlin and Vainer to continue to watch her closely. Their discussions held little interest for Amore, as she watched the people of Fernon. They appeared more than relaxed and at ease as they laughed and enjoyed the splendor of the evening. It amused her, to think that here she was… sitting in a crowd of people, who were totally unaware of who she was. Nor were they ever to find out. Shifting her gaze back to those around her, Amore watched how effortlessly her siblings seemed to ease themselves into the town atmosphere. The only difference was the occasional fleeting look that Vainer would give. Content to listen to the conversations around her, her curiosity grew. The party continued to stretch into the night.

As the morning's rays began to break the hold of night, Governor Tyron decided it was time to head home. Amore dragged her tired body onto her horse as he pawed the ground angrily. Stroking his neck halfheartedly, she turned him toward the group as a younger version of the governor rode up beside her on a beautiful chocolate-colored horse.

"It would be an honor, Milady Amore, if you would ride with your sister and I." He smiled as his eyes danced like a wild wave free in the ocean. His smile was infectious as she felt a smile grow upon her own features and nodded her head. Governor Tyron's son was quite the conversationalist. Thankfully, he focused all of that attention on Aishlin, allowing Amore to enjoy the beautiful scenery of the Valley of Fernon. Her teal gaze tried to absorb everything in sight, from the flowers to the trees and the birds that chirped in the morning air. Eventually they settled on a dark horse that shifted in the distance, a man who Amore could not describe for she only caught a glimpse as the animal shifted, turning sharply on its hind legs and disappearing back into the forest. Blinking, Amore wondered if perhaps she was seeing things. The party she traveled with seemed unfazed. Most of them talked with their companions, while the rest dozed on their horses. Looking back at the spot, her mind began to churn. Perhaps she was too exhausted. Yes, that had to be the answer. Mirage began to tense underneath her and picked up his pace. Flustered, the stallion swung his head before bunching his muscles and rearing, his hooves staying tucked underneath him until they slammed back into the dirt. Scolding the stallion, Amore shook her head and sighed. She had to relax or Mirage was going to be a handful. Not that he was not already.

The trees remained on her right as the path widened to reveal a large stone wall that stretched for a long distance. Vines weaved their way along the wall as flowers began to slowly show their petals. As the front of the company suddenly turned into the courtyard, Amore felt her heart flicker at the beauty of the home of Governor Tyron. The brick home held the look of age, but yet still looked beyond splendid. The courtyard was cobblestone as it led to the steps of the home. Servants hurried out as the company dismounted and the horses led away. If Amore was not so exhausted, she would have wanted to explore. The rider remained at the back of her thoughts as she stepped into the grand hall. A large stairway immediately to the right led to the upper wing. A large hall went straight to the lower living and led toward the kitchen and dining hall. A servant guided Amore up the steps and toward the room she would be sharing with Aishlin. Her tired limbs ached for a soft bed to collapse on. Pushing the door open, the servant girl bowed her head low as Amore and Aishlin walked past.

"Simply beautiful," Aishlin remarked as she walked across the large room. A big bed sat in the middle with tall pillars reaching partway to the ceiling. A dresser sat across the room and past the bed with a large mirror reflecting her image, making Amore wince at the sight of her tired eyes. As she turned toward the east she smiled at the beautiful arched windows that held cushions allowing a person to sit and peer out at the world. Brushing aside the long purple drapes, she jumped as a voice asked.

"Would you like help out of your dress, milady?" the servant girl asked. Amore had already forgotten about her.

"No, thank you."

Aishlin lay on the bed, appearing to already be fast asleep. The servant girl started toward Aishlin when Amore checked her. "Leave her be, thank you, that is all." Bowing, the girl backed up to the door and closed it, leaving them alone. Slipping into a nightgown, Amore ran her hand along the silk as she pulled the drapes aside again to peer out. The view was simply breathtaking. Past the stone wall held the forest of tall trees that reached for the sky itself. Their leaves rustled and shimmered like crystal. The birds continued to chirp in the distance, welcoming the world to open their eyes and enjoy the day. A few wildlife mingled in the morning warmth, bringing a smile to Amore. Quickly stepping back, Amore's heart jumped. The same horse stood in the distance. Watching. Peering back out as the rider tapped the animal's shoulder, making the dark horse disappear back into the woods once more. Dropping the drapes, Amore stepped back and took a deep breath, her teal eyes shifting toward the thick wooden door. She was overreacting. The rider could mean nothing at all! Perhaps she should still tell Vainer. *Why? So he can lock me up?* Vainer would overreact. She loved her family, but they all worried greatly, and most often it concerned Amore. Sighing, Amore turned to the bed and climbed under the thick covers. As her eyes closed, the horse returned, dancing across her mind.

The evening sun fluttered into the room as a breeze brushed the currents aside. Amore drifted in and out of dreams. Sighing in frustration, she slid her legs over the side of the bed and climbed out, changing into a dress. Amore wrapped a shawl around herself and slipped out of the room in order to not wake up Aishlin. Hearing voices coming from the lower level of the house, Amore quickly found the others all gathered in a large room that held lavish couches and a beautiful stone fireplace.

"Amore, glad you could join us." Governor Tyron's wife Lady Reni beamed. The stout, dark-skinned woman glowed with admiration and love as she wrapped Amore into a hug. "My dearest girl, what does that father of yours ever feed you?" she exclaimed, stepping back to examine Amore's small frame. When you stand Governor Tyron and his wife together it will cause a person to take a second look. Lady Reni's head barely reached the height of his chest. His appearance could easily frighten people away, but the man had the heart of a child. Simple, pure, and loving. Governor Tyron could easily pick up his little wife and hold her in his arms like a young girl and it made Amore smile at the thought of him doing such a thing.

"Now, Vainer, I have been meaning to inquire on the meaning of this visit." The governor's tone grew serious at the high risk they all were taking. Vainer shared a look with the older man before Governor Tyron seemed satisfied for the moment. "Either way, we are most joyful to have the three of you. I dare say this is something that surprises me most wonderfully! We will take great care while you are here." The hidden meaning was clearly heard by the two siblings, though Amore was curious to know why Vainer did not answer the man verbally. The governor showed them around his home. A large doorway in the back led to a garden filled with flowers, a stone pathway stretched from here to stables beyond. The grounds of the home were surround by tall brick walls.

"What a splendid garden, Lady Reni," Amore praised as they walked around the pathways. The older woman beamed at her words before gently caressing a large flower that was almost the size of her very hand.

"Yes, I am quite proud of these flowers. Some of them are the biggest in the kingdom." She winked her hazel eyes as she said this, making Amore smile. It would be extremely hard not to instantly like Governor Tyron and his wife.

"You know, my dear! You and the cooks will have your time cut out for you with this one and her sister," Governor Tyron boomed as he put his arm around Amore's shoulders. His dark curly hair bounced in the breeze as he smiled down at Amore. "You look so much like your mother, Amore," he stated softly. "Just as tall, skinny, and colorful."

Amore's heart warmed at the thought of looking like her mother. No one ever said that before, of course anything was rarely spoken of her.

"Would you, Governor—"

"Tyron! Do not make me tell you a second time."

"Tell me about my mother." That made the big man lose his smile for a moment as his eyes saddened before he nodded.

"Later, I shall tell you later." Sighing Amore nodded her head and tried to smile as the hope fled from her. Everyone seemed to avoid the subject concerning her mother like it was the plague or something. At least he had not rejected the idea all together.

Her patience waned immensely as the day wore on, as she tried to hold on to her peace, waiting for when the perfect moment would arise to talk about her mother. Her heart yearned to learn more about her mother, and it frustrated her soul that nobody would let her. As Tyron finally settled in for the evening, and Lady Reni was showing Aishlin how to make a crumble pie, Amore decided that it would be a good time to again inquire about her mother from Tyron.

"Would you be so kind to tell me now?" Amore asked as Vainer and Tyron grew silent from their conversation. Vainer studied her quizzically for a moment before shifting his gaze to the governor.

"Tell her what?" he asked.

Tyron smiled as he leaned back in his chair and placed his feet on a table. A fire flickered behind him in the beautiful fire place that had been built by Reni's great, great grandfather. Also a governor of the beautiful Valley of Fernon. Home to Governor Tyron and his family.

"Your mother, God rest her soul, Riana, was a beautiful woman." As Governor Tyron started out, Vainer had just taken a sip and started to choke on his drink. Amore glanced at her brother. Seeing he was perfectly all right, she quickly focused back on the Governor's words.

"When your father told me about Riana, I thought it was impossible that any woman could make him settle down. She proved me wrong and I'll happily admit to it too." He laughed and shook his head his gaze suddenly shifted to Amore as he smiled deeply. "You are the spitting image of your mother, Amorita."

"I think that is plenty of stories for the evening. Thank you, Governor."

"Vainer!" Amore blurted, annoyed with her older brother who quickly shot her a harsh look. Laughing slightly, Governor Tyron smiled as he caught Amore's gaze once more.

"I think your brother is most correct. The evening is late. I shall tell you more another time." Offering his hand, Amore took it as he brought it to his lips and gave it a kiss. "Good night, young one."

Flustered and annoyed, Amore drifted out of the room and as she pulled the doors closed Vainer's voice reached her ears.

"I must request that you please do not tell Amore stories about her mother."

"There is no harm in it," Tyron contradicted.

Pressing against the door Amore tried to listen closely but Vainer must have sensed she had not moved on as he yelled, "Go to bed, Amorita!" Rolling her eyes, Amore made her way across the main hall until she reached the stairways. A large painting of Governor Tyron, Lady Reni, and their son, Tyson, hung on the stone wall, making her smile at the happy looks on their faces. If only she could be so happy. The room was empty when she entered it and took a seat at the window that overlooked the front grounds and gateway to the home. Amore stared out at the setting of the sun and smiled at the beauty of it all.

The door to the room opened and no one greeted her so it had to be Aishlin.

"What are you so smug about?" Aishlin asked, drawing Amore's attention.

"I did not know I was smug about anything," she retorted as Aishlin sank into a chair to begin brushing her long brown hair. Her green eyes flashed as a smirk crossed her lips. "I think the governor's home is very beautiful," Amore remarked, looking out the window again.

"Remember what we talked about before coming." Aishlin started again for the hundredth time that Amore had heard this statement.

"Oh please! I am not a child, contraire to yours and Vainer's beliefs. I know the dangers that we face if anyone outside of this home finds out where we came from," Amore exclaimed, resting her head against the brick wall behind her.

"No, not that!" Aishlin sighed and shook her head as she stopped her brushing.

"Really? Because most of the other things we talk about do not have anything to do with coming to Avalon," Amore insisted, staring Aishlin down until she relented and sighed.

"Just do not leave the grounds unless Vainer or I are with you. That way we will be most precautious."

Sighing, Amore figured it was best not to argue at the moment as Aishlin began to climb into bed. It had been a long trip for all of them but Amore's mind would not let her rest, at least not yet. Perhaps it was sheer exhaustion that kept her awake, though it seemed funny to her. If one was exhausted, they should be able to sleep a full nights rest. Twisting once more underneath the covers, Amore sat up and shook her head. It was hopeless, absolutely hopeless. Climbing out of the bed as she wrapped a shawl around herself, she settled on the window ledge and stared at the stars above as they glimmered happily before her until her eyes slowly flickered shut as the land began to lighten.

Making her way downstairs early the next morning, wonderful aromas drifted toward her from the kitchen. Lady Reni and some of the kitchen help where busy preparing breakfast.

"Good morning, my dear!" Lady Reni exclaimed as she quickly dumped more ingredients into a large bowl. "Care to help me make breakfast?"

Amore glanced around at the three other people in the already small space and smiled apologetically. "Maybe another time, ma'am. Do you know where my sister went off to this morning?"

Aishlin had been gone when Amore woke up, which was not unusual. Aishlin loved early mornings. It seemed to refresh her even if she had only gone to bed hours before the sun rose.

"Lady Aishlin went to town with Governor Tyron this morning, milady," a servant remarked when Lady Reni did not answer.

"Yes. She volunteered to bring some things back for me."

Sighing, Amore left the busy kitchen and wandered around the grand house before drifting toward the stables.

"Where are you off to this morning?" a voice asked her as she neared the doors to the beautiful stone stable. Her brother stood not far behind her as his gaze never relented.

"I want to see my horse, or am I banned from that too?"

Vainer smirked slightly. "Of course not. Just do not get any funny ideas." With that he continued on his path toward the west end of the property.

Mirage greeted her with a whinny and eagerly accepted the halter as Amore led him outside. The black stallion never really cared for being stalled but would have to put up with it for now. His forelock covered his eyes as he ripped at the sweet grass. She had hoped when she asked to accompany her family that she would get a little more freedom, but by the looks of it, that was not going to happen. She had been greatly surprised to find that their intentions were to come to Avalon and not their original destination. All the same, Amore had been eager to escape the watchful eyes of her father, teachers and guards.

Amore stayed with Mirage until breakfast was called. Vainer had things to do right away after and Aishlin had not returned back from town. Lady Reni was quickly busy with her flowers and the servants seemed to all but vanish for the most part of the day. As Amore sat near Lady Reni as she worked in her garden, her mind thought about the night before.

"Why do you think my brother does not want Governor Tyron to tell me about my mother?" she asked softly.

Lady Reni took a deep breath and sat up, her eyes solemn. "I think it pains them too much to hear about it," Lady Reni offered, and Amore smiled softly. It was a considerable answer but it felt like there was more to it. "I may not be a very good person to ask."

"Yes, but all the other times I have asked, no one will say a word concerning. They just tell me to let it go." Sighing, Amore got up and began to pace the garden. What was keeping Aishlin so long? Hearing the whinny of horses, Amore hurried around to the front side of the house. As she neared her sister's horse came into view and another. Governor Tyron's son, Tyson, about Aishlin's age, rode up on his horse. Amore remembered him from the evening past and smiled with curiosity growing on the inside of her. He was tall like Vainer but stockier. A smile similar to Governor Tyron's spread across his dark-toned face.

"Amore, you remember Tyson, Governor Tyron's son, from the other night," Aishlin introduced as a servant took their horses away.

"Yes, of course I do." Amore smiled, Tyson was very much a perfect version of his father. The young man easily wrapped Amore into a warm brotherly hug before stepping back and winking at her.

"You can imagine my surprise, Amore, when I saw your sister in town at the party. I haven't seen her since—"

"Tyson, enough. You're too much," Aishlin quickly cut him off, laughing, and started toward the house. Winking, Tyson offered Amore his arm as they followed after the older Divon sister.

The day drifted by horribly slow for Amore. Aishlin talked about how she ran into Tyson in the town square. Vainer and Tyson quickly grew into a deep conversation about things Amore had no interest in being forced to listen to, so she drifted toward the garden once more, and took a seat on the bench and stared at the stables. A terrible idea came to her mind which made Amore enjoy every moment of it. How she would follow through had to be timed perfectly. When Tyron returned home, Amore tried to ask him more about her mother but kept getting interrupted by others and the older man did not seem to want to approach the subject tonight. As Vainer walked out of the main room, Amore caught her brother by surprise.

"I am curious, brother, how you did not seem upset that Aishlin was in town alone. Yet if I walk to the stables you're curious to know what I am up to."

Vainer started to answer then stopped and studied her for a moment. If Amore really thought back, it was rare that Vainer ever had a guard follow him around and if Aishlin did it was only one or possibly two.

"She was not alone. The governor rode to town with her and then his son came back."

"That is not the point, Vainer," Amore exclaimed.

Vainer sighed and narrowed his green gaze at her. "It does not matter for what point you are trying to make. If Governor Tyron offered to take you to town, I would not care. End of discussion." With that his long stride carried him away.

It's highly unlikely that he would.

"Go easy on him, Amore," a deep voice said, startling her. Governor Tyron leaned up against the door frame separating the two rooms. "He is just protective over you." He gently squeezed her arm before walking past and to the stairs. Pausing at the bottom he turned to her and smiled. "It will all get better, you will see someday." Plastering a smile on her face, Amore wished him good night before heading to her room. Aishlin was already resting in bed when she entered and rolled over once to spot her before pulling the covers tighter around her shoulders.

"Do not be too long, Amore. You've barely slept these last few days," Aishlin commented before her voice drifted off into sleep. Tonight she would get no sleep, anticipating the time for the moon to reach its peak.

Oceans of Cavar

Glancing back at Aishlin, Amore tightened the cloak around herself before slipping quietly out of the room. The house was silent except for hushed voices that came from the back of the house. Vainer's voice along with an unfamiliar voice reached her ears. Watching the small flicker of candlelight from the archway, she slowly made her way toward the door. Freezing, she listened as a body passed in front of the light. A young girl about her age giggled and carried a pot of water across the opening before disappearing once more behind the wall. Sighing with relief, Amore smiled and slipped into the chilly air. Picking up the skirt of her cloak, Amore jogged across the courtyard to the stables. Her heart pounded with each step she took. Finally she would be able to take a midnight ride.

Alone.

No one else.

Just her.

The bright moon mixed with the burning torches allowing her to find her way easily. Glancing back at the house, Amore pulled the tall door open slightly and walked inside the dimly lit hall. Horses shifted in their stalls and a few nickered but one lasted the longest. Mirage's nicker overshadowed the others. His nostrils vibrated as he greeted her. Rushing to his stall and covering his nostrils with her hands, she whispered "Hush, my beauty. You might wake someone!" She stroked the stallion's head. Bang! Amore jumped and spun around, her heart racing as the doorway to the stables blew open and voices reached her ears. Unbolting Mirage's door and slipping into the corner of the stall, Amore tucked her knees to her chest and slid down the wall, trying to hide in the corner. Snorting, Mirage flickered his ears as curiosity filled his eyes. Nuzzling the top of her dark hair, Mirage snorted and swung his head around as a light flickered through the cracks in his door.

"Hello, boy, trying to sneak out are you?" The stable boy's voice grew quiet, as his fingers gripped the top of the door. "What are you hiding?" His voice grew curious as the door groaned as he started to pull it open.

I forgot to lock the door! Amore wanted to smack her head. Looking up at her horse, she crawled closer to him along the wall.

"Deamo!" she whispered fiercely. Mirage flickered his ears then tossed his head, striking out with his front foot. Snorting, the stallion fake charged the door and reared, his legs tucking along his belly.

"Deamo!" she instructed again, smirking as the stallion responded perfectly. Mirage flattened his ears and lunged while still in his rear. The man stumbled back, slamming into the stalls behind him. The horses jumped in surprise, adding more noise to the chaos. Landing, Mirage snorted and shook his head. Her stallion's halter glimmered in the small streak of moonlight that shone through the door. Amore glanced around the corner. The stable boy was busy trying to calm down the excited horses. Taking her chance, Amore jumped onto Mirage's bare back. With no saddle or reins, she crouched on his neck.

"Let's go," she whispered, patting his neck. Mirage did not hesitate, jumping forward. The stallion turned quickly. Picking his feet up in a high trot he proudly pranced his way down the aisle and out the door just as the stable boy and other servants returned and his shouts followed them into the night. Sitting up Amore tapped her horse into gear. The stallion bolted from a trot to a gallop, brushing past the guards that rushed toward her.

Hitting the open plain, she held on tight to the stallion's thick mane as he extended his stride, enjoying the fresh air that flew past them both. Amore's heart felt like it would burst with joy, her eyes stayed closed with tears from the wind running down her tan cheeks.

"Kakosa!" she shouted past the wind.

Obeying, Mirage slowed his joy run, settling back to a walk. His flesh was warm but no sweat covered his hide. Trees were starting to pop up across the horizon as he lifted his head high, drinking in the air. Snorting, he shifted turning toward the north.

"What is it, Mirage?" Amore asked, stroking the stallion's neck, fingers mixing with his mane.

Pawing the ground, Mirage bobbed his head up and down but didn't move. Trusting her horse, Amore allowed him to lead her where his heart desired. It took a couple of minutes at a walk but the sound of waves crashing against rocks brightened her mood even more, Amore had never been to the ocean before. Emir was surrounded by other countries and a large mountain range, where the coast of Avalon touched the untamed beautiful mass of water.

"Some things have to be seen to see the true beauty of it all." She soaked in the sight of the moon glistening off the waves as they crashed to the sandy shore. Amore quickly lost track of time and where she was. Shifting, Mirage let out a whinny that jerked her back into the present moment. Mirage kept his head turned watching a horse that stood in the distance. The moonlight hit the animal's white coat, making it look like a rose against a burned forest. The horse pranced under its rider's command, its mane blowing around its neck as it cantered toward her. Amore instinctively started to try to pull Mirage back into the woods but her hand grasped at nothing, making her remember her earlier decision. Her eyes searched the hooded rider and the animal. The horse's movements and attire suggested that it was either a warhorse or a prized animal by a royal or king. Amore's heart raced as her stallion refused to respond to her commands. He perked his ears and snorted before finally stepping forward.

"No! Back to the woods!" she hissed under her breath. The white horse was picking up speed until it shot right past, her continuing its gallop down the shady beach. Amore stared in shock. They wanted a race? Mirage pranced underneath her, eyes staring after the horse. Before she could even react the stallion bolted, unsettling Amore. Grabbing the stallion around the neck, she held on for dear life. Pulling herself back up, the stallion had his ears perked as he surged after the white horse. His legs pounding the earth sending shock waves into Amore's legs, Mirage never disobeyed her before which intensified her curiosity. *There's no stopping him now so might as well enjoy myself and not worry*, she thought. Mirage was gaining quickly on the horse but was also running out of room to run. Having already been halfway between the two ends, Mirage did not have much time to shorten the gap between the two. Coming up alongside the horse's hindquarters, his ears flattened in determination as he stretched his legs out farther, his muscles working hard to propel even more speed.

Amore's excitement picked up as her stallion came alongside the animal. She grinned as Mirage started to pass the horse but her smile quickly faded as the rider's hand reached out and took hold of the glimmering halter that hung around the dished black head. Sitting up suddenly, the rider pulled up his horse, forcing Mirage to slow alongside the animal. Furious with herself and the other rider, she held on to Mirage's mane and glared at her captor, not realizing her hood had fallen off during the race.

"Kindly let go of my horse!" she demanded, her voice anything but pleasant.

The rider's face was hidden in the midst of shadows and the hood that still remained upon their head. "I would not speak to harshly to the man who just saved your life." The man's voice was low as a smile spread across his shadowed face. Amore pretended to be shocked about his statement when she wanted to smack herself for making a stupid mistake. *Wait, the riders is...* Amore studied the man. What should she do? Panic or be reasonable? Maybe Aishlin and Vainer were right to watch over her so closely.

Or Amore should just work this out on her own. She was never going to get another chance to actually do something for herself.

"Saved my life?" she asked.

"I would not go that far." The words were soft.

"Meear!" she demanded. Mirage's ears flickered before his muscles shifted suddenly under her legs. Hanging on with her knees, Amore held on tight as her stallion reared. Amore figured the man would have let go. Instead Mirage pulled the man with him as he swung around, hooves pounding into the ground, unseating Amore onto his neck. Her heart pounded as she pushed herself off the stallion's neck and looked at the man lying on the ground. Patting her horse, she smirked. "Good boy. You see, I have him perfectly under control," she commented smiling. Hearing the sound of pounding hooves she looked toward the man's horse as it galloped away, bucking every now and then before disappearing into the trees.

The man sat up and brushed his arms off. The moonlight sprinkled light on his face and for the first time Amore was able to see him clearly. Enough that it made her blush and glance away to regain her thoughts. Looking back at him she tilted her head slightly preparing herself for anything he might say or do but nothing prepared her for this.

"You are very beautiful up close." His voice sounded genuine and soft. His eyes studied her, making her feel even more uncomfortable. By the looks of it, he had to be a lot older than her or older than how she felt when he studied her like that, making her heart jump like it did when her mother gave her Mirage when she was a little girl.

"Thank you." Amore's words came out quiet as the man slowly stood and brushed himself off. Gently patting Mirage's neck, he glanced back toward the woods where his horse had disappeared before looking back at her. His hand lingered on the black silk hide.

"I must be going."

Tapping Mirage's side, the stallion turned to head back down the beach. His whole body jerked to a stop as the man grabbed onto his halter again, holding him there.

Amore closed her eyes and took a deep breath. "Please let go of my horse, I really must be on my way," she said as politely as she could at the moment. The man only smiled, and brushed his hand along Mirage's shoulder coming dangerously close to her knee. Amore's heart hit another note as something glimmered under his cloak. *Sword!* her mind screamed. Amore carried nothing to protect herself. Her mind seemed to freeze on that thought that she missed his words, blinking she focused back on him.

"You're not going to leave me here after pulling me off my horse, are you?" His words seemed to tease, but Amore was not sure of the situation anymore. Her hair started to blow in the wind that was picking up from the north, causing her to glance back down the beach at the open land and sky as dark clouds started to roll over the stars.

"Well," she started and glanced down at him, her words froze in her throat as their gaze locked. Amore was getting sucked in by the man and too quickly. "Get one thing straight, sir, you are to keep your distance." Picking up his hand, she pushed it off her horse's neck. "And you are to stop grabbing my horse's halter whenever you please." She glanced toward his hand. "If you fail these things, be sure my horse is strong and is trained very well." Amore attempted to sound affirmative. As she said those words, Mirage swung his head around and snorted before nudging the man's muscular shoulder.

"He seems rather dangerous." The man smirked, stroking the soft silk on Mirage's forehead. Amore was surprised at her stallion warming up to him so quickly. "May I at least know one thing if I am to respond to your demand?" His voice was light. Amore could not help but relax slightly. "May I know your name?"

"Amore," her voice responded before her brain kicked in. Amore glanced down at Mirage's silky mane before turning her full attention back on him, feeling quite childish in his presence. "I am called Amore." She twisted her fingers into Mirage's mane to keep them from fidgeting in his presence. Her father had always told her as a child to never fidget especially in public.

"That was not so hard, was it?"

Amore stayed quiet for a couple of moments before looking back at him.

"I am called…Xeris."

Amore frowned slightly. Why had he paused before saying his name? Xeris stepped closer until he was standing beside her.

"Are you going to let me up?" he asked.

Amore stared at him in surprise. "I asked for you to keep your distance, sir. We did not discuss that you'd be riding my horse." The hair on the back of her neck stood on end as adrenaline rushed through her body. The thought of how easily he could pull her off of Mirage kept running through her mind. He laughed and gestured toward the sky.

"We'll never make it out of this storm if I walk."

Amore looked up as the clouds rumbled above her. He did have a point.

"I, I…" her words refused to come out of her mouth.

Xeris's hand came to rest in front of her on Mirage's shoulders. "I swear, Amore, on the grave of my father that I will not hurt you."

Amore studied him before glancing back down at her horse as he nibbled at the man's cloak. She trusted Mirage and Mirage seemed to trust this man.

"Okay." Her words were soft but they had come out and she could not take them back now.

What am I doing? she thought, as her heart pounded against her chest. Mirage stood still, allowing the extra weight on his back. Amore glanced down as his arms slowly wrapped around her waist. Her skin felt like it was on fire! Taking a deep breath, she tapped Mirage's sides. "Let's go, boy," she whispered. The stallion sensed the storm and immediately bolted into a canter. As they dodged trees and rocks, Amore had to admit that Xeris was a good rider. He stayed with the horse's motion really well. Whistling to her horse, Mirage picked it up a notch as they hit open land, his hooves pounding into the dry mud as rain started to fall hard and fast. Her vision blinded, she trusted her horse and let him direct their path. The rain continued to hammer the earth as the minutes seemed to fly by. Amore felt Mirage shift slightly and make a wide arch as if to head back, or were they going the same way? *This is not good at all. We are lost.* Trees popped up all around her. The thick branches and leaves held off the heaviest of rain that only a few droplets made it through.

Amore ducked, laying against the stallion's neck as he made his way under a willow tree. The air was cool but at least they were going to be dry. Sitting up she smiled, forgetting about Xeris for those couple of moments.

"Good boy," she praised the stallion, stroking his slippery neck.

"You have one fine animal, Amore," Xeris commented.

Glancing back, she smiled slightly. She could feel herself warming up to him. In a way, Xeris was a lot like Vainer. Sliding off the stallion, Xeris pushed aside the long weeping willow branches as thunder rumbled in between the sound of pouring rain. They would be going nowhere for now. Swinging her leg over Mirage's neck, Amore started to slide off her stallion when Xeris caught her midair. Surprised, Amore grabbed his forearms to steady herself as her eyes locked with his deep blue gaze. She felt herself being slowly lowered to the ground as her hands lingered on his arms. He appeared to be quite the gentleman. Smiling slightly, Amore was finally able to break his intense gaze. Being on the same level as Xeris, she felt her heart skip a beat as she realized how much taller he was than her, not to mention stronger. Her head barely came to the top of his shoulders. Letting go of his arms, she stepped back and smiled politely, trying to force down the heat that was rising to her cheeks before turning to Mirage.

The stallion had moved off a little ways and stood napping by the thick tree trunk. Without really thinking, Amore pulled off her wet cloak, her soaked hair falling down to the middle of her back. Amore felt his eyes boring into the back of her head. Realizing what she did made her heart jump but she refused to show it, fearing her heart might explode. Her dress hung loosely around her shoulders, the once-soft silk now drenched and clinging to her skin. Taking her hand, Amore ran it over Mirage's coat, hoping to shed some of the water that clung to him and to force her mind off of the man with her.

Daring herself to glance back her eyes quickly found Xeris's back to her. He had removed his top coat, revealing the sword that hung loosely along his hip. His stance was straight and he stood with a dignified sort of air to him. Shifting suddenly, Xeris turned around, making Amore quickly look away and study the trees. She had always loved these trees. They had been fun to hide and play under back when life was filled with only joy. Back when her mother was still alive. Her body shook with nerves as she slowly sat down next to the trunk and rested against it. Amore cautiously glanced at him as he made his way closer and took a seat near her. His face was defined and soft. In the faint lighting, she could see his skin had a tan color to it.

"If I may, what where you doing on the beach in the middle of the night?" she asked, carefully watching for his reaction.

He glanced over at her and a smile slid across his mouth. "I think I should be the one asking that question," he teased, his voice holding a hint of laughter, putting Amore at ease. "My horse Leah likes to stretch her legs after a long ride. What about you, Amore? What were you doing on the beach, alone, at night? Running away?" He hit the nail on the head. She was not running away for good, just wanting a breath of fresh air and then she planned on going back.

"I needed some fresh air," she replied, smiling softly as her eyes grew heavy, threatening to close as exhaustion from the trip finally took hold. "You know my brother Vainer is probably going to kill me when I get back," she admitted, studying the darkness around, her mind too tired to comprehend her words. "He is very protective."

"Get some rest, Amore." Xeris gently placed his coat over her. The soft sound of the waves crashing against the sand and rock mesmerized her mind as the moon glistened off the water. The beautiful noise of the waves was like nothing she had heard before. Amore smiled and rested her head back against the tree as sleep took hold.

The hard ground began to make her restless. Jerking awake, Amore glanced around before letting out a sigh and looked at the man beside her. His arms where crossed, as his head rested back against the tree. The sound of rain began to entice her back to sleep, as she wrapped the coat around tighter herself.

⌘

The beautiful morning light hit her face as a gentle breeze lifted the dreams from her. The events from the night before slowly unfolded in her mind. Glancing around the small opening of the willow tree, her heart stopped. Mirage was nowhere to be seen and Xeris was gone. Pushing herself up, Amore scrambled to her feet, oblivious to the fact that his coat still hung loosely around her shoulders.

"Mirage?" she called, hoping her stallion would come. Brushing her long hair back, she realized that she had taken it down last night before heading out riding. Aishlin had constantly instructed her that a lady never has her hair just loosely down. If it was to be down it must be done correctly to be beautiful, not to be another commoner. Quickly tying her hair up into a bun, she pushed the willow branches aside and grimaced at the brightness of the sun. Mirage's black hide gave him away quickly as he grazed happily in a small opening she had not seen during the night. Shaking her head, she smiled and started toward her horse. He did not even bother to lift his head as she approached.

"Mirage, you almost gave me a heart attack." She sighed, stroking his soft, velvety neck. Glancing around, Amore looked for Xeris. "Wonder where he went?" she commented softly to her horse. It was probably best that she did not see him ever again, besides her actions and words toward him. Amore had been anything but a lady of the court of higher rank and blood. She had acted more like a teenager with no care of what was required of a lady, to talk to any man for that fact. Something she had often heard her father, Aishlin, and Vainer say many times.

"What man will want you, Amore, if you keep speaking so boldly to them?" seemed to be Aishlin's favorite sentence.

Amore knew that down the line it was for the best to change the way she behaved, but for now all she had wanted was her freedom. Yet the only thing that crossed her mind was how to get home. Feeling a tingling sensation shoot down her back, she tensed as arms wrapped around her unexpectedly and yanked her backward. She tried to scream out but a hand covered her mouth and a familiar voice sent both relief and chills through her "Hush." Xeris whispered and continued to pull her into the shadows of the woods and behind more trees until he pushed both of them onto the ground. Amore tried to struggle against his arms but failed horribly. Peeling his hand away from her mouth, she took a deep breath.

"Will you kindly explain what you are doing?" she hissed, trying her best to look at him. Xeris placed a finger over his mouth and pointed to where she had just been standing. Mirage lifted his head and snorted loudly, looking away from their direction. Bolting suddenly, he ran disappearing into the trees. The sound of thundering hooves and horses snorting shortly followed him as a band of hooded men galloped by chasing her stallion down. Amore felt her heart stop. *What have I done?* Amore's horrified mind screamed at her. She lay there frozen. She should have listened to Vainer about not leaving the safety of a group. Amore wanted to kick herself. Letting out a harsh laugh, she felt a tear slip out. Xeris slowly pulled her around so she was facing him, making her realize that he was still holding her close to him, extremely close. His un-shadowed eyes seemed to look right past her and into her heart and soul.

"Are you okay?" he asked.

Amore shook her head and studied him. "This was a horrible idea to go off on my own, I should have listened to my brother." *I'm doing it again!* Amore just kept digging a deeper hole for herself. *Stop talking to this man like you've known him since you were young.* Amore watched him getting sucked into the moment then the moment ended.

"Do you always do what your brother tells you to do?" he asked suddenly, surprising her.

Amore stared blankly at him as her mind wrapped around his question. "No, I do not." Amore pushed him away from her and got up. Brushing her dress off of any dirt and dust, she glanced at him. "Thank you." That's all that would come to her mind right now. She was in way over her head and did not know what to do next. Her family usually had guards who followed her so if something had ever happened like this they would take charge. Instead she was stuck with a man she barely knew with no horses to speak of.

"I think it is about time I returned home," Amore said, watching Xeris pick himself up off the ground. "It was a pleasure meeting you." Her voice did not sound like her own, sounding instead like Aishlin speaking for her. Turning around, Amore started to walk.

"Do you know which way to go?" Xeris asked from behind her, making Amore annoyed inside.

"Of course I do!" Her voice snapped a little too hard that it made her flinch. *Good one*, her mind commented.

"Then lead the way, Milady." He just smiled, appearing to enjoy this a little too much. Turning around, Amore walked off frustrated with herself and him. Amore was not sure about the culture of this country, but in her own it was severely frowned upon to show so much emotion and boldness toward any man that was not related or a husband. Frankly if she thought about it, it was frowned upon to even speak to a man unless introduced to them by a close friend or family member. Amore knew that she was burning the whole book on how to be a proper lady. When she returned to father she would take her studies more seriously, maybe.

The silence that filled the air around her was horrible, it was making her mind run wild about how mad Vainer and Aishlin were going to be. How in the world was she going to explain losing Mirage and being gone this long? Glancing around, Amore felt fear trickle through her. The landscape all looked the same, and the trees covered the majority of the sky keeping her from seeing where the sun was throwing off her sense of direction. Sighing, Amore glanced down before looking back at Xeris who silently watched her struggle, never saying a word. Slowly turning toward him, Amore knew she had to ask, no, beg, him for help.

"I may have lied to you." *Why did I choose those words?* she wondered. Tilting his head Xeris looked surprised.

"Really, in what way?"

He was tormenting her for sure! Amore took a deep breath. *You have already been way over the line with him already so just enjoy it,* she thought suddenly.

"More than you will ever know." Smiling softly, Amore shifted and looked the way she had been heading. "I do not know where I am going; I am not able to see the sun well enough that my directions are a little mixed." *No one will ever find out about this!*

Chuckling, Xeris stepped closer, making Amore's heart leap, startling her that she stepped back slightly.

"Come on." Taking her by the hand, Xeris led her in the same direction she had been heading. Ducking underneath a branch, Xeris led her up a small hill then kept walking, releasing her hand. Amore's face was on fire as she felt her hand drop to her side and followed the man. Her eyes bored into his back. He walked with pride and a long stride, making Amore study him a little more. He carried himself like that of a noble, and yet that of a soldier. His hand rested on the hilt of his sword, appearing to be simply out of habit. Suddenly Xeris looked back, catching her watching him that their eyes connected and he smiled. *He is not like any man I have ever met,* she thought suddenly, smiling back at him as he looked back the way they were heading.

"Do you just have the one brother?" he asked as they walked along, the ground slowly starting to dip.

"Yes, I have only one brother," Amore replied, picking up the hem of her dress, realizing then how dirty her dress had gotten. "Oh my," she stated out loud.

"What?" Xeris asked, his voice catching slightly as he whipped around, drawing his sword slightly, making Amore blush again and look away.

"My dress is filthy." Amore felt a smile start to creep on her face but nothing could prepare her for what Xeris did next. Stepping forward he brushed the strand of hair away from her face and smiled.

"I think you look…very filthy." He laughed then and glanced off to the side.

"Ouch, that's not fair. You do not look so wonderful yourself," Amore retorted. Worry filled her as a weird look passed over Xeris face. "Xeris?" she asked, looking around. Grabbing her by the hand suddenly he raced downhill, pulling her along, her heart flying. *Something has to be wrong!* she thought as she tried her best to keep up with him. Bursting from the trees, Xeris wheeled on her, making her freeze in her tracks and let out a scream as he threw her over his shoulder. Her eyes briefly caught the sight of the beach that they had been on the night before, before feeling the cold rush of water surround her as Xeris crashed into the water. Gasping for air as her head came up, Amore quickly brushed the water away from her eyes.

"You!" she yelled, furious. "You made me think someone was after us!" She threw water at him as a laugh came out of her mouth and Xeris grinned. His dark hair spiking in the water.

"You're welcome." He gave a small bow as best he could while maintaining swimming and making her mind flash back to the other night.

"That was you." She commented, staring at him astonished. He let out a small smile and nodded his head the sun sparkling off his eyes. *The sun!* she thought, looking up. It was well past noon now which was not good at all. Amore knew her way from here and she really did not want to face Vainer and Aishlin yet. Looking back at him she smiled sadly and started swimming back to shore. Hitting the beach she walked out of the water and looked back at him. "Thank you, Xeris, for everything." Before her mind could scream at her insanity, Amore gently kissed him on the cheek. She could tell she took him by surprise as well. Stepping away she turned and disappeared into the trees where it had all started. Her heart was pounding but she could not stop the smile that had spread across her face, something that she was not going to let Aishlin and Vainer see.

The land was beautiful as birds chirped happily around her and fluttered from one tree to the next. It was almost peaceful and serene, making Amore relax as she stopped to pick a flower and smell it. Part of her did not want to return back to her siblings, yet she knew it was the best thing to do. Humming to herself as the warmth of the noon day dried her clothes and hair, she was surprised and relieved that she spotted no one else, and it appeared that Xeris had not followed her as far as she could tell.

The familiar brick wall of Tyron's large house showed in the distance and with every step closer she dreaded what was going to happen next. Taking a deep breath, Amore walked through the front gates, she did not make it to the steps before Aishlin came flying from the house and crashed into her, her arms wrapping tightly around her.

"Amore, thank the Lord!" she cried, pushing Amore back. Aishlin studied her with a smile on her face then it changed to the Aishlin Amore knew and quite often feared. "You have a lot of explaining to do, young lady! But first we need to get you cleaned up and someone needs to let the men know that you're back."

After that everything was a blur. The two hours' worth of pampering, then another three hours of Vainer pacing back and forth asking her question after question and a lot of raving of how stupid she had been to pull a stunt like that. At the end of the day and in the peace of the room to herself, Amore was grateful she had not told them about Xeris. He would always be a secret of hers that she will take to her grave. Amore trusted that she would probably never see him again. She only wished Mirage was here so she could at least know he was safe. Sleep fled her once more that night. Aishlin had kept checking on her and it was not until Amore finally convinced her that she was not going anywhere that Aishlin finally fell asleep. Sitting on the window ledge, Amore stared out into the starry night sky. She hoped her stallion was safe and on his way back to her and she could not help but let her mind wander back to Xeris as a faint smile came across her face and her eyes slowly closed.

"Amorita Deandre Aleara Divon!" her sister's voice made her blink and let the sunlight seep into her eyes. She had fallen asleep next to the window and the sun's early rays filled the horizon. Climbing off the ledge she drowned out her sister's lecture on her behavior. Sitting down at the chair next to the bed, she curled what she thought was a blanket around herself as Aishlin started brushing Amore's long, wavy hair.

"Are you even listening to me?" she asked, making Amore jump.

"What?" she asked, glancing back. Aishlin shook her head in disapproval then she suddenly stopped and fingered the blanket around Amore.

"Where did you get that coat?" Aishlin asked suddenly, pulling it free from Amore's shoulders. Spinning around she stared at Xeris's coat, then she looked at her sister, as panic began to fill her.

"I must have found it in the stable last night." She reached out and snagged it from her sister's hands. Holding out her hand, Aishlin gave her a look that suggested Amore was starting to lose it.

"We shall find who it belongs to then give it back," Aishlin instructed.

Amore narrowed her eyes at her sister and shook her head. "I took it, I will find the owner," she commented, turning away from Aishlin.

"You know who it belongs to, do you not?" she asked, stepping closer.

"It's none of your concern," Amore retorted. Aishlin's eyes narrowed in determination, making Amore sigh and roll her eyes. "Yes, I do know who I got it from and I will return it." *Probably not.* Thankfully the servants saved her as a knock on the door filled the room telling them that breakfast was served.

"We'll talk about this later; now let us not hold them waiting. Get dressed and meet me downstairs."

Amore was quite relieved at how welcoming Governor Tyron's family and servants were. Everyone seemed to fall into easy conversation. Thankfully no one asked her any questions about where she had gone or why she did such a stupid thing. Vainer shifted his gaze at her a few times but was easily distracted by Tyson.

The rest of the day, Amore spent mostly in seclusion as she desperately wanted to avoid her sister at all cost. Avoid the unwanted questions, that no doubt, eventually she would have to answer. *I need to thank Tyson later for distracting Aishlin,* she thought as she spotted her sister and the young Tyson walking along the outer wall, talking quietly to themselves. A warm breeze blew around her bringing her the scent of the flowers making her smile. She wished that the gardens at home were as well tended to like Lady Reni's.

❦

As the sun began to set that evening, Amore walked alone in the garden. Since her little adventure, a sentry was posted outside the stables for now. A cool breeze from the ocean swirled around her, picking up her curled locks and resting them across her shoulders.

"A wildflower," a voice said, surprising her. Lady Reni moved away from the burning torches and toward her as she smiled looking at the flowers. "That is what I consider you, Amore. You are planted between so many beautiful flowers but every one of them looks alike. While you, my dear, stand out against each one of them, and not in a bad way." Her hazel eyes twinkled as she looked at Amore with adoration. "Do not tell your father this but you are like him in so many ways." She smiled. Amore stared at the beautiful soft pedaled rose before her.

"I know what I did was not the safest thing to do."

"Hush, I want to hear nothing of it. You can only cage a bird so much before you end up destroying it." Taking Amore's arm gently, Lady Reni led her toward the house. She stopped short and stared in through the window spotting her family inside. "You know what I see when I look at the three of you?" Amore had no answers to give her and she apparently wanted none as she smiled softly. "People who love each other dearly and do not often know how to express it." Patting her arm, Lady Reni continued on into the house, leaving Amore alone once again. Conflicted and slightly confused by her words, Amore's mind pondered on the past days' events and a smile crept onto her face. "Do not forget, tomorrow we are attending the party in Fernon."

Amore loved town parties. It always meant a good way to get to know people without anyone asking why you're talking to a certain person. The small town had been packed all day with everyone from dukes down to the common people of Avalon. In the bustle and dancing crowd, Amore gave up the fight to figure out where Aishlin and Vainer had gone and let herself be pushed by the crowd until she ended up toward the sides. Sighing with relief, Amore leaned up against the wall of a house and smiled at how crowded the town was. She was so absorbed into the music and dancing that she did not feel the hand until it was too late. A strong arm wrapped around her middle and a hand covered her mouth so she could not scream out.

"A lady should not hit people, Amore." The faint, familiar voice reached her, making her relax and stop her struggle. His breath sent chills down her neck. Letting go of her he grabbed onto her hand and started to pull her back. "Come with me." His voice was quiet and hurried. Amore glanced at his shadowed features and back at the crowd before turning to follow him down the darkened alley, the moons light barely reflected in between the buildings. Amore had to pick up her dress as Xeris picked up speed.

"Xeris, where are we going?" she asked, feeling very unladylike running like this, holding hands with a man she had only met once before. Finally he pulled her to a stop just before the woods. The faint breeze sent chills down her, reminding her she had left her shawl behind.

The darkness held secrets that would always be unknown to her. Confused, Amore turned and looked at Xeris who motioned behind her. Turning around, Amore felt her heart stop then start racing with excitement. The tall stallion's hide glistened in the moonlight as he trotted proudly closer, his nostrils quivering a hello as he shoved his head into her arms. Amore held tightly onto Mirage's neck, her hands brushing against his new decorum that covered his neck, saddle, and head. Finally letting go of her horse, she turned around and smiled softly. Xeris must have gone through a lot to get Mirage back.

"Thank you, Xeris, I will repay you," she reassured him. Xeris glanced down and looked at her again, Amore felt uneasy at the look in his eyes.

"Do not worry about it, milady, he belongs to you and always will." Reaching out, Xeris gently touched Mirage's soft velvet forehead. Stepping forward he drew closer to her. "Besides, I tried to ride him and he threw me," he whispered, making her smile.

Amore slowly stroked Mirage's neck and carefully studied Xeris. No one had ever gone through so much trouble for her. Amore felt drawn toward him, something she rarely felt. The men she had always been surrounded by were nothing more than soldiers to her, people who were terrified or greatly respected her father.

"I really do not know what else to say but thank you," she replied, stroking her horse's soft neck as his hand brushed up against hers. His eyes captivated her, sucking her into his world. Everything told her to break his gaze and step away. But she couldn't. Amore had never had someone look at her like they were looking right into her soul. Amore's heart flickered as Xeris slowly took her hand and pulled her closer to him until his arms were wrapped around her waist. Brushing a thin strand of hair away from her face he leaned forward to gently kiss her. Amore's eyes closed against her will as her hands took hold of his arm, her fingers touching a cold metal band around his forearm but she quickly forgot about that as her mind started to fog and she kissed him back. Xeris broke the kiss first and studied her. Amore's eyes opened slowly as heat hit her cheeks. *What are you doing?* her mind screamed at her. She held onto his forearms for fear that they might start shaking if she let go.

"Amore?" His voice was soft and low, making her look up at him. She just looked. Amore's whole body seemed to have shut down. "Rule with me, Amore. Become my queen and be with me forever." His words startled her, making her senses kick in. She really wanted to pull back but did not dare.

"You're…" She hoped she heard him wrong as chills set in. "You are King Xerxes?" she whispered, her heart stopping. Kings often would wear thin bands of gold around their heads when away from their palaces. Without thinking, Amore reached up and touched the cold band on his head. She realized then that he had also been wearing a ring. How did she not notice this before?

"Amore?" a voice called out in the distance, making Amore pull away from Xeris.

Stepping back quickly, she stared at him for a few moments. "I've—"

Hearing her name being called again, she glanced back toward the town. Refusing to look at him again, Amore turned and ran back toward the town that had somehow gotten too far away. Amore's heart was racing hard against her chest as she entered the dark alley. Slowing to a walk her mind tried to figure out what had just happened until she crashed into Vainer. Her brother grabbed onto her arms and studied her carefully, his eyes betraying his worry.

"Amore, are you okay? You look like you've seen a ghost." He glanced back the way she had come as a faint whinny called out. "Is that Mirage's whinny?" he asked, his voice getting excited. Amore grabbed onto Vainer's arm to keep him from walking toward the woods.

"No, probably not. You know, I am not feeling the best, could we return to the house?" she asked, her voice breathless. Vainer glanced at the woods once more before nodding. Taking her arm he led her into the busy street. The people dancing around them had no idea their king stood within their town. Finally their horses came into view and Amore realized she had left Mirage behind. Her stallion was once again out of her grasp and possibly never to be seen again. Amore froze pulling Vainer to a halt.

"How…" Amore started to feel lightheaded. Vainer kept watching her waiting for her to finish.

"How what, Amore?" he asked, his voice hitched slightly.

She couldn't break his intense gaze. She knew she would be unable to keep much from her brother but this was something she did not want to discuss here, amongst the crowd, especially if Xeris happened to be near. The thought made her glance around, expecting to see him.

"Let's go please, Vainer," she asked, hoping her brother would understand.

Nodding, he helped her up and climbed onto his own horse. Turning away from the town Amore could have sworn she saw Xerxes in the shadows watching her. Her mind swirling with thoughts as her heart continued to pound loudly in her ears.

On the way back to the house, Amore kept glancing around watching for any horses and riders. She finally understood now why Xerxes had kissed her. In her country, and Amore was sure it was the same here, a woman or man of low rank, not married, was not to show any form of affection toward those who were not related. Xerxes being a king was not worried about showing affection toward her. Being outside of her country where no one besides the governor and his family knew who she was made her to be like a woman of lower rank. Her mind felt overwhelmed and the sight of the guarded house of the governor was a welcome sight. Climbing down from her horse, Amore headed straight for the house, she hoped Vainer would not ask her anything—yet, anyways. As the door closed softly behind her, Amore stared at the floor letting it all sink in. How had this even happened? Especially to her, it was preposterous. Crazy. Nothing could convince her that she had heard him right and that he truly was Xerxes, king of Avalon. Running a brush through her hair after she had changed for the night, Amore still tried to comprehend his words and the proposal. Queen? It was astounding to even think about it. Queen of Emir, that would be something in itself. Queen of Avalon? Her heart jumped all over again as she took a deep breath. She desperately needed not to think about it. Otherwise, she would get no sleep tonight. Perhaps it was some misunderstanding. Though the very real feeling of the crown upon his head stated otherwise. He did not behave like a king would. *How are they supposed to behave?* she thought back to the king of Emir, King Haman. Amore always thought of him as respectful, dignified, and very mature in thought and character, like a king should be. Xeris, otherwise Xerxes, he did not fit the thought of a king in her mind. Curling up under the covers, she tried to quiet her thoughts as the door to the room squeaked as it opened.

"Amore?" Aishlin called softly as Amore quickly closed her eyes and tried to relax, appearing to be asleep. "Are you awake?" Eventually, her sister stopped and she heard the door close behind her as she let out a long breath and opened her eyes once more. She knew that avoiding the curious mind of her siblings would not last forever. However, tonight Amore just wanted to avoid her own thoughts, and wake up in the morning like nothing had happened. If that was even possible!

Avoiding leaving the grounds, Amore began to run out of excuses for her reasons. Thankfully, no one seemed suspicious beyond her own family to her actions. She was unsure what Xerxes was going to do next. She did not reject him yet she had not given him an answer. Curling her legs close to her body, she wrapped her arms around them and stared out into the horizon. Amore glanced toward the door wondering who was hiding behind it waiting and listening. Vainer kept looking at her strangely the last couple of days but he had yet to ask her anything, Amore knew if she told them they would not let her go anywhere by herself. Amore had feelings for Xerxes, but being the king of his kingdom and her being the daughter of a general in the neighboring kingdom made her realize that it would never work out. Emir and Avalon never got along and the relationship between the two neighboring kingdoms was at its worst. Hearing the door click open was a relief from her tormented mind. Aishlin carefully walked toward her and sat down on the cushion by her feet. At first she said nothing as she kept her gaze lowered.

"You want to talk about it?" she asked, glancing at her ever so cautiously. Amore could see the concern in her sister eyes. Amore sighed and kept her gaze away from her sister.

"You would not understand, Aishlin," she commented, leaning her head back.

"Are you sure about that, Amore?" she asked, her green eyes watching her carefully. "Did someone hurt you?" she inquired, her voice hitching with anger, as her hand came to rest upon Amore's knee.

"No!" She shook her head and smiled slightly. "No one has hurt me, Aishlin, it's just something I need to deal with. Something that you cannot protect me from," she replied, hoping her sister would ask no more. Amore really did not want to explain everything.

"Is it about a boy?" she implored softly. Sighing, Amore looked up at the arched ceiling above her head. *More like a man, no boy in him at all.* "It is a boy, father warned us not to let you out of our sight! Who is it, Amore?" Annoyance shot up through her, this is why she took off that night in the first place. Vainer, Aishlin, and her father did not trust her! *Can I even be trusted to be out alone?* she wondered thinking of the past events.

"Okay, it was a boy but you have to let me learn, Aishlin. You cannot protect me forever!" She glared at her sister before pushing away from the cushion and walking across the bed chamber.

"I do understand, Amore. Yet you must understand we are just trying to—" Aishlin stopped short and let out a quiet sigh. Getting up from her spot she made her way over to Amore and hugged her. "Will you at least tell me his name."

Rolling her eyes she felt a smirk grow upon her face as her sister continued to persist. "Xeris." Amore felt uneasy saying the name Xerxes. She did not know if Aishlin would recognize the name or not. Amore glanced down at her folded hands. "He actually saved my life a few weeks ago when I ran off and lost Mirage," she commented, slowly looking at her sister for a reaction. Her eyes grew big and her mouth opened but she seemed to catch herself.

She motioned with her hand to continue.

"I am confused, Aishlin. He…" *Is king of Avalon, enemy of our father's.* Amore got up and paced the room. What else did she dare tell her sister? Aishlin seemed very understanding right now. Pausing, Amore looked back at her sister. "Wait! What happened to my sister Aishlin?" she asked, walking back over. Aishlin blinked in surprise and started to fiddle with the pillow next to her.

"I do not know what you could possibly mean."

Since when did Aishlin avoid eye contact with her? Her sister shifted on the cushion and fingered the tassels of the pillow beside her, her daring green eyes downcast.

"I think you do, my dear sister. I do not recall a time where you have been so gentle in your approach to me. Usually you just order me around." Amore did not mean to sound harsh but the truth is that's how it was. Aishlin lifted her gaze, her eyes flashing.

"Maybe you should just enjoy it," Aishlin commented very smugly, smiling as she got up and started to leave the room, her dress swirling around her legs as she walked gracefully. Stopping in the doorway, she winked. Amore had never seen this side of her sister before and it was very intriguing. Following her downstairs, Amore stopped short on the stairway and watched Aishlin greet Tyron's son Tyson. They stood extremely close for being just friends. Aishlin quickly spotted her and stepped away from Tyson.

"Are you going to come to town with us, Amore?" Tyson asked, smiling up at her. Quickly descending the rest of the stairs and Amore stopped at the bottom. She desperately wanted to say yes but she did not know what was waiting for her if she left the house.

"Well," *if I stay close to Aishlin and Tyson, Xerxes hopefully will not approach me and ask for an answer I cannot give.* "Yes, I will," she expressed, excitedly smiling. Tyson smiled brightly as he nodded his head. The fresh-smelling grass wafted around her as the horses were brought forth. A mare was given to Amore to ride. The tall horse bobbed its head and wiggled its lips as Amore sat quietly waiting upon the others. The familiar feel of the animal beneath her felt wonderful as her fears seemed to all but vanish for the moment.

It felt good to be out of the grounds, yet it began to feel like every shadow held something behind it. Keeping her chestnut mare next to Aishlin, she tried her best to keep her mind off the king. Aishlin and Tyson were content to talk to each other which kept their minds off of noticing how nervous Amore felt. Hearing the sound of a snort, Amore twisted in her saddle and glanced back. The road behind them stayed bare. The gentle breeze swishing through the leaves was the only sound but the hairs on the back of her neck where standing on end. The busy little town quickly distracted her. Merchants lined the streets, they yelled and offered and invited closer anyone who would pay attention. People even bustled around others offering, pushing items into hands, even a few begged for purchases. Amore was gazing at a beautiful necklace when she felt a pair of eyes watching her. Looking up she glanced across the street to find a man turning away just at the right moment and enter into Governor Tyron's town office. Sure it could be anyone, the town was packed with people, many of whom had been coming and going out of the there square all morning.

"Tyson, who was that that went into your father's office?" she asked, trying to sound anything but curious as she picked up a jewel and began to examine it. Tyson looked at the building and toward a small group of horses standing together.

"It is hard to tell but looking at the unique pattern on the horses' saddles suggest they're palace guards. Odd that they would be so far away from it." He shrugged his shoulders before turning back to what had caught his attention.

The merchant at the stand glanced around before leaning over the table to softly comment, "Not just palace guards, but the general himself." Stepping back he called a loud hello to someone and shifted his attention on to others. Amore turned her gaze back on the governor's son. His stance gave away that he was not one bit concerned about it. He laughed at something Aishlin had just said and very closely stuck to her sister's side before stopping to look at Amore with warmth in his eyes.

"The general is the king's right hand man. One of his closest friends and advisors. He's usually never far from the king," Tyson informed before casually moving on. Amore followed their little party, hoping that her mind was more concerned about this than it needed to be. After all Vainer and Aishlin did not appear worried as they mixed with the crowd. Amore even got distracted after a while and started to converse with a few of the town citizens. No one expressed any worries about the general being in their town. Instead all they could talk about was it must mean a party was going to be happening, and what kind of party at that. After a while Amore's mind bounced back and forth before she gently took hold of Tyson's arm, pulling him to a stop and away from the others. She shifted her gaze around them before turning her complete attention on him. He smiled, already reading her concerned appearance.

"What would he be doing here?" Amore asked, her voice soft and quiet.

Tyson smiled and looked back at the horses that had grown a little distance away before his voice grew mysterious as he leaned closer as if it was a secret that could not be shared. His eyes flaring with intrigue.

"Could be many different reasons, maybe King Xerxes is finally getting married and the general is here to invite my father to the wedding." Tyson laughed at his own words then looked at her seriously. "Do not worry about it so much, Amore, you are all safe with us. Trust me and trust my father," he reassured her.

Taking a deep breath, Amore smiled and relaxed her posture. The general might be here for many different reason and they just might have nothing to do with her.

"Of course how silly of me to worry so. Thank you, Tyson." Amore smiled.

Nodding his head the young, handsome man quickly found his way back to Aishlin, leaving Amore behind in the crowd of people. Drifting off to the side and toward different vendors, Amore simply browsed, her mind thankfully resting on the subject for the moment.

"Did you hear, milady? The General is in town and will be staying with the governor!" an older woman extravagated suddenly, her full attention turned on Amore. Smiling like it meant nothing to her, she faked an interest. "I hear rumors that the King has fallen in love and it could be someone from this very town!" she continued before hustling away to spread her rumors that were not far from the truth itself, enough that it terrified Amore once again. Aishlin and Tyson stood off by themselves, Vainer was nowhere to be found, and Amore drifted through the crowd, allowing them to choose which direction she was going to take until the crowd suddenly parted, allowing Governor Tyron and his guests to walk easily amongst them. Five of the men looked like soldiers, but the one who walked alongside the Governor stood out in Amore's mind. His sandy-colored hair matched well to his tan-colored skin, mixed with a dark green and blue-colored eyes. He was a tall, broad, well-built man who carried himself with long, determined strides. Someone to whom one would not want to toil with. Amore kept her spot within the crowd but was easily in earshot of their conversation.

"Tyson, my son!" Governor Tyron's voice boomed, calling out to his son through the crowd even though Tyson and Aishlin stood facing them already. "Tyson, I would like you to meet General Damon. General, this is my son, Tyson, and our good friend, Lady Aishlin. Their companions are somewhere around here." They all respectfully bowed their heads to each other when Governor Tyron exclaimed. "Amore, there you are! Come meet the general." Amore felt her heart flicker as she walked closer and plastered a smile on her face. Her body moved on its own as it carried her gracefully over to them.

"It's a pleasure to meet you, General." Amore surprised herself by holding eye contact with him after a bow. He smiled and placed a hand behind his back before returning the honor given him.

"The pleasure is mine, Lady Amore." He spoke with grace and poise, that of a well-educated man. Governor Tyron and some of the others started up a short conversation. General Damon's eyes suddenly flickered toward her making her look away and caught Aishlin watching her too. Stepping closer, Aishlin smiled slightly and just glanced at her while showing complete genuine interest in what was being said. Amore did not hear a single word spoken but she could feel the guards' eyes on her every now and again. She finally caught the end part as the governor turned to the man who stood next to Amore.

"General Damon, my son will escort you back to my home when you are ready and I will meet you there tonight." Governor Tyron smiled a smile that could have fooled Amore; if it was not for the slight hint of worry in his eyes before it disappeared she would have believed his happy tone and expressions before he turned around and walked away. Feeling Aishlin's arm slip through hers and lead her along, Amore tried to forget about the general and the other guards as they continued their time in the town square. General Damon was quiet, causing Aishlin to seem to forget about him as she quickly glued herself to Tyson once again. Sighing as she watched her sister, she started to put a few pieces together inside. The way Aishlin was acting the other night to her behavior today. Aishlin liked Governor Tyron's son, she continued to ponder on this when General Damon startled her.

"Beautiful day today, is it not?" the general asked, smiling at her, his eyes showing no intentions to his question. Amore smiled and nodded her head before slowly continuing on in order to keep up with the others. The general grew silent once more, content to simply walk alongside her. Chills shot through Amore's arms as she wrapped her shawl around herself a little tighter. "Do you like this part of the country, Lady Amore?"

"Yes, it is very beautiful. I particularly like seeing the ocean. It amazes me the vast amount of water and all the creatures that must be contained within."

Upon their visit to Avalon Amore had only ever heard about the ocean, Emir was surrounded by vast mountain ranges that reached from one side to the other. Then they were surrounded by other kingdoms like Avalon, Cadaver, and Delmar. Avalon, being unfriendly territory, it was impossible to see it, and Cadaver did not even touch the ocean. Besides, Cadaver was an incredibly unstable kingdom at the moment. Its monarchy had recently been taken by force and no one was sure who took the king's place, and Delmar was a small kingdom smashed between Avalon and Emir.

"Simply stunning, the ocean. It can be both beautiful and deadly."

To what was the point to his conversations, Amore could not figure out. They shared a few more brief sentences that led to nothing in particular. She desperately hoped that she did not appear nervous as the general seemed content to remain by her. Vainer soon joined them and introductions were made, but even her brother seemed to be at complete ease with the men. Amore tried to place the worried thoughts out of her mind, as the General Damon asked to head to the home of the governor and everyone easily agreed with him. It seemed rather silly to her, if some would have said no to the powerful man.

❧

The ride back was quiet, with the occasional words spoken. Even the animals seemed to have gone strangely silent. Once they were back at Governor Tyron's house and in their room Amore was ambushed.

"Amore!" Her voice was whispered but her name sounded more like a poison dart in her ears as Aishlin whipped around at her, her eyes shooting daggers. "I would like to know now why the general has taken such an interest in you, Amorita. Is he Xeris? This interest is far more than just being social!" Aishlin kept rattling on and raving but Amore started to drown her out as she watched the vast tree span out the window and fingered the silky curtains that hung from the ceiling. "Amorita, are you even listening to me?" Her name snapped her back from the moment, making Amore look at her sister who let out an exasperated sigh and sat down ungracefully onto the bed.

"The general is not Xeris." Her voice was soft as she studied her sister for a moment until their eyes connected. Hearing a soft knock on the door quickly broke that connection as Aishlin called for them to come in. The maiden bowed respectfully before talking to Aishlin. Amore looked back out the window and gazed off into the distance. She could tell that the general had spent quite a deal of time watching her and talking to her as much as possible.

"I'll try my hardest to understand, Amore, but you need to help me with understanding by being open with me. Right now, the governor has prepared a grand meal for the general and would like us to join them."

A feast, you could definitely say. Amore took her seat next to Aishlin and waited patiently while the servants brought the food out. On the inside Amore could feel the eyes of her brother, sister, the governor, and the general and she was starting to feel the pressure. The conversations were a blur, most of which Amore could not remember, but one statement did stand out in her mind.

"How long are you planning on staying, General?" Governor Tyron's voice spoke his curiosity and intent on the reason for the visit. The general turned his attention toward him and smiled.

"Tomorrow I will be heading back to the palace. Her Highness Princess Braylin has sent me to personally invite you to a celebration next month on the fifteenth." As the last words came out, Amore looked up and her eyes locked with the general's for a moment before his gaze shifted and looked around at the table. She felt a sense of relief flood through her after finding out the reason why he was here, but it still did not answer many other questions in her mind. Everyone slowly said their pardons and headed off to bed until Amore, Aishlin, and Tyson walked alone in the garden.

"General Damon, come join us," Tyson called as the general walked by, coming back from the stables. The general turned and started heading in their direction. He walked with the statue of a man of war, yet a man who could fit into almost any society on earth. Amore let out a forced smile. She was hoping to avoid the general for the rest of his stay but as he walked closer she felt like that would be impossible.

"Lady Aishlin, Lady Amore, fine evening, is it not?" he asked, looking up at the stars.

"Very fine indeed," Aishlin answered, quickly flashing a beautiful smile that looked like it was fit for the palace. *Aishlin would make a wonderful queen, more than I ever would.* The thought struck her suddenly as she watched Aishlin converse with the two men before they set off at a walk again. Aishlin did act very much like a lady, someone of dignity and one who demanded respect. She loved the court and protocol, where Amore would rather be free to go where she pleased and do what she wanted. Something she never had a chance to do, and Amore started to feel that she wasn't ever going to get that chance.

"What do you think of Lady Reni's garden?" the general asked her, appearing right beside her all of a sudden, startling Amore.

"It is very beautiful. Lady Reni's done a fine job in tending it. You know, I think she takes care of all the flowers herself. It's a sort of passion with her," Amore replied, not knowing where all the words came from but they flowed easily and sounded right.

"Yes, indeed, though I must say that the palace gardens are a lot more splendid and very beautiful. You should see them sometime."

Did his words just hint something? She glanced at him for a moment. Her world was about to turn even more upside down as the general stopped suddenly.

"I think it's time to turn in, I have a long ride tomorrow so if you will excuse me."

Catching her hand unexpectedly the general bowed his head before stepping back and leaving. Amore watched the back of the man disappearing and something told her she would be seeing him again and soon.She could see the curious look in Aishlin as she turned and looped her arm through Tyson's once more as they continued to walk quietly around. Amore began to feel rather out of place, and quietly excused herself as she retreated to her room which was a quiet relief as she pondered the evening's events. Aishlin was not long before returning to the room. A pleased exuberant looked upon her face.

"I wonder why her highness would send the king's right hand man on tasks like personal invites? You would think that he would be too busy to be bothered with petty issues," Aishlin commented as she began her nightly ritual of brushing her long hair.

"It's probably not petty to Governor Tyron that he received an invite from the general himself," Amore answered back a little too quickly, causing Aishlin to turn halfway in her chair, her hands stopped their brushing.

"Amore, I—" She stopped suddenly and gave a small smile. "You know, you're right, Amore, though I must say I am glad that the general will be leaving tomorrow. I think I will talk to Vainer about heading into town in the afternoon and getting some gifts for father." Aishlin went back to her brushing.

Father. Amore had not even thought about her father lately. Was she even ready to go home? It has only been a couple of weeks and Amore did not feel like she was prepared to head back. Even with the mess she had created here, she really did not want to get sucked back into her studies just yet. Her studies on how to be a "perfect" lady of court. Why did her father care so much about it anyways?

"Amore, do you think you will ever see Xeris again?" Aishlin asked suddenly, making Amore jerk her head around and stare at her sister.

"Why?" she asked, her voice a little too high for its own good.

"I was just curious about this…" Turning around, Aishlin held out the coat Xerxes had given her to keep her warm the first time she had met him. Thinking about the last time she had seen King Xerxes, she blushed slightly.

"I will give it back." Standing up she reached out to snag it from her sister's grip but she bolted away too quickly. Spinning to face her, Aishlin let out a devious smile.

"I want to meet him. I think it only proper to meet this Xeris. To meet the man who made my sister blush," Aishlin taunted. She was not acting like her usually bossy self, making Amore let out a soft sigh and sat back on the bed.

"I am sure you would, Aishlin, but I hope that will never come true." The words came out before she could even think about them. Aishlin smile slowly slid from her face as she walked closer. Hugging the beds wooden pillar Amore stared at the blankets on the bed.

"You know, Amore, it's not that Father…that we did not want you to marry someone, I think we've all just been overprotective of you and you do understand that being from the kingdom that we are…why I strongly discouraged you leaving by yourself." Her words made Amore want to roll her eyes something even her mother would have frowned upon.

"You do not get it, Aishlin. At home I do not even get to go out by myself. I'm constantly with someone. I've never had a chance to learn, to make mistakes and learn how to deal with them. Maybe I would not be in this mess if everyone would have trusted me sooner." Stopping in her tracks, Amore clamped up and got off the bed, walking to the window. "I even doubt myself." Dealing with her worries alone had been eating at Amore, especially having a sister like Aishlin who one moment was playful then the next would be serious and trying to act like her mother. Amore just wanted a sister who cared about her but did not go to the lengths Aishlin did.

"What do you mean, Amorita?" Aishlin implored softly.

Sitting on the window seat, Amore let out a long sigh stared up into the sky watching the stars. "I do not want to tell you, Aishlin, because you will overreact," Amore replied, staring her sister straight in the eye. Amore could not stop herself, everything just started rolling all on its own. "You do not know what it's like to never have a moment to yourself, then when you do your moment explodes into something that you cannot control and it scares you because…"

A concerned look passed over Aishlin's eyes. "Amore, what are you not telling me?" Aishlin asked, her voice soft as she walked over and sat in front of Amore on the window cushion, forcing her gaze upon her.

"Why is General Damon, the king's advisor, here?" Amore asked, looking straight into her beautiful sister's green eyes.

"Her highness—"

Amore cut her off, her gaze never shifting off her sister. "What does the name Xeris remind you of?" Amore asked her. A confused look passed over Aishlin's eyes. Leaning back against the stone wall, Amore looked out at the night sky. "Who is king of Avalon?"

"Amore, do not tease me." Aishlin's voice shook slightly.

Looking her sister straight in the eye, Amore shook her head. "I am not, Aishlin." Getting up, Amore walked toward the door, still wearing her evening dress from the dinner. Stopping suddenly, Amore looked back at her stunned sister. "Xeris is King Xerxes. I did not find out until the town festival. To be honest, I did not think I would ever see him again after that day at the ocean." Pausing with her hand on the door, Amore turned back once more. "One last thing and you will know everything. King Xerxes asked me to marry him and he kissed me." Slipping through the doors, Amore slipped down to the kitchen and froze suddenly as voices reached her ears.

"Do you really love her that much?" Vainer voice asked, making Amore inch closer.

"Yes, I wanted your blessing since I cannot ask your father's." The other voice threw Amore off that she could not place it at first but as she listened she came to realize that it was Tyson's voice.

"Then, yes, I give you my blessing. When are you going to ask her?"

"I am going to ask Aishlin tomorrow."

With the sound of their footsteps approaching, Amore hurried through the front door of the house. The door closed softly behind her. She took a deep breath of the night air. This could only mean one thing: Tyson meant to ask Aishlin to be his wife. It sent chills of excitement through her for her sister. Her suspicious were right, how closely they had kept to each other since their arrival. It all made since to her now. Aishlin was truly happy, and it was beginning to show forth in her conversation and approach toward Amore. A guard happened to walk by the front of the house as her breath caught in her throat and she willed them to keep walking as they paused. To her relief, they did not look toward the house as they continued to patrol the grounds. Slipping back into the home, Amore found the common room empty and took a seat upon one of the chairs, pondering her thoughts.

❦

As the night began to wane and the evening events began to wear off, Amore finally made her way back up to the room. Trying to not awaken Aishlin, Amore slid the bolt quietly before slowly turning around with only the moonlight to guide her across the room. Walking to the desk, Amore tried to untie the dress by herself until a soft voice said, "Let me help you." Aishlin helped her change before requesting for her to sit down in the chair and began to brush Amore's dark chocolate-colored hair. When she finished Aishlin walked around front and knelt down in front of her. "Forgive me, Amore, you should have been able to come to me with all of this but I guess I was not being a very good sister."

Amore smile sadly. "Thank you, Aishlin, and of course I forgive you. To be honest I was very attracted to Xeris. He was the first man who seemed to take an interest in me without knowing father. He was so easy to talk to like I was talking to Vainer." Amore played with the hem of her night gown as her long hair fell down her shoulders.

"Any man will be lucky to one day have your heart, Amorita. Just not this one." Aishlin smiled and took hold of her hand. "I remembered the first crush I ever had, I was seven at the time and there was this twelve-year-old that would be studying under father at times and I would follow him around and pester him so much." Aishlin was trying her best to cheer Amore up but it did not help very much.

"What now? I did not give him an answer, when I heard Vainer calling I sort of ran away. When I first saw the general my mind went wild." Pausing, Amore smiled slightly as she looked down at her hands. "I truly hope he is simply here for the invitation and nothing else."

"We will just have to be careful." With that, Aishlin stood up and started to make her way back to the bed leaving Amore to think.

"Aishlin," Amore whispered, climbing into the soft bed and laying on her side facing her sister.

"Hmm?"

"Why do Avalon and Emir hate each other? No one has ever wanted to talk about it," Amore asked, her curiosity starting to grow.

"What does it matter?" Aishlin's soft voice gave away that she was on the brink of falling asleep.

"Do you hate this country?"

"I do not necessarily hate Avalon, I really do not know. I guess growing up with father being the general. Hate is such a strong word. There has always been tensions and disagreements between the two, Avalon and Emir being powerful countries that believe in their own method of ruling. I guess I've never really pondered on why." Aishlin stumbled over her words, something she rarely did, causing Amore to grow more curious.

"No one is perfect," Amore replied, causing a soft hmm for a response.

"Ask King Haman sometime, maybe he will be able to explain it." Aishlin's voice drifted off toward the end, leaving Amore with more questions than answers.

"Good night, sister," Amore whispered before leaning back on the bed to stare at the ceiling until sleep finally took hold sucking her into a dream.

Royalty

THE SUNSHINE SPARKLED OVER THE horizon on the world sleeping below. The beams shedding light into the darkest regions, a beautiful grassy landscape mixed with forests of trees welcomed its warmth. The great branches and blades of grass bending to reach every ounce of sunlight. Its warmth eventually spreading onto a beautiful rock walled home and slipping onto soft currents seeping into the rooms of those asleep.

"Good morning, maladies," a soft voice woke Amore from her peaceful dreams. Her vision blurred for a few moments before being filled with the image of an older maiden. "Governor Tyron requested your presence on a trip to town this morning," the maiden implored before helping both women get ready. Amore twirled around in the soft blue gown as her freshly curled hair swung around her before coming to rest on her shoulders and back. Smiling, Amore checked herself over a few times.

"I must say Lady Reni does a wonderful job sewing dresses. I love that she does not care about her rank when it comes to doing what others would see as simple things in life." The Governor's wife loved to sew and was quite good at it.

"Thank you, Amorita," Lady Reni's voice suddenly filled the room, making Amore grin at the small, dark-skinned woman. Lady Reni's head came to Amore's shoulders, she was quite filled out compared to Amore and Aishlin who where tall and, as Lady Reni often put it during their stay, way too thin.

"Are you ladies ready? My husband is growing impatient." Lady Reni smiled toward the end and winked at the two girls. "Men cannot live with us and cannot live without us," she teased as she led them out of the beautiful house. A beautiful bay mare named Avery stood waiting for Amore to ride, reminding her that her stallion was gone. The mare let out a soft snort as she approached. Stroking her soft, velvety nose, Amore spoke gentle words to the mare before coming to rest upon her narrow back. The mare shifted before shoving her nose out pulling against the reins wanting to join the others as they ventured out of the tall stone gates. Releasing the pressure off the mare, Amore allowed her to follow the others happily. The trip to town seemed shorter than normal. Its streets were busy, but the smell of freshly baked bread filled the air. Aishlin stuck closely to Amore's side not leaving her alone for a moment. It began to dawn on Amore that she had not heard of any exciting news from her sister and spent the next half hour trying to get a glimpse of Aishlin's right hand. No ring sat upon her fingers, and no happy glow radiated from Aishlin's eyes. Tyson must not have asked her yet. Spotting the governor's son in the distance, Amore smirked as he glanced toward them and then leaned closer to the merchant.

"Aishlin, let us find some desserts," Amore exclaimed, suddenly pulling her sister in the opposite direction. Her sister laughed but began to complain about having already eaten too much. Everything looked good and at least it distracted Aishlin enough for Amore to try to find Tyson again. His hands were shoved in his pockets as he waded back through the crowd and toward them. His eyes sparkled as he neared. Vainer was not far behind him. Her brother had been very quiet lately. Amore had known Aishlin would explain everything to her brother and as their eyes met, he smiled slightly but it did not last long. As Aishlin joined Tyson and Amore walked with Vainer, she could feel her brother's tension.

"I have been thinking, my dear sister, that we should be heading home tomorrow. First thing in the morning," Vainer said softly. His gaze stayed upon the people in front of them as they weaved their way through the town square. *If Tyson proposes that means Aishlin will not be coming with.* She had never considered that when she overheard their conversation. She was both thrilled at the idea of her sister getting married and suddenly heartbroken at the same time.

"I think that would be best," Amore concluded, nodding her head and forcing a genuine smile as she took Vainer's arm. Her heart was heavy as they headed back to the house that evening. It would mean escaping her problems but leaving her sister behind. Vainer rode alongside Amore. Tyson and Aishlin spoke in whispered tones and both would burst into laughter. Amore's mind wandered as her eyes scanned the land around them. Clumps of trees lined the roads with little open valleys here and there. A faint sound rang out through the night air, making the hair on her neck stand on end.

"Did you hear that, Vainer?" Amore whispered. Her brother looked at her quizzically when the noise had stopped. He smirked and shook his head.

"Must be an animal," he remarked before drifting back into his own world. Amore continued to listen until she was sure it was a small animal in distress. Stopping her horse she glanced back down the road they had just traveled upon. The fading light of the sun gave her no clues to the owner of the cry. Turning back to the group, Amore hesitated. The others were already quite a distance ahead of her and no one had seemed to notice that she had stopped.

"Let's go, Avery." She clicked to the mare underneath her. The bay mare spun beautifully on her hind legs spinning them in the opposite direction. Amore's heart would never let her up if she had left an abandoned animal. Amore's confidence quickly faded as her mare tensed beneath her and lifted her head high, ears flickering forward as a snort came out. The cry continued to come from within the woods' border, seemingly so close yet so far out of reach. Without warning the mare bolted, unseating Amore. Grabbing onto her neck, Amore pulled the mare up. Avery swung her head but settled down underneath her. Before Amore could reposition herself squarely on the mare's back, she let out a scream as someone started to pull her off the saddle. Amore fought back against the person but was nowhere strong enough as a second hooded person showed up. Amore felt her hope slip as the bay mare galloped away, taking with her a chance to run. Her adrenaline kicked in as Amore felt a blindfold come around her eyes as her attackers dragged her backward. Her heart felt a faint flicker of hope as she heard her name being called out in the distance. That hope faded as she felt herself being lifted up and set down in front of someone on a horse. The animal bolted into an instant gallop taking her away from safety. Her captors did not slow the animals for what could have been hours. Amore's adrenaline kept her wide awake but time and where she was was a stranger to her. Finally the animal slowed and the arm around her waist shifted as the person must have been looking behind them. Hearing the pounding of hooves, Amore knew that it was not a rescue party because they would still be galloping away. As the sound softened, the snorts of horses did not comfort Amore. Feeling the man behind her climb down, Amore tried to move her hands but they stayed bound together.

Amore's heart pounded as she felt her captors pull her off her horse. They spoke quickly and in hushed tones. Feeling a hand brush against her cheek, Amore jerked her head away as the blindfold slid from her eyes. Her eyes adjusted quickly to the faint moonlight until they came to rest on…General Damon.

"General?" she asked, bewildered, but Amore was afraid she knew his answer. She glanced around her at the guards that had been in the town with him. King Xerxes was tired of waiting for her answer, so he had her kidnapped. That had to be what was going on. The general cut the bounds off of her hands and gave them to the guard next to her before looking her straight in the eye.

"You must forgive me, milady, but someone is anxious to see you," he apologized.

I knew it! she thought as the general gestured for her to sit.

"We will let the horses rest for a few hours then continue on. Get some rest, milady, we are in for a long ride."

"This is not exactly a proper way to treat a lady," she said, testing him to see how determined he was to complete his mission. He must have understood the look in her eyes because she ended up having a guard watch her while they watered the horses at a nearby creek. Amore let out a faint sigh and studied the guard as his eyes never shifted from her.

Good job, Amorita! What a mess you've gotten yourself into. She studied the terrain that surrounded her. There was no way she could outrun a group of six guards on horses and all of them had their animals in hand. Would Aishlin or Vainer try to rescue her? It was doubtful, but Amore had to think of something before she was trapped behind the tall palace walls. Amore's eyes flickered as she tried to figure out where she was. The open land suggested nothing but rolling hills and grass plains. Amore could not see a tree in sight, and Governor Tyron lived surrounded by mostly woods. Slowly sitting down, Amore watched the general as he spoke with his men. The moon was in the center of the sky by the time the general felt compelled to move on, with her chances of escape diminishing with each moment as they resaddled the horses. The guard that had been keeping an eye on her shifted his attention toward his own horse. Getting up, Amore brushed her dress off and glanced around. The open land shone too brightly with the moon in full light, and there was no place to hide that they would not easily find her in and raise up a lot of unwanted questions. Turning her teal eyes on General Damon, she weighed her options but came up empty.

"Do I at least get my own horse to ride?" she asked, but her eyes told her the answer. Six guards, six horses.

"If we plan on getting there before nightfall tomorrow, I doubt it," the general stated bluntly as he led the dark tan mare forward. Standing at the mare's shoulder, he motioned for her to go first. Amore swung up onto the back of the mare coming to rest behind the saddle. General Damon gave a blank unamused look and motioned with his hand toward the front.

"If you would be so kind." His voice held the tone that he did not have time to be babysitting her.

"Are you worried, General, that I will fall off?" she asked, pretending to be surprised.

"Milady." He paused for a moment and looked down, resting up against the horse for a moment before looking up at her. "I have strict orders to bring you to the palace. I plan on fulfilling those orders one way or another." His tone grew hard toward the end. Feeling that it was best to oblige, Amore slid her way to the front of the saddle as General Damon quickly climbed on behind her. The mare shifted, impatient to start again. The land continued to remain bare, and the moon glistened off the tall blades of grass in the open land. As she attempted to watch the landscape, hoping to pinpoint landmarks to remember, Amore's eyes slowly closed each time she blinked.

⋘⋙

Feeling a warm sensation on her skin, Amore jerked awake. Her heart leaped at the sound of a brook and wind rustlings through leaves. The sun was welcoming them over the horizon as the horses walked peacefully along. Glancing down Amore felt her heart jump violently at the arm that was wrapped around her waist pressing against the beautiful silky light blue dress.

"You have been sleeping for a few hours, milady," General Damon pointed out, taking his arm away now that she was awake. Amore refused to respond as heat rose to her cheeks. How in the world did she even fall asleep on a horse, with a man she barely knew, trusting him to keep her safe? "We rest here," he instructed, pulling the dark dun mare to a stop. The land still had rolling hills but now a few selections of trees stood casting shade upon them. The long grass felt wonderful against her hand as she waded through it. The horses ripped hungrily at the blades. A few of them snorted and let out a whinny, drawing her attention back to the road they where on. A large work horse ambled along pulling a wagon with one person driving the animal and three others sitting in the back. The man respectfully bowed his head and kept his gaze ahead but the girls in the back glowed as their eyes rested on Amore and whispers began to fill the air between them. Amore watched as they continued on, her gaze staying with one of the younger girls as she suddenly hopped off the back and raced toward her. Amore smiled as she bowed low and held out a beautiful red rose. Gracefully accepting it, Amore bowed back as the girl blushed and turned to dash after the wagon that had barely gotten any farther. Amore fingered the soft petals and continued to smile as she drank in the scents of the rose and rested up against the oak tree. Her mind filled with wonder and she did not ponder the opportunity of escaping as the men were turned away to their animals and conversing with each other.

"Come, milady, it is time to be going," the general called, bringing Amore back to the present. Continuing to hold the rose, Amore remounted the mare and let the sun warm her tan skin. They had to be getting close to a city for the road they traveled was soon occupied by others that quickly moved out of their way, their gazes downcast until they passed then the whispers and wonders would begin. Small buildings began to dot the land, as the city walls that were adjacent to the palace showed up quickly on the horizon. Amore felt her heart prickle at the sight of the stone walls. They had arrived sooner than expected because the sun was still high in the sky and the city appeared to be quite busy. General Damon's mare let out a loud snort and perked her ears forward as she began to prance underneath them.

"Welcome to the City of Roselyn, Lady Amore. Named after the King's Mother God, rest her soul, Queen Clarice, favorite flower," General Damon boasted. Encouraging the mare forward, General Damon headed straight for the main gate.

"You are not going through the main part of town, are you?" Amore asked, startled, as she tried to glance back at him. A devious smile spread across his face as he nodded his head as a few of the soldiers passed him.

"Of course, there is only one way to the palace itself," he insisted, but the look that his eyes held suggested otherwise. "Do not worry about your appearance, milady. You look just fine." Amore doubted it but what choice did she have. *Do not leave Governor Tyron's house in the middle of the night!* her mind chirped in. Nudging the horses into a trot, Amore was surprised at how gracefully the mare moved underneath her. She barely caused a jolt to run through her legs as she moved easily over the terrain as it turned into stone pathways.

"Make way!" one of the soldiers yelled as the crowd parted and the sound of hooves hitting rock rang loudly. Silence fell over the crowd and Amore felt every eye turn toward her. Her heart felt like it was going to stop altogether as the crowd began to follow them. The city of Roselyn was massive in size. The street slowly began to work its way up, as the city seemed to grow with each passing moment before finally reaching the gates of the palace itself. A beautiful bridge sat behind the tall gates that stood open but guarded. Amore wanted to look below as she could hear the roar of a river beneath them. The courtyard held tall mature trees rustling their leaves in the warm breeze. Tall drapes reached from the top of the palace down to the ground. The palace itself appeared to be a city inside itself. The people had stopped short at the gates before the bridge, leaving just the general and his men inside the empty courtyard. She expected the general to stop when his soldiers did. Instead, the guards standing at the tall, dark oak doors swung them wide as his horse continued right on in into the grand hall itself, or that's what Amore figured when she spotted the large chair sitting on a podium at the head of the room. A large eagle behind it stretched its massive wings along the width of the room, as it looked ready to take flight.

A servant rushed forward to the take the mare as the general dismounted and helped her down.

"Tell her highness her guest has arrived," General Damon instructed as another servant girl rushed forward. Bowing low, she dashed away, disappearing behind tall pillars that lined edges of the room. Placing a hand behind his back, he motioned for Amore to walk forward as the servant led the mare away down a hall that was hidden from their sight. Amore felt completely underdressed for such a beautiful room. Windows stood high up on the walls where no one would even be able to reach them, lighting the room well with the natural light of the sun. The floor was a mix with all kinds of colors and patterns that a person could stare at for hours. The walls held beautiful paintings from everything from people to landscapes to animals. Amore was studying the wall when a strong female voice exclaimed from behind her, "Ah, finally you are here," making Amore whip around. A tall, dark-skinned woman stood on the platform with a beautiful smile plastered across her face. "Thank you, General." She dismissed him as he bowed his head before disappearing behind one of the pillars. Amore was stunned and unsure of what to do. "Welcome, Amore Deandre!" She walked forward and wrapped Amore into a quick hug before stepping back. "I am quite pleased to meet the woman who has stolen my brother's heart." She beamed. *Xerxes did not send for you, his sister Princess Braylin did!*

"Your Highness!" Amore snapped out of her state of shock and gave a bow. Princess Braylin let out a laugh.

"I suppose you are wondering why you are here," she implored and Amore nodded her head before turning her gaze back on the beautiful princess. "Come, let us dine together. I am sure you are famished from your trip." Turning around, Braylin walked past the beautiful dark oak chair and led through tall double doors that led to a hall and a large outdoor garden stood not far after.

"I must say, Your Highness, the palace is beautiful." Amore's eyes could not take in enough of the hallways and the carvings along the walls.

"Thank you. My father, God rest his soul, doted on elegance," the princess expressed as she stepped out in the sunshine. Birds chirped from the trees that lined the other side of the garden wall. The wall Amore passed was cut in half with pillars lining in between the gaps where rose bushes twisted their way up. Taking a seat on a soft cushion that sat on the grass, Amore shifted her gaze around as the princess appeared quite content to simply stare at her.

"I am sorry, Your Highness, but you were going to explain why I was brought to the palace," Amore inquired, shifting her gaze hesitantly at the princess. Princess Braylin sat perfectly straight, her long hair held together by a pink flower as it twisted through a braid.

"Yes, of course. My brother, King Xerxes, told me all about you, Amore. You see, my brother and I do not have secrets so wipe that bashful look off of your face," the princess declared, smiling. "I thought to myself I need to meet this woman, because no one has ever caused my brother to be so...distracted."

Amore let out a faint smile as she took a slice of bread from the table as her stomach growled in protest.

"Thank you for such kind words, Your Highness, but I doubt I caused the king to be so distracted," Amore responded before taking a small piece off the bread and eating it.

"Of course." Her unrelenting brown eyes flashed in the sunlight. Amore felt it was impolite to ask but she had to know the princess's intentions of bringing her to the palace.

"Milady, if you do not mind me asking—"

"You are staying in a room that I had prepared for you," the princess interrupted, smiling apologetically. "I am sorry, my manners are apparently in need of checking!"

"That is all right, it is of no importance, Your Highness," Amore reassured. Amore was not even sure how to ask how long would she be staying.

"If you have eaten your fill, you can rest now. I am sure you are exhausted after your journey," the princess concluded. Amore had barely even eaten the slice of butter bread but felt relieved to get a chance to rest.

"Thank you, Your Highness." Amore stood up after the princess did, who could not seem to stop smiling as a pleased look passed over her face.

"I think we are going to be wonderful friends, Amore," Princess Braylin stated as a servant girl came forward to show Amore to her room. It was not far from the breathtaking garden to which Amore felt grateful as her body realized how tired it was. The servant girl offered to help her undress and get ready but Amore dismissed her, feeling uneasy as it was.

The bed was extremely soft as she lay underneath the soft sheets and a warm breeze pushed past the silky curtains that hung down over her window view of the horizon and more of the palace. Rolling onto her back she stared up at the ceiling. *It does not seem possible. That I could be here, in the palace of Avalon.* Part of her still did not believe it, did not want to believe it. It made her curious to know that it was Princess Braylin who had her brought to the palace. What could be her reasons? Her eyes slowly began to grow heavy as she allowed the soft bed to relax her, until her eyes finally closed.

Hearing a soft knock on the door, Amore's eyes slowly opened and took in the room around her. Sitting up quickly Amore gasped as she looked around and everything came rushing back to her. Her heart still hammered as the voice of a servant called, "Are you all right, milady?" through the door.

"Yes, come in," Amore replied, sliding her legs out of bed as an older woman came in and bowed low as she easily balanced a tray in her hands.

"Her highness Princess Braylin thought you would be hungry and sent this for you." She set the tray on a wood table in the middle of the room. Then backed away to the corner and smiled brightly. "If I may be so bold, milady, I am quite pleased you are here. We are finally going to have a queen again." The servant's words barely caught in Amore's ears as she sat at a chair next to the table and took some eggs from the platter until the last words finally took hold of her mind.

"Queen?" she asked, startled, her dark blue eyes whipping around to stare at the servant who continued to beam. "I beg your pardon, but whom?" Amore implored, watching the older woman.

"You are teasing, milady, as if you do not know. I am Clarice, the head of your maidens, and it is an honor to be serving you, milady!" Clarice exclaimed her eyes filled with joy. Amore turned back to the food she had brought and her appetite fled.

"Is everything all right, milady?" Clarice asked and Amore quickly reassured her everything was perfect while her mind ran wild. "If you are done, milady, Princess Braylin would like you to join her this morning at—"

"This morning! How long have I been asleep?" Amore blurted out, startling the older woman.

"Since yesterday afternoon, milady."

Amore leaned back against the chair she was sitting in and pondered on her words.

"Do not worry, her highness thought you would be tired especially when riding with the general." The maiden continued to rattle on as she helped Amore get ready. She would not take no for an answer when Amore insisted she could do it on her own. Before long Amore felt like she was ready to attend a celebration as Clarice showed her the way.

Princess Braylin was conversing with some servants as they approached and quickly shooed them off when Amore neared.

"Amore, glad to see you so refreshed. Sleep well?" she inquired.

Does she ever frown? Amore wondered as the princess continued to smile. If Amore knew her better, she would have thought that Princess Braylin had something up her sleeve.

"Very well, thank you, Your Highness," Amore responded. Clarice bowed and left, leaving them alone. The room Princess Braylin was in was the same room Amore entered last night.

"You saw the grand hall yesterday but today we are starting preparations for celebration on the fifteenth," Princess Braylin answered Amore's unasked questions as servants were busy preparing.

"The celebration General Damon invited Governor Tyron and his household to?" Amore implored and the princess nodded.

"Yes, that one. It is less than a week away and we have a lot to do." Braylin began to order some of the servants to clean the windows, a feat that Amore wanted to watch but decided it was best to keep up with the princess.

"Your Highness, I know you said that you wanted to meet me. I need to ask why all the secrecy?" Amore inquired, daring to ask before her nerve let up. Braylin stopped suddenly and turned around, her long multicolored dress swirling with her.

"Secrecy, oh, General Damon." Braylin nodded her head as if understanding some deep meaning to it. "Yes, when I first sent him out inviting Governor Tyron to the celebration which had to be done anyways, I was hoping that he would have brought you back then but he said your family and even Governor Tyron made a clear statement about…how do I word it, you were unavailable."

"Governor Tyron said I was unavailable?" Amore asked, startled, making Princess Braylin chuckle softly as she gracefully moved throughout the room inspecting every detail.

"Not in those words exactly but General Damon did find it interesting that Governor Tyron mentioned you when General

Damon never mentioned anything about you then he said that they glued themselves to you and never left your side for a moment. Always listening and watching."

Story of my life, Amore thought as her eyes got distracted by a beautiful painting being carried across the hall.

"So when he came back, I basically ordered him to figure it out." Braylin, amused, very easily told more servants what to do. Everything was second nature to Princess Braylin.

"I am honored, Your Highness, but—"

Braylin cut her off. "You know what I would love, Amore! If you would dance that evening with the entertainers, please do not give an answer now. Think about it at least."

She must be hiding something from her, Amore could feel it. "Of course, Your Highness."

"Please, Amore, call me Braylin. I just know that we are going to be closer than sisters," she hinted before carrying on with her task. Amore watched with amazement at how easily Braylin handled everything and with such a pleasant tone. In the short time being here Amore could tell the servants enjoyed being around the princess. Following Braylin around the palace allowed her to figure out some of the halls. It would take time to memorize what led to where.

"I want to introduce you, milady," Braylin winked and motioned for four women to come forward, "to your maidens. They shall serve you night or day, whenever you wish. Liana, Namur, Crystal, and Talia. Talia is Clarice's daughter."

Every one of the women bowed low. It was going to take some getting used to having a group of women follow her everywhere, and judging from their appearances most of them were older than she was except Talia. She looked significantly younger. Clapping her hand, Braylin dismissed the women as they hurried away before leaning closer to Amore. "They are all very good women. Crystal can be a bit of a handful at times. She was the daughter of nobility at one time." Motioning for one of her own maidens to step forward, Braylin instructed for lunch to be served. "Talia is a bright young girl. Very promising. I think you'll find she makes a wonderful conversationalist," Braylin continued, giving Amore some insight to the women who would be serving her.

"How long have they all been here?" she wondered out loud and Braylin smiled slightly before moving on showing her more areas of the palace.

"Some their entire life, others only a few years to be told."

"Do any of the servants ever leave?" Amore asked.

In Emir, servants rarely stopped working in the palace and oftentimes the ones who replace those who could no longer work were their children. It turned out to be the same in Avalon as well. It began to dawn on Amore that even the servants in her father's household had been there since she was a young girl. She never pondered the commoners and had not put much thought toward the working class of the nation. She had always been caught up in her own world and her own problems.

"I am honored once again, Your Highness, but I feel that I do not need any maidens," Amore tried to reassure, hoping to get more of the meaning behind everything but the princess simply smiled and said once more, "Call me Braylin, please!"

Celebrations

HER WEEK AT THE PALACE went quicker than she had anticipated. It was two days until the celebration and Braylin kept Amore busy. Nothing to do with helping but everything to do with beauty treatments, and Princess Braylin had ordered a new dress for Amore to wear in the dance. She had seen the other dresses but they did not even come close to comparison with the one Braylin was having made for her. It spiked Amore's curiosity on the dawn of the celebration and Amore was requested to relax in her room. Leaning forward on the banister on the deck outside her room, she watched the baby foxes playing below. The open grounds below her window overlook were continually filled with exotic pets. Amore smiled as the thought of venturing below crossed her mind. Carefully opening her door, she checked to make sure the hallways were clear. Pulling a shawl over her head, she dashed out and slipped along until the steps appeared to take her to the garden, hearing voices brushing along the stone. Amore stumbled into the hallway and hurried partway down the spiral stairway before coming to a stop. Taking a deep breath, she waited, listening. The voices grew louder before fading once more as the people continued walking. Smiling, Amore got up and continued down the steps, her dress dragging along the stones. Coming to a dark closed hallway, she spotted the sunlight sprinkling in through the archway. Grabbing the iron handle on the half door, she smiled as she closed it behind her. The animals continued their play as she took a seat next to a tree and watched.

At first the foxes wanted nothing to do with her before one of the young ones' curiosity grew and ventured toward her. The whiskers twitched as he crouched low until it bounded away, attacking a blue butterfly. It helped her to pass the time away until she heard a soft voice.

"I love it down here." Braylin smiled as she took the seat next to Amore and watched the animals in the sanctuary. "My mother loved this place as well. She started it all with her first exotic animal." Braylin's eyes grew distant, lost in thought before she smiled and turned her attention to Amore. "Are you ready?" *Yes and no.* Getting up, she brushed her dress off and smiled. Braylin led her to the grand hall as her excitement grew at the sound of the party. Would Vainer or Aishlin be in the crowd with the governor?

The thought was fleeting as Amore stepped into the room adjacent to the grand hall as the other dancers rushed around her getting ready. They had already helped Amore prepare. She had asked them not to, but all they would say was "Princess's orders." As the music started, Amore followed the rest of the dancers out onto the floor. She was used to dancing in the courts back at home so she was not nervous until her eyes hit the king. He had returned. *Of course, the party is to celebrate his return!* Amore thought as she twirled around the room with the others. At least he would not be able to recognize her under the jewelry and shawl that covered her face. Forcing her mind on the steps that came next, Amore was able to put Xerxes out of her mind for the moment. As the dance required, all of them together spun to face the king. To Amore's surprise, Xerxes appeared quite bored with it all. Braylin leaned over to whisper something in his ear and motion forward one of the dancers with her hand. Amore stood watching along with the others. Her heart picked up as Xerxes took the dancer's hand and followed her to the floor. His eyes had brightened after whatever Braylin had said. She felt her heart flicker as he looked intently at all of the dancers. Raising her hands to clap them together and make the bells on her hands jingle, she formed a circle with the others around him. Keeping her eyes down or off to the side, Amore avoided eye contact with him. After a few minutes she could feel his eyes boring into her making her heart want to stop as the girl next to her stepped forward to dance with him for a moment then stepped away again to rejoin the line. Amore felt her legs move on their own bringing her closer to him. Spinning around in front of Amore, she felt him catch her hand bringing her to a stop facing him, her eyes locking with his. A smile spread across his face as he slowly pulled down the shawl that covered her face. Amore felt her body go numb refusing to budge an inch. Out of the corner of her eye she could see the dancers start to dance again. Without warning Xerxes leaned forward and kissed her. Amore felt heat rush to her face as her eyes flickered. Breaking the kiss Xerxes picked her up and spun her around. Wrapping her arms around his neck to keep from slipping out of his arms, her heart felt like it was going to stop beating altogether as the crowd cheered around them for their king. Setting her on the ground, he kissed her once more. Amore did not know how to respond. Her mind was blank and her heart was pounding, drowning out any thought or reason. Slipping his arm around her, Xerxes lead her up the steps. Spinning around, Xerxes raised his free arm.

"Drinks for everyone!" His voice sounded quite pleased as the crowd cheered happily. Amore's eyes glanced cautiously over the crowd. Her skin was on fire where his arm was still wrapped around her waist. Sitting down, Xerxes pulled her down with him. Crashing next to him, she cautiously glanced at him, her eyes trying to block any emotion or thought that was passing through. His eyes held a sparkle in them that she had not seen before.

"I cannot believe you are here," he said, finally letting go of her.

I cannot believe it either. Thankfully, their gazes broke as he glanced over at his sister. She held up her glass to them and smiled. *Braylin had set it all up.* The thought annoyed her but Amore had agreed to dance tonight. *What do I even say to him?* she thought, suddenly realizing that the last time she had seen or spoken to Xerxes he had proposed to her before she could say anything. He kept talking, saving her for now.

"I've thought about you every day, Amore." His hand brushed back her hair and the diamond-strand earrings she was wearing. He froze suddenly staring at them for a moment.

"Something wrong?" She couldn't believe she had said something. Xerxes blinked, seeming to come out of a shocked state. Smiling he shook his head and a giddy sort of look came over him.

"No, everything's perfect." His hand fell down to her shoulder. "So what do you think of my palace?" he asked, looking around them. Amore glanced around taking in the scene. Men and women were dancing and celebrating, enjoying the evening's events that continued to unfold.

"It's beautiful, Your Majesty," she commented glancing, toward Braylin, who winked at her. Picking up a cup, Xerxes handed it to her and smiled. She forced a smile and took a sip, her eyes focusing on the red wine. Standing up suddenly, Xerxes clapped his hands together and a horn rang out, quieting the crowd in an instant. Amore's eyes froze on him as he turned to her, raised his glass with the crowd, and smiled at her.

"To the future Queen Amore Deandre."

His words hit her hard. Keeping her same expression she stared at him as the crowd shouted out "To Queen Amore!" Amore felt her hand raise her glass then bring it to her mouth to take a sip. She had no way out of his proposal now, the whole royal court knew, along with his entire kingdom tomorrow. Reaching out his hand, Amore slowly took it and stood up. Pulling her in close to him he smiled and kissed her gently on the lips. Holding her close he lifted his glass up his eyes staring into her making Amore feel like a young girl standing next to him.

"To us."

His voice was soft as he took a sip then offered his glass to her. Amore felt her hand shaking as it took his glass and brought it to her own lips. Drinking in the strong, potent red wine, she forced a smile. Amore was not a fan of drinking but right now she felt like downing the entire glass. The crowd cheered wildly for their king but Amore's eyes stayed frozen on one person in the crowd. He did not cheer nor even smile. Instead he stared at her, his expression empty. Breaking her gaze he turned back mixing into the crowd, almost disappearing. Amore wanted to run to her brother but knew that would be a stupid mistake as Xerxes spun her around dancing with her.

Amore felt unsure of what to do as many people came and greeted the king and congratulated him. She felt her heart almost stop as Governor Tyron and his family walked closer, bringing with him Vainer and Aishlin. Amore stood along with Braylin as she quickly stepped forward to greet them.

"Welcome, I am so glad you could join us," she exclaimed as each person bowed low. Amore stood behind Braylin as her gaze caught Aishlin's. They flashed a worried look before fading into a shielded court look that she knew too well. All emotion was buried inside and placed by a well-trained version.

"You must be Crown Queen Amore's family. Welcome. You must stay with us for a while to celebrate this wondrous occasion," Braylin invited, causing Amore to briefly glance back at Xerxes who was in a deep conversation with another before looking back at her siblings.

"It is an honor to meet you, Your Highness," Aishlin said, bowing low as Braylin smiled wide.

"My King," Braylin called, causing Xerxes to break his conversation and look their way. "You must invite these guests to join us!" According to protocol, only the king was allowed to invite anyone past the steps. Xerxes nodded his head and gave a quick motion with his hand before turning his attention back to the men he was talking to. Amore felt her heart lift a little as her family walked up the steps and to some cushions that waited. Everyone waited until Braylin sat and to Amore's surprise for her as well. Taking the soft plush cushion that sat next to Braylin,

Amore's emotions raged inside of her. She kept a calm, level face but was very unsure of what was to come next as their little group fell into a silence.

"How are you, Your Highness?" Aishlin asked suddenly, catching her by surprise. At first Amore thought she was speaking to Braylin. Aishlin never addressed her as someone of superior rank. Blinking a few times, Amore felt a smile slide onto her tan face. If it was possible, the whole world seemed to vanish around them for a brief moment.

"Very well, thank you."

"I must thank you for allowing her highness to come and visit me. It has been such a joy having her here," Braylin cut in before Amore could say any more. Braylin and Lady Reni started talking about the gardens at the palace as Aishlin shifted next to her as her green eyes flashed toward Amore who sat apart from them as Xerxes walked over. Everyone quickly got to their feet. Amore felt heat raise to her face as her family bowed low.

"My King, this is my brother Sir Vainer and my sister Lady Aishlin." Amore quickly did the introductions as her heart leapt violently inside of her chest. Xerxes gave a small bow of his head before his gaze quickly directed toward Vainer. His expression was very difficult to read.

"It is a pleasure to meet you, Your Majesty," Vainer said. "I trust you are taking good care of our sister," he added, his eyes and tone turning humorous but Amore knew he was serious. If he had the chance he would be marching Amore right out of the palace and back across the border.

What are they going to tell father? The thought suddenly dawned on her.

"Of course, I believe I am the lucky one to be congratulated tonight." He praised Amore as his hand took hers and he brought it up to his lips and kissed it. Amore felt her gaze entangle with his for a moment before she shifted her eyes to her sister who had her gaze turned toward the ground.

"Thank you, Your Majesty." Amore blushed as his warm hand lingered in hers making her arm and hand burn, tingling sensations rippled through her skin.

"My king, I have invited our guests to stay, if this is all right?" Braylin added as Xerxes turned his attention to his sister and Amore felt his hand tighten for a moment before it relaxed again. Amore looked up at him as he slowly smiled and gave a quick node of his head his crown staying perfectly in place.

"Of course, you must stay." His response sounded almost pleased but the feeling that was slipping around inside made her uneasy. Governor Tyron made apologies that he could not stay. Lady Reni on the other hand appeared more than pleased.

"We would be honored to, Your Highness!"

Amore felt her heart skip a beat at the thought of being able to spend time with her family again. Maybe they could give her advice on handling the terrible mess she had created and continued to do so, also before the royal family and court found out who she really was—the daughter of Avalon's arch nemesis, General Divon. Catching gazes again with Aishlin, she frowned slightly at the look her sister had. It was one where she wished she could speak through their minds like they believed they could when they where children. Feeling Xerxes shift, Amore followed suit and took the spot next to him. Amore sat completely straight, hair still mingling with her outfit that she had at the beginning of the evening.

"As I understand, Vainer, you have studied the art of sword fighting," Xerxes said, studying Vainer. Amore's mind ran wild with where he could have learned that delicate fact as Vainer responded perfectly and the smile that flashed seemed like it fit in the palace as any other.

"Yes, Your Majesty. I find it most challenging on horseback. Her highness Amore's stallion is particularly good at it."

Did Vainer just challenge King Xerxes? Amore wondered as she stared at her brother in surprise. She had yet to see her stallion since the town party and the mention of him brought a warmth to her heart.

"I do believe, brother, your horse is very good at stunting," Amore retorted before she realized she had spoken out of turn. Shifting her gaze down, Amore felt goose bumps run down her arms. The group around them grew quiet for a moment.

"Tomorrow we must see how well the horses match each other. Tell me where you found such fine creatures, my queen."

Xerxes addressed the question at her, surprising her. Turning her gaze upon him she let out a smile. His features were soft and humorous. He looked completely at ease talking with each one of them.

"It is rumored, my king, that they come from the rarest blood stock found in the mesabe desert from the legendary stallion Bane…or so it is rumored." Amore extravagated causing a laughing smile to come out of the king.

The rest of the evening appeared to be in slow motion for Amore. She felt herself respond out of habit as she sat next to Xerxes and responded when the time was necessary and thankfully no one grew suspicious. Her siblings answered beautifully, better than Amore felt she even answered, but it did not surprise her. Vainer and Aishlin lived the court and knew the protocol of many kingdoms.

Eventually everyone grew weary of partying and most slowly drifted home while the rest seemed happy to clasp right where they were. As it stretched into the morning hours, Amore felt the whole night's events start to take its toll. Thankfully Princess Braylin spotted it.

"If it is all right, my dearest brother king, I do believe our guests and her highness are growing weary of the party spirit." Braylin's voice still held its steady demeanor of a royal princess. Xerxes glanced at her and smiled as he nodded his head.

"Sweet dreams, my queen." Leaning back on his chair behind him, Xerxes appeared tired but waited until they all stood and walked off before closing his eyes. Taking her arm in hers, Braylin led Amore out of the court room. Amore felt her legs want to give out but forced herself to keep walking. The dark hallways were lit only with lanterns and candles every few feet. Braylin called a few servants forward.

"Show our guests to their rooms," Braylin ordered as the servants bowed their heads low before turning to lead the way.

"Rest peacefully," Amore quickly said before Vainer, Aishlin, and Lady Reni followed the servants away down a hall that led away from Amore's room.

"That was an interesting night," Princess Braylin commented, her voice revealing her happiness after the others disappeared. Amore stopped suddenly, pulling Braylin to a stop.

"Your Highness, I do not know what your brother may have told you but I never did give him a definite answer," she implored, trying to get Braylin to explain what had happened. Braylin only smiled and leaned up against the wall.

"I know everything. My brother and I have no secrets. I also know my brother loves you dearly, Amore. When he came back here to the palace, he seemed quite miserable. That is why I brought you here. Xerxes is not one to force someone he loves to do something, so I knew if I did not make it happen you would still be at Governor Tyron's house and he would be a miserable ruler." Princess Braylin let out a laugh and smiled quite contently.

"Tonight." Amore wanted to understand everything that had just happened to her. Her tired mind quickly evaporated. If the royal court saw her as someone unfit to wear a crown they would be quite upset with Xerxes if he married her.

"Tonight went perfect! You will be queen for sure, Amore, everything went according to plan. I figured you would be a little hesitant to wear the earrings and drink from his cup." Braylin smiled brightly at her. Amore tilted her head and tried to think back. Xerxes was shocked when he saw the earrings.

"What do you mean, Your Highness?" she asked, imploring for more information. Braylin reached out and pulled the diamond-strand earrings forward.

"The royal court knows what these are. My mother, before she died, gave these to Xerxes with explicit instructions and Lord Byron heard as well. She told Xerxes that he was to give these earrings to his future wife as an engagement gift." Dropping the earrings back, Braylin started to walk away, leaving Amore standing there, startled. "Good night, Queen Amore," Braylin called back to her as she continued on her path.

The empty room was relieving to her tired body as she lay upon the bed. Amore was officially engaged, to a king no less. A knock at the door startled her as she quickly sat up, "Come in." Clarice bowed as she stepped through the door, followed by the youngest of Amore's maidens.

"Is there anything we can help you with, Your Highness?" Clarice asked as Amore shook her head.

"No, you are both dismissed. Thank you."

Clarice smiled and nodded her head before informing her. "Talia shall remain in the little side room tonight. A maiden shall always be near for you, Your Highness." She nodded her head to Talia, who bowed low and hurried through the small doorway on the other side of the room. Amore had been curious to know what the room was for. Lying back on the bed, she sighed as she closed her eyes, hoping that sleep would envelope her and take away her worries.

❧

A late morning sun sparkled through her window forcing her to open her eyes. Memories from the night before came flooding back. *The earrings are an engagement gift.* The words suddenly rang in her mind. *When Xerxes saw the earrings he must have figured I said yes.* The thought tormented her mind. *What would father think of me now?* she wondered. Sure she would be queen, but queen of the wrong kingdom. Slipping out of the covers, Amore slowly put her feet on the ground as a knock came to the door. Talia quickly showed up in her room startling Amore, reminding her that from now on someone would always be near to her. Letting out a sigh, Amore called out.

"Who is it?"

"Madam Clarice, Your Highness." The voice of the maiden rang out strong and clear. Sighing, Amore told her to come in. Wanting to slink back into the bed, Clarice smiled as she came in the door. "Congratulations, Your Highness," Clarice praised as she picked up the dress from the night before. Frowning slightly, Amore watched her and Talia.

"What do you mean?" she asked. If you ever wanted any information, ask the servants. They knew everything that went on between the palace walls. Turning around, Clarice smiled at her and shook her finger at Amore. A playful giddy look in her eyes, the maiden seemed to enjoy her station in life greatly and showed it often.

"You know what I mean, Your Highness. Now let's get you dressed. Your guests are already awake."

Amore slowly climbed out of bed as Clarice's words rang in her mind. Her guests? Of course, her sister and brother. She had completely forgot about them. Amore let the maiden help her into the dress. Her mind jumped between everything last night to her excitement that she had her family back for now. After the dress was complete, Amore sat in the chair so Clarice could fix up her hair. Thinking about the previous night, she dared herself to inquire further to the maiden who already warmed her way into Amore's heart.

"Clarice, what does it mean when one drinks from the king's cup?" she asked. The older woman suddenly grew quiet. Even her hands stopped in the midst of the tangle that was Amore's hair this morning.

"Well, it could mean a few things, if you're talking about the king handing a cup to another to drink a peace offering or what happened last night?" Clarice asked. Spinning around, Amore stared up at the woman.

She really did know a lot. Studying her for a moment, Clarice smiled. "Turn around Your Highness and I shall tell you." Reluctantly Amore turned back around. "When you drink from the king's cup like you did last night after he toasted to you as future queen," she paused for a moment, letting the words sink in, "that is a symbolic gesture to the court of his engagement to you." Amore let the words hit her heart. So she was officially engaged to the king.

"You are absolutely positive?" she asked softly, her voice not sounding like her own.

Clarice laughed. "Of course, Your Highness. You sound like you're being led to the gallows." Finishing putting her hair up in a beautiful bun, Clarice stepped around to face her and view her masterpiece. Looking Amore in the eyes, she smiled. "You're going to make a beautiful queen!" She sighed and clasped her hands together over her heart.

Amore smiled faintly. Standing up, she brushed the wrinkles out of the dress and looked at the door. *Now or never.* Amore's hand grasped the iron door handle as Clarice suddenly shouted in excitement. "Your Highness, wait!"

Turning around in surprise, Amore expected the worst. Racing forward, Clarice held out the diamond–strand earrings and carefully placed them in her ears. Amore could feel the last strand brush against her shoulders.

"Now be gone with you, Your Highness," she instructed, opening the door for Amore.

Stepping out into the hallway she instantly felt someone following her. Glancing back she spotted General Damon appearing quite relaxed as he fell into an easy step beside her.

"General." Her greeting sounded harsh but she was going to make the best of it. He smirked at her and nodded his head, his green eyes flashing with mischief and something that Amore could not put her finger on.

"Your Highness, I have been requested to join you today with your guests. The king has been detained this morning and sends his apologizes."

Detained? Amore wondered. *Why would I need General Damon to accompany me with my own family? Does he not trust me or my family?*

"They are waiting in the east garden, I will keep my distance to not disturb you, Your Highness."

Amore made her way toward the garden that she enjoyed. It was the biggest and the most beautiful. The warm breeze floated through the arches and down the hall as she approached Lady Reni, Vainer, and Aishlin, all sitting deep in conversation. Amore glanced back as she left the hallway through the arched flowered doorway as General Damon stopped, staying in the shadows. The sunshine felt good against her skin as her hair somehow stayed perfect as her feet carried her across the lush green grass, the scent of roses and lilacs filled her noise making her smile.

"Amore!" Lady Reni exclaimed excitedly, then she blushed slightly and stood up, bowing low. Her dark blue dress made her look twenty years younger. "I am sorry, Your Highness." Her voice still held her excitement as Vainer and Aishlin stood as she neared, making Amore feel rather different on the inside, a feeling she was afraid she was going to have to get used to as they all paid her respects.

"Do not worry, Lady Reni. How did you sleep?" Amore inquired, trying to act ladylike with her hands straight at her sides, Amore's posture stayed the same. At least that was one thing that got through to her. *Never slouch; it is an absolute disgrace to a woman who slouches in public!* The teacher's words rang in her ears.

"Very well, thank you, Your Highness. Her Highness Princess Braylin has asked me to join her for breakfast. I just wanted to say good morning to you before I go." With that Lady Reni headed off, passing by the general and let out a loud, "Good morning, General," as she passed. Amore smiled. She adored Lady Reni. She had such a free spirit and appeared to have no cares in the world. Amore watched the older woman until she could no longer be seen before turning to her siblings. For the first time she was completely unsure of how to react around them. Under the careful eye of her future husband's right hand man, Amore made the motion for them to take a seat. Amore blushed as they waited until she sat first, her nerves stood on end.

"How have you been?" Amore asked her eyes unwavering at her siblings' gazes.

"Quite pleasant, thank you. Amore, what happened last week?" Aishlin asked quite boldly. It was not a secret so she should be able to tell, right? Amore pondered her memories before selecting her answers carefully.

"Her Highness had wanted to meet me and had requested the general to escort me." Amore paused briefly before shifting her gaze to the left without moving her head. "They have been most kind, I can assure you." Amore tried to not make her voice rise or fall too much but she had the feeling they got the hidden message. Amore wished she could speak freely with Vainer and Aishlin. "How long are you planning on staying?" she asked hopefully, but her hope faded as they glanced between each other.

"We head back to Governor Tyron's home tomorrow morning." Vainer fell silent as servants ran out with trays of food making Amore's stomach grumble reminding her that she had not eaten. The servants placed the three trays down then bowed low and backed all the way up to the archways again. Amore watched them before letting out a faint smile.

"Eat, the food here is spectacular." But her apatite seemed to flee as a question bounced around in her mind. Her siblings ate slowly. They all grew quiet until their stomachs were content. Amore fingered the tan sparkly gown, her ears at least filled with the sounds of birds singing and animals chattering in the distance.

"I would love for you to meet someone!" Amore exclaimed spontaneously, standing up. Startled, her siblings got to their feet as Amore beamed. Turning sharply, the future queen marched across the open garden. Her maidens quickly scrambled from their spots to follow behind them. Finding the stairways she had only found the day before, Amore led them down it and to the animal sanctuary. Letting out a soft kissing sound, the small baby female fox came scattering forward, letting out a soft sound in greeting. Amore picked up the warm furry little creature.

"This is Scarlet. We became wonderful friends yesterday."

Aishlin gushed over the beautiful creature. Vainer, on the other hand, simply smiled before strolling around the sanctuary.

"Where do all of these creatures come from?" he asked, looking up at the exotic birds that sat in tall trees with a netting over the top.

"The royal family has been keeping them for generations now. They have purchased them through private traders or even a few Princess Braylin has particularly fallen in love with." The noise of someone clearing their throat behind her made Amore turn to find General Damon standing in the doorway.

"I am sorry to intrude, Your Highness, but King Xerxes is ready for you to join him." The general stepped back to allow them to precede with him back through the palace. His stride was even and relaxed while Amore felt every nerve inside her standing on end. What if they grew suspicious of her family? Someone was bound to figure it out that Amore and her siblings did not belong. Something would expose them like their quality of horses. Something.

As they broke free of the palace, and into the large stable yard filled with horses and soldiers. Xerxes stood in the center conversing with a captain, before his gaze spotted them. The captain bowed and hurried away, as he motioned them closer. Amore stopped short as Vainer and Aishlin continued on to speak with Xerxes. As custom, her family bowed low, keeping their eyes downcast until the king addressed them. She pondered those before her, to see her brother speaking with the king teased her mind. Vainer flashed a smile that Amore knew all too well. It made her worry. What were they speaking about? Xerxes stood tall as his intense gaze never shifted from her siblings. Her brother was very daring and always bold. Even now he stood up straight as he held himself like visiting royalty. Aishlin always held herself with pride and decorum but today she seemed more content to just listen.

What could possibly be worse? The undeniable fact that you are stuck within the palace of someone your heart is torn between love and fear. Or the possibility of her brother having something cunning up his sleeve and it bothered Amore. The impression she was given as she watched those before her was of distrust between Xerxes and her siblings.

To what is the purpose to all of this? she wondered as Braylin came alongside her. A stable boy brought Vainer's his tall bay horse as he bobbed his head and pushed against Vainer. Leah, the king's mare, stood in the distance with another stable boy. Braylin seemed oddly quiet alongside Amore.

"He does not trust them, does he?" she asked, surprising herself. If it surprised Braylin, the princess did not show it. She remained silent as she watched her brother and Amore's siblings.

"I cannot disagree with you on that. It is hard for my brother to trust," Braylin admitted, watching her brother with love. Amore allowed her words to sink in.

Does that mean he does not trust me? she wondered, not that she could blame him. They barely knew each other. In fact, Amore knew nothing of King Xerxes beyond a few rumors that she actually listened to back home. Beyond that nothing else. Amore started to pay more attention to the man she was betrothed to.

"He must not trust me very well." She had to say it. The thought was eating at her. Along with all the other things that were eating at her.

"Actually no, I think he trusts you very much. You did something to him," Braylin reassured. What in the world could she mean? What could have Amore done to him that she would feel such a way. Amore wanted to inquire further but kept quiet as she watched. *He trusts you and you're lying to him.* The thought provoked her heart, but she could not speak the truth. It would create more than just a problem for her.

Aishlin slowly made her way toward them, bowing low to Princess Braylin before coming alongside Amore. Amore studied her brother as the two men talked.

"What, dear sister, are they talking about?" she wondered. Aishlin simply smiled and let her arms fall alongside her beautiful green tinted dress. Her long hair tucked in twisted bride against her neck.

"What else do men talk about besides politics, war, and other interesting factors?" Aishlin remarked, smiling. Her eyes sparkled slightly, making Amore flash back to what she had overheard before her trip to the palace. Had Tyson actually proposed to her? Could Amore's own engagement have hindered her sister affections? The royal family knew Governor Tyron's family well. If Amore was ever found out, it could hurt the governor greatly. Hurt her sister in the process, if she had gotten engaged to Tyson. No matter what, Amore wanted to know.

"Do I owe you congratulations, sister?" she implored, Aishlin looked surprised but she knew the woman too well as she smiled brightly.

"I do not know what you are talking about."

It sounded suspicious but how much did Amore dare ask her sister. It was all harmless, after all. Aishlin and Tyson getting married, what harm could come in asking. She was marrying the king of Avalon after all. Unless she found a way out of it.

"Oh please," Amore lashed out, grabbing Aishlin's right hand to find it bare. Her own mind reminded her that no ring was placed upon her own finger. Instead the earrings announced her engagement. Dropping her sister's hand as Aishlin beamed with delight Amore clasped her hands behind her back. "Fair enough. Princess Braylin, do you know the purpose of this morning's…I am not even sure what you call it."

"To be honest, I have no idea. Lady Aishlin." Braylin's voice drifted off as Amore stared at the two men. Both of their horses continued to rest waiting for whatever reason they were brought there for. She could only imagine what they could possibly be discussing, men so different in appearance, and ideas. Vainer's tall bay shifted, pushing into his rider's shoulder. Xerxes's eyes flickered toward her; he smiled and motioned her forward. Surprised, Amore consented, her eyes flickering toward the stables as Mirage appeared being held by a stable boy. Shortly after him two more horses followed. A smile spread across her mouth at the sight of the beautiful animal, as he bellowed out a whinny in greeting and shoved his nose into her hand, eyes focusing on her.

"Ready?" Xerxes asked, appearing beside her and startling her. Turning her attention to the king, she frowned slightly.

"For what, my king?" she asked curiously. King Xerxes smiled.

"For a ride."

This surprised Amore and at the look on Braylin's face it did the same to her. As a stable boy helped Amore mount up her heart fluttered slightly. She would have never imagined nor even dared dream up such an event. Her family riding with Avalon's king, princess, and part of Avalon's army. Would anyone back in Emir even believe such a tale? Even imagine it possible? No doubt they would not condone such an occasion. Mirage snorted underneath her and bobbed his head as they rode out of the gates. Mirage settled down but continued to lash his tail back and forth.

Horses and riders began to surround them as they left the safety of the palace walls. If anyone tried to attack them it would be a death wish, and the same for anyone wanting to escape. The ride they were taking was beautiful. Amore wished she would be able to enjoy it more. As she kept busy maintaining Mirage under control. Whispering softly under her breath, Amore spoke the language of her home. His black ears swiveled listening. He began to settle as Xerxes joined her. Leah, his mare, snorted and flickered her ears back at the stallion, making Amore smirk.

"Is he all right?" Xerxes asked and Amore forced a beautiful smile. How was she to explain that her uneasiness was causing her stallion's behavior?

"Yes. He shall be fine once we get farther along," Amore lied and felt badly for doing so. As her gaze drifted around their party, she caught her sister's eyes as Aishlin smiled slightly before it disappeared. Could it also be that Amore's heart pounded inside of her as memories raged in her mind unnerving her greatly. Mirage was one to pick up on everything Amore felt. At this moment she wished she could turn her thoughts off and drift away in the scenery as they rode toward a deep ravine. You could hear the rushing of water below. A grove of trees lined the ravine hiding it from plain sight. The soldiers around them began to move into a gentle canter. Amore ran her hand over the soft neck of her stallion before encouraging him forward. He hesitated before responding with a beautiful canter, his attention shifted toward the white mare beside him as he let out a flirtatious nicker before being checked back into place. They continued their ride until they reached a beautiful overlook of the ocean. The horizon seemed to have absolutely no end and no beginning. The wind off of the ocean was a welcomed relief from the summer heat.

"Sir Vainer, would you care to take me up on my offer?" Xerxes asked suddenly, surprising those around him. Braylin gave her brother a strong quizzical look as Vainer shifted in his saddle unsure.

"Of course, I think it would be a most welcomed challenge, Your Majesty," Vainer said, smiling brightly like it was a long awaited revenge.

"My brother king, are you sure this is most appropriate?" Braylin asked, turning her mare around to face her brother. Amore wanted to protest as well but became distracted as General Damon came to a stop on her left side.

"General, where were you off to?" Amore inquired. The man simply half smiled before resting in his saddle. King Xerxes urged Leah forward as the guards made a large ring.

"First person to be knocked off his horse loses," General Damon announced as a soldier rang out a bugle. Amore could not believe her eyes. It was like watching two young boys. The horses pranced in place moving easily as the men began to sword fight. Amore could only imagine the worst possible ending. One of them was going to get severely injured.

"General Damon, are you sure this is the best thing to do!" Braylin protested, riding closer. The general shifted his attention to the princess. His expression remained blank and he simply shrugged.

"It is what his majesty wants. I have nothing to say about it."

"Men!" Braylin exclaimed, rolling her eyes.

Amore's heart fluttered as she watched the two clash. She could tell Vainer was getting frustrated at how much Xerxes was beating him. Vainer's tall bay Masque grew agitated, his tail beginning to lash as his ears flattened. Without warning the bay suddenly reared, throwing his rider before coming down upon Leah. The mare scrambled out of the hooves as the king got thrown in the path of the horse. Masque swung his head with his ears pinned and began to snake out toward Xerxes. The guards quickly drew their swords but Amore had already reacted when she saw the bay go up.

"Camso."

Mirage responded quickly, his ears flattened as Amore gave the horse complete control. The black stallion slammed into the bay before he could land upon the man below. Screaming, Mirage ripped into Masque as the stallion stumbled and scrambled back. The bay swung around to buck at Mirage but was matched by a hard kick as Mirage swung around charging at Masque. Amore gripped the stallion's neck trying hard to keep from being thrown.

"Calmese."

She stroked his silky black neck as Masque trotted away, his head swinging back and forth with a vengeance. Vainer continued to lay on the ground, his expression pained. Xerxes had quickly gotten to his feet and stood unscathed off to the side. Swinging off of her horse, Amore hesitated as Aishlin hurried to his side and shifted her gaze toward Xerxes. What did she do? Check on the man standing who was her betrothed or her brother who lay on the ground. Xerxes made his way to her and smiled half heartedly but looked stunned.

"Go on." He motioned and Amore rushed to Vainer's side as some of the soldiers helped him up.

"Are you all right, brother?" Amore asked. Aishlin had his arm wrapped around her neck as she helped support him.

"Yes, just a little bruised, is all. I have not taken that kind of a fall in a long time." He managed to smile slightly. "My apologize, Your Majesty, I do not know what got into him."

I do, Amore thought as she watched her brother limp away. Xerxes walked up to her again leading Mirage as the black stallion shoved into his shoulder. Masque could sense Vainer's frustration and the hidden tension within her brother. The horse immediately went to his loyalty and fought the person his rider was focused on.

"Are you all right?" Amore offered, looking at him cautiously. He nodded and smiled slightly.

"I think my pride is the most injuries that I have." He stopped and stroked Mirage's neck. "Your stallion, Amore, is most impressive, just like his rider." Xerxes smiled again as he slowly swung onto Leah. Sitting once again back upon her stallion, Amore shifted her gaze cautiously at Aishlin before turning it to Braylin. She did not look one bit surprised as she shook her head and quickly stated so when it was just her, Amore, General Damon, and King Xerxes.

"What where you thinking, brother dearest?" she demanded, striding quickly after the two men. Amore started to slink away but was reprimanded by the princess. "No, you don't, Amore! What could have possibly been the point to all of that? Please someone explain it to me," she asked, outraged. Xerxes allowed the abuse from his sister as he waited until she had let everything out.

"It was nothing more than a little fun, Braylin," Xerxes said yet the impression Amore had gotten from everything was that it was a lot more than that. His gaze suddenly shifted toward her as he smiled. "Walk with me." As Amore took his arm, she glanced back as Braylin continued to complain to the general. Shifting her attention back to the man she walked by she was beyond words to say as they walked in silence.

"Are you sure you're all right?" Amore asked. Xerxes smiled and suddenly pulled his arm free to wrap it around her shoulder as he kissed her gently on the temple.

"Thanks to you and your stallion, yes." He grew quiet for a moment as he took her arm again before stopping suddenly and turning his deep colorful eyes on her. "Would you show me what else your stallion is capable of?" His question seemed innocent enough. What possible harm could come of it? Amore's mind raced slightly before a soft "of course" escaped from her mouth. Now that she had spoken it, she could not take it back. Especially not after he smiled and turned to continue their walk. Amore's mind began to wonder through the past few days and something began to dawn on her that she just had to ask.

"If it be all right, Your Majesty. I have a question for you."

"Xerxes, and yes, of course." He smiled at her sweetly, making a smile slip onto her own face before her thoughts grew distant again.

"How did you know? Last night during the festival, how did you—"

"Know which one you were?" Xerxes finished for her. Amore nodded and stared off into the distance. He stopped suddenly bringing her to a halt and causing her attention to shift back to him as their eyes connected and he grinned. "By the way you refused to look at me. All of the other girls dared in glances but not you." With that he continued to walk before smirking suddenly and adding. "Besides, knowing my sister, it was not hard to figure out that you were the most decorated and beautiful woman out there."

The dress, Amore realized. It was a different color. She had also been wearing a banded crown underneath her shawl. Her mind drifted to the ear rings still hanging from her ears.

"About last night…" Amore started slowly, daring herself to face him as she spoke. Stopping, he smiled, his eyes warm and inviting any question from her. Yet it caused her mind to freeze and her reactions to slow down.

"You handled last night beautifully, Amore, like a true queen," he praised. Amore smiled but was disappointed she was unable to speak what was on her heart.

Last night, it was all so sudden. Completely confusing. I did not understand the customs. I did not mean it. I think I did not mean it. Amore felt something different inside herself, everything began to slide. Losing its hold. She wanted to tell him everything. It was all there just waiting to be told. He frowned suddenly and studied her a little more deeply.

"Are you all right?"

Blinking, Amore plastered a smile on and nodded. "Yes, just lost in thought." It was true, she did not have to lie that time. Gently stroking her cheek he smiled contently before stepping back.

"Good. Now, there is something important we must discuss," Xerxes stated before getting interrupted by Captain Ramses. Amore had met him previously and could not stand to be in his presence for very long.

"My Lord King, I must beg your forgiveness." The captain bowed low until Xerxes motioned for him to stand up straight. "I must speak with you urgently." Xerxes gave her a faint smile before nodding his head as the captain began to back away waiting for his king to join him.

"My apologies, my queen, can you spare me for a moment?"

"Of course."

Gently kissing her hand, Xerxes spun around and strode over to the captain, his strides long and defined. Turning away slightly, Amore looked at the carvings along the walls. The stone was smooth against her fingers tips but her senses kicked in hoping to catch anything.

"Are you most certain of this?" Xerxes asked softly enough Amore barely caught his words.

"It is expected that they shall arrive next month, Your Majesty."

"Fair enough, you know what to do."

"Of course, my king."

Glancing in their direction, Amore caught the captain place his right arm across his chest then bow low before hurrying off. Blinking Amore turned away uninterested.

"You must forgive me once again, Amore," Xerxes said, walking up behind her. "Deans, find the general. I must speak with him immediately." Gently taking her arm, Xerxes spun her to face him as he smiled softly. "Until later?" he asked and Amore nodded. Giving her a kiss, Xerxes motioned for her maidens and guards to come forward. "I do believe your brother is resting in his room. Perhaps you should check on him." Bowing respectfully to Xerxes, Amore followed the maidens to the room her family was staying in. The passage seemed to stretch across the palace until they reach the room. Guards stood outside the door and quickly came to attention as she neared. Amore nodded as one of them knocked and an answer rang out. Amore felt awkward at first as the doors pulled shut behind her. One of her maidens followed her in while the rest consented to wait in the hall.

"Liana, would you wait with the others?" Amore asked. The woman about her age respectfully bowed and hurried out. Finally it was just the four of them. Completely alone for the first time. Releasing a long breath, Amore smiled and walked across the room allowing her shoulders to sag slightly as she collapsed in one of the chairs.

"How are you, Vainer?" Amore asked, studying her brother who sprawled across another chair. He smiled brilliantly and deviously.

"I am perfectly fine, dearest sister. Just some bruising, nothing major." His gaze grew serious as they continued to look at each other. "What about you?"

"I am fine. Masque came nowhere close to hitting me."

"No, not the horses!" he protested, rolling his eyes.

"I am fine," Amore reassured. She glanced at the door and began to wonder how much could be heard through the wood. Her family seemed to take the hint and shifted in their chairs.

"Most beautiful palace indeed," Lady Reni remarked from the window.

"How are you really?" Aishlin whispered as she took the seat next to Amore.

"I cannot imagine what kind of craftsmanship this place had taken or how long for a matter of fact," Lady Reni continued as she walked across the room to admire the wall that held no spectacular designs like Amore had seen in other rooms. Glancing at her sister, Amore wanted to cry but held it back.

"Good, I am treated very well. Guarded closely," Amore reassured again, still not revealing her true feelings. Vainer gave her a hard look that said, "We know you better." Sighing, Amore smiled. "All honesty, I am terrified. I am not the best person to be a queen. I have never enjoyed royal protocols like yourselves,"

Amore explained quietly. Wanting to desperately change the subject as Lady Reni continued on about the gardens, Amore forced a sincere smile forward as she looked at Aishlin. "How about you, dearest sister. Any good news for me?" Amore asked, hoping to change the subject to Aishlin's possible engagement. Frowning, her sister studied her quizzically.

"I still have no idea to what you might be referring to, Amore. Care to elaborate?"

Amore glanced over at Vainer who stared at the ceiling staying out of their conversation.

"No, I think I shall not," Amore replied, smiling slyly. Tyson must not have purposed to her. Glancing down at her hands, Amore's heart began to hurt. "Have you thought of what you are going to tell father?" she whispered. Aishlin sighed and shook her head in frustration before getting up and pacing the room.

"No, in all honesty, Amore. We hope to have to tell nothing to him," Vainer expressed quietly. Amore let out a sigh and shook her head. Father would eventually know, whatever Vainer's excuse to be made upon her absence. The only valid excuse was to either tell him the truth or to tell him that she was—that was something Amore did not even want to imagine him going through.

"What about the truth?" she asked softly before cautiously looking at Vainer. She knew her brothers' dislike for the Avalonians, even though he had been doing a fairly great job of hiding it during this time. Vainer sat up in his chair and shook his head.

"Are you crazy? Father would not handle the news well. He does not care for…" His words fell short as he glanced toward the door. Her heart flickered at the thought of what could happen if anyone found out. It was something Amore hoped to completely avoid. "Perhaps, you have had an injury that prevents you from traveling home."

"Would he not just travel to Beliz himself then to make sure I am all right?" she asked as Vainer let out a frustrated sigh and

Amore grew quiet. It was not an easy thought. Her father would be most curious to know how she was doing either way. It would break his heart if Vainer had to lie and tell him that she was… dead. Which could easily become the truth at any moment. Even so, she did not want her father going through anything like that. *I could write him a letter. Perhaps it will delay him until I can think of some way of breaking the news to him.* "I'll think of something," was all he could say as he rested back once more, staring blankly across the room. Knowing her brother, Amore really did not care to think what he may come up with.

"Lady Reni, have you ever seen anything more splendid than the grand hall?" Aishlin asked loudly and Lady Reni began to gush about every detail she saw. Amore rested her head back and stared at the ceiling in defeat. Hearing a knock at the door that came all too soon, Amore invited them in. It had not given her even close to enough time. Liana bowed low respectfully.

"What is it, Liana?"

"Dinner is prepared, Your Highness." Bowing her head low, Liana stepped back. The walk to the hall was an unnerving silence for her. Her conversation with her brother filled her thoughts throughout the meal to which, hardly anyone seemed to speak.

The meal was delicious but the tension in the air was thick. Xerxes excused himself long before the dinner was over and made a quick apology. Braylin remained silent for the most part until their guests cleared the room and headed back to their chambers for the evening. Amore started to take suit when Braylin stopped her.

"How has your family enjoyed their stay?" she inquired when it was just them and the servants. Amore smiled hesitantly before drifting back across the room. She took a seat as it appeared the Princess was quite comfortable remaining where she was.

"They admire the palace. Especially Lady Reni," Amore expressed. Braylin smiled slightly and nodded her head, half interested in the conversation she herself had started.

"How does your family come to know the governor and his family?" Braylin asked suddenly, her gaze staring steadily at Amore.

Smiling, she struggled for words. *Come up with something or this is going to end horribly for more than just you.*

"Our families knew each other a long time ago. I do not know for sure if I can say when for I do not know myself." Amore tried and it must have sounded all right for Braylin smiled suddenly, her eyes twinkling.

"My apologies, Amore. I do not mean to seem so unfeeling." Braylin sighed and stared across the room. "Lady Reni said she knows your mother quite well." Amore felt her heart twinge and smiled sadly as her gaze drifted to the floor.

"Knew. My mother is no longer with us," Amore said softly. The words surprisingly hurt as she spoke them. No one had ever inquired of her on her mother's behalf. Was this perhaps what Lady Reni had mentioned. That it hurt her siblings too much to even hear stories about their mother?

Braylin smiled sadly. "I am sorry. I know far to well what it is like to lose a loved one."

Amore had yet to hear very much of the king and queen. Of course she barely knew the woman who sat before her.

"Your father, is he well?" Braylin implored, her gaze softening. Suspicion started to grow on the inside of her.

"Yes, thank you for asking." Desperately wanting to change the subject, Amore shifted her attention toward Braylin's parents. "How is your father?" she asked. Braylin grew oddly quiet before the princess smiled slightly.

"Both have passed on, God rest their souls." Standing up abruptly, Braylin smiled brightly before stating a quick, "Good night, Your Majesty." Braylin playfully bowed before exiting the room.

Crown Princess of Delmar

AMORE WAS NOT READY FOR her family to leave. As the morning sun warmed up the land, servants brought forth the horses. Wrapping her arms around herself, Amore pulled the shawl tighter as her gaze tried to fill with water. She stood alone until they would join her, once ready. As usual her guard's and maidens stood near waiting and watching. *If only I could go with them*, she thought. How long could she keep up her charade? Amore had been almost certain yesterday that they where on to her but she must have satisfied the curiosity. For now.

"Your Highness!" a voice rang clearly in the morning air, drawing Amore from her thoughts of despair. She smiled at the older woman. Lady Reni was a woman to be admired. As she bowed respectfully to Amore, the stout, dark-skinned woman beamed with excitement as she leaned closer and gave Amore a strong hug. "You will see. Everything will work out," she whispered softly before placing a kiss on both sides of her face. "Your mother would have been so proud of you." Her eyes sparkled with sincerity as her soft hands cupped Amore's face before she started toward her horse. As the servants helped her on top of the older stead, she smiled brilliantly. "Your Highness, an honor as always," she said as Braylin joined Amore. The darker-skinned princess smiled as ever and moved forward to have a few parting words as Vainer and Aishlin walked closer. Her heart fluttered at the thought of this possibly being her last good-bye. As she hugged her siblings close and struggled to let go, she felt Aishlin slip something into her hand before stepping back, both girls fighting to hold back the tears.

Vainer held her close for a few moments before whispering quietly, "Atone palate." *Be safe.*

Before he stepped back, Amore handed him the folded letter she had written to her father. In case he would need it. Explaining to him that, Amore wished to remain in Beliz. She would continue her studies with her uncle, who was a very intelligent man and would return home soon. Her summer would be busy, so there would not be time for writing, that she loved him and would miss him greatly. Her heart hurt as his fingers folded around the letter, and he smiled faintly at her before turning away. Maybe Amore could become so well-masked in her emotions like her brother as he turned from her.

The horses danced in anticipation of the coming trip, their hooves stirring up a soft wave of dust. The horses arched their necks and flung their tails into the air as they moved toward the gate, Amore felt like her heart was being ripped in two when the gates closed behind them. She stood watching like she could see through the thick iron gates and see them until they reached Governor Tyron's home. Amore was unaware of how long she stood there watching until someone came up behind her. His hands took hold of her arms, sending jolts through her.

"May I be so bold to ask something of you?"

Amore turned around to stare at him in surprise before cautiously saying, "Of course."

Xerxes smiled and glanced toward Mirage. The black stallion hung his head over the wood fence and flickered his ears as he spotted them looking at him. Her heart leaped as she smiled. His coat glimmered in the sun and his mane and tail sparkled.

"Will you show me?" he asked.

Amore had already said of course to his favor, she could not turn him down now. So she nodded, but felt torn. Her family had trained a lot of their horses in the way Amore did. It was a great advantage in battle, besides if you were wounded you could direct the animal without reins or if you got separated you could call them back to you using the language you created to converse with the horse. Also the special language was so no one else, especially the enemy, could command the war horse in such a way. A stable boy brought the stallion forward, and shied away as the black horse swung his head, almost flattening the boy to the ground. Mirage snorted before striking the ground with his hoof, scarring the dirt with each strike.

"Mirage," Amore scolded the stallion and took the rope from the boy. Mirage nipped angrily at her for being gone from him for so long. "Beta, sheza comesa!" *Enough, settle down!* Pushing his muzzle away as he flickered his ears, a long breath released from him but he continued to twitch in his own skin. Ready to explode. Xerxes gave her a curious look. Amore had forgotten about him and spoke in her secret language to Mirage. Blushing, she rubbed the stallion's neck and leaned against him.

"I have a secret tongue I use with him." How did he make her feel so open to share pretty much anything? Was that what Braylin talked about when she said that Amore did something to Xerxes? Amore really doubted it, the man before her still somewhat resembled the man at the beach but a little more dignified and a lot more grown up. Xerxes smiled then and gently rubbed Mirages noise. Taking her foot, Amore bumped Mirage's knee. The stallion flickered his ears unresponsive as he continued to stand, his back leg coming to rest on the tip of his hoof. "Stubborn!" she retorted, smacking him gently on the shoulder. Bobbing his head, he snorted as if he knew what she was saying. Tapping his knee again, he finally picked up his leg and lowered his knee to the ground. His left front leg stretching out as his nose tucked into it. Xerxes smirked and nodded his head approvingly.

"How do you get him to rear like you did at the Ocean of Cavar?" he asked, enjoying the display. Mirage knew a lot of things, many of which Amore really did not want to reveal. However, he already knew of that one so…

"Meear!" Shaking her head as he bobbed his up and down giving a half-hearted bounce off the ground. His front hooves barely coming off the dirt. "Meear!" she demanded. This time he startled even her as he shot straight up into the air. Scrambling back both of them got out of his way, as his hooves struck out. Landing with a thud, he swung his head hard before giving a playful half rear, half buck and galloped away. His tail arched, enjoying his brief moment of freedom. Amore could not help but laugh at her horse as he proudly trotted up to other horses in pens flirting with any horse that would pay attention to him. Sadly none paid the stallion much attention. Letting out a sharp whistle, Amore watched as he shook his head in defiance and snorted, turning to face them. His ears perked as he studied the humans. Whistling again, Amore shook her head as he continued to ignore her and trot proudly around the opening. His tail arched until it touched his rump.

"I am sorry but it appears he has a mind of his own today." Amore laughed as she watched the display. Xerxes chuckled and shook his head, enjoying the stallions clear defiance, and attitude.

"Magnificent creature, Amore."

"Please do not tell him that. He already has an ego." Amore smiled, feeling completely at ease beside Xerxes with no one else around other than the usual. Xerxes laughed as his eyes sparkled in the sunlight. Finally the magnificent animal cantered up to them swinging his head as he approached before slamming his hooves into the ground and stopping short in front of them. Stroking his head as he lowered his dished face Amore stared into the eyes of the horse before her. Completely free, yet so willing to stay near her. Mirage was bringing a welcomed distraction for her attention as they grew silent with each other.

"Are all your family's horses so well trained?"

Indeed they were. Amore's heart grew heavy at the thought of lying once again. She feared that soon she would either grow heavy with the secrets she contained or grow numb to her conscience continuing to remind her that she did not care to lie.

Perhaps she could think of a way to avoid the whole truth but allow partially to come forward. "My mother was very talented with these magnificent creatures and they appeared to adore her. They seemed to work better for her than anyone else and it drew people's attention. Yet no one was able to match what she could request of a horse." It was a lot of her mother's ways to how her family's horses bonded with them, or so that is what her family told her. Amore picked it up quickly, but always wondered about her mother's capabilities. Mostly she wanted to know her mother better.

"It would have been an honor to know your mother," King Xerxes praised, making Amore smile warmly at the thought and almost want to laugh at the idea of King Xerxes and her father together. Never would two such men come to an agreement.

The quietness of the garden was the perfect place to settle in to read the letter. It had been eating at her to read it, yet patience won out until she was finally alone. The maidens talked amongst themselves, no doubt ably conversing about the recent events of the palace. The letter was folded tightly, but soon her beautiful sister's handwriting occupied the page.

To My Beautiful Sister Amorita,

I have no words to comfort you, dearest one. As far as I can see you have made him fall very much so in love with you as we feared. Follow you heart, dearest sister, it will not lead you wrong during this time. Vainer is planning on going home in a couple of days fearing that it would be the best thing to do. We tried to think of different ways to be able to bring you back with us but I worry that this is up to you now and I'll pray that your life will always be blessed and bountiful.

Please, Amorita, forgive me! Seeing you now has shown me that you are a lot stronger than we ever gave you credit for. I do have to add that I desperately wish we would have not allowed you to come. You deserve the truth. Father believes we are visiting our cousins. You were not suppose to come, but when Father insisted on you coming how were we suppose to tell him? Let me reassure you we simply wanted to visit Father's old friend Governor Tyron after receiving a letter from him.

I pray, dearest one, that I will get to see you again soon.

Love with all the love the world can contain,
Aishlin

Amore took a deep breath as she leaned on the rock ledge that overlooked the valley below. Amore had begged her father to allow her to accompany her siblings to her cousins. Her father was very reluctant, yet he was persuaded by Amore. After they had departed, she had learned of their expedition when the guards suddenly vanished one night. Set up in advance by Vainer himself, the guards would take a little vacation then show up again when it was time to return home.

Resting upon the wall, a gentle breeze floated around her bringing the wonderful aromas of flowers and mixtures of scents. The maidens assigned to her lingered about, laughing and talking. Her gaze then found a young boy drawing near to her, bowing low in respect.

"Is her highness ready for lunch?" he asked.

Amore declined and the boy hurried away. She was not in the mood for anything to eat. As she gazed back out into the horizon, she caught the movement of the maidens sitting down to eat. Her attention remained with one maiden in particular. Her dark skin stood out against the other three maidens, her hair black as the night. She sat perfectly straight but what caught Amore's eye mostly was how the maiden Crystal handled herself. Ever dignified, elegant, and most incredibly reassured of herself. Not something most would see in a maiden serving others. Turning her gaze away so she would not draw the maiden's attention, Amore pondered Braylin's words. "She used to be the daughter of a noble." The short time that Amore had maidens, she could see in the younger girls' eyes that she did not particularly care for her position in life. She had not heard the maiden say so directly. Of course she was not such a person to even think anything toward the other women. She barely knew them, and her own life before the palace would hopefully forever stay buried.

"It is the truth!" the youngest of her maidens claimed, sounding rather upset about something. Talia looked upset as Crystal let out a soft chuckle.

"I meant it only in fun, Talia. You do not need to get flustered about it," Crystal remarked, smiling still. The considerably younger girl looked away holding back her frustration as she remained quiet.

"May I be excused, Your Highness?" she remarked suddenly, surprising Amore as the young girl turned her attention on her.

"You may."

The young girl quickly got to her feet and bowed to Amore before hurrying away, making Crystal chuckle as she remarked to Namur.

"I did not think she would get so offended about it." Namur narrowed her gaze but kept her mouth shut as she looked away. Amore began to wish that she had heard what had happened to have hurt the young maiden. Amore kept her gaze turned away from the others, but paid closer attention to the conversations that ensued. They grew silent before Namur finally spoke up.

"Liana, would you be so kind as to show me how to make that bracelet."

"Of course." The two maidens began to discuss the steps to making it.

Crystal remarked loudly, "Surely you both cannot be mad at me as well?"

This drew Amore's attention as she turned to watch the display. Namur slowly raised her eyes as she stared quite intently at the younger girl.

"What I feel, Crystal, is not of importance," she remarked.

Crystal leaned back on the cushions and smiled, seemingly very satisfied with herself. Namur looked over at Amore hesitantly before returning to the project with Liana. Amore watched Crystal for a moment as the younger girl had her eyes closed and rested. Talia returned shortly later and sat down without any words spoken.

"Tell us a story, Talia," Namur soon inquired of the younger girl. Talia smiled slightly and flashed a quick glance at Crystal.

"Perhaps another time."

The palace had grown quiet with the passing of time. Everyone seemed to relax. No soldiers followed her and her maidens seemed to grow more comfortable in her presence and often were requested to allow her some space. Princess Braylin had been busy with who knows what and Amore was left to ponder her life. She spotted Crystal in the distance with some of the other women of the palace, many who Amore had yet to meet. She was nervous around the nobles' wives, and thankfully most still gave her space. To the point Amore even inquired the princess about it.

"It is beyond me at times, they will come to the palace if their husbands are here for a particular reason. Other than that they stay within their own homes in the city or countryside," Braylin had remarked. "At times they would even bring their daughters. Some more so than others."

Amore studied the women of the palace at a distance. They were all very beautiful, some more than others. Would it be possible for the king to possibly fall in love with another? The idea both amused her and hurt at the same time. She was allowing herself to grow too attached to the idea of marrying Xerxes. She fingered the soft petals of a flower she had plucked from the garden before bringing it up to her nose and drinking in the wonderful fragrance. It made her think of Lady Reni's garden and her family. Vainer should have been across the border by now. Had Aishlin gone with him or gotten engaged? Had everything been cast aside because of her mistake? Was it too risky for her sister to marry the governor's son if everything turned south for Amore?

"Your Highness," a voice startled Amore from her world. Blinking she turned to spot the general as he smiled at her.

"What is it?" she offered, perplexed. The general clasped his hands behind his back. The man's posture spoke of dignity and elegance. If one could be found in a soldier.

"The king requests for you to join him this morning," General Damon informed smirking. Joining the seasoned soldier, Amore smiled suddenly and offered the flower to him. "What is this for?"

"Perhaps you could give it to someone. Or keep it for yourself," Amore remarked. She liked to tease the general the few short times they were together. They never could quite agree on many topics and it amused Amore's bored mind.

"Interesting," was all he replied. Amore's mind drifted back to the women who mingled in the garden as they waited for things to do and her smile grew wider for a moment. Some of the women were palace officials' wives, or dignitaries' wives who happened to be visiting at the moment. She had spotted a few wives of the guards but rarely saw them or heard anything about them. Looking from the women to the man beside her, Amore's smile grew as she eyed him.

"Have you, General, ever thought about getting married?" Amore asked.

The flower had disappeared and the man beside her barely blinked an eye as he promptly stated, "Of course not," as he kept the pace brisk enough but Amore could not help but keep her smile as she pondered the idea and tried to even imagine the general with a wife. She would have to be something special to put up with the man beside her.

Making a soft hmm, Amore allowed the silence to grow between them. General Damon was a very well-educated man and he had to be. Advising a king did not come easy and with these passing days since the engagement and her family's departure from Roselyn, Amore had briefly seen the king a few times. Some demanding business had taken his attention away from her and sad enough Amore was relieved to feel less pressured for the moment, allowing her mind to drift as they continued to walk the palace halls. If one did not know where they were going, they could get lost amongst the halls, stairs, and rooms that filled the grand palace.

"This way, Your Highness," General Damon stopped suddenly.

Amore had yet to be in this part of the palace. A tall, arched column covered in vines led to a covered bridge. Empty torches sat outside the covered bridge waiting to be lit once the land darkened. The bridge slopped once more and came to a massive door. Her gaze connected with the general's out of curiosity and he pulled the round door handle opening the tallest door Amore had seen inside of a building. Stepping through she had expected for the general to follow but as the door closed behind her she stood alone in the hall. Carefully making her way forward, she eventually walked into a large circular room. Tall silk drapes hung from the ceiling over the doorway and multiple equally impressive windows. A fireplace hugged one area of the room while large beams reached for the ceiling but came short. Massive drapes hid what was placed upon a platform in the middle of the room. The wood was an incredibly deep, rich color. Glancing around the empty room, Amore inched her way closer until she reached the step to what she finally realized was a large bed. *This is his private chambers.* It dawned on her then. The room was beautiful. The domed ceiling held the drapes and carvings. Hearing foot steps Amore spun around and stumbled off of the platform her gaze catching Xerxes as he walked through one of the open doorways.

"General Damon," she started but quickly stopped as he smiled.

"Yes, I asked for him to bring you in here."

Stunned and unnerved, Amore grew quite unsure of what to say. So she went with the first thing that came to mind. "The carvings are beautiful." She truly meant it. The room was elegant, even more so than the palace of Emir. She had to admit that the palace of King Haman had nothing on Avalon's palace. Whoever was behind it all truly had a unique gift. She wanted to explore the room further but decided it was best to remain were she was. As Xerxes neared, Amore felt her heart flutter. He seemed to be able to make her want to be like a little girl and blush deeply every time his deep blue eyed gaze turned toward her.

"Come with me," he expressed softly with a warm smile as he led the way back through the open arch and out into a large, private garden. Mirage stood in the center grazing happily on the rich grass that grew up in the wide open area. A beautiful decorative saddle sat upon his back, and the bridle was equally as magnificent. "I was hoping that perhaps your stallion may let me ride him if you were around." He smiled brightly. Mirage had thrown her father many times before he even gave up riding the horse. For whatever reason, Mirage was peculiar about whom he allowed upon his back. Vainer, said he felt that the horse was simply too spoiled. When Amore offered for him to ride Mirage, Vainer quickly declined and said that he did not have a death wish.

"Your soldiers may charge me with murder, my king," Amore joked, feeling very uneasy about Xerxes riding her horse. Partially because he could very easily get hurt and the other part, the more she allowed him into her life the harder it was going to be to keep her distance. Mirage lifted his head and snorted as they neared and Xerxes chuckled.

"He cannot be that bad."

Why is he so interested in riding Mirage? Amore wondered as she gave in and held Mirage's bridle. The stallion flickered his ears back and snorted, pushing his nose into Amore's arm. His lips nibbled against her skin.

"You have to ask him, he does not do well with demands." She slowly stepped back. Mirage's back hoof rested on its tip as he rested it on the ground. His head turned to watch Amore as she back away. Xerxes asked for a walk and the stallion remained motionless for a moment before obliging and moving forward, surprising Amore greatly as he moved easily for Xerxes who smiled brightly. True to his previous nature, without warning Mirage exploded and Xerxes held on for the most part before Mirage threw him and cantered away. As Xerxes laid their motionless, Amore became greatly worried as she hurried to his side. He stared at the sky, as she crouched down next to him.

"Does anything hurt?" she asked, almost afraid to touch him. He smiled slightly and shook his head.

"Just a little sore."

Turning his head to look at her, he smiled and reached up to cup her face with one of his hands. Without thinking, Amore wrapped her hand around his as he held it there. Mirage trotted closer and stopped next to him. Lowering his head he snorted and sniffed Xerxes before grazing on the grass beside the fallen king.

"I think he is laughing at me."

The idea made Amore chuckle, erasing the tension she was feeling inside of her.

"I did warn you," she laughed. "Do not feel so bad, no one has been able to ride Mirage except for me."

Stroking the stallion's head, Amore glanced down at him again as Xerxes seemed content to lay there watching her.

"What is it?" she asked, growing concerned until he smiled.

"I want to try again." Xerxes got to his feet, moving a little slower this time. Climbing back on the stallion, Xerxes turned to her and offered his hand out as a grin plastered across his face. Swinging up behind him, Amore gripped the back of the saddle. Mirage shifted and patiently waited. Reaching around behind him, Xerxes gently grabbed her arm and pulled it forward so she held onto him instead. This time she did not hold the blush from her face, because thankfully he would not see it. Asking the stallion once more, Mirage moved off easily into a beautiful canter and responded perfectly. Only once did he hesitate and Amore reprimanded him for it. She began to enjoy the time and even began to laugh as Mirage easily went through several maneuvers with two passengers on his back. It took them a while before they noticed General Damon standing on the balcony steps. Pulling Mirage up, he slowed to a stop in front of the general.

"I beg your pardon, my king, but you wanted to know when they reached the outskirts of Roselyn," General Damon informed.

*Who reached the outskirts of Roselyn?*Excitement grew on the inside of her.

"Thank you, General."

General Damon nodded and retreated back up the steps. Grabbing onto Xerxes's arm, Amore swung down and was followed shortly by Xerxes.Mirage let out a snort as he lowered his head to rip at the grass once more. His coat glimmering in the sun as his skin twitched chasing away the fly.

"Who is coming?" she implored as a servant was called to take the stallion away. Smiling he took her arm and they made their way back up to his chambers.

"The royal princess from Delmar. It will be an honor for me to introduce them to my future queen," he answered. His skin felt warm against her hand, as she tried to chase away the chills that ran through her at how closely he walked alongside her. *Do not be so childish.* She thought as she fought the blush that raced to her face.

As they reached his room, he turned to her and smiled happily. *Does he know what he does to me?* She smiled as she felt herself relax under his gaze. Every time he was near her, Amore felt completely at ease. He made her feel quite safe. Yet very unnerved at the same time. *Is that normal?*

119

"I shall see you shortly, my queen." After gently kissing her cheek, Xerxes left. Her footsteps echoed in the room as Clarice stood waiting by the doors for her.

"We have a lot to do, Your Highness," Clarice spoke, as soon as she stepped foot into her room. The maidens began to work, preparing her for the visiting royalty. Amore still felt funny from time to time, allowing the women to prepare her for almost anything. Rarely did Amore have to accomplish any task herself.

"Do you know anything about our visitors?" Amore inquired, the maidens around were beautifully dressed as well. A few of them cast looks at each other and smiled as Clarice answered her.

"A little, Your Highness." She stood off to the side as the others worked, watching. She let out a smile as Amore looked up at her. Clarice was an amusing woman. She showed Amore nothing but respect, but the older woman was more like a friend to her than a maiden. Amore knew if anyone else found out among the palace maidens, it would not be received well.

Fighting back a smile, she said, "Is that all you are going to tell me, Clarice?"

"No disrespect, Your Highness. But it is not my place to speak." Her smile slipped then, Clarice looked rather serious as Amore nodded her head and let the matter drop.

It was not long and Amore's hair was beautifully done. The dress, like all the others, was beautiful. A small diamond-filled crown was placed upon her dark brown hair. *If only Father could see me now? Would he be proud of how I behaved?* Her father remained in her mind as she walked towards the grand hall. She was grateful for the lessons her father had impressed upon her to take. It helped her to not feel so out of place.

◈

Her heart pounded in anticipation as she neared the grand hall and joined Xerxes as he stood by the doors. Her heart leaped even more at the sight of him. Nothing about him at this moment, resembled the man she had meet at the ocean. Still, he made her feel like a young girl on the inside. *How can he make he feel so different each time I see him?* Taking her arm in his, Amore felt her last taste of her old life as a general's daughter slowly slipping away with each step. Each step brought her closer to being caught up in Xerxes's world. One of the court protocols and rules that Amore was expected to follow. If this court was anything like the court back home, she would be able to get by but every kingdom was different. The Grand Hall looked beautiful as ever. A large crowd had gathered but all appeared to be on their best behavior. Xerxes led her to the middle of the platform and stopped. Dropping her arm, Xerxes placed his hands behind his back and stood waiting. Amore felt out of place standing next to him, and she glanced over at Braylin who stood on his other side. She stood slightly behind him and gestured for Amore to step back. Following her lead, Amore took the step back and then waited. The doors swung open as trumpets sounded and every eye turned. Amore's eyes instantly found the royal couple. The visiting king appeared quite confident but Amore felt her eyes stay on the queen. To her surprise, she appeared to be very young and her eyes glanced from side to side. Her posture gave away her nervousness, making Amore look around the room. Soldiers stood shoulder to shoulder creating a protective path for the royal couple. They also stood along the front of the platform protecting their king. She knew there were soldiers behind them as well. Compared to the visiting royalty, Xerxes was heavily guarded. Amore tried to look at them how Xerxes saw them—a young, inexperienced royal couple, looking to a larger kingdom to help them out. They finally stopped and bowed. Xerxes motioned the guard to bring them closer. Amore shifted and glanced down for a few moments before looking up, instantly meeting the gaze of the queen. The girl held her gaze for only a few moments before looking at the glassy stone floor. Her fair skin seemed a little faded, as her light brown hair was wrapped up into a bun.

"Presenting their Royal Highness, Lord Zander and Crowned Queen Almeria of Delmar," an official of the palace introduced them. Xerxes nodded his head and smiled perfectly. It amused Amore to see how many difference faces those in the court life would often show, and here in Avalon was no different.

"Welcome back, Lord Zander and Crowned Queen Almeria. I would like to introduce you to my future wife, Crowned Queen Amore Deandre."

Gesturing her forward, Amore bowed her head respectfully to the couple as they did the same. Stepping back again, Amore glanced over at Braylin who gave a faint smile but her eyes held her disgust. Amore hoped she did not do something wrong. As Xerxes did a few more introductions to Lord Byron and Lord Timothy, he offered to give them a tour of the palace.

"That would be wonderful, Your Majesty," Lord Zander spoke. As Xerxes turned to show them the way, servants quickly went in front and behind. As Xerxes and Lord Byron stepped forward, Amore waited for Braylin and Almeria to join her. They were to walk behind the men while they talked. As they walked down a few halls, Braylin hocked her arm around Amore suddenly and leaned into her.

"If you do not mind, brother, I'm not feeling well. We shall relax here then catch up with you in a moment," she spoke out. Xerxes glanced between the two before nodding his approval and continuing on. Braylin continued to lean on her as the group continued on. Amore even caught the faint glance that Princess Almeria gave them. As they slowly got farther and farther away, Braylin suddenly stood straight. Amore stared at her in surprise.

"Are you all right, Your Highness?" she asked, worried. Braylin did not even bother to look at her.

"The nerve of that sick, disgusting man!" she hissed. Amore glanced after the men before looking back at her, her blue eyes wide with curiosity.

"Lord Zander?" she asked. Braylin stared daggers at Amore, making her step back, prepared for Braylin to strike out.

"Do not speak that name to me, Amore. It leaves a horrid taste in my mouth," she snapped, fixing her dress before continuing on. Amore just stared at her and glanced to Braylin's maiden who still waited for them to continue on.

"Lord Zander was keen to marry the princess when she was fifteen. Without warning, he suddenly left the palace and had not been heard from since," the maiden informed, filling in the blanks.

"I heard that, Kashia!" Braylin sneered. Amore smiled faintly and followed after Braylin. *No wonder why she's upset*, she thought, catching up to the princess.

"All I will say is I wonder how he trapped that young girl into his schemes! Do not trust that man, Amore. Whatever you do, do not be alone with him either." She took her arm again to keep up with her act. Amore helped Braylin along and kept her eyes focused. She had a feeling her life was about to get even crazier but at least it was giving her a chance to breathe between everything that was happening. They followed the men at a distance as they led out to the stables and outside the main palace walls. The royal stables was a large open ground with tall brick walls surrounding them in the distance. It was the most open place Amore had been allowed to go in such a long time. Guards instantly surrounded them all as they walked toward the paddocks and the horses that stood beyond them. Amore felt the breeze hit her face and soaked up the feeling. It was the first time being beyond the palace walls in weeks. As they got closer, Amore finally understand what Xerxes was saying to Princess Almeria. A beautiful bay mare stood patiently next to one of the stable boys.

"This mare is for your wedding present. She is one of my finest mares and the calmest."

For the first time, Princess Almeria smiled as she stroked the mare's face but quickly stepped back after a harsh look from Lord Zander. Amore spotted her stallion off in the distance as he did.

Letting out a fierce whinny he galloped closer, striking out as he neared the end of the pasture line. Lifting his head high, he let out a whistle before bolting and galloping off. Coming back he slid to a stop before crashing into the fence.

"Now that's a horse, Your Majesty. Where did you get him?" Lord Zander asked, walking closer to the stallion. Mirage pinned his ears and snaked out to bite the man's hand as he reached it over the fence. Amore caught a faint smirk across Xerxes's face before it disappeared.

"He's not my horse, Lord Zander, but Crowned Queen Amore's stallion," Xerxes commented, making Amore smile that he was not about to take credit for her stallion. Lord Zander looked surprised at first but quickly hid it and stepped away from the fence.

"Impressive, Your Highness. Would you ever consider letting him go?" The question surprised and annoyed her. Amore kept her smile intact. Mirage would never leave her hands. If it was possible she would see him buried before ever giving him to another.

"No, Mirage was born with me and shall die with me," she responded bluntly, not caring that she should have waited for Xerxes to respond first. Lord Zander only smirked.

"Of course." He smiled before Amore glanced over to Xerxes who seemed pleased at her response. Turning to the princess he smiled slightly showing her complete kindness.

"Would you like a ride on the mare, Your Highness?" Xerxes asked. The young girl perked up but it quickly faded as Lord Zander answered for her.

"We are a little tired from our journey, perhaps the women should rest while we talk a little business," Lord Zander practically ordered. Braylin was about to reply but Amore nudged her and glanced at the princess. She did look weary and Amore could not blame her.

"I think we should take a little rest. Princess Almeria, would you like to join us?" Braylin asked, stepping forward and almost collapsing onto the young girl's shoulder. "Oh my dear! Thank you for catching me! I think Amore's a little tired from hauling me around. Would you be so kind as to help me back?" Braylin practically dragged the young girl with her as she marched up the hill. "Come along, Your Highness!" Amore smiled at Braylin and followed behind them. A group of the soldiers quickly reformed around them as they walked back up the hill as they entered a hallway. Braylin kept holding Almeria's arm. A few soldiers stopped following but a good group crammed into the hallway with them. Amore felt every slight brush against her as they walked alongside protecting her from the young girl. If that girl did hide some sort of weapon, she barely looked strong enough to make it enter someone's skin. Finally they reached a private garden with cushions circled around a small table. Amore carefully sat as Braylin forced the girl to sit with her. The soldier's formed a medium-sized circle around them and Amore could see Braylin was about to explode.

"Leave us!" she commanded, glaring at the soldiers as one of them tried to object but quieted quickly as her eyes narrowed. They backed farther away, disappearing into the archways but always watching. Turning to the woman next to her, Braylin's eyes softened. "Are you hungry?"

The girl nodded and smiled slightly but her eyes held fear. Braylin snapped her fingers and a servant ran out with a tray of meat, cheese, and crackers, setting them down in front of them. He bowed low and ran back to his spot, waiting.

"Eat, Your Highness," Braylin instructed the young crowned queen. Amore could not help but study the young queen. Leaning back, Amore took one of the pieces of cheese and slowly ate it. Her eyes widened slightly as Almeria had eaten a majority of the food placed upon the tray. By the look of Braylin's express she could see her surprise. After the tray was empty, it was clear how exhausted the visiting princess was. Princess Almeria remained quiet as they all slowly fell silent with each other. She slowly looked around at the palace surrounding them. Braylin gaze remained steady as she appeared just as relaxed as any other time. Amore enjoyed watching Braylin and how she handled situations life threw at her.

"I wish to speak with General Damon, if you will excuse me," Braylin expressed, standing.

The princess scrambled to her feet and quickly said, "Of course, Your Highness," before slowly sitting down once more. So many questions lingered in Amore's mind as she studied the young girl before her. The food was cleared away, and once more they sat alone. Amore hesitated. Princess Almeria looked in need of rest. But the thought of how young she looked pricked at her.

"Your Highness, if you do not mind me inquiring, what is your age?" Amore asked cautiously. It was impolite, no doubt. The young princess looked up and caught Amore's gaze for a few moments before looking down again.

"Seventeen, Your Highness." Her voice was quiet as a faint quick smile spread across her lips. Amore narrowed her eyes for a few moments before smiling in return. She was only twenty and the girl had to be at least five years younger looking then her. *She looks barely older than fifteen.*

"I must say, you appear very young for your age. Though no doubt a gift," she expressed, smiling, as the younger girl in front of her attempted to smile as well. Her ocean-colored eyes looked clearly exhausted.

"Thank you, Your Highness."

"Would you—" Stopping short, Amore got to her feet as she could see Xerxes walking closer behind the princess. Princess Almeria quickly stood as soon as Amore did and bowed respectfully as the king neared. She seemed to grow even smaller in his presence.

"What can we do for you, my king?" Amore asked as the princess kept her head low. Xerxes smiled as he shifted his gaze from Amore to the princess.

"When you are ready, Your Highness, a room has been prepared for you. Did you enjoy the meal?" Admiration for Xerxes began to build inside her as she watched how sweet and kind he was to the young woman.

"Yes, Your Majesty. The food was most excellent. If it would be all right, I am most tired. I would like to go to my room now." Almeria's cheeks filled with a deep red, her eyes the color of a wave tossed in the ocean.

"If you need anything, Your Highness, please feel free to ask me," Amore offered. Princess Almeria nodded her head and gracefully bowed out as a maiden came to show her the way. Her heart skipped a beat as she stood alone with Xerxes. She attempted to scold herself for feeling such a way. He turned to her then and smiled. His eyes sparkling in the sunlight as he stood with his hands behind his back.

"What do you think of her?" he asked. Amore smiled sadly and pondered the royal princess.

"I think she is rather young. She told me that she was seventeen but she just seems so much younger and so oppressed, scared almost of everything and everyone. If you want my honest opinion, that is," Amore admitted, looking out as the servants cleaned up the garden. "I'm sorry for speaking out today also in front of lord Zander." Xerxes leaned against the stone archway and watched the servants.

"Do not apologize, Amore. My mother was quite outspoken and my grandmother hated it but I know that my father would not have been such a great king if she had stayed quiet when she was supposed to."

Amore smiled at his words. It warmed her heart to hear little bits about his own family, when so little was spoken of them.

"My father would have had a heart attack if he had seen how I have behaved these last few months." Amore seriously needed to work on not allowing him so intimately into her own world. *How does he even do that?* she wondered. He made her feel like she was around Vainer and that she could talk quite freely around him. Share anything with him. Just open her heart and allow him in.

"How have you behaved?" he asked curiously as his smile slowly grew. Amore wrapped her arms around herself and she could not help but smile. Her eyes flickered away before looking at him straight.

"Would your mother have approved of the way we met?" she asked, her voice soft as her mind flashed back to that night. "I seem to speak my mind with you, when I should mind my own thoughts." Her words grew quieter in the end as he smiled.

"Amore." He stepped closer and placed his hands on her waist. "We should be open with each other, no secrets. Secrets destroy families and kingdoms." Leaning forward, he kissed her cheek gently. "I approve of how we met because you would not be here now," he whispered, his breath sending chills down her neck as her eyes closed against her will. She felt her guard starting to slip on the inside as he kissed her cheek again, moving closer to her lips. Before he reached them, however, a voice interrupted them.

"Beg your pardon, my king," the general's voice rang out. Xerxes sighed and stepped back, releasing Amore. Amore felt lightheaded as she stood there, afraid that if she moved she would fall forward and crash into Xerxes. "We have a few things to discuss." The general stepped respectfully back and looked away. Opening her eyes, Amore stared into Xerxes gaze and a sense of longing filled her unexpectedly.

"I shall see you later." Stroking her cheek, he turned and left. Amore stared after him, still trying to regain her sense of awareness. *What just happened?* she wondered, stepping back and using the wall to catch herself.

Walking down the hall, Amore let the peaceful quietness soak into her. She replayed their conversation in her mind. *I need to stay away from Xerxes as much as possible. This is all getting too dangerous.* Walking down a dark hall, Amore glanced around. Each moment she let herself get caught up in those moments with him was one step closer to possibly hanging herself in the end. *No secrets.* How about, your future wife is the daughter of General Aleara Divon? A Lady of the court of King Haman, one of Xerxes's enemies.

"No secrets," she spoke out loud as she came to the end of the hall and looked around. The thin windows showed the outside world and a wooden door stood off to the side. Glancing back to make sure no one had spotted her, Amore pulled at the handle. The door refused to budge at first then suddenly gave way and swung open. Picking up her dress, Amore walked up the narrow, circular hallway until she reached a second door. Pushing it open, she felt the warm breeze hit her as she stepped out onto the tower roof. Its tall stone barrier kept her from falling off the edge but the view was breathtaking. Smiling to herself as the sun beat against her skin, Amore leaned onto of the stone barriers and looked down. The palace roof blocked her view of the ground but Amore didn't mind. She wanted to see the horizon anyway.

"Your Highness!" a startled voice made Amore jump and spin around to see a surprised young guard bow his head as she turned. "I'm sorry I did not think anyone was up here."

Amore smiled and nodded her head.

"I am not supposed to be up here, am I?" she acknowledged as the guard looked at her quickly before glancing away respectfully. "What is your name?" she asked curiously. He seemed startled at first then smiled shyly.

"Leon Carter, Your Highness." His voice squeaked, making Amore smile as he slowly moved farther onto the landing.

"I should be on my way." Amore walked past him as he quickly got out of her way.

"Your Highness," he called softly back to her as she started down the steps. Turning around, Amore waited for him to continue. "If you would like, Your Highness, when I leave I shall leave the door unlocked so you can come up here and look at the horizon," he offered, making Amore smile on the inside and out.

"Thank you, Leon."

Turning away, Amore walked happily back down the steps and through the hall. Her maidens and guards came dashing forward then startling her.

"Your Highness!" Liana exclaimed, out of breath, eyes wide. "I was afraid when we could not find you." Her gaze softening as she lowered her eyes and they assumed their positions behind her. Only Amore noticed that Crystal was missing from the number but did not question it for now. The maiden still acted like she was the daughter of a dignitary at times, and Amore often overheard her speaking to the others how one day she was going to marry a prince. Slipping back into the sunlight, Amore wandered the halls and gardens before growing bored. Dragging her hand along the stone walls, she glanced around her. Princess Braylin had not come back from talking to the general. Xerxes was now talking to the general and Princess Almeria was napping.

Walking down an unfamiliar hallway, Amore studied the walls. On one side the windows showed a drop-off to lower parts of the palace and the other was a solid wall. At the end of the hallway was an opening with a sentry posted. The guard bolted to his feet as Amore neared and stood at attention, waiting.

"What is through that door way?" she asked, studying the young man who stumbled for words.

"The servant quarters, Your Highness."

Thanking the sentry, Amore turned around and began to walk back. She was curious to see that part of the palace but decided it was best not to without a reason behind it. Spotting the young Talia in a spacious sitting area, she quietly made her way closer not wanting to disturb the young girl and whatever she was reading. Jumping in surprise, Talia scrambled to her feet and bowed her head.

"How may I help you, Your Highness?" she asked and Amore smiled as she looked at the scroll in her hands.

"What are you reading?"

The young girl looked surprised before blushing. "History of the palace and Avalon, Your Highness. I hope that is all right."

Laughing, Amore motioned for her to sit and took an empty chair. "Of course it is all right with me. My tutor always told me to learn my history so I would not be doomed to repeat it." Her tutor told her a lot of things, many of which seemed a little farfetched.

"That has a lot of truth to it, Your Highness," Talia said, shifting nervously. "Did you like learning?" She studied Amore.

Smirking, Amore sighed and shook her head. "Sadly, not very much. I remember everything I learned but did not care for it very much. I was too concerned about other things in life."

The young girl's eyes grew wide as she leaned closer in her chair. "Like what?" she whispered, her voice excited, making Amore feel a little silly.

"Well, I guess for one thing, horses. I have loved horses since I was young. I always thought that they brought freedom, I suppose. Then…" Amore laughed at the thoughts. Her focus had been about riding and having freedom. A few times it had been thoughts of boys, but it was mostly pushed to the side because the boys who surrounded her were mostly men and all soldiers, with an occasional visit to the court which entertained her enough to enjoy the company of some of the dignitaries and nobilities' sons. That was before Aishlin would arrive in the room, and the attention would turn toward her, which Amore did not mind because she really did not want to get married into the court life. She preferred wide open spaces with no one in sight for miles. "I am sorry, I got lost in thought."

"What type of things did you learn?" Talia questioned. The girl had a bright mind and it was plain to see that she loved to learn.

"Geography, reading, arithmetic, history, protocol of the court, how to be a proper lady." Amore chuckled in the end. Talia sat back in her chair and sighed slightly as she grew distant.

"What is it like to be of nobility?" she asked, her words dreamy.

Amore studied the young girl as she stared at the ceiling. It never dawned on her to ponder such things. Of course Amore had never really had to work a day in her life. The only work she would have to do was for education and that of dancing, languages, and such.

"I suppose...I really am not sure how to describe it. Confusing at times, demanding, and not a lot of time to yourself. Yet rewarding, I imagine." It mostly flustered her, yet the dresses she wore and the jewelry were splendid. The capability of getting up long after the sun rose. "Talia, you and the princess look so much alike in age," Amore expressed, studying the young girl. In fact, they looked very close in age. "Care to join me for a moment?" Amore asked, standing. The young maiden scrambled to her feet and followed Amore closely as she walked the halls scanning for Princess Almeria. She finally found her out by the stables, petting the beautiful mare that had been gifted to her. Soldiers surrounded Amore immediately before she demanded for some space and they widened the circle.

"Your Highness!" Amore called so she would not startle the princess. Princess Almeria turned and blushed slightly, stopping her petting of the mare. "She is a beautiful horse, what have you decided to name her?" Amore inquired, running her hand down the silky neck.

The princess's eyes grew thoughtful as she studied the mare. "I have not thought about it." Her words were soft as she stared into the eyes of the mare and a faint smile broke out. "I can see my reflection in her eyes." She actually seemed excited for the first time.

"Azure."

The voice behind them drew both their attention. Talia blushed and lowered her head. "I am sorry Your Highness."

"What does that mean?" Princess Almeria asked, her eyes still turned on the mare.

"Precious one in one tongue, blue in another," Talia said softly. The princess smiled as she softly said the name.

"Azure. I like it. Thank you." She turned her gaze on Talia and bowed her head kindly. Talia smiled brightly and lifted her gaze as she glanced at Amore who smiled. Sure enough, the girls were the same height and same body stature. It only affirmed Amore's decision that Princess Almeria was claiming to be older than she was or that she was a lot smaller for her age.

"Talia, would you be so kind as to accompany the princess today?" Amore asked and Talia quickly nodded, excited. As she left the two girls started up a wild conversation and burst into giggles. The soldiers followed Amore back until she reached the hall then only one tagged along. Servants along the way bowed to Amore before continuing on their path. A wondrous smell drifted toward her from the Deben, where all of the food was prepared. Her stomach complained as she continued walking. Her dislike for Lord Zander quickly grew as her eyes spotted the visiting nobility in one of the smaller gardens standing too close to...her maiden Crystal. The girl giggled about something he said and moved closer. Out of the corner of her eye, she could see the guard behind her tense at the sight.

"Am I interrupting something?" Amore announced as Crystal giggled once more then bolted away from the man and shook her head, her expression annoyed. Bowing, she quickly turned and hurried off. Amore watched her go before turning her attention to the man.

"Nothing more than a little conversation, is all, Your Highness." The tone suggested otherwise, and the way he said Your Highness made her nerves stand on end.

"I would be most appreciative, sir, if you kept your distance from my maidens," Amore requested. She wanted to turn sharply away and walk off, showing great disrespect for him, but she refused to, knowing it would not look good for her. The lord took a step closer and the guard behind her moved toward the front, catching the man's eye as he stopped and bowed.

"Of course, Your Highness." His eyes narrowed. Amore only lowered her gaze for a brief second before turning and walking away. After a few steps, she glanced back as Lord Zander stared after her before turning and walking off. The guard behind her muttered something and Amore was sure it was unpleasant and acted like she had heard nothing at all.

"Your Highness!" Liana's familiar voice called and she hurried closer to them, picking up her dress so her feet would not step on the beautiful hem. Bowing, she stood straight and quickly repeated. "Dinner shall be served in two hours in the Florae Hall."

"Thank you, Liana." The maiden continued to stand in front of her until Amore asked, "Anything else?" The girl, just a couple of years older than her, grinned and nodded her head. Liana led her back to her Amore's chambers and the sentries pulled open the doors. Inside waited more maidens and a beautiful dress sprawled out on her bed.

"Princess Braylin picked out the jewelry for you as well, Your Highness," Liana. informed as the women began to help her out of her current dress and into the one that waited. Its dark blue color was accented in black. It glimmered like all of her other dresses. After everything was secured in place, she would sit for the next hour and half while her hair was taken down, brushed, and replaced into long, flowing curls. A small diamond crown was then placed upon her hair and wide twisted gold bracelets laced her forearms and wrists. The necklace and earrings seemed out of place upon her skin. The maidens dressed beautifully as well but Amore felt like she was getting ready for a wedding. The time drew near and she followed Liana to the Florae Hall.

The hall was filled with all of Avalon's important dignitaries. She was excited to see Governor Tyron and Lady Reni amongst the crowd of people. As she walked in everyone bowed low respectfully to her. She wanted to greet Governor Tyron but knew it would come with time. The first to approach her was one of the highest ranking officials in the palace. She had yet to truly meet a lot of the officials of Avalon. Briefly at the celebration, but not truly. The first man was sort of tall, with light brown hair and fair skin. He bowed low before standing back up straight.

"I am Lord Byron, Your Royal Highness!"

Amore was about to stretch her hand out to him, when Clarice checked her and Amore stopped short. Thankfully the officials appeared to not notice. "I am in charge of watching the laws of Avalon, and making sure protocol is maintained."

With that another came forward and bowed low. "I am Lord Timothy, Your Royal Highness. I am charged with the privilege of overseeing the land of Avalon, and to make sure she flourishes always."

A few more approached and repeated what their station was. Until a man stepped forward that made Amore want to cringe at the arrogant look in his green eyes. He bowed but not as low as the others.

"I am Lord Marcel, Your Highness. I am in charge of overseeing all of Roselyn and what is within it." Even though his words were short and he left quickly, it left a bad taste in her mouth. As the rest of the officials acknowledge their positions, Amore smiled brightly as Governor Tyron approached. Lady Reni waited respectfully in the background until later.

"I am Governor Tyron, Your Royal Highness." A bright smile was upon his face as his eyes flashed slightly. "I am in charge of the bountiful city of Fernon. It is most wondrous to see your royal highness again." With that Governor Tyron bowed again and left to find his place. Before Amore could move to take her place for the meal, Clarice stepped forward at Amore's request.

"It is against protocol and considered very offensive to touch one of royalty. Especially the king's intended," she whispered quietly for only Amore to hear. Her expression must have appeared surprised as Clarice smiled slightly. "It has been in place for many generations. You do not want to know the consequences that are still in place as well." She said the last part even quieter. It was not long and the king finally appeared. The officials all bowed low and shouted their praise for their king. As Xerxes turned his eyes upon Amore, she felt her heart flutter at the look in his eyes as she bowed. Taking his offered arm, Amore followed him to her place. The food was served, and the guests praised the abundance of the meal. When their praise's turned toward Amore, she felt heat trying to rise to her face but forced her pounding heart to quiet and smiled at the wondrous comments they paid her. She was extremely grateful when the praise of her beauty turned away onto something else. Nothing prepared her for a higher official to stand up and raise his glass.

"To the king, may he live forever!" The proclamation echoed through the room as as everyone proclaimed it and waited to drink as the man continued, "To the king and his beautiful bride, we all wait in anticipation for such a great day of their union!" The crowd cheered and Amore felt her bright smile stay in place. As they continued to cheer, she caught Governor Tyron's hand in the air, yet the look in his eyes made her quickly look away and catch Xerxes smiling warmly at her, drinking in the praises of his people. Unable to hold his gaze too long fearing her heart would melt, Amore drank to the toast after the crowd settled down and was quite relieved when entertainers came out to please the crowd. She could feel Braylin's eyes on her and glanced over at the princess briefly as she smiled and looked away. Amore allowed her mind to get lost in the music and laughter of the entertainers. Shifting her gaze to Xerxes, he smiled at her and motioned for her to join him.

Taking the seat next to him, he pulled her close suddenly and whispered her ear, "You handled that wonderfully." His breath was warm on her neck. She did not know what to say, or truly how to handle all of the attention that had been given to her tonight. She had figured the feast and gathering had been in celebration for the visiting royalty yet nothing had been made mention of them yet. Xerxes once more watched the others as his arm still looped around her waist and Amore flickered her gaze at Princess Almeria as she sat quietly watching everything, appearing a little overwhelmed at it all. Avalon was considerably bigger than Delmar. Delmar barely covered a portion of Avalon's vast land and wealth. Emir and Avalon matched each other in size and power. Perhaps the princess was not used to the commotion of the party. The princess's gaze suddenly turned toward her and she seemed surprised that Amore was looking at her. Lowering her gaze, she bowed her head slightly and did not meet Amore's gaze again. She then turned her attention briefly to Lord Zander. He was caught up in the amusement of the entertainers and laughing quite contently many times. Her gaze then drifted to Lady Reni. She was leaning close to another official's wife and was sharing something with her, her face bright with a smile. As she caught Amore's gaze, she lowered her head respectfully but quickly caught her gaze again. The older woman smiled brightly, her eyes filled with joy and excitement.

As the party slowly quieted down, Amore desperately wanted to greet Lady Reni but kept her position by Xerxes until he was the first one to be drawn away into a conversation. Even then she still waited, not wanting to break any protocol she may not know about until finally she was able to be released. As she slowly made her way toward Lady Reni trying not to appear in too much of a hurry, she was quickly intercepted by Lord Zander and paused respectfully to hear what he had to say.

"I must ask your forgiveness, Your Highness, for my behavior today. The trip has been long and tiresome. It seems to have affected my judgment greatly." He bowed low and actually appeared to be sorry.

"You are forgiven, Lord Zander, and it is understandable, no doubt."

He still unnerved her but at least it seemed like he was trying to make amends. As he continued to make conversation with her and Amore responded the way she felt was necessary, she could see Braylin watching them and a most displeased look was upon her face.

"Excuse me," Amore remarked as Lord Byron walked over to talk to Lord Zander. Casually, Amore made her way over to Braylin, stating her hellos to the appropriate people before finally reaching her side. Standing alongside the princess for a moment, Amore remained silent before finally commenting softly, "You seemed most displeased with me, Your Highness."

Braylin made no reply as she warmly greeted one of the dignitaries' wives.

"It is not you that I am displeased with, contrary actually. I think you are doing a marvelous job." She grew silent once more before stating, "Fine day, is it not Madam Grandeur?" An older woman walked up to greet them before stating what a fine day it was indeed and started up a long conversation about how the weather was turning out for this time of the year and she expected it would turn even hotter before the year was over. Making her excuse, the older woman bowed before wandering off to talk to another and Braylin quickly and softly continued, "I am greatly puzzled by that man. Did you know he actually approached me today and offered sincere apologies for what happened between us when we were younger? He made it sound like we were young children that did not know what we were doing."

Amore hurt for Braylin. She must have been wounded deeply by the man and to see him now after so many years engaged to another must be hard. Could it be possible that Amore had gotten Lord Zander all wrong? Was it her sincere admiration for

Princess Braylin that made her uneasy about him? As she watched the visiting nobility, she pondered this as her eyes turned toward Princess Almeria. The two had barely spent any time together since dinner and the young girl stood solemnly amongst officials appearing to listen to whatever their conversation happened to be. Motioning for Liana to come forward, Amore requested for her to ask the princess to join them. When Princess Braylin was free from her conversation, Amore quietly asked, "I would like to ask your help."

Braylin smiled and nodded her head. "Anything."

"I feel it would be best to learn more of the protocols of the palace. That way I am not breaking any laws without realizing it."

The princess looked surprised but smiled warmly as she nodded her head. "That is a wonderful idea."

Amore turned her gaze back toward Princess Almeria, as Liana approached with her head low and made the request. The princess appeared slightly relieved as she walked back toward Braylin with Liana.

"Did you get a chance to ride Azure today?" Amore asked, trying to get the young princess to open up after she had bowed once she joined them.

She smiled faintly and shook her head. "No. Perhaps another day when I am not so tired from the trip. Thank you, Your Highness." She still appeared very tired but was handling everything rather well. Maybe Amore had gotten the princess all wrong as well. She began to doubt her own judgment.

"If you do not mind my inquiring, Princess, how did you and Lord Zander meet?" Braylin asked. The princess appeared surprised at the question then took a shallow breath and glanced over at her betrothed.

"He helped me greatly after my parents' death. He was a wonderful advisor to me during that time and helped me to show the kingdom I am ready for the throne," she answered as her eyes never left the man. Amore studied her expressions but could get nothing but a distant longing and hurt.

"I am most sorry to hear about your parents," Braylin sympathized.

Princess Almeria smiled and turned her teal gaze on Braylin. "Thank you, Your Highness." Princess Almeria grew distant for a moment before Braylin drew her back into a deep conversation. Lady Reni finally made her way toward Amore but before she had the chance to reach her, Xerxes approached. Princess Almeria bowed low and remained that way as he stopped in front of them. The young princess seemed greatly surprised when the king addressed her personally.

"I hope my dear sister is not corrupting you with her ways, Your Highness," he teased.

Princess Almeria's head shot up and she stared in surprise at the older princess. "No, she is not, Your Majesty," she reassured him.

Princess Braylin shook her head. "Pay him no mind, Your Highness. My dearest brother king likes to tease me."

The princess nodded her head but seemed to be in complete awe of whatever King Xerxes remarked. Contentment filled Amore as she watched those around her conversing with each other. How Braylin and Xerxes treated each other intrigued her greatly.

"It was an honor that you joined us this evening. I hope you have been enjoying your stay so far?"

Princess Almeria smiled brightly, warming up to his words. "It has been most pleasant, Your Majesty. I really enjoy the lovely mare that you have given to me."

They continued on in conversation until Princess Almeria made her apologies and moved on. Xerxes shifted to stand next to Amore as Princess Braylin also went to talk with another.

"I think she admires you greatly, Your Majesty," Amore remarked softly, turning her eyes upon him. He stood straight with his hands clasped behind his back. He was overlooking the crowd with a faint interest, almost as if he was wishing they were not all gathered together. He smiled at her words but made no comment further on it.

"The officials seem to think very highly of you," she continued. "Who would not?" She caught herself then and blushed, looking away. She felt his hand on her chin as he gently turned her face toward him, his smile warm.

"I think it is you they are very pleased with tonight." His words brought back all of their praises toward her and Amore felt overwhelmed, making him grin. "You are honest, Amore, and the officials can see that." His words felt like a knife into her heart as she tried to hold the smile as he thankfully turned his attention back on the people.

Honest? she thought. *What kind of honesty did they see?* She felt anything but honest as she stood there mixed in a crowd of people that would easily turn against her if she spoke out her full name and who her parents were. *I am anything but honest right now.* His words haunted her mind as she stood beside him. He looked concerned suddenly as he looked at her once more.

"What is it?" he asked, and Amore tried to quickly bury any emotion she must have been showing.

"I feel very unworthy of your praise." She actually meant it. Grinning, Xerxes leaned closer to her.

"You can share anything with me, I will not hold it against you." He must have been flirting with her.

"It cannot be that easy, my king." She tried to add playfulness to her words. He smiled and took her hand bringing it up to his mouth as he kissed the back of her hand.

"Then I shall gladly win over your heart, until it is."

You may not want to know everything, she thought. *For surely then your mind and your heart would change.*

An easy silence filled the air between them as the party continued. The people seemed to be enjoying the time and grumbled when it was time for it come to a close. She had not been able to talk with Lady Reni but it was already placed in the back of her mind as she walked down the hall with Xerxes to her room. Stopping in front of her door as the guards bowed low and her maidens stood back waiting, Xerxes smiled and gently kissed her check.

"Until tomorrow then?"

Amore nodded, smiling. The maidens helped her get ready for bed until she dismissed them all. Making her way to the window as the bright moon illuminated the land, she stared out into the darkness. Tonight her attachment toward the king had grown, but she could feel her fear grow as well. She had never imagined her life to turn out in this direction. She only hoped that her secret would be buried until she had lived a good, long life and buried in peace. That was the only end she wanted to accept.

Hidden Secrets

With the passing of time, Princess Almeria grew stronger, recovering from her trip. She accompanied Amore and Princess Braylin frequently, and seemed to be in better spirits. It began to make Amore question her original assumption about both the princess and even Lord Zander. It seemed like after the dinner that night and his apology that he was trying to make amends for his behavior and appeared to be most pleasant that Amore grew even more conflicted as Princess Braylin refused to give in to her complete distrust of the man and often retold it to Amore when they were in private.

"Perhaps he has truly changed from his ways," Amore remarked as Braylin shot her a harsh look and shook her head.

"Do not be so naïve," she retorted.

The brightly lit room made the deep colored stone feel warm and inviting. Amore grew lost looking at the stone as the silence grew between them once more.

"Tell me about your home. I have come to realize that I know not a lot about your origin."

Her heart froze. She had wondered when this day would come. Someone had to be curious. She could tell that her silence was increasing Braylin's curiosity.

"What would you like to know?" finally came out of her mouth. Had her face gone pale? Could Braylin, knowing Amore a little better, see how terrified she was on the inside? Would she be able to tell if Amore provided a false story? Braylin smiled slightly as she turned her attention away from Amore.

"What was your home like?"

"Beautiful. It was made of stone but nothing like this."

"Tell me about your mother."

Amore's heart hurt at the mention of her mother. She at least would not have to speak falsely there. This time she must have showed more emotion then she had wanted to.

"Oh, I am sorry, Amore! It is all right you do not have to say anything if you do not wish to," the princess quickly apologized.

"Even if I wanted to I would not be able to share much about her anyway," she confessed and smiled sadly. Braylin nodded her head and her eyes were sad.

"My mother was a beautiful woman. Everything about her commanded respect. My father…" Braylin suddenly laughed at a fond memory. "My father would tell us stories when we were younger when they had first met. He said that she startled him greatly. He loved her from the moment he set eyes upon her." Taking a long breath, she smiled slightly. "Tell me about your father." Amore actually smiled then.

"He is very loving, and extremely protective. My brother said he was not always that way but when my mother died, everything changed." Amore smiled slightly as she gazed off. "My father always wanted me to become my best at everything. I think that is why I disliked my studies so much."

Braylin grew oddly quiet for a moment, her eyes distant and thoughtful.

"I never thought of how your family must have reacted when I had General Damon bring you here. I pray your brother must have sent word to your father." Her voice sounded genuinely concerned. Vainer had to have made it close to home by now, if not intercepted by soldiers. What was he even to tell father?

"I did not even think to ask," Amore remarked without realizing that she had said it.

"We shall send something to your father immediately then. Invite him to the palace!" she exclaimed, smiling.

Amore felt her heart stop. To what could she give the persistent Braylin an excuse worthy enough? She would no doubt hear the truth spoken through her words this time.

"I do not think he would come. He does not care to travel great distances."

The excited light in the princess's eyes died slightly. "What a shame, for I would have dearly loved to have meet him. Xerxes no doubt would not approve of going very far during this time either." Braylin dropped the subject and grew deep in thought. Amore tried to settle her racing heart as she stared across the room and to the open window. Getting off the chair she made her way there and gazed out.

"I have always wanted to visit the mountains," the princess continued, smiling slightly. "I have always thought that the majority of this palace had to have come from somewhere. Of course with the mountain ranges being in Emir, that is impossible." She grew quiet once more, smiling at the idea of the mountains. Amore had indeed been to the mountains before. Part of her relatives lived next to them. Her father would often take her with him on his journeys when she was younger and they had visited many towns in and by the mountains.

"Have you ever been to the mountains?"

Amore could hear the curiosity filling her voice. Searching for any information concerning the future queen of her country.

"No." Thankfully enough her voice remained steady as her nerves made her insides shake. Digging her fingers into the palm of her hand, Amore forced a smile as her gaze meet the princess's. A thought began to prod Amore's mind, one her sister had not been able to answer. Slowly turning around, Amore gazed at the beautiful princess before her. Why did Avalon and Emir hate each other? Amore could think of no bad thing about the Avalon's rulers.

"Princess Braylin," Amore inquired before her nerve lost out. Braylin smirked slightly and turned her gaze on Amore. "Would you care if I asked you a...cautious question?" The princess's smile grew as her gaze became curious.

"Of course."

"What is the reason of the hatred between Emir and Avalon?"

Startled, the princess remained quiet as her eyes grew thoughtful. "That is indeed a cautious question to be asked. I feel in my experiences with Emirians that our views are very different." She grew quiet. "Why the sudden curiosity?" she implored and Amore smiled just to seem just that. Curious.

"You talked about the mountains, so it caused me to think and wonder." How many experiences did the princess have with Emirians? Would any from the Emir's royal court ever have to deal with her? She had to ask. How would she convince her way through a situation like that? She never would be able to unless those who came from Emir kept their mouth shut. Permanently.

"Does the palace often have dealings with Emir?" Amore continued, watching the princess closely.

"Not as of late. In the past, in order to attempt to solve any accusations, either side would call forth a meeting. Nothing ever became of those meetings other than the proof that we share very different opinions."

If only you knew, Amore thought as she turned away once more to look out the window.

"Do not concern yourself in needing to worry about Emirians. I doubt we shall ever see anything of them for some time," Braylin seemed so confident in the negative opinions of Amore's people. So assured of their strong differences that the two kingdoms would never come to peaceful terms. Her words buried deep within Amore's heart, reinforcing the thought that no one must ever know of her country of birth. No one could ever find out.

⟡

Her conversation with Braylin lingered in her mind throughout the day. *What if something ever happened between the two kingdoms? What then?* Amore did not like the idea. If Avalon and Emir's conflict with each other grew, eventually it could lead to war. What then? What would Amore do? Who would she stand with? Shaking her head, she took a deep breath. *I hope I never have to come to that point.*

Amore felt her heart sink at the sight of the stack of scrolls both Talia and other servants carried. She had asked Talia to find them for her, not wanting to bother Lord Byron too much. Knowing the young girl would need help, she had sent Crystal with. Seeing that the older maiden walked empty handed and other servants carried the scrolls reaffirmed her sinking belief about the beautiful maiden. Crystal took her seat as the scrolls were set in front of Amore. Giving Talia a quizzical look, the young girl flickered a hesitant smile. "I did not think there were this many," she expressed, letting out a long breath. "Is there anything else I could do for you, Your Highness?" Talia asked, eyeing the large scrolls.

"No, thank you, Talia." She desperately wished she had not even inquired about them in the first place. Amore slowly opened the first one and began to read. For the most part, many of the protocols made sense and matched Emir's in a way. However, there was quite a few that puzzled her greatly.

"Beautiful day, is it not Your Highness?" Zander called, drawing her attention away from the scroll she was reading. Gently rolling it up, she handed it off to Liana and smiled slightly as she looked up at the crystal clear blue sky. Birds floated in the breeze before disappearing into the bright hot summer sun.

"Yes, it is." She shifted her gaze looking for Princess Almeria. The young princess appeared to not be with him, making him smile slightly. *I wonder what he could possibly want?* The visiting guest seemed to approach her more and more as of lately, drawing her into conversations about anything in particular. Each time, Princess Almeria was never with him.

"Almeria is enjoying the beautiful mare this morning," he answered her unasked question. Amore was glad that the princess had time to spend with the mare Azure. They seemed to match each other so well in temperament.

"I am glad." For the first time since his arrival, Amore actually felt comfortable in his presence as he continued to make mention of things here and there. Zander actually had quite the sense of humor, making even the maidens giggle a few times. What increased her curiosity was the annoyed look inside Crystal's eyes as she continued on with what she was currently doing.

"That is most amusing," Amore remarked after he finished a rather interesting story. *What would Braylin think of you right now?* she wondered suddenly and felt the smile slip from her face for a moment before plastering it back on to not draw attention. He stood quite relaxed and his expression humorous, appearing to be quite at home within the palace walls.

"It was certainly a sight to see, Your Highness," he remarked, smiling brightly before bowing low as he offered out his hand. Keeping her hands at her side, Amore felt her smile slip as she kept her gaze steady upon him. As he realized she would not take his invitation, he stood straight again while his smile still remained the same.

"Good day, Lord Zander," Amore remarked softly as he bowed once more and turned to leave. Her heart flickered slightly, wondering if he knew the protocol of Avalon. If so, then how easily he seemed to break one. Taking a deep breath, she turned her attention back on the scroll. It was going to take some time to learn all of the royal protocols and laws of Avalon.

Desperately needing a break from reading, Amore soon found Braylin alone in a large open room. Whatever she was doing she kept it closely to herself and well guarded.

"It all seems rather hopeless." She collapsed on the couch. Braylin let out a laugh as she shook her head before turning back to the large canvas before her. "What are you doing?" she wondered as she studied the tall woman.

"Never you mind and think about your studies." She chuckled as she leaned over the table.

"I would rather not. Frankly I wish I had never asked about them in the first place," she retorted, staring up at the beautiful colorful doomed marble ceiling.

"Yes, it can be most frustrating to have to study them. Is there anything specific that you want to ask about?" she implored, still working on the canvas, yet fully aware of what Amore was talking about.

"How about all of it? How is one supposed to remember and follow all of those?" Her mind was overwhelmed with the scrolls she was reading. At least several were rewritten and ones she could set aside to not concern herself with. Sighing, she leaned back resting on the couch. Thankfully it was only Braylin and herself in this room. No other ears to listen to their conversations.

"Follow what?" a strong male voice asked, startling her. Xerxes made his way closer as Amore laid back down to continue stare up at the ceiling.

"Protocols," Braylin remarked, "Amore is wanting to set the whole library on fire," she continued, making Amore chuckle.

"You are exaggerating," she retorted as Xerxes smiled and leaned against the backing of the couch Amore was on. "Though it does not seem like a bad idea. If no one can read them, no one can follow them."

Letting out a long sigh, Amore sat up, feeling rather self conscious laying there with Xerxes looking at her.

"Protocols are important to making a kingdom run," he remarked, smirking. Amore's mind flashed back to a rather odd one that she had read and she gave him a quizzical look.

"All of them? I really do not see how certain days one is only supposed to write with one hand and not the other is supposed to help any kingdom." As she was speaking, Braylin burst out laughing.

"Is that really still in there?" she asked, a wide grin upon her features before she shifted her eyes up at her brother. Turning back around she chocked back the laughter. "When I was younger, I convinced my dearest brother to have a royal protocol written. Never thought they would actually go through with it and leave it there for all these years." She could not contain her laughter, making Amore smile.

"Though it is not an official protocol because my father never sealed it, I do wonder why it is still in the scrolls," Xerxes remarked.

"Perhaps Lord Byron should check his scrolls and see which ones are not effective anymore," Braylin insisted, still enjoying the fond memory of her past.

"How is Princess Almeria?" Xerxes asked from behind her still. How did the room seem to grow so much smaller all of a sudden?

"Good, I believe. I have not seen her as much as I have seen of Lord Zander. He seems to show up a lot as of..." Her breath caught in the throat as she felt his fingers brush against the back of her neck. Her mind froze as his fingers twisted around the strands of hair that had fallen from her beautiful braid bun.

"Where have your guards been?" he asked, his voice sounding soft and distant. Her mind remained blank.

"I..." *Stop it!* she scolded herself as she saw a glorious smile spread across Braylin's face. "I have not had any following me for some time now," she finished and took a deep breath quietly. Her heart beat skipped a few times.

"Really?" His voice sounded loud in her mind. "I shall have to see to that." Gently kissing her cheek, he smiled. "I shall see you both later." Her heart continued to pound even long after he had left.

"Who has been bringing you the scrolls?" Braylin asked after some time had passed. Yet the pleased look upon the princess's face remained.

"Talia and Crystal," feeling heat rise to her face as Braylin continued to grin. She made a soft hmm sound but said no more. Resting back once more to stare at the ceiling, her mind drifted back to the conflicts with Emir and Avalon which tore at her heart.

"What are you thinking about?" Braylin asked as the quietness began to eat at Amore. Sitting up once more, she clasped her hands on her lap and sighed.

"Do you..." Stopping short, she smiled and shook her head. "It is nothing important that cannot wait until later."

Getting up, Amore made her way back to the garden. The scrolls were gone as Talia informed her that Lord Byron had retrieved them and would bring back the correct ones. It was some time before Amore saw Lord Byron making his way through the halls with scrolls in hand.

His expressions looked completely apologetic and very dismayed.

"I am most sorry, Your Highness. I am not sure how the old written protocols got mixed in with the ones you have been studying." His eyes shifted quickly toward Crystal before he bowed low once more as the much smaller stack was handed to Talia. Crystal did not seem concerned as she studied the object in her hands. Admiring her handiwork.

"Thank you, Lord Byron." Amore nodded her head as the lord turned and walked away. Talia looked greatly flustered as she shook her head.

"I do apologize, Your Highness, if anything I had brought to you was no longer in effect." The young girl's apologies made Amore smile. She liked Talia greatly. She was very sweet, and Amore got along well with the tan-skinned girl. Her sunlit brown hair rested against one of her shoulders as her green eyes glared across the way to the older maiden who seemed oblivious to the conversation.

"Do not worry about it, Talia. I am relieved to see that the pile has shrunk considerably." The young maiden smiled and nodded her head. "Would you care to help me with them?" she asked, making a light grow on her beautiful young face.

"Most certainly, Your Highness." It was then that Crystal's expressions seemed to change from a oblivious to annoyed.

With Talia's help the protocols were easier to remember. It was not long after the conversation with Xerxes and Braylin that two guards began to follow Amore as soon as Amore stepped out of her room until she returned back in the evening. At least it seemed to keep Lord Zander at bay, as well as most of the others in the palace besides her maidens and Braylin. Not that no other seemed to converse with her that much anyway. Princess Almeria returned from her horse later that afternoon. She seemed to be in pleasant spirits as she joined Amore.

"How was Azure, Your Highness?" Talia asked excitedly as she joined the young princess once more like Amore had asked of her. Talia drew Almeria into a deep conversation and it still confirmed Amore's original thoughts that the two young women were equal in age. Talia seemed to put the princess at ease more than anyone else could, and it pleased Amore greatly to see that. Talia seemed be such a free spirit in a way. She could see the strong resemblance between her mother Clarice and the young girl. It amused her mind to wonder about the potential in her. She seemed very well learned and, like Braylin had said, a wonderful conversationalist. The room they were in slowly became a favored place for her. Wonderful scents of flowers and fragrances constantly filled the air. The room was beautifully decorated to every extent possible. Many gold furnishings to the finest wood to be found.

"What would you do, Talia, if you were crowned a princess?" one of the maidens teased the young girl. Talia smiled brightly as she laid back against the cushion.

"Oh, to even think about it is wonderful enough." The young girl flashed a smile.

"One never knows, Talia, when you know nothing of your own ancestry," another remarked, still swirling the idea around. "Perhaps you are a descendant of a king from far away." As the woman continued to play with the idea and chuckle over some of the suggestion that came up, Talia threw a hesitant look at Amore and Princess Almeria. A worried look filled the young girl's eyes.

"I am content to where I have been placed in life," the maiden remarked, looking at Amore before quickly looking down as a redness filled her checks. Growing embarrassed by the talk. Amore smiled and wanted to comfort Talia that she took no offense from the women's talk.

"We did not mean to embarrass you, Talia," one of the maidens apologized as the young girl fiddled with her dress. "Perhaps we may have gotten a little carried away with it."

Talia looked up and smiled. "That is all right." Her mother walked into the room then and smiled as the maidens fell silent in her presence. Clarice frowned as she looked around before sitting down nearest to Amore.

"Did I miss something important?" she asked, glancing up at Amore.

"No, ma'am," the maiden who started it all quickly remarked as she turned her eyes to a project she had set aside previously. Clarice nodded her head before she looked at Talia and smiled as her daughter drew the princess into conversation again.

"Clarice," Amore remarked softly, drawing the respected maiden's attention as she moved alongside Amore. "I wish to speak to you privately."

They went to the garden alongside the room, smaller than most but just as beautiful. She pondered her owns words as she thought through the protocols she was learning. As Clarice joined Amore, she studied her with a warm gaze.

"What is bothering you, Your Highness?" she asked. It had been Clarice who first mentioned about Amore being a queen. She still seemed rather excited about it and expressed it often to Amore.

"How am I doing?" she asked, looking at Clarice. The older woman was beautiful even for her own age. Her skin was on the darker side while still remaining fair. She was at least a foot shorter than Amore, who was tall enough on her own. "As one is required of a future wife of a king?"

The maiden grew silent as she pondered Amore's question before smiling. "I find, Your Highness, that you are doing very well." Her smile was bright as she studied Amore. "Do not worry yourself too much, you shall find your own way of handling things. Learning the protocols is a wonderful place to start." Amore nodded her head as Clarice continued, "Are you worried the royal court will not accept you like the king has?" she asked, startling her. Amore had pondered the thought of not being found worthy in the court's eyes but with Braylin's own reassurance and even the praises she had received did not allow that thought to remain. Nor did it appear that Xerxes at any time would easily fall for another within the palace.

"No, that is not it." So what was her question even about? "Thank you, Clarice." The maiden nodded her head and returned to the others, leaving Amore alone. Whenever Amore thought about being queen, it pricked her heart. She had grown considerably attached to Xerxes, but what about everything else that was involved in his life? What if she had to choose between the two? Between her father and…Xerxes. Could she make such a choice? The thought plagued her mind as she returned to the maidens. They were conversing about little things of interest, nothing interesting enough to pull Amore from her thoughts.

A strong breeze from the ocean was sweeping away the heat of the summer, keeping those within the palace cool for the time being. Getting up from her place, Amore began to wander the palace in hopes of chasing away her thoughts; the maidens remained quiet behind her until Amore dismissed all of them. Only Clarice remained with her, which suited her. Clarice kept watching her but respectfully remained quiet, waiting to see if Amore wanted to speak. If only her childhood friend Annalisa was here, she had always been a great listener and a wonderful friend. *No doubt she would be excited for me.* Annalisa was one who always seemed carefree and happy as Amore had wanted to be.

"Your Highness." A young boy hurried forward and bowed low. Amore could spot a woman older than her waiting in the distance watching.

"What is it?" she asked, turning her eyes back upon the boy in front of her. He kept his eyes to the ground as he made his request.

"Milady wishes me to ask of you to join them in a welcoming to the future queen, a party only for the women, Your Highness." Flickering her gaze at Clarice as the older maiden's head barely shifted forward in a nod.

"Tell your mistress that I accept."

The young boy nodded his head and hurried away. The woman smiled and bowed her head before turning to show her the way.

Clarice softly whispered in her ear, "That is Lady Tamar, Lord Byron's wife."

As Amore stepped into the beautiful sunlit room, she suddenly felt rather out of place. The woman bowed respectfully as she neared. Lady Tamar stood straight and smiled brightly.

"We figured it was time to properly introduce ourselves to the future Queen of Avalon since we have not had the time to yet do so." She offered Amore the best seat in the room. Slowly sitting, she tried hard not to study each of the women. She had seen most of them within the palace from time to time but they usually kept to themselves.

"I am Lady Tamar, wife of Lord Byron. This is Lady Marcella, wife of Lord Timothy." The fair-skinned woman kept her gaze down as she bowed her head and a redness flushed her fair skin. "Lady Gemini, wife of Lord Marcel." Amore tried to remember all of their names but soon just nodded her head and said a warm greeting as Lady Tamar clapped her hands and took her seat as well. Princess Braylin sat nearest to Amore but she felt greatly uncomfortable. It pleased Amore to see that Princess Almeria joined them as well, sitting near to Braylin. Most of the women in the room seemed to be quite a few years older than her. Amore soon found out that she was the same age as some of their daughters. Their conversations stayed pleasant for the most part while from time to time it shifted to the intrigue within the palace. It was plain to see that Lady Tamar was extremely confident in herself and a majority of the other wives seemed to follow her lead.

"Her highness has been most quiet throughout the afternoon," Lady Tamar remarked, smiling at Amore, making her feel rather uncomfortable as the women turned their attention toward her.

"Perhaps she is just too polite and does not wish to interrupt us older women," another lady of the court remarked as Amore's heart skipped a couple of beats. *They think you are inferior to them.*

"Contrary." *Oh what is her name?* Amore kept going to not show she could not recall the woman's name. "I have been enjoying listening to the conversations." Braylin flashed a quick smile before taking a sip from her cup. "Do all of you have homes within Roselyn?" she asked, hoping to turn the attention away from herself once more. *What do I even say to them?* Amore was taught to respect the elders in her town and at the palace. Though often she would not get along so well with her sister, but that was to be expected.

"Most of us do indulge in city living but others prefer to be outside of Roselyn's walls," Lady Gemini remarked smugly. "Though perhaps our daughters may someday enjoy court life as well," she added, looking to her daughter alongside her, equal to Amore in age, and just as beautiful. Lady Gemini's daughter had barely spoken any words since the start and kept quietly to herself unlike her outspoken mother. "How is it, Your Highness, that you yourself have yet to set a date for your marriage to the king? No doubt all of us have heard that he is actually allowing you to determine the time," she asked, keeping her steely eyed gaze upon Amore. "You can certainly imagine our surprise that the marriage has yet to take place."

Her heart was pounding as Amore struggled to keep her expressions the same. *They are on to you.* She was nervous, greatly nervous when she thought about that day. Part of her still hoped that he would somehow fall in love with another, while the other part continued to fall deeper in love with him herself. What did she know about being a queen? She hoped the amount of time that the silence fell between them was not as long as it felt inside of her as she smiled.

"There is a lot to learn about being a queen," Amore remarked, surprised that those words even formed in her mind as she spoke them. It seemed to satisfy them for now but it still left chills along her arms as she quickly took a sip of her drink to calm her racing pulse.

"No doubt with our current visitors as well, a time shall soon be determined," Princess Braylin concluded before turning the attention toward another lady of the court. "Lady Lana, I hear congratulations are due with your son to soon be married to a duke's daughter." This drew the quick attention to the excitement over the news that apparently no one else had heard before. Braylin smiled quickly at Amore as relief flooded her. The tension she was feeling slowly resided as no one asked her any more questions. Princess Almeria continued to remain quiet unless someone addressed a question to her. The time could not have gone by any slower for Amore, it seemed like eternity before the woman began to slowly make their excuses and depart as the evening sun lowered itself in the sky. Until it was just Amore and Braylin left within the room.

"I cannot thank you enough for changing the subject like you did," Amore expressed to the princess who was only a couple years older than herself, though she acted well more mature than Amore felt today. Braylin smiled and let out a soft chuckle.

"You shall learn how to handle them as I do. Thankfully, it is not often all the women of the court are together like they came today. Most of the time you shall only have to deal with certain ones," Braylin stated as she turned, her brown eyes curious. "I do wish to inquire upon a question Lady Gemini asked." Amore nodded her head as nerves worked through her once more. "Have you chosen?"

Dropping her gaze, she studied the gold tray placed in front of her and the handiwork of the person who must have molded it. "To be honest, I have put a lot of thought about it. Though I have not made a decision as of yet."

Braylin smiled as she nodded her head. "Nervous perhaps?" she asked. Slowly looking back up at her, Amore smiled faintly as Braylin chuckled. "Do not concern yourself too much, you shall make a most wonderful queen. I can tell."

"How do you know for sure?" she asked, her voice soft. Braylin smiled as she studied Amore's gaze.

"By that question alone, Amore…"

Their conversation confused her as she pondered the princess's words. Braylin seemed to be secure in her position in life. So confident in who she was, that nothing appeared to bother the royal princess. The courtiers respected her and the palace servants adored her. Was everyone able to see beyond Amore's facade and see how nervous she grew around the officials and the powerful rulers in Avalon? Though it did surprise her that Xerxes did not make her nervous like the others did. The only thing she grew concerned around him was falling for him even more than she had. That someday, her truth would be known and then…. Would he still love her enough to look past who her family was? Where she came from? The palace was quiet as the evening set in, the halls lit with burning torches as the silk curtains sat still with no breeze to cool off the hot evening air. Amore was tired but too warm to go to sleep yet, so she walked the halls slowly. Thinking.

"Your Highness," a voice called, pulling Amore to a stop. A very decorated soldier stepped forward as he bowed his head low. She faintly recognized him as she waited to hear whatever he may want. "Is everything well with you?" he asked, standing straight once more.

"Yes, I find that walking helps to wait out the weather."

He smiled and nodded his head before looking down for a moment.

"I suppose you do not recall who I am. There were a lot of people that day, no doubt." Amore felt terrible that she could not recall who he was as he quickly continued. "I am General Tiberius, in charge of the palace security and commander of the eastern armies." He looked back at the two guards that followed Amore and smiled faintly. "If you ever need anything, Your Highness, do not hesitate to ask."

Amore nodded her head as the man smiled and gracefully bowed out of her way. As the distance grew between them, Namur slowly spoke up.

"General Tiberius is a most gracious man, Your Highness. Trusted by the king and General Damon."

Motioning for Namur to come closer, Amore's curiosity grew the best of her.

"He stays mostly with the eastern army but often returns to the palace. He served greatly as advisor to King Remien."

If his army stays in the east, perhaps they often were the ones who confronted with Emir. Had the general ever met her father? If she thought about it, Xerxes and Braylin could have easily met her father as well. As the hot summer temperatures refused to loosen its hold, Amore finally returned to her room in an attempt to sleep. The usually soft bed seemed to only make the matter worse. She groaned with frustration as she sat up. No air moved in the room, nothing to help her cool off. Her mind drifted to one of the many private bathing chambers she had often used. The water brought in from the river usually had a decent temperature to help cool her. However, the work involved quickly squashed that idea.

"Is her highness feeling well?" Talia asked softly as she appeared in the doorway leading to a smaller chamber for a maiden to sleep in case Amore needed something.

"I cannot sleep."

"Would you like me to read to you, perhaps it shall help you to sleep?"

"That is all right, Talia, you may go back to sleep." Amore smiled at the young maiden's offer.

"If it be all the same, Your Highness, I cannot sleep myself." She looked just as miserable as Amore did. "At least it will help me to keep my mind off of not sleeping."

Chuckling softly, Amore nodded as a smile spread across Talia's face. Turning around quickly, she hurried to the separate room and soon returned with a stack of scrolls.

"On the third of Torin, reports showed a high level of rainfall which will increase throughout the coming weeks. Citizen's are eager to…"

Amore listened to Talia as she continued on about the crops, and how the abundance of crops had been very good last year. She began to feel herself drift off to sleep when Talia mentioned Emir, startling her back awake.

"A conflict with Emir has risen, several citizens complained of Emirians damaging their crops and wrecking part of their harvests. No proof has been found to back these claims, though evidence shows of tampering to the crops of the Town of Elvira, near the border of Emir. On the eighteenth of Alos, a conflict concerning Emir arose in another town along the border. This time it was concerning Emirian soldiers coming rather close to the town. General Tiberius Damon reported that the soldiers were indeed on Avalon territory. Once confronted, the soldiers claimed to have accidently crossed over during a storm. General Tiberius Damon reports of no such weather in Elvira. Escorting the soldiers back to Emirian territory, General Tiberius confronted Emir's commanding general, Alexander Divon, concerning the soldiers. The exchange was less than pleasant and the general appeared to not discipline his own soldiers. General Tiberius made a full report to King Xerxes on the thirtieth concerning the matter. A council was brought forward to discuss the issue and decided upon. If the event occurred again, the Emirian soldiers would not be returned to their country. The blame would be placed squarely upon General Divon's shoulders for not keeping his own men in line."

Amore's heart was racing as Talia continued. The next part worried her greatly.

"Reports of more Emirian conflict has arisen. Decision has been made by the palace to—"

"Thank you, Talia. That is enough for this evening."

The young maiden nodded her head and returned to her own room. Although her eyes were heavy, Amore could no longer sleep as her mind swirled around with the details in the chronicles. Everything she had read concerning Emir was not in pleasant terms. Nor did any seem to be pleased with any actions concerning Emirians, or her own father. The night dragged on as her mind refused to quiet until the break of morning. By late morning, Amore began to feel the exhaustion from having not slept but was able to hide it even from her closest maidens. Talia looked worse off, as the young girl looked rather sluggish and irritable. The others did not seem to be much better as they all look tired. The heat from the day before continued on into the morning, as Amore found a comfortable place to sit and try to get a little rest, to the delight of the maidens as well.

Turning down breakfast, Amore kept her spot in the shade as the tiredness from the evening slowly began to subside and ease away. It was too hot to eat anything and the only relief that brought her any comfort was the breeze that had begun to slowly build up as the morning went on. Lord Zander made his way closer, a beautiful warm smile upon his face as he bowed low to her. Amore watched him carefully as she felt a smile began to grow upon her own face.

"What is it, milord?" she asked.

He stood straight and smiled brilliantly. "I have come to realize my great mistake, Your Highness!" His words startled her as she grew curious to his intention. Motioning for a servant to step forward, Lord Zander took a square box from him and smiled brightly. "A gift from the princess and I, for her royal highness to wear."

With that he popped open the box, revealing a beautiful ruby necklace that lay within. *What do I do?* She panicked for a moment as she motioned for one of her maidens to take it from him and bring it to her. She glanced over at Clarice. The older woman's expression gave her no hints, forcing Amore to handle it on her own. It seemed funny to Amore that the princess was not with him to present such a gift. But she did not ponder it long as the maiden bowed low and handed her the box. It was beautiful indeed. Slowly closing the lid, she handed it to Clarice and smiled.

"Be sure to express my gratitude to the princess as well, Lord Zander, as I will indeed tell the king of your generosity," she expressed as his smile grew.

"Wonderful, Your Highness, and if it pleases you I brought something for your maidens as well." The women's expressions grew excited as they waited and Amore nodded her head. "Good!" he exclaimed, and motioned as a few more servants brought forth trays of desserts and small boxes for each of the maidens. The boxes contained little trinkets, jewelry and other things. The maidens began to compare the things they had gotten with each other as Lord Zander bowed once more and left them to enjoy their gifts. When he was out of sight, Amore turned to Clarice who was nearest to her.

"Was that the appropriate thing to do?" she inquired softly. With everything she was starting to learn about protocols, Amore's thoughts were greatly confused about what was considered good or bad. Clarice hesitated before smiling slightly.

"It was most fine indeed, Your Highness. Though I would rather it have come from another man," she concluded as she smiled. "Do not worry yourself. You said the right things, and handled it well." Amore was conflicted but allowed the subject to drop as she watched the maidens laugh and attempt to make some of the trinkets work. She began to enjoy herself as her eyes spotted Xerxes standing across the garden and he smiled at her. Standing up, Amore made her way toward him as her heart beat began to pick up.

"What is going on?" he asked, his voice amused over the maidens in the distance. Looking back Amore smiled slightly.

"Presents from Lord Zander and Princess Almeria," Amore answered. He looked surprised as he smiled.

"Really?" he remarked, placing his hands behind his back.

"He even brought me something," Amore continued as her heart beat faster. Motioning for Clarice, Amore said thank you as the older maiden bowed low as she neared and handed the box to her. Handing the finely crafted wooden box to Xerxes, she watched his expression as he opened the lid. He looked surprised but not angry, which had to be good.

"Was that appropriate of me to accept such a gift?" she asked slowly as he studied the ruby-studded necklace. Xerxes smiled suddenly as he looked at her. Setting the necklace back inside, he handed it back to Clarice as she turned and hurried away.

"Yes, though it surprises me where he got such precious jewelry like that," he remarked. "It is not a type of gift one generally gives to another man's intended," he continued making her heart sink. He chuckled suddenly and pulled her close in a hug. "Do not worry yourself, Amore." Looking up at him Amore got lost in his gaze. "I can see that you are trying to be honest and would not think you to be unfaithful to me." His words grew softer toward the end as he slowly leaned closer. Before he could kiss her, Xerxes froze and shifted his eyes as a soldier made a soft coughing sound. The maidens were watching and the guards around them seemed to look away out of respect but an odd look flashed across his eyes. "Come with me." His words were softly whispered as a smile took the place of the look. Taking her hand, Xerxes began to lead her through the beautiful palace. His pace was even and defined.

The halls slowly began to change over to a covered path with tall pillars holding the sun from their heads as the palace walls all but seemed to fade away to an open stretch of green grass. She could still see the protecting walls in the distance, but it actually felt like she had stepped away from everything as Xerxes suddenly turned, a wide long stairs lined with tall basins that would hold a fire at night to see led them down the hill. The beauty of everything continued to astound Amore as the palace seemed unending. There were no questions to Avalon's success and wealth.

"Are you enjoying yourself?" he asked, smiling at her.

What was not to enjoy? Amore had more than enough in everything she could ever want. The entertainers always came up with new ways of amusing them. Not to mention the games and different things to create. No matter how hard one tried, for Amore's sake anyways. At times, it could become rather monotonous. Though with everything going on with the visitors, it had helped to ease away the thought of not doing very much creatively. She was starting to miss the long rides with Mirage which she had so often enjoyed. Helping her father's men with the training of the young horses. Getting into trouble with her close friend who had only lived a short distance from her home.

"Is something the matter?" he asked, studying her gaze as she had yet to respond to him.

"I have no complaints, if that is what you are asking." She smiled.

"Then what is it?"

How was she even to respond what was in her heart? The only thing she had begun to learn about being a queen was reading the protocols. She had yet to find anything that mentioned the role of the Queen of Avalon. Though she was not yet done with her studies. How was she to tell him how nervous she became when she thought about being such? She had never been one to enjoy the daily goings of the court back home. Aishlin thrived in that area. She adored the splendors of the court.

"What is expected...of a queen?" she asked hesitantly. He stopped and smiled at her warmly, though he pondered the question before answering her.

"As far as you being queen, you need not to worry too much. You shall not have to make any hard choices." That was part of what she was afraid of when she thought about everything. Was she even going to be able to contribute anything to help run the kingdom, or was the title more of a show of status? He chuckled suddenly as he studied her as he leaned closer to softly whisper. "I do not think you shall have any difficult fitting into the role of queen."

Is that a compliment? she wondered as they started walking again. It began to dawn on her that they were truly alone. For the first time, in a very long time. A large gazebo sat within the middle of the opening, its massive pillars holding up an equally impressive roof. A mixture of colors swirled across the floor. She thought back to Lady Gemini's statement. How long was Xerxes willing to wait for her to decide? How long was she going to wait? Though she attempted to convince herself it was in hopes of deterring his affections toward her, Amore began to wonder if it was even possible. They had not spent much time together alone. Each time, she could not get him to leave her thoughts. Nor convince herself not to feel anything for him. The hope of possibly ever leaving the palace to return to Emir seemed less likely with each passing day. Each moment she was drawn more into this world…this life. A life she was actually beginning to enjoy. Even with all of its troubles and all of the secrets still buried so deeply inside of her.

His gaze lightened enough that she wondered what else was buried beneath. His smile slowly grew as she thought back to the ocean and the first time they meet. Here in the role of a king, he seemed so much more mature and very wise. But part of the look in his eyes revealed who he had been when they first met. The person he rarely allowed seen.

"Are you concerned about it?" he asked, studying her and making her feel like a young girl again.

"I would not be telling the truth if I said no," she smiled slightly as she looked away to ponder the idea. Being queen, ruling a kingdom and being loved by a man.

"What about it concerns you?"

Everything. Looking at him, Amore kept her smile as she studied his gaze. *How badly I want to tell you.* She could feel it there, the truth. Everything just wanting. Say something. Perhaps he would understand. Perhaps he would not be angry with her. Maybe they could both look past the divisions between the kingdoms, bringing peace to the land. Before she could speak the words that so desperately wanted to be spoken, a servant called out, interrupting the words that were just waiting to be spoken.

"My king."

Xerxes sighed as the light slowly faded disappearing once more.

"They are waiting for you."

"Who is waiting?" she inquired, hoping to get a glimpse into the world she was not allowed to see.

"The officials have decided to have a gathering to honor the royal visitors in the palace."

Taking her arm, she could see the same look that often took place during these gatherings she had witnessed before. A look that made her wonder if he wished they could be back at the ocean like when they had first met and his life was far away. Beyond his current grasp at the moment. *Does he ever get much time alone?* she wondered. Rarely Amore herself even was, unless she was in her own private chambers. Even then someone was always nearby. She could not imagine what it was like for him.

The gathering had started out small but with momentum began to grow more than just that. Though no official ceremony took place, rather an intimate gathering of the officials and important people of Avalon who were close enough to make it. The grand hall looked splendid like always and the sweet savor of many delectable foods teased her. Princess Braylin remained by her for most of the time until the visiting royalty walked closer, and Braylin grew annoyed. Before he could reach them, the princess turned and walked off to converse with another. Amore flickered her gaze to the lord as he bowed low and smiled slightly at the princess's clear dislike of him.

"I do not blame her, Your Highness. We did not leave things off very well last time I was here," he remarked before Amore said anything. He looked after the princess before turning his gaze upon her. He actually appeared quite charming, growing Amore's confusion about him. If only the princess would open up more why she cared not for the lord. Sure, his actions when he first arrived were a little unpleasant, but it could easily be explained by the exhaustion from the trip.

"How are you enjoying your stay?" Amore inquired, growing uneasy in the silence. The guards around her shifted but remained ever present. The maidens seemed to not pay the visiting dignitary much attention.

"Very pleasant, Your Highness. I was wondering if I could inquire something of you." Amore nodded her head and he smiled. "Your stallion, were did he come from?" Amore tightened her jaw before flashing a beautiful smile.

"He was a present given to me." She would give him nothing else. Nodding his head, he bowed as General Damon approached. He seemed like he had more that he wanted to say but kept it inside.

"If you will excuse me, Your Royal Highness." He quickly moved away as the general bowed his head slightly to her watching as the lord walked away. Amore tried to read his eyes but could not. The general was a hard one to really understand so easily by simply looking at their expressions.

"How are you, General?" Amore offered. The general had been absent from the palace for quite some time. She was sure on the business of the king, no doubt. Investigating possibility of the ever-growing rumors.

"Fine, thank you, Your Highness." He stopped for a moment and lowered his gaze. "I would like to give you some advice, if that is all right."

"Of course."

"One can grow weary watching a flower until it blooms." He smiled slightly at her confused look. "I was in Fernon not too long ago, and Governor Tyron sends his regards. Said to tell you that your family has returned home safely and will count the days till they can see you again." So Aishlin had gone home as well. Perhaps it was best, yet it did not make her feel any better.

"Thank you, General, for the message, and I shall ponder your words." His greenish blue tinted eyes flashed as he stepped forward.

"How is her highness doing?" he asked quietly. Amore shifted her gaze briefly at Braylin and pondered her words carefully. Of course the general probably knew Braylin far better than she did.

"She is as she always has been," Amore commented, making the general smile as he stepped back. General Damon made a few more mentions about his visit to Fernon before moving on and Amore watched as he eventually made his way to Princess Braylin's side and began to discuss something with her, making her smile and glance toward Amore for a moment. Turning her gaze, she spotted Zander conversing with more of the officials and King Xerxes. She began to ponder about the man as he appeared to be making a lot of friends among Avalon's highest ranking officials. He appeared very at ease amongst them, as the majority of their attention seemed to be focused upon him.

"What is known about Lord Zander?" Amore pondered out loud and the maidens around her glanced at each other.

"What do you mean, Your Highness?" Namur asked, making Amore realize she had spoken out loud. Smiling slightly, she watched the group of people that had gathered together. Lord Zander laughed at something one of the officials had said and grew back into the deep conversation he was having with Lord Timothy and Lord Marcel. Lord Timothy suddenly stepped away and walked across the garden to his wife and began to speak to her, while the remaining two kept talking. Amore watched until Lord Marcel shifted his eyes toward her and Amore looked in another direction, hoping that they had not caught her watching them.

Smiling as Princess Almeria walked across the grounds, Amore motioned for the young woman to join her and began to talk, hoping to find out more about the young crowned Queen of Delmar. The young woman appeared reluctant at first but slowly began to open up to Amore. Not completely, but more than she had before.

"What is Delmar like? I have never had the honor of seeing it," Amore inquired and the young girl smiled.

"It is beautiful. The weather is wonderful all year round. The land is mostly flat with some rolling hills. Nothing like the mountains in Emir."

Amore tried to hide her excitement as she carefully asked, "Have you been to Emir before?" The thought of possibly having seen the princess before entertained her mind. Princess Almeria's eyes grew concerned as she blushed.

"Yes, when I was younger. We visited Emir once to see the mountains and meet some of the officials there," she recalled, appearing apprehensive talking about such a country.

"Hmm, what do you think of Avalon?" Amore asked, changing the subject as the curiosity of those around her seemed to perk up. Princess Almeria smiled brightly.

"I think it is very beautiful. I have yet to see the ocean. I cannot wait to do so before we leave."

Amore shifted her gaze toward Lord Zander. She knew very well Braylin's opinion of the man, a little bit about what King Xerxes thought. Perhaps the princess would be able to help her growing conflict concerning Lord Zander.

"What of Lord Zander? Is he liking Avalon? I heard that he has been here before." Amore tried to be careful with the questions she asked. She did not want to cause any strife or give the wrong impression. The light in the princess's eyes shifted slightly as she turned her gaze on her betrothed.

"He likes Avalon greatly," she remarked, her words sounding forced and Amore grew concerned.

"Does he treat you well?" she implored softly.

The princess's eyes flashed as she quickly stated, "Very well Your Highness." She smiled to lighten the mood she had created.

"That is good to hear. I am happy for you, Your Highness." They fell into an easy silence but Amore's mind began to turn. The princess seemed very upset when Amore asked, and happily dropped the conversation concerning her intended.

Later as Princess Almeria neared him and they began to talk, Lord Zander did not appear too happy. About what? Amore had her suspicious but that was all she had. Suspicions.

Eye of the Beholder

As THE PALACE ENTERTAINERS CONTINUED their performance, Amore glanced over at Princess Almeria. The maidens seemed to enjoy it but the princess only faintly smiled and quietly laughed a few times. The wonderful smelling food was served. Amore remembered the gift Lord Zander had said they both had given to her and Amore had never thanked the princess for it.

"Princess Almeria, I want to thank you for the gift you and Lord Zander gave to me." The princess looked surprised. "I apologize for not sharing my gratitude sooner," she continued as the princess looked down before glancing over at Zander across the way from her. It seemed like this was the first time she was hearing about it as she looked confused. Braylin looked curious as well as she appeared to not really be listening.

"You are most welcome, Your Highness," the princess smiled slightly as she continued to eat. Her beautiful colored eyes were conflicted in appearance.

"If you do not mind me asking, where did you find such a beautiful item like that?" she asked, watching the princess's reactions. She wondered if Princess Almeria even knew that Lord Zander had entreated her and her maidens with gifts. The princess hesitated and struggled to find an answer as Amore continued quietly, "You did not know of the gifts he gave?"

The princess took a deep breath. "No, but I am most glad he did," she reassured.

Amore caught Braylin's expression before looking back at the princess. Looking over at Clarice, Amore pondered having the necklace brought for the princess to see.

"Would you care to see it then? So at least you may understand my gratitude," Amore offered. The princess hesitated before turning her ocean colored eyes upon Amore.

"Yes, that would be very nice, Your Highness."

Amore turned her gaze to the man, as she felt the suspicion begin to grow on the inside of her. There was definitely more to the man than he portrayed to others. More perhaps than even Princess Braylin realized in her distaste for him.

It was not long and Clarice returned with the box, handing it to the princess. Clarice returned to her spot and Amore watched the princess carefully. Braylin was watching, eager to see what lay inside. As the princess opened the box, she choked for a second and then seemed to recover herself and smiled as she closed the lid once more.

"It is very beautiful," she concluded. Her jaw was tight as she took a quick deep breath and smiled brightly.

"May I see it?" Braylin inquired.

Amore nodded her head as the princess handed Braylin the box. Her eyes never changed as she studied the necklace before smiling brightly. "Very beautiful indeed!" She motioned for Clarice to take it away as she put her hands back in her lap and kept a smile upon her face, making Amore suspicious of Braylin's reaction. The princess remained quiet as she took a sip from her drink and stared blankly at the dancers now in the hall. Startling her, Braylin's eyes looked furious as she narrowed her gaze glaring at Amore as she leaned closer.

"What are you doing taking such a gift from a man like him!" she exclaimed quietly so only they could hear. "I can only imagine what my brother is going to say when he finds out!" she continued, not even giving Amore a chance. Xerxes appeared quite absorbed into the atmosphere as well as those around him. Enjoying the food and amusement.

"Braylin!" she exclaimed softly, stopping the princess in her rant. "He did not seem to mind when I told him, which was almost immediately after."

The princess's gaze softened slightly as Amore continued, "I was trying to be respectful, I thought it was coming from both of them. Now I can see that it was not."

"It most certainly is a grand gift to be given so freely," the princess remarked, her tone softening as she sat back once more and flashed a beautiful smile like always as Princess Almeria looked at them for a moment. Amore sighed as she thought about the necklace and Princess Almeria's reactions. If it ever happened again, Amore would be more careful next time. *I wish there had never been a first time.* Trying to immerse herself back into the celebration, Amore felt terribly relieved when she returned to her bed chamber for the night. She pondered the princess's reactions as her eyes slowly closed. Letting out a soft moan as she rolled onto her back and looked out the window; the world was still very dark outside. Her stomach complained as Amore pushed herself up and sighed. She could not recall who was spending the night in the maiden's room, but they appeared fast asleep as Amore peaked through the door. Taking the chance to be alone, Amore got dressed and slipped into the hallway. The sentry at her door was leaning against the wall with his head dropping as his chest rose and fell; she held back her chuckle as he slept standing up. Wrapping her shawl around herself, she slowly walked the halls. Her stomach continued to complain but slowly started to settle itself as she walked. It had to have been something she had eaten the night before. It felt wonderful to actually be somewhat alone.

༻❀༺

The halls held a beautiful glow to them from the bright morning sun that began to eliminate the palace. Startling her, Braylin suddenly appeared beside her and laughed softly at Amore's expression.

"You are not the only one who knows how to get out of her room without anyone noticing." Braylin chuckled. Amore looked back to see that no guards or maidens followed the princess.

"How is it that you can so quietly get around without anyone knowing?" Amore questioned as the princess beside her smiled.

"Something I learned as a child, especially when the cooks made the most wonderful smelling desserts." She chuckled and shook her head. "Though I feel today, it is more you who are distracted enough not to notice. What is bothering you?"

Amore felt rather bashful to admit that it was her stomach that was causing her discomfort this morning. "Nothing more than little a discomfort this morning," she managed.

Braylin nodded her head. They grew quiet with each other and simply enjoyed the warmth of the morning sun as a beautiful breeze off the ocean kept the heat at bay. Amore could not help but ponder the look upon Princess Almeria's face. It bothered her greatly. Just when she had seemed to be getting the princess to slowly open up around her, she hoped the necklace would not seclude the princess once more. Taking a deep breath, Amore enjoyed not having so many people around her.

"How long until you think they realize we are not where we are supposed to be?" Amore asked smiling at Braylin, who shrugged and let out a sigh, enjoying the peacefulness of the quiet palace.

"To soon," she remarked and nodded her head, drawing Amore's attention to General Damon walking quietly down the hall. Both women stopped as the general noticed them and headed in their directions. "Before you even begin, Damon," Braylin started as the general stopped in front of them, "I have one question for you. Who broke the statue of King Tibirian?" The general's gaze stayed steady upon the princess before he shifted his eyes upon Amore as he slowly smiled.

"Are you having a pleasant morning, Your Highness?" Amore curiosity began to get the best of her.

"Yes, though I am curious to know the answer to Princess Braylin's question." The smile slipped slowly from his face and grew upon Braylin's as she eagerly started to answer.

"You see, my dear friend General Damon will never admit to his shame of being under the influence of a beautiful girl who convinced him to tip over the statue," she teased.

"Before you spread rumors of my faults, princess, I would be sure to share the full story."

"Oh, but then, your relationship with the future queen could forever be tarnished." Their gazes locked with each others for a moment as the general narrowed his eyes before smiling suddenly and bowing his head to Amore.

"Excuse me, Your Highness," he said as he was moving around them. Namur hurried closer followed closely by two guards who stopped short as the general began to speak to them. Turning her attention back to Braylin, Amore raised her eyebrow as the princess smiled and continued to walk on.

"I may have tricked the young Damon when I was ten to tip over the statue…he was a little less wise in those days." She chuckled softly. "I grew up with Lucas Damon, long before he became a serious, dedicated soldier. Perhaps, it is because of I that his father started to have him trained at a young age to be a soldier." Braylin chuckled again.

"It is hard to imagine him any different than he is now." Braylin's smile only grew at the statement as they walked into a garden, causing both of their maidens to hurry forward, and breakfast was brought forth. Amore's stomach churned at the smell so she kept slowly walking until Braylin finished her breakfast and joined her once more.

An argument from her maidens began to fill the halls. Crystal began to pick on Talia once more, irritating the young girl. It was starting to happen more frequently especially when Amore was not directly in the area.

"Do not be so childish about it, Talia," Crystal remarked to the younger maiden. Crystal seemed to enjoy pestering the younger one. Talia often took it with great stride but Amore could tell that it bothered the younger girl from time to time. Today was no exception. Talia narrowed her gaze before replying rather bluntly and seriously, which was not Talia at all. She was softer spoken and never straightly told anyone off.

"You have no right to treat me as such!" she retorted, her furious gaze staring at Crystal. "If you wish to continue like this, be assured I have been here longer than you have." Their argument easily filled the halls as the maidens in the garden slowly quieted once more with Namur settling the conflict between the two.

"How are things going with Crystal?" Braylin asked suddenly as they stopped a good distance from the garden again. Crystal was laughing alongside some of the other women. She had been most interesting. Amore tried her best not to hold anything against the maiden, when she herself held so many secrets within. Pondering her answer, Amore studied the woman.

"She can at times be quite rough with Talia," was all she could really come up with. Braylin looked surprised. *What about Crystal and Lord Zander?* she wondered remembering suddenly.

"Really?"

Amore watched the others. "Yes. She is very opinionated, other than her attitude toward Talia I have had no problems concerning her," Amore concluded. Braylin made a soft hmm sound and grew quiet. *Are you only covering for her because of your own guilt inside?* she wondered as she studied Crystal. She had many things she was concerned about toward the maiden. But she felt in no place to judge how the former noble's daughter reacted to certain things.

"Perhaps it would be best to dismiss her for a while," Braylin remarked, nodding toward Crystal as she started to turn her attention back on Talia once more. It made Amore's heart jump as she thought about confronting the maiden. It would not be seen well in the eyes of those around Crystal's sphere of influence and with the other women in the palace. Once dismissed, she would not be able to return until Amore called for her. But as Amore stepped out into the garden, alone, Crystal was about to start again with Talia. Amore neared and they all bowed their heads. With her heart pounding in her ears, Amore took a deep breath.

"I wish to speak with Crystal alone."

The others scrambled to their feet and hurried away. Crystal picked her head up and met Amore's gaze. Her expression was unconcerned and bold. *Just say it before you lose your nerve, then she will know how uncertain you really are.* "I think it best if perhaps you are relieved for some time." Her expression slowly began to change as she let out a chuckle.

"Surely this cannot be because of Talia?" she asked, raising an eyebrow.

"Your contempt toward the others—"

"It was nothing but a joke! I did nothing wrong to be blamed, cast aside!" she defended herself as she scrambled to her feet and Amore's heart launched again as she kept her gaze even.

"I will not stand for it. It was more than that—" the maiden cut her off again and this time Amore grew annoyed.

"You are dismissed!" her voice grew loud and stern, silencing the maiden before her. She allowed herself to calm down for a moment before adding nicely. "For now." Crystal kept silent this time as her gaze fell and she nodded her head. Giving a quick bow, the maiden turned and hurried away as guilt began to eat at Amore's insides.

"It was the right thing to do," Braylin reassured her as she joined her once more. *Then why do I feel so rotten on the inside?* The maidens returned in quiet spirits as they joined around Amore once more. Though Amore had dismissed Crystal, she began to wonder how much freedom the maiden was going to have. How much would she still be able to mingle amongst the others.

The peace quickly settled between her maidens with Crystal's dismissal. Guilt tried to settle upon her for having yet to call the maiden back to her. Was it so terrible to enjoy the relaxation of those who were content around her? Nothing seemed to settle Amore's thoughts, so she wanted to disappear for a while from the eyes of those around her. Heading towards the stables, Amore desperately wanted to disappear from the guilt growing inside of her. Voices drifted throughout the hall, filling the air between the stillness of the afternoon. As Amore neared she began to hear the confident voice of Crystal. Slowing her pace, Amore's curiosity got the best of her as she listened to the maiden's words.

"Who is this woman that the king has chosen to reign over us? How is it that we know nothing of her? Does not the king think any of us worthy of his affections?"

She knew that Crystal did not share warm feelings for Amore. She had yet to hear of the maiden speak out rightly against her.

"Would any of you make the king wait so long to be married? Why is she waiting?" she continued. Slowly walking closer, Amore could see the back of Crystal as she spoke with some of the officials' wives and there very beautiful daughters. No one seemed to notice her yet as one of the officials' wives responded.

"It is true that we do not know very much about the future queen," the woman agreed. Amore could not remember who her husband was. A couple of the wives finally took notice of her and quickly averted their eyes and bowed their heads, causing Crystal to stop in her rant. Bowing, the women quickly dispersed as Crystal slowly turned around. After moments of what would be considered most disrespectful, the once noblemen's daughter bowed low and boldly walked away afterward. Her eyes were not even sorry for the words she had spoken as she disappeared into the shadows. Amore could not hide the hurt that she had spoken out so boldly about her, but it was truth the maiden had spoken, the words she was spreading abroad. Lowering her gaze, Amore took a shallow breath as her heart squeezed inside her chest. Crystal had been used to being served, not serving another. She knew the maiden did not care for her position in life. Why so outright against Amore? She had never shown any lack of countenance toward the maiden. Nor treated her any different from the others.

"Please, Your Highness, do not listen to that ungrateful child!" Namur quickly spoke, obviously seeing that it had affected Amore.

"Thank you, Namur." What was she to say? The maiden was very much so right in her own way, but yet what else had she possibly been spreading to the wives of the officials? No doubt they would soon tell their husbands. Lord Timothy and Lord Byron's wives had been a few of the women in the crowd. Namur nodded her head and stepped respectfully back to her place, but the look in the maiden's eyes was pure anger. It had been some time since Amore had relieved the maiden. She had been hesitating greatly upon restoring Crystal to her position. She could see the peace restored amongst the others amidst the departure of Crystal. Perhaps she had allowed too much time to have passed, growing the maiden's contempt and hurt.

Amore continued to softly try to understand Princess Almeria's world. No matter how much the princess seemed to reassure her, it never sat right with Amore. From the look in her eyes, to her actions. Especially how Amore began to notice the little changes that occurred whenever Lord Zander was around. Though he kept up his usual bravado, Amore slowly began to see through more and more of his mask. Being able to see clearly into what he must truly be like.

Crystal seemed to disappear from sight once more, and Amore heard no other words spoken against herself for some time, but that did not help the sting of her words. A sense of loneliness tried to fill her as something important kept Xerxes busy. It seemed like eternity for her from when she had last spoken with him. Something—that as being his wife and queen—

Amore might have to get used to, especially if she was nothing more than just a symbol of status to those around her.

"Braylin." Amore called softly as the princess was walking away from Amore. She stopped short and smiled brightly. It seemed like even Braylin had tasks to be accomplished within the palace. Glancing around at those who surrounded them gave them some space. "What is keeping the king so preoccupied?" Her smile faded as she looked down before turning her eyes back upon Amore.

"Troubling news from some of the regents and governors of the towns." The always pleasant tone in her voice was missing as her gaze drifted away. Braylin started away as Amore caught her arm.

"Please." Their eyes meet as the princess let out a deep breath. "I wish to know what is going on. Though I may not be Queen yet, I would like to know." Taking a deep breath, Braylin nodded and brought Amore to an enclosed private room. Letting out a breath again, she looked Amore in the eyes.

"There are rumors of the towns being raided. Xerxes has called some of the governors of the larger cities to the palace to discuss this rumor. That is all I know." As the Princess left, Amore sat heavily into one of the chairs. Who could possibly be raiding Avalon? Though the army was powerful enough to put a halt to it, could they find those responsible?

"Your Highness, someone would like to speak with you." Her maiden requested as Amore sat up and nodded her head. Governor Tyron stepped through the door, making her heart leap as she smiled brightly and stood as he neared. He bowed, making Amore's heart warm as she stepped forward to hug him, then stopped herself short and smiled as he stood straight.

"What brings you to the palace, governor?" she asked, even though she knew why. His eyes warmed as he studied her, before pulling a small letter from his coat.

"My king wishes to speak with me. I have this for you, from your brother." He held out the letter as Amore smiled and took it from him, eager to know what her brother had to say. "It is good to see you, Amore." He slowly turned and left as Amore ripped open the letter.

Dear Amore,

I have decided to give your letter to father. He trusts his brother and will not think it any different if you remained with him. I just hope that Uncle Timothy will not be returning to the city any time soon.

Vainer

The short letter was quite typical of Vainer; he was not much for writing. Tucking the letter safely away, Amore sighed. Hopefully, Father would be spending most of the summer at the palace, so then he wouldn't even notice her absence from home anyway. Braylin stayed busy as the palace seemed to grow still with time. Governor Tyron made sure he said good-bye to her before he left the palace, and for the first time in a while, Amore felt torn again as the governor departed. His presence reminded her that Amore really did not belong with those around her. It made her uneasy once again, especially when the rumors turned toward blaming Emir for the raids.

⋙⋘

As sleep fled her that night, Amore decided to awaken early, before the rest of the palace would, and allow herself to grieve in a way as the abounding rumors seemed to increase. The halls sat quietly, as nothing stirred to disturb her thoughts. The sheer distrust and hatred toward Emir began to work at her heart. Unsettling Amore greatly. Keeping everything inside herself began to slowly eat away at her resolve. She could see the curiosity from time to time in the maidens' eyes but had been able to turn it away. The land was still dark, as night still clung to the sky. Birds were not even singing yet as she slowly made her way through the palace. Somehow she had slipped out of her room between the dozing guards. The stillness of the air seemed to be just what Amore desperately needed. She was tempted to head to the animal sanctuary but decided for a large garden that overlooked a large open area. It was a great place to see the sun rise, if you had awakened early enough. Amore pulled the shawl around her shoulders tighter as she took a deep breath of the fresh air. It gave her the sensation that everything was at peace and nothing would ever go wrong, something she loved about being out early in the morning to watch the sunshine sprinkle its warmth across a land that desperately needed it. Leaning over the stone wall, she glanced at the world below. The river wound its way through the streets, and the city still remained silent, waiting for its people to wake. Hearing voices that broke the stillness, Amore frowned and turned her gaze toward the hall she had been in moments before. Ducking behind a large tree that sat in the garden, she listened, hoping to not be noticed.

"Are you certain of this?" a voice asked. It took Amore a few moments to realize that it was General Damon speaking. The second person remained quiet as time seemed to freeze for Amore as her heart pricked.

"Yes, everything points to Emir."

They could not be talking about me? The thought screamed at her as the second person's voice gave way to be Xerxes.

"I know Emir is a powerful country and we do not always agree but raiding? It seems a little below their standards even," General Damon reasoned, trying to convince both himself and the king of this. Emir raiding Avalon had been at the top of the rumors, but hearing the words out of their mouths made the possibilities hurt.

"It seems otherwise. Gather together the council. We must discuss this." Xerxes's voice grew grave as he spoke the words.

Amore felt her heart sink. Emir raiding Avalon, it was more than below their standards, it was preposterous. Her mind tried to search through her memory. There had been soldiers before who became rogue and did become raiders in Emir even. Could it be possible? Blinking, she listened again to their conversation, not wanting to miss anything.

"War?" General Damon asked.

It broke her heart as Xerxes remained quiet, answering silently before speaking.

"It may lead to just that."

Both men grew silent and Amore thought they had walked on. She waited longer to make sure they would not know she had heard their conversation. She was about to step out when she heard Xerxes speak again. "Where is she this morning?"

"I am not sure, but I will find her for you," General Damon answered. Amore knew then that they had turned the conversation to her. She felt her heart jump. She had to figure out how to sneak away so she would not be found here.

"No." His tone hurt. Yet that had been her goal all along, was it not? "Leave her be for now." Their voices grew distant as they continued talking. Taking a deep breath, Amore peaked around the tree and bolted. Dashing right through where they had just been standing and down the first hall she could find. She should have been more aware of where she was running. Running into something or someone, she felt their arms reach out to catch her keeping her from falling. Amore blushed slightly in embarrassment then she felt her heart stop. Lord Zander's smile spread across his face as he held her still. The glint in his eyes could make a lion cower.

"Your Highness, are you all right?" he asked, pretending to be worried as he looked down the hall. Amore had snuck out bright and early this morning, so none of her guards were with her, and her maidens still figured she was in her room sleeping peacefully. Pulling back, Amore fixed her shawl and composed herself.

"Of course," she remarked as she began to step around him. Blocking her path his expression grew graver.

"Be careful, Your Highness, you never know who is wondering these halls." His tone cautioned, Adrenaline started seeping into her veins as he remained motionless.

"Are you threatening me?" she asked, stepping back. He moved with her closing the gap.

His hand reacted quickly, pushing her against the stone wall. Amore struggled to get away from him but he kept her pinned between him and the wall. His hands tightening around her forearms causing pain to shot through her.

"I would suggest to stop meddling in my business." His tone grew hard as he leaned closer. Amore's mind tried to think of what to do to get her out of this situation as his hand slid to her throat, causing her mind to shut down as she stared widely into his gaze, his breath hot against her face as he leaned closer again. "I can see what he sees in you, you're a very beautiful woman." He paused, and Amore's mind figured what would happen next as his lips grew closer to hers. She could not move, her body frozen in fear. Stopping short, he smiled. "I would hate to see anything bad happen to you."

With that he retreated, dropping her. Amore gasped, realizing then that he had actually squeezed her throat. Collapsing to the ground as air rushed in, her mind flashed through memory after memory. She could not make them stop as she sat there. She did not even realize that someone now kneeled beside her. They pulled her arm around their shoulders and helped her to stand. Her gaze flickered down the hall to a man standing at the end. Silently, had he been there the whole time? Had he seen everything? Before she knew it Amore was in her own room with Almeria looking her over, her small cold fingers gently examining her neck. Her eyes wide, filled with fear.

"Thank you, Almeria," she managed, feeling weak. The princess stepped back to grab something cold and wrapped it around her neck. The water dripped down her skin as Amore held it in place.

"There will be no bruising on your neck, Your Highness, but I am afraid your arms are." She drifted off and looked down her body subconsciously, touching her own shoulders. Amore studied her then and realized, she was not the only one to be attacked by him.

"Has he hurt you before?" she asked softly. Almeria glanced at her before turning away to grab some sort of cream to rub on Amore's arms. She had not answered but it rang loudly. "Why are you still with him?" she inquired, Almeria sighed and sat on the bed beside her.

"Fear, I guess. I am too scared to leave. My people need help and he had been so willing. He was very sweet at first but as time went on and after we got engaged he became violent. He threatened me that if I ever said anything I would regret it," she explained softly. "I am more afraid of how much my people admire him than what he would do to me personally. So I do nothing." Her tone grew tired. She had been holding everything by herself for so long. Amore wrapped her arm around Almeria and hugged her.

"I will help you," she whispered. The young girl shook suddenly. Pulling back she shook her head.

"No, Your Highness. I could not imagine anything bad happening to you," she pleaded. Amore smiled slightly and looked at the purple fingerprints on her forearms. She would tell Xerxes or General Damon. "Please do not tell anyone!" she exclaimed suddenly, like she had heard Amore's thoughts. "He has a horrible temper, and somehow he knows a lot of things and people." *Of course, he has traitors!* her mind thought. They could even be within the palace. Amore would have to be careful. She did not want Almeria or anyone caught in the crossfire. "Promise me,

Your Highness, that you will do nothing. Just do not go anywhere without your guards!" she pleaded again, her expression terrified.

"I promise that I will wait until the timing is right," Amore promised. Almeria nodded her head and sighed. Amore stayed in her room the rest of the morning. Thankfully her throat was only red for a while before it disappeared. However, she would have to be careful about her arms. Taking a darker shawl, Amore wrapped it around herself, keeping it over her shoulders like she would have been cold even though the weather was beautiful. The palace remained silent throughout the rest of the morning hours. It was still early but the day felt like it should be ending. Her maidens followed her closely as she walked the halls looking for Princess Braylin. At least this time with others around her she should be able to avoid Zander. Whispers filled the rooms around them, as servants and guards talked about everything going on in the kingdom. Rumors of raiders hitting small towns, towns-people grumbling about the monarchy. Arguments about Emir, whether or not Emirians could be trusted. Amore's heart sank at the hatred toward her home. How long would she be able to keep up with her charades? How long if this keeps up could war be avoided? *It seems like I may be caught in between my father and Xerxes after all.*

"Marian, have you seen Princess Braylin this morning?" Amore asked one of the princess's maidens. A dark red-haired girl dashed forward, her head low and eyes downcast.

"No, Your Highness." The maiden's voice was soft. To where could Braylin have gone? She desperately needed to discuss something with her. In the distance Amore could see Captain Ramses. The soldier patrolled the corridor that led to the stables. Amore did not like the man. He had a lot of pride and treated others like dirt. She could not understand how he got away with everything that he did. Or maybe she could as he spotted her and bowed low, a beautifully placed smile upon his mouth. As she passed he stood back up. Amore could feel his eyes following them. A servant opened the wood door allowing her to pass. As soon as she passed a group of soldiers instantly surrounded her as she walked toward the black stallion that awaited her.

Mirage's nostrils vibrated with glee. He tossed his head as she neared before shoving his velvety nose into her outstretched hand. Being with her horse gave her longing for home and her family.

Longing to swing up onto his bare back, Amore checked herself looking down at the beautiful gown she wore. Back home she would not have cared but with royalty visiting and with so many watching her every move, Amore doubt that it would be considered appropriate for her to do so. "Someday," she whispered, kissing his nose as a warm breath surrounded her face. Letting out an excited whinny, he swung away from her and trotted to the end of his paddock, his ears perked up looking to a mare that was being led toward the stables.

It took some doing before Amore found Braylin tucked away in a secluded corner of the palace. She was alone, a faint smile flickered across her face as Amore neared.

"I see that you have found me." She laughed before letting out a long sigh and looked around the quaint little room. "My favorite hiding place, or so it used to be until now." Slowly sitting alongside Braylin, Amore wrapped the shawl around herself a little more and leaned against the wall as she studied the empty room.

"I have a question I need to ask of you." She eyed the princess as Braylin seemed rather quiet—unusually quiet. Nodding her head, Braylin turned her attention upon Amore. "How long have you known our guests?" Uncertainty filled her as Braylin's eyes grew curious.

"The Princess?"

Shaking her head, "No, I know you do not care to even think about our guest. But I would like to know more about—him."

Braylin studied her for a while, her eyes becoming serious as Amore quickly avoided her gaze.

"What has he done?" Her tone was annoyed. Amore shook her head and faked a smile that felt awkward.

"Nothing."

She winced as Braylin slapped her on her arm, hitting the bruises. She shifted her gaze toward the door once more, causing Braylin to look back before smiling with satisfaction at a secret that Amore did not know.

"Father had this room specially built for strategy meetings. The walls and doors are thicker than most oak trees at the full length of their days," Braylin reassured, laughing as she spoke the words. *How do I even word this without revealing too much?* she wondered. Braylin frowned as Amore continued to remain silent.

"He has not hurt you, has he?" she exclaimed, bolting to her feet. As Amore did the same.

"No!" she hastily replied, but it was too late. The expression on the princess's face read everything as she began to examine Amore. Pulling back the shawl from her shoulders revealed the rainbow of colors beneath. Pulling the silk shawl back in place, Amore took a deep breath and told Braylin everything that had happened with Lord Zander. Braylin's expression grew from shocked to furious.

"Please breathe a word to no one, Braylin. I fear that Lord Zander is more powerful than we have given him credit for."

The always composed, dignified princess paced the room, muttering a few things that anyone would blush at.

"We must figure out something. Princess Almeria does not deserve to be at the mercy of that man!"

"As far as what the princess says, her people adore him," Amore remarked. It was not going to be an easy task. Working in secret would make it even harder. Sighing, Amore shook her head and wondered how her life could get even crazier. "Are you feeling well?" she asked. Braylin let out a sigh and nodded her head.

"Yes, I came in here as I needed to get away for a little while." She smiled then. "Come, let us go back out before anyone else misses me." The walk back through the palace was quiet. It was not long before both of their maidens returned to their sides as well as the guards. Making it rather difficult to move freely. As Braylin returned to her own private chambers, Amore found a quiet place to think.

It was always a moment of peace to not have others constantly following. Watching, listening. It would probably terrify Amore to know what the servants of the palace knew about those within its walls. Maybe that was a good thing. Liana, Talia, and Namur were the only ones with her today, which would make it easier for her to keep her ideas to just them.

"Can I trust you with a special task?"

Their eyes grew excited as they glanced at each other as her voice grew quieter so only they could hear.

"Of course, Your Highness," Liana said and Amore smiled.

"Good." Looking around the room to make sure no other ears were near, she leaned closer. "I am sure you all know every well what goes on behind these walls and if not, others do. Find out what you can about our guest for me. Do not speak a word of this to anyone else. Understand?" The women nodded their heads. "Well, go on and be careful. Talia, I do have something else to ask of you."

As the two older girls hurried away, the young daughter of Clarice stayed behind, waiting. Her eyes sparkled with anticipation.

"How is your mother? I heard she was not feeling very well." Clarice had been absent the past few days and it worried Amore. The older woman had grown on her considerably. She was very popular among the palace, and one of the kindest people she knew. Talia smiled softly and her eyes grew distant.

"I am not sure, Your Highness. I do not think she is physically ill, but perhaps it is something deeper. She does not wish to discuss anything with me, and every time I have asked she will not talk about it." The young girl's eyes grew hopeful. "Would you speak to her, see if you can find out what is wrong?"

"I am willing to try but cannot guarantee anything. Now your task, the library and the scrolls. Find out what you can concerning Delmar's laws, if we have anything, or Avalon's, concerning engagements."

Nodding her head, the young girl dashed off. Hopefully no one would ask her why she was reading such things, when the girl was so often found in the library during her free time to which she did not have to serve Amore. Having just the guards follow her made Amore regret her earlier decision. She should have never left her room without them. The servants' quarters were on the other side of the palace grounds, a considerable distance to travel daily. As she neared the tower stairs that would lead her to the level that the widowed or unmarried female servants lived, the sentry stood up straight as she neared.

"Amore!" Her name rang out suddenly. Xerxes stood on the opposite end and motioned for her to come. Sighing softly, Amore placed a smile on and made her way toward him. Her mind flashed back to the conversation she had overheard this morning. "Where are you going?" he asked, curious, as she neared.

"To visit Clarice. I heard she had not been doing well these past few days and I was concerned." He smiled at her words and offered out his arm for her to take. Together they began to walk the halls slowly.

"I have been meaning to apologize to you, my queen. With everything that is going on we have not discussed us."

It was constantly on the back of her mind but lately was overshadowed by Princess Almeria and Lord Zander that she had actually came to forget about it. "Perhaps after our guests leave, we should take some time to ourselves." He smiled and Amore thought about the man she had met at the ocean's beach. He was somewhere inside of Xerxes, covered underneath layers of protocol, duty, and everything that was expected of him.

"That would be wonderful." Amore meant it. She often fought herself with allowing her attachment toward Xerxes to grow, but against her strongest will he seemed to melt away her defenses easily. Taking her hand in his, he kissed it for a moment before frowning at the dark shawl.

"Is something wrong?"

I wish I could tell you! She wanted to, but she wanted to respect Princess Almeria's wishes at the same time. Why did everything seem to have to be a secret with her?

"No, I was just a little cold this morning. Nothing to worry about."

His eyes narrowed slightly but he did not question her any more as they walked through the warm morning air. She enjoyed the peaceful moment with him before he had to leave her once more. He said his apologies and left, leaving Amore with a kiss upon the check and her heart feeling rather low. It surprised her that she felt the time was far too short, but knew that he was busy with a lot of things, taking away his attention from her.

The first chance Amore received she took it to make good upon her promise to Talia and to herself as she went to visit Clarice.

"Come in," a soft voice called.

Clarice sat across the petite room at a small window. She scrambled to her feet as Amore came in and tried to smile brightly. "Your Highness! What do I owe such a pleasure for this visit?"

Amore motioned for the older maiden to sit. Clarice hesitated until Amore insisted.

"How are you, Clarice?" she asked, watching the woman who had served her loyally since she had arrived. Clarice looked tired around the eyes as she tried to smile again. "Your daughter is quite worried about you." Clarice started to protest and Amore put her hand up to stop her as she smiled. "As am I." Clarice's usually darker tanned skin seemed lighter than usual. Her green-eyed gaze stared out the window. She seemed to contemplate her words before speaking.

"I am all right physically speaking, if that it was you are worried about," she reassured as she gave a smile and stared at the floor then looked at her hands, avoiding the real subject to why she had been ill these last few days. Glancing around the room, Amore wanted to sit but the room already was too small and it would seem very improper to sit on the small bed.

"Is there anything I can do for you, Clarice?" she offered, and the woman smiled as her eyes swelled with tears. As Amore stepped forward, wanting to offer the woman a hug, she grasped Amore's hand firmly and stared up at her pleadingly.

"Promise me something, Your Highness!"

Surprised, Amore grew worried as she nodded her head and agreed. Clarice sighed happily. "Make sure my daughter always has the best opportunities in life. The best that is available to her in her situation in life." Her words began to make Amore grow concerned as she studied Clarice's face.

"Clarice, are you sure you are all right?" she asked, concerned.

Ignoring her words, Clarice grew more firm. "Please, my queen!"

"Yes, as a personal favor to—"

"Thank you, Your Majesty! I shall never forget what you have done for a humble servant such as myself."

"A friend. Clarice, I shall do this as a favor to my friend."

The older woman smiled at Amore's words and looked away for a moment before letting go of her and standing suddenly.

"Well, best be time that I get back to work then."

Amore left Clarice to prepare, as she stepped out of the maidens' room, and the guard awaited her to her left. She caught the faintest voices talking and someone was giggling. Her curiosity grew but she did not have to wait too long as Crystal stepped out a room followed shortly by Captain Ramses. They both froze when they saw her. Crystal held her head up in defiance but the captain at least looked a little bit shamed. Without any words spoken to them, Amore turned and left. The guards quickly took their positions as she walked deeper through the palace. The wing that Clarice lived in was one for widows and the unmarried maidens of the palace. Captain Ramses had no place being there. If she remembered correctly, no man was allowed behind the sentry posted at the beginning of the hall. The guards had been an exception when they had accompanied Amore. How much did she dare overlook Crystal's downright contempt for Amore? Her maidens returned and nodded their heads as they took their place. Finding a quiet room, she asked for the guards to remain outside, stating she wanted to rest. The maidens took their spots around her as Amore waited.

"What did you find?" she asked Namur first.

"Very little, Your Highness, beyond the fact that Captain Ramses and Lord Zander have been seen together a lot lately."

Amore turned her attention to Talia and she shook her head.

"I have yet to find anything concerning what you have asked of me."

"Thank you. I do not feel you need to search any further."

Dismayed at the lack of knowledge, Amore began to wonder if she would be able to inquire of the king without drawing too much attention. Perhaps the princess would shed some more light upon the subject.

"Did you find out anything, Your Highness?" Talia asked as soon as Amore was alone. Smiling sadly, Amore shook her head.

"I am sorry, Talia. I am more concerned than when I first went to see Clarice."

The young girl's face grew afraid and Amore squeezed her arm. "Do not worry yourself, your mother has decided to return to her work." Her reassurance fell short for both herself and Talia. Thanking her, Talia bowed and hurried away. Watching the older maiden from a distance, she seemed to walk perfectly fine. She greeted the other servants warmly and smiled brightly at her daughter.

Amore found the princess in a secluded garden. She appeared to be deep in thought until one of her maidens drew her attention to Amore. At the look in Amore's eyes, Braylin dismissed all of the maidens and motioned for her to sit.

"What is it?"

"I was wondering if it would be a good time for you to tell me more about…our friend."

The princess's eyes grew heavy as she looked away before she could start Amore motioned for Princess Almeria to join them. The young princess looked unsure but consented and sat down. Braylin took a deep breath as she began to explain how she had come to know Zander.

Braylin had meet Zander, at the time he was nothing more than an official for a lord. She was at the age of fifteen, and his charm was the first thing she noticed about him. He was incredibly handsome and very smart. She was happy when Zander would accompany his lord to the palace on business and they often easily fell into conversation. They continued this for many months to come, and Princess Braylin fell more in love with him and how he had great plans for his future. It was not long after that they got engaged. Xerxes was unsure about the sudden announcement but Braylin convinced him of her love for Zander and her brother respected her wishes and said nothing. Her father was pleased with the bright young man that his daughter was interested in. As her father took more interest in Zander, he began to spend less time with Braylin and grew mean and cold toward her. Braylin never shared with anyone the things Zander inflicted upon her. She buried them deep below shame and disgrace for falling for him, yet she was still caught up in his charm until the day he realized he would get no share in the inheritance Braylin would be generously given by her father. That everything would go to her brother when he became king.

"He made great apologies, broke the engagement, and disappeared. Father never knew that he had proposed, only Xerxes did." She sighed and shook her head. Turning her gaze to the young princess, Braylin reached out her hand and squeezed the girl's arm. "Do not make the same mistake I did and allow him to get away with everything. I should have told my family what he did to me but I was and still am greatly ashamed."

The princess's eyes were downcast as she listened to the story. Amore felt great concern for the young girl. How long had she gone along with whatever Lord Zander said?

"I had always felt so childish for falling for him." Her words were incredibly soft as her head hung. "I thank you, Your Highness, for sharing with me about Zander. I need some time to think." Getting up, the young princess bowed and turned to leave as Amore stood.

"May I walk with you?" Smiling, she nodded her head, almost appearing relieved that Amore wanted to join her. It made her realize then that the princess had no guards and only a few maidens provided by King Xerxes during her stay.

Accompanying the princess back to her room, Amore kept quiet. She felt there was nothing more that needed to be said. As they walked two men stood in the distance talking to one another. The second man Amore quickly recognized as Captain Ramses as he quickly disappeared down a hidden hall. It was then that Lord Zander noticed Amore and she felt chills run through her as she turned her gaze away and she could see a smile spread across his mouth as he bowed his head respectfully and stepped back as they walked past. The young princess had grown stiffer by the moment until he was past them and they were further down the hall.

"Your Highness," a voice called. A servant dashed forward and bowed low. "The king wishes to speak to you," he informed and hurried away.

Xerxes was in his private chambers when Amore was brought to him. He was writing something when he motioned for her to come closer. Rolling up the letter he smiled as she neared. "What can I do for you, my queen?" His voice sounded sweet but yet it did not hit the same tune as it had before.

"It is concerning one of my maidens." *Also concerns our guest of honor.* How badly she wanted to share with him the things that had happened and what both Almeria and Braylin had told her but she would still remain quiet. *No secrets.* His words flashed through her mind weighing her heart down even more. His smile faded, and Amore began to wonder if he felt the same as the maiden did. Xerxes had graciously allowed Amore time to adjust to the palace life and told her it would be upon her timing that the date would be set. Yet she had learned a lot of the protocols and laws. To Braylin's remarks, she was doing wonderfully as any queen should. So Amore had no excuse to why she still waited.

"Clarice." Her heart sank again. Why could she just not open up to him like she could before? It seemed like their meetings grew more frequent and less affectionate. "She worries me." Less truthful by the moment. Xerxes smiled then.

"Yes, I heard about the maiden's health. The palace physician has taken a look at her." His words grew quiet as he looked down. It was what Amore had feared. Clarice was ill.

"What is wrong with her?" Amore inquired as he did not answer. Xerxes set his pen down and looked at her softly.

"He does not know. He figures it has to do with being low in spirits for a reason that she will not say."

Sighing, Amore looked away and stepped toward the balcony before stopping in the doorway. The weather was beyond warm, yet she still wore what she could to hide the fading bruises on her forearms.

"What else is on your mind that you are not telling me?" he asked, surprising her. Turning toward him, she tried to smile. *More than I can tell you.* His gaze grew strong for a moment as he waited for her to answer. "Is it about Crystal?" he offered, startling her greatly. Of course he would eventually hear, if he did not already know from the beginning. He nodded his head. "I was waiting for you to come to me first before I did anything," he remarked and slowly stood. "I shall deal with it the sooner the better. What else?"

"I saw Captain Ramses coming out of a room with her in the servants' quarters when I was visiting Clarice," Amore remarked and began to feel guilty, like she was spreading a vicious rumor. He actually looked surprised at that statement.

"Did anyone else see this?"

"No, the guards were waiting at the end of the wing."

What difference is it if you are in his private chambers to you spilling out what was happening in the private chambers of another? A thought chirped in her head as she looked around. Xerxes looked perplexed by the knowledge.

"Good, mention it to no one else."

If I add any more secrets to my list, I shall be nothing but hidden secrets. Placing her hands behind her back, Amore fought with herself before slowly asking.

"Are the rumors true? Is Avalon being raided?" Amore inquired as her nerves stood on end. Xerxes flashed his gaze up, surprised by her question. She had heard of rumors about raids and bandits, then the conformation that came from Braylin. The surprised look quickly vanished as he smiled slightly.

"Do not worry yourself on such rumors. Majority of them have no truth to them." Stepping around the table he was at, Xerxes kissed her temple but the tenderness of the affection felt forced. If her spirits sank any lower, Amore was not sure how much more of it she could take.

Raiders

Horses danced in anticipation. Guards murmured to each other in unease. It was very unusual but permission had been given and the horses prepared. Amore had been very surprised to hear that King Xerxes was allowing her to accompany Princess Almeria on a ride outside the palace walls. The princess had not been able to spend much time with the mare Xerxes had gifted her. The bay mare was quiet against the prancing guard horses. The animals reached out to bite each other in frustration. The weather was pleasant, the sky held a few clouds shielding the sun from its warm rays. The black horse underneath her danced with anticipation for a good run. Having such a picky horse made it difficult for the servants to exercise such a creature, thus Mirage practically cantered in place as his neck arched until his chin touched his glimmering chest.

"Calmese," she whispered, trying to calm the excited stallion as he did a rear striking out with his front hooves. Leaning forward with the motion, Amore let out a flustered sigh and shook her head.

"What dialect is that, Your Highness? It is beautiful," the princess inquired, Amore smiled slightly and studied her beautiful black horse.

"My mother taught me this secret tongue. She said that only two beings knew of it, her horse and her. That way no one would ever be able to command him like I do," Amore explained the best she could without giving anything away that would incriminate her. She had to admit, Princess Almeria was an excellent rider. The young girl's small frame fit the little bay's quiet attitude very well. The beautiful landscape stretched for miles. The last time Amore had ridden this ridge had been with her family. The company of guards from the palace rode loosely around them, watching, waiting. Amore felt an uneasy feeling hit her as Mirage picked up his head and swung it toward the north, his large nostrils flaring to drink in the wind.

Stroking his neck, the horse beneath her vibrated slightly when he suddenly jolted, swinging around and into a full rear. Wrapping her arms around his neck as best she could, she held on as he stayed up in the air. Landing with a thud he swung his head and began to prance. His tail slashed the air with vengeance. The guards' horses picked up quickly on the stallion's agitation, unsettling the already frustrated soldiers.

The air was suddenly filled with shouts and exclamations. Men poured out of the trees, hoods covering their heads as they raised swords into the air. Their animals danced with excitement. The amount of raiders easily overwhelmed the guards, or so it seemed at the moment. The stallion beneath her reacted before she had a chance to think. He bolted, coming close to colliding with a guard's horse. Knocking the animal out of his way, his black ears pinned in determination as he refused to listen to the bit and charged ahead, startling the raiders and guards. Mirage galloped with vengeance to his strides, his long slender black legs reaching far with each pounding step. The cry of the raiders behind her seemed to propel his momentum. Glancing back, dismay filled her. The guards fought off the remaining raiders as Princess Almeria's mare carried her away with guards galloping madly after her. The rest chased after her. The stallion's legs seemed to eat the ground with each pounding wave sent through his muscles. His ears pinned as his tail arched whipping in the wind like a flag. Her heart began to pick up with the relief they would get away.

Relief. It can both be fuel and poison for the person feeling it. As relief released its grip and fear replaced it, Amore pulled the powerful stallion up finally as men poured out of the tree line in front of them. Mirage's neck arched as he snorted and pawed angrily at the ground, his rider frantically looking for ways to escape. The only way now was the ravine. It was a step run and incredibly dangerous, yet compared to the men in hoods around her, the ravine looked like child's play. She knew what she had to do but feared it at the same time as her horse spun in circles ready to explode. He knew the danger, he had been ridden into fights before when Amore was young and her father used him as a cavalry horse before he became too difficult for him. Glancing toward the cliff once more, she loosened the reins as the raider released her intentions. Before anyone could react, Mirage bolted, dirt flying up behind his hooves as he tore toward the drop-off. Amore's heart flew as his muscles bunched beneath her and he came off the ground. Even though Amore completely believed in her horse and the power of his frame, her heart sank as his hooves pounded into the soft dirt, causing it to slide as he galloped down the cliff. Her head bounced against his rump, as his reins flew in the wind.

They where almost there! Unbelievable!

Before any joy or pure excitement could flood her, everything came to crashing halt. She did not know what caused Mirage to stumble as they neared the bottom, all she recollected was seeing the ground coming up to fast and meeting it too hard.

The world was mixed with ground as everything hit slow motion, the black blur of Mirage rolling over her to the sensation of the cold slap of water as the currents took hold and tried to drag them under, waiting to claim their lives. How she held on to the stallion was beyond her as air filled her lungs before being dragged under again, this time separated from her beloved horse. Her hands grasped at the water depths, continuing to close around nothing until finally grasping the familiar leather strap.

Clasping tightly around it, she felt herself begin to be dragged toward the surface, or possibly to river bottom, she could not tell, until the air hit her, and wild black legs thrashed out, coming close to striking her as they slammed into dirt finally. Before long; Amore was not sure when they came to a stop, only that the sky looked beautiful, its clear blue crisp color made her feel like she was looking into eternity. Nothing hurt here. No pain, no sorrow.

Simply peace.

She vaguely could see Mirage struggling to his feet next to her, his black hooves landing near her somewhere. The stallion struggled to keep his balance before lowering his head to push into her shoulder. His warm breath was unfelt by her skin. Something dripped from his forehead and onto her. Still she felt nothing but a sensation that it was okay to fall asleep.

As the peacefulness around her began to subside, Amore clung to it and did not want to leave. Her blue eyes slowly took in the world around her. The wood ceiling was one she had never seen before. Its dark wood was frayed and looked well worn to the years of use. Attempting to sit up, Amore groaned and froze. Her body felt like she had been run over by a thousand horses. Her mind was blank to what had happened, and how she even arrived at this place. Slowly moving her head, she winced as the world blackened slightly before clearing again and the nauseous feeling left her. The room was faintly lit, enough for her to see the surroundings. It looked like a storage room, shelves lined with food and blankets on one corner and the other with more small beds like the one underneath her. As the door cracked open she was surprised to see it was on the ceiling. The hem of a dress showed first until that of a young girl appeared with the flood of light from the world above. The girl hurried forward, a worried look flashing over her face, as something cold sloshed onto Amore's forehead.

"I am so glad you are awake." The girl's voice filled the silence of the room as the bed sagged as she sat beside Amore's hip. A smile flickered across her face. Her hand brushed against Amore's head making her wince. "That's quite the nasty bump. I don't think I've ever seen anyone in such a shape as you." Her words mashed together. Amore tried to search her mind as everything slowly came back. Oddly enough, she did not remember the fall. The last thing she remembered was nearing the bottom of the ravine then the river before lying on her back staring up at the stars.

"What...happened?" she choked out, her voice sounding not like her own. The girl shrugged her petite shoulders before taking the rag from Amore's forehead.

"Not sure really, some of the men found you and your horse along the river. They called the horse loco, wouldn't let no one near you until he finally clasped."

Mirage clasped? Amore sat up suddenly and the world around her began to spin as the girl gently pushed her back down. "Easy now, he'll be just fine. I overheard one of the men saying that he must have pulled a muscle in his shoulder. Probably why he hobbled on three legs. Other than that just a couple of cuts and he'll be okay. He actually looks better off than you," she explained, trying to smooth over Amore's worries. Amore attempted to overlook her own wounds but the lighting in the room refused to show anything. "There's nothing majorly wrong with you according to the doctor. Just a lot of bruising, cuts, and the bump to your head. He also said you would probably be sore and stiff for a long time. You ran a fever for the first few days that you were here but thankfully that broke last night and you're finally awake," the girl rattled on as a smile of happiness covered her face at her last words.

How many days have I been asleep?

"How...long have I been here?" Talking hurt her insides as her muscles complained at working. The girl's eyes looked away thoughtful as she counted in her mind.

"Two days. Today will be the third." Glancing toward the stair-ways at the corner of the room, she leaned closer, her eyes growing wide with curiosity. "Are you really royalty?" she whispered, her voice soft. Amore's hand reacted on its own and slowly moved to finger her forehead where the small banded crown she had been wearing on the ride was gone. "We figured you were from the palace by the decorum on your horse and the crown along with all your jewelry." Her voice was filled with awe as she thought of the possibilities and things Amore must have experienced.

Before Amore could say anything else, someone called out, "Jenna!"

The girl's eyes grew wide. "Excuse me," she apologized and dashed across the room and back up the stairs, the door closing behind her, shutting Amore back into darkness. She was not sure how long she laid there, her mind spinning with all the details. Taking a deep breath, she swung her legs slowly off the bed and forced herself to sit up. Nausea struck her, forcing her to stop when she sat up and bow her head into her hands until it passed. Her stomach grumbled at not being fed. All Amore wanted to do was get out of the darkness. Reaching out for the wall at the head of the bed, Amore used it to stabilize herself to stand. Her mus-cles shook and complained before forcing her to sit back down. Frustrated, Amore crashed back onto the pillow and sighed. Between sleeping and not knowing whether or not it was day or night, Amore was unsure how much time passed before the girl showed up again. This time the smell of food brought a wel-come relief.

Sitting up slowly, Amore gradually took the bowl from her before being forced to allow the girl to hold it. At least Amore's arm allowed her to feed herself. The soup was hot but felt good against her throat. After finishing all that she could she smiled her thanks as the girl set the bowl aside.

"Daniel thinks it should be safe for you to come out now. The raiders have not shown up in a few days. Well, since you arrived, actually."

"How long has it been since you were last down here?" Amore inquired before the girl continued to talk. She smiled and helped Amore to stand.

"I think about ten hours. Every time I checked on you, you were asleep."

Amore felt weak as she let the younger, smaller girl help her up the stairs and out into a bright room. Her eyes squinted against the sun as she took a seat on a soft cushion. The room was set up with tables and chairs everywhere. The house was built out of a beautiful thick tree wood. Amore admired the coloring to the bark.

"Great-grandfather built this home. He was in better society than we are so he could afford it. It was handed down to my father, and hopefully I will inherit it someday. That is, if we don't lose it in order to pay taxes! Oh, I am sorry, I wasn't supposed to say that," she explained as she took care of the dishes, setting them in a large tub to be washed later. "We use it as a town gathering place now, our rooms are upstairs. And the storage room you were in to be safe."

"From the raiders?" Amore asked and the girl nodded. "What is your name?" she finally inquired as the girl smiled and took a seat.

"I am called Jennavieve. Most of my friends call me Jenna, you may call me Jenna." Jenna grinned as she twitched in her seat. Amore could tell that the young girl wanted to ask her so many questions but was trying to be polite and not intrude. "I think I have met you before!" she exclaimed suddenly, bouncing in her seat as her eyes grew wide. Amore tilted her head to the side and rested up against the wall behind her.

"When would that have been?" she asked, knowing Jenna would be more than happy to explain.

"I think it was still in the springtime, I am not very good at remembering the days and calendars," she expressed, smiling. "You were with the General Damon, and I had given you some flowers." Her eyes were searching, waiting for Amore to remember. So much had happened since the springtime but it slowly came back to her and she smiled.

"I remember now." The girl's face glowed with warmth as she blushed slightly and nodded her head.

"Yes, I thought it was so wonderful to meet someone who had to be royalty. Please tell me, are you royalty?" she inquired, again reminding Amore that she had not answered her before. Amore glanced around the empty room. Did she dare say anything? Would these people even care? Perhaps they would, but she could not get around explaining the decorum on Mirage and the crown placed upon her own head. Even her maidens were not dressed that nicely.

"Yes, but I greatly appreciate it if you said nothing. I do not want any fussing over me, or anyone placing themselves in harm's way," Amore softly ordered as the girl bobbed her head and smiled really big. The doors to the café opened suddenly and in walked a short older man. His expression was grave as he spotted them.

"Hello, Jenna." He walked with a limp to his step until he stopped in front of Amore. "How are we feeling this morning?" The older man began to examine her bruises and cuts.

"Much better, thank you."

"Good." He glanced back at Jenna before taking a seat next to the young girl as she handed him a glass of water. He looked perplexed as he took a sip. His eyes glazed over slightly as he waited before speaking. "With all of the activity between here and the palace, I have to make sure. I have to know who you are, ma'am," he finally spilled out. The older man studied her unrelentingly and Amore glanced over at the young girl. She had to say something. They could not get into trouble over her. Could they? Sitting up a little straighter and wincing, Amore took a deep breath.

"I am Amore—"

"The king's betrothed?" the man blurted, startled before growing pale as he leaned back. Amore glanced down. He knew who she was simply by her name. Yet did not recognize her. Maybe no one in this town had been to the palace. Of course Amore was not allowed to go terribly far and the ride with Princess Almeria had been a huge exception.

"Yes." Judging by the expression on his face, Amore knew he was trying to figure out how she got into the situation she currently resided. "The raiders attacked Princess Almeria and I two days ago. As far as I remember, my horse went over the ravine, and then I woke up here," Amore explained as shortly as she could. The man still appeared overwhelmed as he got to his feet and walked slowly toward the main door, muttering under his breath to himself. Amore could faintly hear the words "What are we going to do!" repeated over and over.

"I did not want anyone to know, sir. I do not wish to cause anyone unease or harm," Amore apologized, slowly standing. It was then she realized that she was wearing a simple brown gown. Who in the world had changed her clothes? Glancing at the young girl, she smiled slightly and looked down, answering Amore's unasked question.

"Your Highness, you do not need to apologize. I do fear for what might happen if the raiders find you here. With this rain, it is impossible to bring you ourselves safely to the palace. Between the soldiers and raiders it would take a few days' journey."

"How far is the palace?" Amore asked, glancing between the two. Jenna shrugged and the older man continued to stare out the window.

"At least a day and half ride. In a wagon it would at least be two days, if not more," Jenna exclaimed.

The door to the café suddenly burst open and a rush of people came in. By the looks of it and the shocked expression on the older man's face, it was the townspeople. Many greeted her and asked how she was. Thankfully neither the older man nor Jenna said anything as Amore offered, "Thank you, I am doing better." They were so friendly and open toward her that it warmed her greatly.

"Everyone!" the older man called out, drawing the attention of the ten people so everyone turned to face him.

"I would like you all to meet…Mira. She works in the palace," the older man lied and Amore smiled, nodding her head, approving of it for now. The older man sunk in his chair as those around Amore continued to greet her before turning to Jenna. An easy conversation filled the room, Amore tried to follow as much of it as she could before growing weary. She continued to listen as the conversation turned towards the raiders, and the crowd began to murmur with unease. From what was said, the raids had been happening for longer than Amore had even realized.

"There is talk of war with Emir because of their blatant acts." One man exclaimed as the other quickly agreed with him.

"It is about time that something is done!" others added as Amore's heart began to pound loudly in her ears. The conversation turned to how expensive the campaign would be, but those who indulged in the topic seemed certain that Avalon would triumph in such a matter. Panic tried to fill her until Amore stood. Breathing deeply, she slowly made her way towards the door. The world outside was gloomy and dark matching her thoughts and the conversation. The rain continued to pound the soaked earth as Amore stepped out underneath the porch of the building. The fresh smell helped to relieve her mind as she leaned against the post, observing the town.

The Village of Tylia was quite small, a few buildings here and there. Homes lingered not far from the town. Amore sighed as she glanced toward the biggest building of them all. Judging by the large doors it had to be the stable. Hearing the splattering of mud, Amore glanced down the street to find a lone horseman trotting toward her, head down against the driving rain. She was unsure whether to turn and go back inside or keep her position and watch. Thankfully, Jenna solved her problem and came up beside her before crying "Father!" and dashing out into the muddy street to meet the horseman. The older man appeared next to Amore then.

"I apologize, Your Highness, no disrespect to you. I just fear how the town would react knowing who you really are." Amore smiled slightly before watching the man get off his horse and hug the young girl.

"It is all right, sir. The less people know the better. I do not need anyone risking their life for me," she explained. The man chuckled uneasily before shaking his head.

"That's just it. If anything happens to you and the king finds out we did nothing, all—" He stopped short of his words and looked ashamed. "It will not be a pretty end for us or anyone else, for a matter of fact."

"Why?" she asked curiously. "I can understand him being upset but how would it affect everyone?"

The man looked at her surprised before tilting his head. "You don't know?"

Startled, Amore shook her head before studying him as he looked back out toward the man that stared at them as he approached. Jenna led his mount away to the stables.

"Maverick, so good to have you back!" the old man exclaimed as the rather broad man stepped up on the porch. Amore did not like the look in his eyes as his gaze flickered at her, almost sizing her up before turning to the man beside her.

"Doc, taking in more strays, are we?" he asked, his voice deep and gruff. Amore felt slightly offended by his tone and words. Something about the man put her at great unease.

"Maverick, I would like to introduce you to Crown Queen Amore," he said quickly, obliviously understanding the look he was giving her. Usually people gave a great deal of respect when hearing the beginning part of names that hers was attached to. Instead, the man's expression darkened before his eyes flashed at the man he called Doc.

"What is she doing here?" His words shook as he glared at the older man. Amore went from unease to startled to annoyed. She could easily make his life horrible if she really wanted too. The older man tried to rebuff the broad, hate-filled man.

"Maverick, careful!" Doc cautioned. Amore stood straighter, or somewhat straighter before her muscles complained.

"Why, so they can make my life more miserable than it already is?" he snapped, glaring at Amore. "Since I have been begging to talk to someone in authority then so be it, I guess you'll have to do. Take my home and you'll regret it," he snapped at Amore before whipping around and storming off. Amore stood stunned as she watched the man disappear at the end of the row of buildings. Doc started apologizing for him. Amore glanced over at the man before gently brushing aside his apologies. What touched her even more was the horrified look on Jenna. Her shoulder slummed as she stood in front of Amore, head low.

"Please, do not take heart to my father's meanness. He once was a very nice, good-hearted man."

Amore gently put her hand on the young girl's shoulder and smiled sadly. What was she to even say? Something about the man still left a bad taste in her mouth. The young girl helped her back into the café and up the steps to a room where she would be staying temporarily. Jenna helped her into something more comfortable to sleep in. The young girl's eyes grew wide as Amore took a sharp breath at the large bruise along her ribs.

"Is that really painful?" Amore took another deep breath and winced, nodding her head. Covering up once more, she slowly sat on the bed.

"Thank you, Jenna." The young girl nodded her head as she simply stood still before her.

"Why do you think that they wanted to hurt you?" she asked softly, turning her eyes upon Amore. She had not even thought about it as she shrugged her shoulder.

"I cannot answer that, Jenna." Jenna sighed and nodded her head before stepping forward and wrapping Amore into a hug.

"I am glad you are okay." With that, the young girl turned and left, blowing out the candle for Amore as she slowly lay on her back and stared into the darkness. Her body slowly dragged her into an exhausted pitiful sleep.

◦◦◦

Feeling a gentle hand on her forehead she jerked awake and felt bad for startling Doc as he leaned back. His face looked like he had grown older through the night as he tried to smile weakly at her.

"How are we feeling this morning, Your Highness?" he asked, his voice sounding frail and worn. Amore told him and he nodded his head. "That is good to hear. I have to apologize once more to you and ask for your forgiveness. The town was told last night who you really are. It set them back, but it had to be done. It was only fair to them."

Amore slowly sat up and looked around at the small room.

"If you can find me another horse, I will be on my way," Amore said. A thought floated around her mind. She was completely unguarded. If she turned toward home no one would have anything to say about it. She could run and never look back, escaping her life. Even as she entertained the idea, something was still bothering her. The way Jenna's father had treated her and the way Doc had seemed to grow frailer by the passing moments.

"I must strongly object, Your Highness! It is too dangerous for you to make such a trip, especially in your condition. Besides, we do not have any soldiers or anyone trained well enough to protect you. Maverick has sent some of the young men on the fastest horses we have to the palace. Hopefully they will make it," he added softly in the end, barely loud enough for Amore to hear.

"If you do not mind me asking—"

"Call me Doc, please, Your Highness."

210

"Doc." She smiled then and grew deep in thought. "What did Maverick mean about taking his home away?" she implored.

The older man smiled sadly and looked around them. "This home has been in his family for generations. With raiders tormenting the crops and hurting our income, the palace demanding payment for taxes. As I am sure Jenna has so kindly explained this house here has been made from some of the rarest trees that are no longer in existence. Other than the fact that if the taxes are not paid we will all lose our homes. So this house was offered by the officials as a payment for us all. Maverick went to the palace last week to try and sort it out. By the way he spoke toward you yesterday, they never even saw him."

Doc grew silent, allowing for it to sink in before gently patting her on the knee before quickly withdrawing his hand like she had slapped him. Amore was surprised. Being in the position of life with her own family she never worried about income or taxes. Moving from court life to palace life it had never crossed her mind. She was even more surprised that the raiders have been around for a while.

"Why has no one told the palace about the raiders sooner?" she asked softly, staring at the floor. The older man chuckled before shaking his head with regret.

"Why bother? No offence, Your Highness, but the officials do not exactly see eye to eye with us commoners." With that he slowly stood and bowed as much as he could to her before straightening and shuffling toward the door. Moving even slower than before. Amore hoped she was wrong but she felt like she was the cause for it all.

Her muscles did not complain as much as she stood and slowly dressed. It took some doing as her body did not want to move as freely as before, but eventually, the plain dress covered her tender body as Amore ran her fingers through her hair. Her hair was a mess and desperately needed to be cleaned. Taking the brush from the small desk she ran in through her hair until at least it laid smooth before putting it into a braid. At least that was the best she could do. As she descended the stairs the room grew deathly quiet. The once bubbly group avoided eye contact with her and bowed low as she walked past. She had been used to respect at the palace but for some reason this felt odd, out of place. Maybe it was the dress, or the fact that her skin was a bit dirty or the bruises that lined her arms and head. So as she escaped out onto the porch once more, the air was cool, still fresh with the smell of rain as the gloomy clouds lingered in the sky. Amore made her way across the muddy street and toward the stable. The townspeople hurried out of her way, bowing to her as she walked. Slipping alone into the stable, she sighed with relief as she walked to Mirage. He did not greet her as normal. Instead his head hung toward the wall with his hindquarters facing her. He looked like he desperately needed a grooming. Sliding the bolt on the door, she called to her horse softly. His head came up and he shuffled toward her, his front leg refusing to touch the ground. Her heart sank at the size of his right shoulder. It was swollen and very hot to the touch. His breath was hot against her skin as he lowered his head and tried to lean against her. Wrapping her arms around his neck, she finally broke down and cried. The weight of everything that happened finally gripped her. She had come close to never waking up again. They both should have died taking a steep ravine like that. She was not sure how long she cried on him before the door to the stable opened. Brushing back her sobs and the tears she kept her back to the door and gently hand brushed the dirt off of his coat. Hearing the sound of a grunt that could only come from a man, Amore turned around to find Maverick with his head low his eyes staring at the dirt.

"I must apologize, Your Highness. I should not have spoken to you in such a way yesterday. If you could find it in your heart to forgive an old fool like me, that would be greatly appreciated." He flickered his gaze up at her and tried hard to smile. He reminded her then of her father, in a few ways. She could tell it was hard for him to admit his follies. Nodding her head, Amore smiled softly.

"All is forgiven." Looking back at her horse, Amore's smile grew sad. "I must ask a favor of you." His head shot up and a surprised look flashed over his eyes. "He will never make the journey back. It would be much safer for you to care for him, than you would me." She held up her hand, silencing him. "Please, do not argue with me on this. We both know this is true. Take good care of him until I can return to take him home." The man seemed lost for words, so he nodded his head. "Now which horse would it be good for me to take?"

"Your Highness, I sent out some men to the palace last night. At least wait until tomorrow before doing anything stupid." He caught himself with the last word but Amore smiled.

"So be it…" She was about to say no but by the look of the young girl in the doorway she knew it was best to give in. A joyous look flashed on her face as she squealed before clamping her hands over her mouth. Her father whipped around as Jenna smiled bashfully over being caught. Jenna could not stop talking the rest of the morning. She asked Amore a million questions and did not give her time to answer before rattling on to the next one.

"Jenna!" she exclaimed, smiling as the girl jolted to a stop with her questions and blushed. Thinking of the jewelry and crown that she had worn, Amore smirked at the idea that crossed her mind. Leaning closer she whispered to the young girl, barely able to finish before she dashed off. Maverick sat across the room watching. His gaze was hard to read but if Amore had to put something to it, she figured contentment. He caught her watching him as he gulped shifting, he turned away. Jenna's chestnut hair bounced as she raced back into the room, very unladylike. It only made Amore like the girl even more. Handing the cotton pouch to her, she sat back. Carefully opening up the band that held it close, the jewelry was sparkling. Pulling out the banded ruby crown, she grinned at the wide-eyed look of the young girl. Gently placing the too-big of a crown on her head, Amore readjusted it before sitting back. Getting up she graciously bowed as low as she could, enjoying the little game. If Jenna's eyes grew any wider, Amore wondered if they would pop as she returned the bow clumsily before dashing over to her father. Jenna whipped around and twirled like she was dancing, before the crown slid past one of her eyes and sideways. Dashing back over to Amore, she beamed happily.

"Do I get to keep it?" she asked, awed. Amore smiled but shook her head.

"I am sorry, Jenna. However, tonight you may wear it as long as possible." The girl's smile had dimmed before growing again as Amore offered out her arms to dance with her. Jenna took her hand and Amore instructed for her to place her left hand on Amore's arm. "Ready?" she asked. Jenna's head came to Amore's chest. She had to be around the age of at least twelve. Starting out slow, Amore spun Jenna around the room before slowly picking up the pace, laughter floating out of her. This was the most fun she had in a very long time. Her muscles began to object, forcing her to stop sooner than she wanted to.

"Aww!" Jenna pouted before her father slowly stepped toward her and offered a bow to his young daughter.

"May I have this dance, princess?" he asked, his voice soft and filled with love. The tough exterior melted away as he stared down at the young girl. As Amore watched the two, the world around them blurred as her heart melted at the sight flashing back to when her father used to dance with her. Amore came close to missing the sight of a certain man walking past the window that made her heart stop and she scrambled for cover of the counter. Her attempt to hide made the others freeze, and she vaguely saw the crown being pulled from Jenna's head and hidden by someone else. The door to the café opened, and Amore's heart froze.

"What can I do to get something to drink!" Lord Zander's voice boomed, his tone annoyed and furious. *What is he doing out here?*

"Right away, sire," someone piped and scrambled to get something from behind the counter. Amore pushed herself farther back, trying to blend in as one of the town girls grabbed a tall bottle of liquor and a glass before pouring him something above Amore's head. "I'll need a fresh horse as well!" he demanded. Amore could hear the door slam as someone dashed across the street.

"Is there anything else we can help you with?" Maverick asked, his tone serious. Lord Zander laughed darkly making chills run through Amore's arms causing bumps to rise to her skin. "Your daughter is beautiful!" His tone was not meant for a compliment. Thankfully Maverick kept himself in check as the obnoxious man stated, "I wouldn't let her wander too far away now, you hear?" before shuffling around the room and the door opened once more before slamming. Amore felt the breath she had been holding escape but she refused to move. Finally someone called all clear and she crawled out from underneath the table and slowly stood. The townspeople had stunned expressions as they glanced over at her. Maverick was fuming over the man who had left before his steel gaze flashed over toward her.

"Who was that man, Your Highness? If he was an official from the palace why did you hide?" he checked his voice. Amore's heart grew heavy as her mind whirled.

"Lord Zander is a visiting dignitary but an evil man," Amore remarked, rubbing her arm unconsciously. "I will deny ever speaking such words!" she quickly added, glancing around at the people in the room.

"It is all right, Your Highness! You can tell by the essence around such a person," the girl at the counter remarked. Amore glanced over at her and smiled slightly. Looking down Amore slowly wrapped her arms around herself.

"I would be most appreciative if no one ever spoke that I saw Lord Zander. It would bring up more unwanted questions than I can answer at the moment. I would like to caution you all to never tangle with that man."

"Won't he say something about being out here when the army comes for you?" someone asked. Amore grew thoughtful before smirking slightly.

"No, I feel that Lord Zander is in a place he is not supposed to be." Amore's smile grew as her eyes narrowed. If he wanted to play dirty with her, then she would play the same game. By the way he did not announce himself or ask if anyone had seen her, Amore knew that he was not out here trying to help find her.

"Your Highness, do you think he has anything to do with the raiders?" Jenna blurted out. The thought had not really crossed her mind but it was a huge possibility. Amore smiled slightly as Maverick checked his daughter for asking such a thing.

"It is all right. I do not know, Jenna, but I would like to find out if I can."

An odd silence fell over those in the room. The rest of the day, Amore consented to rest and answer the inquisitive Jenna. She inquired continuously until her father gently interrupted the young girl.

"Why do you not help the princess to her room to rest? Then later you can ask her some more."

Jenna pouted before nodding her head as Amore chuckled softly. The young girl grew quiet as she helped Amore into her room. She could tell that Jenna still had thousands of questions still waiting to be asked as she slowly left. Resting, Amore stared at the ceiling as she pondered Zander. What could he be possibly be doing out here? How would he even explain being absent from the palace unless he was supposed to help find her? Why had no one else been to Tylia yet? It was not that far from the palace, and the rain had stopped sometime during the night. Amore slowly drifted to sleep until a warm hand gently woke her. Jenna sat alongside her on the bed as a smile filled her face.

"I brought you something that the doc wants you to drink." She wrinkled her noise as she handed Amore the cup. The bitter-tasting herbs made her want to cringe as she sipped the hot drink. "I'm glad I don't have to drink it." The same twinkle in her eyes showed as she gently wet her lip with her tongue. "What is it like being in a palace?" she asked, eager to hear more.

"Jenna!" the doc's scolding voice caught the girl short as he stepped into the room and she let out a long sigh, taking the empty cup from Amore.

"I never get to have any fun." She pouted as her shoulder shagged, making Amore want to laugh as the doc shook his head and slowly closed the door.

"To be a child again," he smiled as he walked closer. He motioned for her to stay where she was. "If it is all right, I need to…check you over." He seemed rather hesitant as he gently began to examine her head before his fingers pushed softly on her ribcage, making her wince.

"What color was your side this morning?"

"A purplish black?" he sighed and nodded his head as he finished examining her. It was like he kept hesitating before touching her skin.

"You are incredibly lucky." He remarked after he was done and Amore slowly sat up. "There is nothing broken, nor does it seem like you have lost any functions in movement or mind. There is no swelling anywhere besides the bruising you received, which is nothing considering your ordeal."

His words left a feeling of weight upon her shoulders. She was only sore from the bruising and her muscles felt like someone had tried to stretch her. How had she been so lucky to not have come out even worse?

"If you feel up to it, there is an inquisitive child downstairs who has been rather impatient to speak with you." He chuckled and shook his head as Amore stood. Sure enough, Jenna stuck to her side and at least waited patiently until Amore was seated before asking any more questions. The town was packed into the building and some of the other kids drew her attention away for a while. Exhaustion soon filled her as she became rather tired with the amount of people in the room.

⚬⚬⚬

To her great relief the town slowly shifted out, allowing Amore to think in peace. This was going on her fourth day. The men had been sent out almost a full day now. They should be reaching the palace by late tonight. As she sat on the cushion, her mind grew back to her dilemma. Should she take this opportunity and make a dash for home or stay? Her heart hurt slightly at the thought of leaving Xerxes and the craziness between them but her mind screamed at her about the chance she was getting to escape certain doom. That chance would slip out of her grasp faster than she could ever call it back.

"Your Highness! Princess Amore!" a woman cried from outside, Amore felt her heart almost stop at the thought of something horrible happening as she hurried toward the door and out onto the porch. Maverick was out on the street and everyone quickly scrambled out of the way at the sight of high waving banners and mud flying beneath the hooves of palace guards. The horses were decorated to every extent possible. Amore slowly made her way out onto the street as her eyes hit the person in the middle. The guards quickly parted to canter past her, as Leah swung her head high into the air. Before she even came to a stop, Xerxes was out of the saddle and hitting the ground. Amore blushed as he swept her up into his arms and spun her around. His grip strong as he slowly set her back down, jolts of pain whirled around her. The bruises still fresh against her skin. Stepping back his hands held her face. She felt greatly surprised by the extreme amount of worry and fear in his eyes.

"Are you all right? How are you? Are you well?"

Amore nodded and let out a small smile as her eyes became moist. She glanced down at her arms as he gently fingered the bruise on her hair line before pulling her close again. "I am all right." Her words were muffled against him. She could actually feel his heart pounding against his chest and it made her feel safe and secure as her eyes closed, wanting to get lost in the sense of security. Feeling Leah nudge her from behind, Amore pulled back and rubbed the mare's nose.

"Where is Mirage?" Xerxes asked, glancing around. Amore lowered her gaze and smiled sadly.

"He is fine but will not be able to make the journey. They promised to take good care of him," Amore explained. Xerxes helped her up onto his horse before swinging up behind her. He said a grateful thank you to the people before swinging around his horse, his arm wrapping tightly around her as Leah jumped into gear. The sun was low in the sky. They would be traveling through the night and into the next day. Glancing back, she spotted Jenna race to the end of the town and hug herself. Amore realized then that she did not get to say good-bye or thank you.

⌇

The ride left her exhausted and worn as her body complained greatly. Amore tried to sleep, but every subtle movement and Xerxes's arm around her kept making her clench her jaw to keep her mind away from the pain before everything around her blacked out. As her eyes slowly opened once more, a soft light filled her eyes through the curtain in her room. Every part of her hurt, as she slowly tried to push herself up before giving up and sinking back into the softness of her bed. Never before in her life did she hurt so much, and it every part of her was sore.

"Your Highness!" Clarice appeared alongside her bed. "I am glad to see you are awake! How are you feeling?"

"Everything hurts." She chuckled softly before stopping. Slowly sitting up, Amore winced as her muscles tinged. Clarice protested before helping Amore rest up against the head of the bed. "I feel so weak."

"I am surprised you are even able to move, though I wish you would not." Amore smiled slightly as Clarice fussed over her. Food was brought as the wonderful aroma's filled her room. At least feeding herself was something she would be able to do. Braylin arrived with the servants carrying breakfast for her, as everyone quickly left, leaving it to be just the tree of them.

"You gave my brother quite the scare, Amore." Braylin and Clarice exchanged a look as the maiden smiled faintly. "What in the world happened?" Amore explained everything that she could remember, even about the curious Jenna.

"Xerxes never approved of such a ride." Her heart flickered at Braylin's words, though she had her suspicions who had arranged it all. *Zander,* his appearance in Tylia was no coincidence in her mind. Amore grew flustered at how easily she tired, and Clarice soon kicked out the princess so Amore could rest. When she awoke, Clarice informed her that the physician had been in to see her. Xerxes had tried but Clarice had refused to allow him into the room. The thought made her chuckle. The next couple of days remained the same until Amore felt like she would go crazy if she remained in her room for any longer. The maidens protested as they helped her into a simple dress, her body still hurt, but she had to get out of her room. A knock echoed off her door as Amore frowned.

"Who is it?" she called out.

"Almeria, Your Highness." Amore had not even thought about her at all, and guilt filled her. Excusing all of the maidens, she smiled as the princess slowly entered the room. Clarice gave Amore a stern look as she closed the door behind herself.

"How are you? I mean…are you all right? I feel so guilty for not inquiring sooner." Almeria's eyes saddened quickly as she walked farther into the room. Amore continued standing, though her muscles wanted to sit as the princess turned her gaze upon her once more. She did not want to show any sign of pain in front of the young girl.

"Please, Your Highness, do not feel guilty! I should be the one apologizing. It is entirely my fault and I feel terrible about it." Her eyes began to water as Amore's heart hurt for her. She wanted to wrap her in a hug but feared she would wince at the same time.

"Do not be ridiculous, Princess Almeria. You would not have known what could happen." Amore reassured her, the young girl was taking too much of the blame upon herself. If Amore could help it, she would not allow her to know how much she hurt. Almeria's eyes looked weary and hurt as she slumped into a chair. Wetting her lips with her tongue, Amore pondered her thoughts before carefully asking, "Almeria, where was Zander these last few days?" She should have asked Braylin but she had forgotten.

She picked her head up slowly and shrugged. "I do not know. When I returned to the palace, he was not here. He has yet to return as well."

Amore found that to be very strange, taking a deep breath, she looked the princess in the eyes. "I think it is time, Almeria, to let them know what Zander is truly like." Fear filled her eyes as she took a deep breath and nodded her head. "If you wish, you can remain here until I return. After tonight, I will make sure a guard follows you as well." As soon as she stepped out of her room, Clarice started to protest until Amore silenced her and she followed quietly. The guards remained close until she was brought to where Xerxes was. Gently knocking on the door, she felt her heart flutter. Protocol stated about not approaching the king unless called. Maybe since he was nowhere near the royal court, it would not matter. He was studying a map intently. Rolling the map up, he smiled at her and motioned for Amore to come closer. His gaze lit up as he quickly wrapped her into a hug.

The guards and maidens stayed outside the room as the door was closed behind her.

She enjoyed the warmth of his arms but could not help but grimace at the same time, making him relax and step away. Amore did not want the moment to end and sighed softly until his hands wrapped around the back of her neck, just below her head as his fingers gently pressed against her skin, relieving the tension in her muscles.

"My mother used to press her fingers like this when we were unhappy. It always felt wonderful." It was the first time he had ever mentioned anything about his mother. If the soothing effect did not have such a strong effect of her mind, Amore would have inquired further. She even began to forget why she had come into the room. Slowly opening her eyes she smiled up at him.

"I need to speak to you about something." Her voice was soft as he smiled. His blue eyes held her gaze, making her mind stumble over her thoughts. "It concerns Lord Zander." The smile fell as he sighed.

"Before you continue, I want to tell you something first." His hands stopped the relieving pressure on the back of her neck as he gently fingered the bruises on her arms. "Zander had set up the ride. I had not been informed until afterward, though he apologized for overstepping his boundaries. I had him followed when he left the palace, I cannot find anything against him concerning the raid. However, he has gracefully bowed out of the engagement with Princess Almeria." He took a deep breath and looked at the bruises for a moment.

"I do not trust him, Xerxes." Their gazes meet once again and Amore felt herself grow lost in his eyes.

"I believe Lord Zander will not be seen again in the palace. From what the soldier informed me, the princess will benefit from the engagement being broken." Surprise filled her as he gently pulled her close again, hugging her a little more carefully this time. "I am never letting you out of my sight again." The words were whispered, words that were not meant for her to hear. She smiled as she allowed herself to get lost in the moment. *Tell him about what he had done to you.* She chocked at the thought. She should tell him, that way Zander would never be able to return to Roselyn and hopefully Avalon again. It seemed almost too easy that he had departed so quickly. Amore had planned to explain her reasons to Xerxes, why Zander could not be trusted, to tell him what he had done, but Xerxes already informed that he had left. Yet Almeria was now free from her obligation, so would it be necessary to inform him of Zander's afflictions? Embarrassment filled her as Amore kept her mouth shut. *He does not need to know if Zander has left. Surely he should not be back again.* "What are you thinking?" he asked softly as he gently kissed her forehead. Amore started to respond when she spotted Clarice walking closer, as Xerxes did as well.

"I must beg your forgiveness, Your Majesty. The crown queen needs to rest. She has been away long enough." Clarice bowed her head low, as Xerxes looked Amore in the eyes and smiled.

"Do you wish to return?" he asked as Amore glanced over at Clarice and shook her head. The maiden stood straight and frowned as Xerxes shrugged his shoulder. "There you have it."

"My king, I must protest, Her Highness needs rest!" Amore smiled as she turned her attention to Clarice. From the beginning, Clarice had been unhappy about Amore leaving her room so soon. It felt nice to have the maiden so concerned about her health.

"I heard that Clarice refused a request of the king," Amore remarked, looking up at Xerxes as he smiled, reading her intentions before turning his head to one of the most respected maidens in the palace. "No doubt, retribution must be made." Clarice crossed her arms as Amore's smile grew.

"What must be done to make this offense, right?" he asked, smiling as he looked down at Amore once more, his arms still holding her close to him. Gazing up at the ceiling, she smiled as she pondered her thoughts.

"She must be dismissed, and then I would be able to stay out as long as I please." Amore smiled, looking at Clarice as she spoke her opinion.

Xerxes chuckled as Clarice's gaze grew even more intense. "If you have had your pleasure of teasing me, can you not see my king how she tires already?" Amore looked once more up at him. She did feel exhausted already, but did not want to admit it. It made her feel rather weak.

"She is right, you need your rest." He gently kissed her then as Amore sighed and nodded her head. Allowing the maidens to escort her back to her room, she jumped in surprise as Almeria scrambled to her feet getting off of Amore's bed. Her eyes wide with curiosity.

"What did he say?" she asked uncertainty filling her words. Amore smiled as Clarice started to fuss over her once more.

"Zander has already gracefully bowed out of the engagement and left Roselyn." Surprise filled her as her mouth dropped slightly. Before they could say anything else, Clarice had the princess escorted out and Amore quickly back into bed. She muttered something under her breath as she disappeared into the maiden's room, making Amore chuckle with fondness over the woman.

Truth be Told

WILD STORIES BEGAN TO FILL the palace the next day about Lord Zander breaking off his engagement with Princess Almeria and promptly leaving Roselyn and hopefully Avalon as well. She was glad to see him go but flustered by how oddly easy that had been. It should not have happened so…unchallenged. It was like Lord Zander had not even put up a defense. It was kept under wraps about the real meaning of the reason for the breaking of his engagement but at least Princess Almeria is now free of him.

"I cannot thank you enough!" she exclaimed later. She beamed like Amore had never seen before. A new light came back to her eyes and she looked genuinely happy. Her smile grew faint as her eyes studied Amore. "I thought, maybe it was fear, but he would have not gone so easily," Almeria remarked.

Amore had pondered that and decided it was best to put him aside for now.

"No need to spoil a perfectly good day. How shall we honor such a day as this?" Amore grinned. The young princess strode across Amore's favorite garden and twirled around like a young child, making the maidens giggle before growing quiet again. Collapsing onto one of the larger cushions, Almeria laughed.

"Who cares? I want to do whatever I please," she announced before entering a conversations with one of the maidens. Nothing would have pleased Amore more to see the young girl so free and her mind drifted toward another carefree girl and she gasped. Jenna, and her village. She had never said thank you, nor done anything in return for the kindness. Nor had she heard about how Mirage was doing. Through the archways of the garden Amore could spot one of the officials walking through.

"Lord Crile," Amore called to the older man. He was the third highest man among the palace officials underneath Lord Byron and Lord Timothy. Lord Crile typically dealt with tax matters. The man stopped and bowed low as Amore approached.

"What is it, Your Highness?" he asked, his voice sounded worn. Smiling, Amore motioned for him to continue walking.

"I have a request to make of you. Has an issue concerning the Village of Tylia come to your attention?" The older man nodded and Amore's smile grew wider. "Good, I wish to ask you to pardon their debts and release any withholdings from them. Consider it a most appreciated gift," Amore asked.

The older man stopped short and grew thoughtful before smiling sadly. "I am sorry, Your Highness, but I do not hold that much power. Perhaps you want to bring it up with the king?" He winked before bowing and stating, "Good day."

"Good day, Lord Crile." Turning around, she made her way back down the hall and started toward the garden before stopping short. "Creston, do you know where the king is this morning?" she asked one of stationed guards.

"In a meeting with the general, Your Highness."

Thanking the guard, Amore pondered Jenna and her beautiful little town when she became distracted by the maidens around her. She then began to wonder whatever had happened to Crystal. With everything else that had been occupying her thoughts, she had completely forgotten about the maiden. "Namur." Namur was the oldest of the maidens, besides Clarice. She was also more reliable than many of the other maidens within the palace. Namur got up from her spot to come closer, to listen to whatever Amore needed. "Whatever happened with Crystal?" she asked softly as she looked over at Talia. The young girl had almost blossomed greatly since Crystal's departure. Amore felt guilty for having not even really noticed her absence from the palace. Namur's gaze drifted lower for a moment as she smiled slightly.

"Due to the respect the palace had for her father, she was escorted out of Roselyn in disgrace…never to return to Roselyn or the palace again. It would be a high offense for her to approach you ever again," she informed as Amore nodded her head. "Life, no doubt, will not be easy for her, if word's spread far of a disgraced maiden that was removed from your presence." Namur added as Amore's heart flickered heavily.

"Thank you, Namur." She began to wish she had not even inquired concerning her. Letting out a sigh, she turned and headed toward the middle of the garden, pondering her thoughts of all that was said.

❧

It was barely midmorning and Amore had already grown exhausted by the mild efforts of her day. Her maidens must have sensed it as well when they coaxed her to rest. She did not want to stay in her room anymore, so she found a comfortable, peaceful spot away from the main area of the palace. The soft cushions felt good against her still tender muscles. Her eyes began to grow heavy as she struggled to stay awake. She reminded herself it was due to the injuries that still had yet to heal. Many of her bruises still remained upon her faded tan skin. Her mind slipped into a sweet, peaceful dream.

The air was warm as birds sang in the distance. The tall summer grass surrounding her father's home waved in the breeze as it blew around her. Amore sat on top of the hill watching as her brother ran closer to her. With each step closer it turned out to be Xerxes. She smiled brightly as he sat down alongside her and overlooked the Emirian countryside of her hometown, Believe.

"It is beautiful here," he remarked, smiling warmly at her.

Amore smiled as she looked out across the grass lands. *Why did I think he would not understand?* she thought as they sat together.

"Amore?" he whispered, softly making her frown as she turned her gaze on him, she slowly began to awaken realizing that she had just been dreaming to find him sitting truly alongside her whispering her name. Her maidens were gone, no doubt because he was there. Smiling as she slowly focused on him as he gently stroked her cheek.

"I heard you were asking about me," he inquired, smiling as he sat straight so he was no longer leaning over her.

Amore smiled and remained where she was as she asked, "I wanted to ask something of you." She waited until he nodded his head, his eyes curious. "The debt's against Tylia and their people." She paused for a moment as her eyes drifted toward her hand as he slowly started to play with her fingers. "Forgive their debts, as a very grateful thank you upon my part," she asked, looking up at him again.

"Consider it done," he expressed, making her sit up quickly using her arms to hold herself as she smiled brightly.

"Wonderful." She paused for a moment as he studied her. Glancing down hesitantly, she dared herself to ask the next part. "Could I be the one to bring them the news?" She slowly looked up into his eyes as she asked. The smile faded as his hands gently held onto her forearms.

"I do not think it would be very wise." She could see the fear in his eyes as her own mind flashed back to the ravine. She knew what his answer would be. She understood completely as well. Yet it dampened her spirits but not for too long.

"I know," she whispered, smiling. Chills ran down her arm as his hand slowly dropped. He grew silent making her look at him fully as his eyes where thoughtful.

"Perhaps, with news of Mirage's improvement, we shall go together, to receive the stallion back," he promised, making her smile. No doubt it could easily change but it was good enough for her for now.

"Thank you," she studied his gaze as he smiled. Her heart fluttered as he leaned closer. She expected him to kiss her. Instead he kissed her gently on the cheek before standing.

"Get your rest." He smiled before walking away.

Swinging her legs off the couch, Amore watched him until he disappeared. She was surprised by how she had wanted him to kiss her. He did not even call her "my queen" like he had done so many times. *One can grow weary of waiting for a flower to bloom.* The general's words resounded back in her mind as she looked down. Surely he had not meant that the king was growing weary of waiting for her decision? Turning her gaze back to the spot Xerxes had disappeared from, her heart began to hurt. As she pondered her thoughts, her maidens returned and took their spots. Her three head maidens watched her carefully as Amore slowly laid back and stared at the silky curtain above her. Her mind lost in thought until she slowly began to hear some of the other maidens' hushed conversations.

"They say it is Emir that is behind everything," one woman remarked to the other. Both women rarely accompanied Amore. For whatever reason, these past few days they have been.

"I do not think Emirians can be trusted," the other agreed.

Amore sat up, her gaze steady upon the women that had yet to notice. "Are they sure it is Emir then?" she asked, watching the surprised expression of both women. They grew quiet, obviously hearing it from rumors no doubt.

"No one is sure, Your Highness," Namur remarked, shooting a hard gaze, scolding the two women.

One of the women grew brave as she asked, "Does her highness favor Emir?"

Amore wanted to state boldly that without a doubt yes. Emir would not be behind raids, especially one that nearly took her own life. Controlling her emotions, she turned her teal-eyed gaze on the woman who quickly avoided her eyes.

"I feel that we should know true facts before sharing them with others. For then no hindrances or unwarranted anger is caused upon our parts. Even then, we should be careful. At times it is best to remain silent versus sharing everything with everyone," Amore remarked, watching the woman as a blush came upon her face. Amore glanced at Namur who looked greatly displeased by the other women as she shifted her gaze at Amore before dropping it quickly.

"Very well said, Your Highness," she quickly remarked. Amore did not doubt that her words would be spread abroad and possibly twisted to suit the rumors' needs. Lying back once more, she tried to calm her pulse as her mind swirled with the thoughts. Reminding her of what she had heard before the ravine. *Could war really be happening?* The thought made her heart hurt as tears tried to blur her vision.

As night approached and sleep fled her, Amore slowly made her way to the tower after explaining to her maiden that she could not sleep. The guard waited below as Amore gently closed the door behind her. The darkness felt peaceful as the moon brightened the land around her so she could see. Wrapping her shawl around her shoulders tighter as a chilly breeze brushed against her skin, staring up at the stars, she felt herself get lost in the beauty of it all.

"Amore," a soft voice interrupted her thoughts, making her look back to find Braylin. "What are you doing up here?" she asked, looking around at the palace and the city of Roselyn. "I found this place not so long ago. I like to come here and think," Amore admitted, smiling softly before looking through the night at the town below.

"My mother loved it up here," Braylin commented, startling Amore, on the rare occasion Braylin allowed her a glimpse into her own past. Smiling, Amore sat on the edge of the stone wall and sighed.

"I was told once that my mother liked to look up at the stars every night." Amore smiled sadly as Braylin took a seat next to her.

"Amore, I need to ask you something." Braylin's voice was reserved, making Amore turn her full attention on the beautiful princess.

"Of course."

Taking a breath, Braylin turned her gaze making their eyes connect and the look that Braylin gave her made her worry. "Do you love my brother?" She did not even beat around the bush and her question made Amore catch her breath and look away.

"I…" The words caught in her mouth as her mind started to run wild. *Lie!* was the first thought that came forward. Amore was never comfortable lying and these last few months had been a lot more than she could handle. "It's complicated." The words surprised even Amore.

"Uncomplicate it for me, Amore! I have watched you and from what I see you do love my brother but are afraid of possibly loving him?" she asked, making Amore stand up and walk across the small circle. *It is so complicated.* Amore felt a few tears slip out as she shook her head.

"You cannot understand." Amore forced the words out and her emotions down, emotions that had been eating her alive. All the things she had been hiding from Braylin, Xerxes, and every single person in this palace and town.

"Are you already engaged to someone else?" she asked, her voice worried. Amore shook her head and stared out into the night as more tears started to come against her will. She wished with all her heart she could say that she was engaged; then again it would not explain most of her actions.

"I am not who you think I am." The words came out before she even had a chance to think. Clamping her mouth shut, Amore wiped the tears away as she felt Braylin's intense gaze. The chilly night air engulfed her, numbing her skin.

"Who are you then?"

Amore felt trapped. How long would she have gotten away with this? Would she have ever been able to escape her coming doom? *Maybe I should tell, get it over with. Stop prolonging the inevitable. I cannot live with all these secrets forever.* Taking a deep breath Amore looked straight before stating.

"I never planned on meeting Xerxes. All I wanted to do was get away to have a breath of fresh air, away from people who watched me every moment. We did not mean any harm; all we wanted to do was visit some friends, how harmful is that? Then we would return home. It was a stupid mistake, I know that now. Slipping away so late at night in a kingdom I have never stepped foot in before. To answer your question, I guess, yes, I was feeling something deeper than I ever felt for anyone toward your brother but fear had always made me watch my step and lately with everything and the words I heard Xerxes speak made me realize I had to keep my distance to try to escape," her voice started to crack. Amore slowly turned her gaze down as Braylin tried to speak.

"Amore, I do not understand. What has my brother said? If you love my brother then why are you so afraid? What would we do that would hurt you so?" Braylin's voice expressed the confusion that she was feeling.

"Princess Braylin. Avalon's enemy is the country Emir, correct me if I am wrong." Amore grew serious as her heart started pounding. She could tell the name meant something to her.

"Of course."

"I am from Emir," Amore's voice quivered as she spoke those words, worry filling her veins. Braylin looked startled at first before letting out a laugh.

"Amore, that is not so bad! You had me worried for nothing." Braylin's voice sounded relieved as she leaned against the half stone pillar beside her.

"But there is such hatred between the two kingdoms," Amore exclaimed, startled by Braylin's reaction. Her hair blew back in the breeze that lifted over the palace walls and swirled around them both before disappearing once more.

"Amore, you are from Emir and our countries are not on… speaking terms. It is not like you're the daughter of General Divon."

Amore choked on her breath as she said those words and she must have made some sort of noise because Braylin looked at her funny. "Is there more?"

"Yes, but I am afraid you will not be happy about it." Amore fingered her beautiful sparkly gown twisting her fingers into the silky lace. Falling to her knees Amore took a hold of Braylin's wrists and let her head fall hitting Braylin's knees. "Have mercy on me, Your Highness. Show me the same kindness and generosity that you have shown me before!" Amore cried. Feeling Braylin's hesitating hand on her hair, Amore slowly turned her gaze up locking it with Braylin's confused eyes. "I am General Divon's daughter. Deandre is my mother's maiden name. I am called Amorita Deandre Aleara Divon, daughter of General Alexander Aleara Divon, and Lady of the Court of Emir." Amore felt like her heart was about to explode as she watched her words sink in to Braylin and her eyes grew wide. Braylin's gaze stared off into the distance, her whole face turned white in the faint moonlight, stunned for words.

Her mouth slowly opened as she tried to speak. "I…I need time to think," she finally expressed, standing up. Amore let go of her and stayed kneeling on the ground. Braylin retreated down the steps, leaving Amore there. Unsure of what was to come next, Amore stayed there until the early morning hours before heading back down to her room. Her bed was a welcome sight as she collapsed into the softness, her mind and emotions exhausted from the night's events. *What is to become of me?* was the last thought to cross her mind before she drifted into sweeter dreams.

The following week was rather uneventful and dull for Amore. Each morning after that evening, she had expected to be thrown in the dungeon, and each morning nothing happened, letting out a sigh as she awoke on the last day of the week. The room was warm with the afternoon sun, and the maiden's no doubt were already awake. Slowly sitting up, Amore took a deep breath and stared out the archway leading to the small deck that overlooked the animal sanctuary below. She had not seen Princess Braylin at all that week and it began bother her. Princess Almeria still remained at the palace but concluded she should be returning home soon. King Xerxes and his advisors were out at the training grounds and did not plan on being back until next week. The consequences that possibly awaited her, made Amore wanted to curl up underneath the covers and refuse to face the day. *If Princess Braylin had decided to have you imprisoned, they would not wait for you to awaken.* Her mind tried to reassure her. She heard a soft knock on the door and the voice of Clarice rang clear.

"Your Highness, I have been requested to assist you with getting prepared."

Amore called for her to come in.

"Prepared for what, Clarice?" she asked softly. Her long brown hair rested on the pillow.

"Your wedding at the rotation of four days. We must begin your preparation now!" she exclaimed. Amore slowly stood and began to undress before Clarice stopped her. "No, no, Your Highness! You will be taking a scented bath!" She helped Amore place a top coat over her night gown. She started putting up Amore's hair when the door suddenly opened and in walked Braylin.

"Give us a moment, would you, Clarice?" Braylin asked. The older woman nodded her head and gracefully bowed out, closing the door behind her. Amore felt her heart flicker as she lowered her gaze. Braylin walked slowly across the room before looking out the archway.

"I have given a lot of thought to our previous discussion." Her voice held a reserve to it. "At first I was leaning toward the idea of…well, we will not even go there. But one evening I was in the library and I found a chronicle from my mother. You can imagine my surprise." Braylin paused and sat slowly on the chair in the corner of the room. She would not look at Amore, her gaze drifted off toward the side of the room but a smile slowly spread on her lips. "Shortly before passing my mother had written that she felt her life would be ending soon and that one day a queen would rule that would be rid of this poison that has polluted our lands. A queen who would show bravery and fearlessness in times of need. I have dared myself to believe that she was talking about you, Amore." This time Braylin turned her gaze on her. Amore tried to hold the connection but shame forced her to look at the stone floor.

"I am no such person, Your Highness," Amore responded, softly frozen in the chair where she sat. Unsure of where this was going, Amore stayed quiet. She had said her piece that night and it was time for Braylin to do so. "What is your decision then?" she wondered aloud.

"I have been thinking on how you have behaved during your time at the palace and I find no accusation against you. Even with being who you are, you have showed nothing but respect for my family and our ways." Braylin paused and her gaze drifted to a distant thoughtfulness. "You are going to marry my brother, you are good for him and I believe for this kingdom as well." As she said those words, she stood up and went behind Amore. "If you do not marry my brother, I promise you, I will reveal everything to him," Braylin added before walking to the door and opening it. Amore watched her as she turned back and gave a devious smile. "She is ready."

Standing up, Amore followed Clarice to a beautiful pool that was covered in flower petals. The maidservants and Braylin turned around so Amore could undress in privacy. The large pool was surrounded by silky dark purple curtains that rested on the ground below. Slipping into the surprisingly warm water and drank in the scents of the roses and other flowers.

"You are to remain in this pool until I return and are to bath in it twice a day. Clarice will instruct you on what else to do, Your Highness," Braylin ordered before nodding her head and disappearing. Clarice brought forward some sweet smelling soap for Amore to wash her hair with. Amore's skin started to wrinkle quite so before Braylin returned with a gown that took Amore's breathe away. It was a golden white mixture with jewels spread all over. One of the maids brought a towel forward and helped her into it as she looked at the dress.

"It is beautiful." Words could not express.

"Good. Let's get you in it then!" Least to say it fit her almost perfect, although it needed some mending as the seamstress started her work. The next few days consisted of that and more as Braylin arranged everything.

"Your Highness!" a maiden called after her as Amore wandered the halls. "Your Highness, you are wanted in the grand hall," she cried out, trying to catch her breath.

Amore's heart picked up as she followed the maiden through the palace. As the large doors to the grand hall swung open, her eyes took in beautiful flowers that arranged everything and the rose petals that lined the path she would be walking in two days. The only thing Amore had difficulty understanding was the king was still not back.

"What do you think?" Braylin asked.

Amore smiled as she glanced cautiously at Braylin. She still felt insecure around the princess with her secret known to her. She had not been able to act the same way as she had before.

"It's beautiful, Your Highness."

Braylin smiled softly and let out a long breath.

"I do have one question, if that is all right." Braylin motioned for her to continue. "Where is King Xerxes?"

Braylin smiled wide that time and glanced down before walking forward. "You will see him on the day of your wedding when you walk down the grand hall. It is tradition that the intended do not see each other the week before," Braylin explained before looking back at her. "You are not having second thoughts, are you?"

"Of course not, Your Highness." Amore lowered her gaze. She had no doubts that Braylin would reveal all to the king if Amore did back out.

"Very good, and please, Amore, call me Braylin." Turning to her, Braylin took hold of her shoulders and kissed her on both cheeks. "We are to be sisters."

Smiling, Braylin turned and left. Lingering in the grand hall, Amore took a deep breath as the reality of it hit her. She wanted to wade across the flowers with her bare feet but dared not to mess up the amount of work it must have taken. The fragrances of the flowers filled the air, taking a deep breath a sense of peace wafted over her as she smiled. The mixture of scents was wonderful; enough that Amore wanted to stay in the room but eventually departed as the servants began the rest of their work. Tomorrow, everything would change in her life. It sent chills through her as her nerves and doubts tried to fill her mind.

Her heart pounded as she was awoken early to prepare one last time. The dress fit perfectly and felt rather light and airy. Her eyes stared at the all the jewelry placed on her head and around her neck and wrists. Her curled hair lay partially on her back, the rest tucked into a beautiful bun. Amore felt like she was going to be sick as she walked out into the hall. Beautifully dressed girls walked two by two in front of her and behind. The soft melody of singers soon reached her ears, singing a beautiful song in a language Amore had never heard before. Trying to calm her shaking hands, she stepped down the long hallway and finally into the grand hall that was filled with loyal subjects from mostly dignitaries to a few commoners. Princess Almeria stood near the front, her beautiful dress and crown sparkling in the bright sunlight that streaked through the windows. Amore smiled as best as she could as her eyes looked ahead. The girls continued their formation until halfway down the hall before bowing low to the ground as Amore's body moved on its own. Xerxes's smiled melted through her, causing a real smile to take her false one. She took the steps slowly as instructed but time seemed to stand still as she reached the top and Xerxes offered out his hand. Amore could hear nothing as her eyes stared into his. The only part she caught was when the priest asked her to repeat after him.

"Crown Queen Amore, do you solemnly swear to uphold the people of Avalon, to protect its people, and to love its king till death do you part." *Till death, something that could happen sooner rather than later.* Amore repeated the words as her eyes stayed glued on Xerxes as he repeated his vows as well. Amore took a deep breath as the large crown was placed on her bowed head.

The priest continued, "It is my great honor to present to the people of Avalon their Queen!"

Finally Amore looked to the crowd before turning back to Xerxes as he leaned forward and kissed her softly. Taking his arm, they walked together back down the grand hall and out into the court. It was beautifully decorated. The smell of flowers continued on through the court, as Amore tried to take everything in but had to stay focused as people came up to her. Congratulations abounded with each passing moment. Amore had so many people kiss her hand she feared that her skin would dry out. She had not much of a chance to even spend with Xerxes throughout most of the afternoon, until he approached her.

"May I have your hand in a dance, my queen?" he asked, smiling at her, one of his hands behind his back while the other waited for hers. Amore smiled and glanced down.

"You may, my king." Her eyes flickered up, catching his as he smiled. Music quickly rang loud and clear as Amore took her stance and they started to dance.

"You look very beautiful, Amore. I feel very lucky to have won your heart." His statement was soft and intimate. It was moments like this that made Amore forget the times of how overprotective Xerxes could be. "You are a very intelligent woman," he continued, making Amore's heart want to burst.

"Please, I do not even come close to the praises that you have bestowed upon me." She still could not help but smile as he kissed her on the forehead.

"Do not underestimate yourself, Amore. I certainly will not." They danced in silence for a few moments before Amore could not help but ask.

"Are the people able to celebrate today?" Xerxes studied her for a moment before his gaze looked thoughtful.

"I had not thought about it."

"Princess Braylin has not allowed me to have a say in what happens today, of course I only thought about it now." Xerxes chuckled at the statement about his sister as he fondly looked over at her.

"Yes, she cannot be easy to say no to. What would you like to do, my queen?"

Amore gazed off at the sky for a moment before smiling. "There must be a feast for them as well and we must declare this a day of celebration, a day of rest and fun." Amore was surprised at herself. She changed completely around Xerxes. Her worries and fears seemed to vanish for the most part and her mind could only think of possibilities.

"Consider it down, my love."

Motioning for the general, Xerxes stopped dancing, causing the music to stop and the people around them grew quiet as they waited. Xerxes whispered something to his general who smiled and nodded his head.

"It will be done, my king."

Placing his hand on his chest, General Damon bowed before turning and going about the business that was ordered to him.

Offering his arm, Xerxes walked over to the cushions that awaited them. Taking their spots he instructed for the party to continue.

"What other demands does the queen have, for this is her day to make them."

"Demands, my king?" Amore paused to think as her eyes watched the crowd enjoying the beautiful day. "I do have one more demand to ask of you." She turned her gaze to his and took his hand. "That I will always have your heart, no matter the events of life." Amore planned on taking her secret to her grave if she could, but life oftentimes had different plans. Xerxes smiled and cupped her cheek and pulled her close kissing her on the lips.

"Consider it done," he whispered in between kisses. For the rest of the day all her fears vanished as she got sucked into Xerxes's world. Amore was glad to be able to stop for a moment and catch her breath as Xerxes was drawn into conversation by another. Her eyes spotted Lady Reni and Governor Tyron making their way closer. She grew excited as her eyes danced around looking to see perhaps if anyone else was with them. She reminded herself that Governor Tyron had sent word of Aishlin and Vainer returning home. They bowed low, making her smile.

"How are you?" she asked as they slowly stood straight once she invited them to. Lady Reni smiled brightly as she studied Amore's gaze.

"Wonderful, my dear!" she exclaimed. She stepped closer and squeezed Amore's outstretched hand as she asked softly, "Did I not tell you things would work out?" She seemed unworried about anything. Stepping back, Lady Reni glanced at her husband who stood in the same spot he was before. Governor Tyron's gaze never left her. Though a smile remained upon his face, she could tell there was a great concern deep within.

"It is wonderful to see you again, Your Majesty." His smile was quick and warm like always. How desperately Amore wanted to hug them both but kept her hands along her sides. For a brief moment, she felt incredibly out of place, dressed so beautiful with more jewelry than Amore had ever worn before. The feeling fled as Xerxes walked back over. His eyes filled with joy as he stopped alongside her.

"Governor Tyron," he expressed as they both bowed low to him.

"We are most pleased, my king, in the union between you and your bride," Governor Tyron said, sounding pleased. Amore tried to watch his expressions and eyes but failed as she shifted her gaze to Lady Reni, who kept a beautiful smile upon her face as her gaze meet Amore's.

"What did I tell you?" she said softly as the others drifted into a deeper conversation.

Amore could not help but smile as she playfully asked, "What would that be my dear lady?" Frankly she was not sure what Lady Reni was saying. What had she told her? Lady Reni's smile grew as she winked at her, making Amore feel quite loved by the woman, who could easily be a second mother to her, now that she had meet Lady Reni.

"Everything would work out just fine, did it not?" She let out a soft breath and her gaze softened. "Do not overthink anything. Trust yourself, Amore. Trust him." She flickered her gaze at Xerxes, making Amore look. His gaze looked intensely interested in the conversation he was having with Governor Tyron. "Love can conquer any army." Amore barely caught her last words and frowned as the older woman smiled and bowed respectfully before walking away as Governor Tyron came alongside her. They stood there quietly with each other before Amore got up the nerve to ask.

"Could I inquire something of you, Governor?" Amore asked softly.

Tyron smiled as he nodded his head. "You do not even need to ask, Amore." Her name was softly spoken as his eyes sparkled. Trying to gather her thoughts, she pondered them for a moment before looking up at him once more.

"You have yet to tell me anything concerning my mother." His smile faltered as he dropped his gaze. She could hear the same words that he had spoken to her before. Perhaps another time.

"Your mother was a beautiful woman," he said softly, smiling warmly at the thought. "Everything about her could easily put anyone at peace and she knew how to use that to her advantage," he teased before shaking his head. "Your father loved her dearly and it nearly broke him the day she died."

Her heart hurt as she thought back. It had been Amore's fault for her mother's death. If only she had listened the first time. For such a young age, she had been quite independent. If only…

"You are the spitting image of your mother, Amore, and like her in so many ways." His words warmed her heart, making her smile.

"Why then did my family never want me to know anything about her?" she asked, studying him.

Tyron sighed and shook his head. "Perhaps to protect you from the pain of only ever knowing of your mother without truly knowing her." Tyron smiled as he bowed his head before slowly moving off. "I shall tell you more another time, Your Majesty," he smiled and left to find his own wife. Amore tried to picture her mother, but soon gave up and put it aside as she watched Xerxes walk closer. He looked over at Tyron for a moment before looking back at her.

"What were you two speaking about?" he asked, smiling as Amore looked at the broad man.

"Secrets," she smiled, and he chuckled. "About my mother."

Evening approached and fires were lit to light up the courtyards. Princess Almeria agreed to stay a few days before having to return to her own country. Amore had not even thought about what was going to come, that for the first time in her life, Amore would not be sleeping alone.

Alliances

THE DAY WAS FILLED WITH gray clouds but that did not dampen the spirits of those gathered together. Celebration was in order as Delmar's future queen wanted to make a covenant with the King of Avalon. Binding their kingdoms together to protect each other, come to the other's aid. In all Delmar was getting a lot of protection from Avalon more than Avalon was getting from Delmar in the deal. However, King Xerxes was quite pleased when Princess Almeria made the request. She was going to need a lot of aid during this time as she journeyed back to her kingdom with little to no protection and Xerxes had been more than happy to align the two kingdoms. Princess Almeria looked beautiful and quite content as she stood near the podium. Being set free from Zander's grasps, she seemed to blossom overnight, becoming a lot more confident and focused. It pleased Amore greatly to see how happy the young princess was. She hoped as well that Princess Almeria would be able to hold her own upon returning to her home, facing the challenges of being a ruler at so young an age. The officials gathered together, and the hall filled with Avalon citizens. She did wonderfully in front of the large crowd. She did not appear to be so nervous as she was the first time stepping into the grand hall. The exchange was made and the young princess bowed low to both of them. Her eyes briefly caught Amore's before she turned to sign her name upon the parchment awaiting her to bind the kingdom together. She bowed to them once more as the announcement was made and the people's excitement filled the air. The crowd intermingled with each other as many took their places for the food. The princess's eyes danced as she turned toward Amore.

"I want to thank you greatly, Your Majesty," Princess Almeria stated once again as she beamed at Amore, her crown glimmering in the light. Amore remembered the first time she saw the young princess. She was everything Amore had felt in the princess was true. She had been incredibly nervous, scared. Her hair and skin seemed slightly faded even after regaining her strength. Now she glowed, as her teal eyes flashed brightly toward a group of men who talked amongst themselves.

"His Majesty the king has been most gracious to send some men back with me on my trip to keep me safe." Her gaze shifted toward Xerxes and Amore smiled at the fond look the princess gave him, making her own eyes drift to her husband. Xerxes was conversing with Lord Timothy and General Damon.

"I am very pleased to have come to know you, Princess," Making the young girl blushed slightly and looked at her.

"I do not wish to imagine what would have happened to me if you had not been watching out for me," she remarked, smiling sadly. Her courage had grown greatly since the engagement was broken. "I wonder if I may ask something of you?" Almeria asked hesitantly.

"Anything."

"That necklace Zander had given to you." She paused as she looked Amore in the eyes. "May I have it back?"

Amore had completely forgotten about the ruby necklace, it had long since been placed in the back of her mind.

"Of course you may. I would rather not keep it with everything that has happened," Amore called for Talia to find the necklace. "When you saw it the first time, you recognized it, am I right?" Amore implored as Almeria smiled shyly and nodded her head.

"Yes, you are most perceptive, Your Majesty."

"Please, call me Amore." Amore liked stating those words as the smile grew upon Princess Almeria's face.

"As you may call me Almeria." She stopped as Talia returned and handed the box to her. Opening the lid, she smiled sadly as she studied the jewels within. "You see, this was the necklace my father had given to my mother," she expressed softly as she closed the lid once more. "I had not known it had even left the chamber it was kept in." She grew solemn before turning her gaze upon Amore. "How did the king take the news?" she softly asked. Amore knew right away what the princess was implying. Looking down, Amore grew ashamed. She should have told Xerxes right away but something held her back from doing so. She did not know what, but she had yet to be able to bring herself to telling him.

"I have not told him anything concerning." Amore stopped and smiled sadly at the shocked expression of the princess.

"Why ever not? I wish I would have entrusted you sooner, perhaps then—" She stopped and glanced over at the king. He had his back to them as he was discussing something with the officials. Almeria lowered her voice and said, "Perhaps then, you would have never gotten hurt."

Amore smiled. She could tell the princess still felt responsible for everything that happened to her, even though she had reassured her many times before that it was not her fault.

"I have come to find that no matter how much we wish, we will never change the past," Amore reassured once more, making Almeria smile as she nodded her head.

"I will remember that."

"Almeria, may I inquire something personal of you?" The princess smiled with curiosity and nodded her head. "What is your true age?" It had bothered Amore from the beginning the age Almeria had claimed to be. Perhaps now she would tell the truth. Almeria laughed softly and smiled brightly.

"I am only fifteen; no doubt you were able to see through that as well." Amore had figured her to be younger. Yet she was still small for own age but it made Amore feel better knowing she would have a chance to mature freely in her own time.

Almeria soon excused herself and made her way over to Braylin to express her gratitude to her as well. Watching the princess talk happily with Braylin, Amore could not help but smile. Almeria was going to make a wonderful queen. No doubt it was not going to be easy but deep down, Amore knew that Almeria would make it. Not only that, but thrive as well. Before Almeria's departure home, word finally reached Amore that Mirage had recovered well enough to make the trip back to the palace. True to his promise, Xerxes made the arrangements for both of them to accompany Princess Almeria as far as Tylia. Then the princess would be sent on her way, and Amore would finally have her horse back within her reach.

The bay mare Almeria had given the name Azure rode easily amongst the company of soldiers. The mare beneath her snorted and swished her tail as the hot sun continued to bear down upon them all. Xerxes rode ahead and had been rather quiet through the procession. The familiar path Amore had ridden with General Damon looked different in the full summer heat. The tree branches gave a grateful shade but the tall grass Amore had waded out into now looked dry and in desperate need of rain. It was fascinating to Amore how only a short time before the region was being drowned in rain now it seemed like ages as the land needed it once more. The mare stumbled beneath her, catching Amore off guard as the mare quickly recovered. Sweat started to form on her shoulders and neck, though they had kept the horses at an easy pace. A deer poked its head up causing a couple of the horses to snort in surprise as the animal flashed its short tail watching them cautiously before moving to a safer distance. No doubt as did many of the villagers and townspeople they happened to see out in the sun.

"Many thanks, Your Majesty," Almeria said, bowing her head when it came time for her to take a different route. Part of Amore hurt to see the younger girl go as Almeria flashed her gaze at her for a second and smiled brightly. "I will not forget what you have done for me," she stated softly as Amore felt her heart flicker with joy.

"Be safe and trust in yourself," Amore advised as the princess's smile grew. At least fifty men would be accompanying the princess back. Part of that company would be those who Xerxes trusted to help Almeria establish herself rightfully as queen. No doubt to also mind over Avalon's interest in its newest alliance and establish any trade that would benefit both kingdoms. Almeria would always have a special place in Amore's heart that she would cherish forever. Hopefully she would be able to see her again sooner rather than later.

As the Village of Tylia came into view, Amore's excitement grew. She expected the town to be quiet, like it had been when she was last there. As they neared the town, a large group of men and horses stood on the outskirts. She heard one of the soldier mention something about horse traders. The chestnut mare beneath her came to an easy halt and snorted as her ears flickered forward watching the large group of horses. The men bowed low as well as the townspeople that were gathered around. Their expressions were beyond shocked. Xerxes shifted atop his mare Leah as he instructed for one of the soldiers to fetch Mirage. Maverick slowly made his way closer, bowing low as the guards allowed him through.

"Your Majesties, my king, an honor for you to come upon our humble town. I cannot thank you enough for your graciousness upon us all," he remarked keeping his head low.

"The queen requested it specifically, as a grateful thank you from us both," Xerxes remarked, smiling as he glanced over at Amore. Amore heard her name being called excitedly and requested the guards to allow through the young Jenna. Her light brown hair bounced as she stopped next to the mare and beamed up at Amore.

"I knew you would come back!" Her eyes sparkled as she smiled brightly. Pulling her hand from behind her back, Jenna held up a familiar pouch as Amore smiled. She had completely forgotten about the jewels and crown she had been wearing then. Taking the pouch from the young girl, Amore smiled brightly as she handed it off to a guard who came up alongside her.

"I brought something for you," Amore remarked as the young girl continued to watch her expectedly. "But you must wait to open it until later." She handed a small brown pouch to her. The girl beamed, nodding her head before taking off, making Amore smile brightly as she watched her. Maverick had dispersed back toward the townspeople. Xerxes was watching her as she turned her gaze upon him and he smiled slightly before looking back at the horses. Amore eyed the animals. Many of them looked nice and others looked hopeless but her eye caught one in particular. A young horse at the side of the group had his head low. His coat looked dirty and gruff. He looked like a meager animal, not worthy enough for a king to pay much attention to. Yet, something about the animal stuck with Amore as she pointed him out to Xerxes. He gave her a quizzical look. Several ropes were tied around the horse's small neck as well as the halter upon his head.

"Fair enough, bring him forward for us to see," he called. One of the traders nodded and dashed to the colt. As he neared the little animal's head raised as his ears came back. As the man started to try bring the colt closer, he planted his feet and refused to budge. Pulling back suddenly, he threw the man off balance and made him stumble, crashing to the ground, bringing laughter from the crowd. Even Xerxes chuckled as he watched. Gently touching his arm, Amore smiled slightly. He looked thoughtful before reluctantly nodding his head. Getting off of the mare, Amore made her way through the soldiers as a few of them scrambled off their animals to follow her as she stepped free of their barrier. The man blushed deeply as she neared and held out her hand. The rope was covered in dirt but Amore paid no mind as she relaxed her body and waited. The colt still had his feet planted and his eyes dull as he slowly began to lick his lips. Turning her attention to the guard, she requested for an apple. It took a while before one was brought forth. Smiling again, she turned her attention back to the colt. Reaching out her bare hand, she allowed him to blow a warm breath against her skin before slowly stroking his dirt-covered face. As she smoothed away the mud and fur, his delicate face beneath barely showed through. His head was incredibly refined, like her own stallion. Even a little white speck showed through the mud.

"My queen, your apple," the guard remarked as Amore continued to look the colt in the eye.

As the colt still remained standing, a man remarked out loud, "Your Majesty, if you can get the colt to move, you may have him as a gift!" She could tell by the tone in his voice he did not believe the colt would move for her as she grinned.

"Thank you, Asher," Amore said as she took the apple from the guard. Offering it to the colt, he picked at it for a moment before sticking his lip up in the air, making the men laugh. Whispering softly to him, the colt flickered his ears around before biting into the juicy fruit and quickly finishing it off. The colt's back came about to her middle, making him no more than five months old. Without a second thought or words, Amore turned and began to walk. For a split second the rope tightened before the colt moved with her, leaving the men speechless as she made her way back through the barrier of soldiers and to the mare that awaited. She sat back upon the mare and the colt began to sniff noses with the chestnut. She could see the astonished look upon the trader's face before he quickly shook that look and his gaze narrowed slightly, making her smile. Xerxes's expression remained the same as a faint smile flickered across his eyes before he shifted his attention toward the town as a loud whinny startled the crowd. Mirage danced in anticipation next to one of the guards. His coat shone brightly as his tail arched, his head held high, making it difficult for the soldier to maintain the creature.

"I hope he has not caused the town too much trouble," Amore remarked softly, making Xerxes chuckle.

"I sent some soldiers here to care for him along with the stable boy that handled him before," Xerxes remarked as he nodded toward a younger boy upon another horse. The soldier rode closer and the guards around them gave them a wide birth as the stallion snorted loudly, his ears flickering forward at the sight of the colt alongside Amore's mare. His neck arched as he reached down, making the colt shrink, and began to clack his teeth. Kissing to her stallion, Mirage flickered his ear at her before snorting and looking away.

"I cannot believe I am saying this, Your Majesty, but I think he is mad at you," the guard remarked, studying the stallion in surprise. Mirage tucked his head away from her ignoring her. Sighing, Amore shook her head and smiled. Reaching down she began to stroke the colt's neck and pulled the extra ropes free from his neck, as her horse swung his head back around and perked his ears before licking his own lips and pushing into her arm, making the colt scramble trying to get out of the stallion's way as he swung his head up into her lap and snorted. Stroking his soft silky head, she smirked. Out of the corner of her eye she could even see Xerxes's astonished expression.

"Let him go," Amore commanded surprising the guard before he nodded and dropped the rope. Untying the rope she handed it back to the guard who looked apprehensive. Giving his head a toss, Mirage turned and waited.

"I was told, my queen, that the colt came from Emir's commanding general's own private herd," the trader spoke up suddenly, a wide smile upon his face.

Amore pushed down the reaction that tried to come forth and studied the man as he turned his gaze away. Before looking at

Xerxes, he looked unamused at the man's statement. Annoyance flashed through his eyes at the mention of General Divon.

"A colt of such caliber looks rather poorly," Xerxes remarked, making the smile of the trader slowly slip from his face as he nodded his head. The trader's words rang in her ears and her mind as they began the journey back. As their groups slowly moved out, Mirage stood in his spot for a moment before swinging his head and licking his lips as he bolted, cantering after Amore. Slowing to a trot, he settled in to follow her. After a while, he started to limp on his shoulder but kept the pace until the group slowed back to a walk. She could hear the soldiers' amused and impressed statements about the black stallion that followed her around like a dog. Amore allowed the mare to follow Leah as she studied the colt alongside her to the stallion. Mirage's head was level as he easily walked along. After some time, Mirage began to nose the colt and gently nip him. The colt at first continued to clack his teeth before eventually ignoring the stallion. It was not long and the colt quickly became attached to Mirage, as they rested the horses and Amore gently brushed the dirt of the colt. Her mind did not even think about the dirt coming off and upon her own beautiful gown. As she worked, the faint, deep, rich color of the colt slowly came forth. Mirage stood nearby grazing as he swished his tail. The colt shook his head and gave it a toss. Untying the rope, Amore let him go, as the young colt trotted after the big stallion and stopped to graze alongside him. Moving slowly, Amore joined the stallion. Lifting his head from the grass he let out a soft snort and nuzzled her arm before going back to grazing contently.

She did not hear their approach until a voice said, "I am most curious, Your Majesty, my queen, why you chose such a gangly looking creature for a horse." The duke looked at the colt. The colt did not look like much now but Amore knew what he could look like.

"Perhaps you should look beyond the surface to what is underneath. You may find potential in that gangly creature, milord."

"I have never seen anything like your stallion Mirage. Most impressive," the duke continued as the stallion turned around, nudging Amore's arm. Mirage snorted as he slowly wedged himself between her and the man. He picked his head up as the man held out his hand like Amore did with the colt. Instead of perking his ears, Mirage flickered them back as his eyes grew intense.

"I do not think he likes you," Xerxes remarked from behind the man, startling him. Dropping his hand, the man bowed as the king stopped next to him.

"I was just admiring to her majesty of how impressed I am with the stallion. I can see now why she treasures him so." The duke paused as he stood straight once more. "I must say, my king, that horse thinks the queen is his own mare. No offense, Your Majesty!"

Xerxes chuckled as he reached out to stroke Mirage's face and the stallion stood still before moving on to find a new place to eat. The duke bowed once more before walking away, his eyes watching Mirage until Amore could no longer see the man. Xerxes watched the colt before turning his eyes upon her and smiling.

"What intrigues you with such a creature?" he asked. The colt swished his tail as he ripped at the grass, his coat still covered in dirt though Amore had spent quite a bit of time brushing him. He reached out and nipped the black stallion alongside him, hoping to get a reaction out of Mirage as the older horse ignored him and continued grazing.

"There is something about him. Something special," Amore admitted, *Could he have come from father's herd?*

Xerxes made a soft hmm before stating, "Really? Was that the same thought you had when Mirage was young?" The questions startled her as she thought back to that day. Her mother led the fiery young black horse alongside her. Amore had been playing out on the hills in the tall grass watching the herds. No matter how hard she tried to recall what her mother looked like in that memory, she could only focus upon the beautiful colt alongside her.

"I was very excited when I was given Mirage, though when he was younger he proved to be exactly as he is now. Independent."

"Did Mirage come from your family's horses?" It was an honest question, but the thought of the possibility of linking the words of the trader with the colt to the same dainty exotic look of her stallion to her father General Divon unnerved Amore.

"His mother did, yes. However, we are not sure who the sire was. She had gotten out one night and came back in foal," Amore admitted, it was the truth. The beautiful dark-colored mare was greatly favored by her father. She was small and well-built an envy of many. She typically was a very well-behaved horse, Amore learned to ride upon her. On that rare night, Mystic got out. The reasoning behind it Amore never learned but when the mare was finally retrieved deep within the mountain range, she was in foal, producing a solid black colt.

"Perhaps someday I shall be able to see these horses of yours," he remarked, smiling warmly at her. The thought was amusing to think of such an occasion, Xerxes meeting her father. *That would be something indeed*, she thought as she watched the horses. *If war broke out, they would surely meet each other than.* The idea was terrifying and Amore desperately wished she had not thought of it.

That evening as she stared up at the tent's ceiling, Amore pondered the man's words. She had yet to see any horse that matched the dished face of her own stallion outside of her family's private horses. Her father guarded the bloodline closely. The offspring of the lines had wonderful temperaments, incredibly intelligent, loyal, and loving. Much like her own stallion, they bonded closely with those who took care of them. Defending the soldiers like no other horses did. Rolling over, Amore stared at the back of Xerxes's head.

"Do you think what that trader said was truth?" Amore asked after a while, not even sure if he was still awake. Did she even dare ask? It was bothering her, thinking of how someone might have raided close to her home. Close to her father. Her mind was trying to place which mare the colt might have belonged to. *Had father been close to home? How long ago could it have happened? The colt looks strong enough to be without his mother, unless they took the mare as well.*

"It is highly doubtful," he observed finally. "I am sure the man is trying to pass the colt off as worth more than he is." Amore bit her tongue from making a sharp comeback as she stared at the tent's ceiling. She knew the colt's potential. Why could no others see it? He was silent for a while before asking. "Why the curiosity?" His words seemed harmless enough.

"It made me wonder," she remarked, which was true. *How would you react if I told you the truth?* she thought, studying him. She had grown more relaxed within the palace but the ever-dawning thought kept with her. How would Xerxes react? She knew of his dislike for Emirians. Slowly rolling over, Xerxes studied her for a moment before smiling. "Could you imagine such a thing being truth?" she asked.

Blinking, he grew thoughtful before looking up at the ceiling. "I am certain that the reclusive herd of the general is very well protected," he reassured.

Does he know my father personally? Amore wondered, thinking back to a conversation she had once with Braylin. Long before the princess even knew who she was.

"Have you ever seen any of his horses?" Amore continued on before quickly adding. "I just keep thinking about the possibilities of it all."

He chuckled and shook his head before rolling back over. "Get some sleep, Amore."

Turning over Amore studied the tent's wall. Sleep fled her as her mind continued to think. Wondering how her father was. If

Avalon was being raided, was Emir as well? Who could possibly be behind all of this? As the night dragged on, Amore slipped out of bed. Wrapping a cloak around herself, she stepped out of the tent into the warm night air. The guards at the entrance scrambled to their feet as she walked past them. Mirage stood near the tent, tethered to a tree. The guard watching over Mirage, Leah, and the other officials horses bowed his head as Amore took the rope tied to Mirage and led him away. The colt quickly followed. Stopping in a somewhat secluded area and taking a spot in the grass, Amore studied the stars. Out of the corner of her eye she could see the guards standing, watching. It was some time before Mirage came alongside her, tucking his knees to the ground. He slowly laid down alongside her, his shoulders next to her as he continued to rip at the grass. Out here, in the night, Amore felt somewhat alone. Enough to allow a sense of peace to rest upon her as Mirage let out a quiet moan and lay completely down in the grass. Running her hand through his mane, Amore drifted back to her home in Believe. The times she would spend out on the rolling grassy hills watching the mares and their new foals. She loved that time of season, for her father would keep the herds close to the house, ever watchful of each mare and foal. Then it would be time to train the next generation, something Amore would be allowed to help with as long as her father would not know of it. She loved spending time with the horses. They did not care who you were, what you may look like. Whether or not you were acting dignified enough. They did not care about palace or court life, all they wanted was someone to care for them. To connect with them.

"My queen," General Damon called out, smiling as he neared. She motioned for him to come closer. He crouched down as he studied the black horse lying beside her. His eyes looked rather impressed. Which would be considered a great compliment coming from General Damon. "Your stallion is very impressive," he remarked, smiling, making one grow upon her own face.

"Are you actually paying me a compliment, General?" she inquired.

His eyes flashed up at her for a moment as a smirk flickered across his mouth. "I paid a compliment to your horse, Your Majesty. Do not let it go to your head."

She laughed then and studied Mirage as his eyes slowly flickered closed.

"How is it that you get him to do that?" General Damon asked. It was rather simple but she did not want to state that. It worked well when you were trying to hide from a certain someone. When you no longer wanted to do your school work. "Perhaps you could show me sometime?" He grew quiet for a moment before his eyes connected with hers and the look within surprised her. Like he knew something, something about her. "I do not think I have ever seen a horse like yours, save for one occasion that was quite some time ago." Her heart picked up and skipped a couple of beats. Her father trained his horses just like Mirage was trained. It worked greatly during a battle. Great for getting by without being noticed.

"Really?" she asked, her voice soft as he nodded his head before letting out a smile.

"Though I doubt that it has anything to do with your stallion, Your Majesty," he commented standing back up straight and walked away.

The sun would be up soon as well as the rest of the camp. Returning to the tent, Amore dressed. Just as she finished, wild screams filled the air. Dashing from the tent a guard quickly stopped her as a tall, red-colored stallion slammed into Mirage. She recognized it as the duke's stallion, a horse the official prized greatly. Mirage strained against the ropes holding him as he let out a scream and kicked out, missing the other stallion. Xerxes hurried out from behind her, as the guards tried to separate the enraged horse. Mirage reared striking out before landing with a thud and trying to swing around as the red-colored stallion kicked out hitting his shoulder. Amore winced.

"Cut him loose!" she cried as the other stallion continued his attack. Leah, tied next to Mirage, was trying desperately to get out of the stallion's way. Finally the ropes snapped and Mirage bolted, slamming into the white mare until her rope snapped and the three horses galloped away. Her heart pounded against her chest, as the duke came racing forward.

"I do not know how he even got loose!" he exclaimed, stopping next to Xerxes. Soldiers raced after the horses as Amore thought about Mirage's injuries and her heart sank. It had recovered enough to make the trip back to the palace at an even pace. Not on a mad dash across the countryside.

The duke's horse was soon returned, his hide covered in sweat as his large head bobbed down, snorting. The soldiers remarked seeing nothing of Leah and Mirage. The days slipped by as they continued looking before Xerxes decided it was time to be going. Soldiers would keep looking for the horses. The chestnut snorted and flickered her ears back at the colt as he danced alongside the mare. His ears flickered around as he let out a high-pitched whinny calling out for Mirage. They returned to the palace and Amore's spirits sank lower. No news of either horse was given. Xerxes reassured her that they would be found but it did not help ease her conscience as she thought about the cuts she had seen on Mirage and his previous injuries. Braylin appeared excited that they were back but the look quickly vanished as Amore could not return the smile and continued on through the palace. How had the duke's stallion gotten loose? How had he happened to come all the way across the camp to take it out upon Mirage? There were plenty of other stallions within the company. To purposefully pick out Mirage, it did not add up with her. The colt danced alongside her as he arched his neck and snorted, eyeballing the palace walls. His little tail arched completely over so it touched his back.

She needed no further proof that the colt belonged to her father. It did not help the feeling she got, knowing that her father's horses had been raided. Nor that raids were happening near her home. Near to her family. *If there are talks of war within Avalon and if raiding is happening in Emir…could King Haman be speaking the same?* King Haman was not much of a man of war. Her father handled that for him. Nevertheless, he would take action if Emir was in danger. Her heart began to beat faster as Amore shook her head.

"What is bothering you, Your Majesty?" Liana asked, reminding Amore that the maidens were with her once more.

"Nothing. Thank you, Liana." Stroking the colt's neck, she let out a sigh as she set him free in a small pen. He trotted around before lowering his head to sniff at the dirt before letting out a snort. Lowering himself to the ground to roll, he destroyed Amore's hard work. Braylin slowly made her way closer and stopped at the pen.

"He is beautiful," she remarked as the colt stayed resting on the ground, his coat covered in dirt once more. Amore wanted to laugh as she shook her head. "What happened?" Braylin asked as the maidens moved farther away, giving them some privacy. Explaining to her what had transpired, Braylin looked puzzled. Taking a deep breath, Amore dared herself to ask.

"Do you know anything more about the raids?"

Her gaze fell as her smile slipped from her face before it returned once more and she stood up straight again. "The reports have grown considerable as of late."

"What about…war?" Braylin glanced back at the maidens before softly answering her.

"There has been talk about it, but that is all that has been. Talk. It has crossed my mind before, but I try not to think about it for too long." Taking a deep breath, she smiled once more. "Come on. Let us not think of such dreary subjects." Motioning with her head toward the palace door, Amore nodded and followed as Braylin began to speak of all the wonderful things that could happen in the days to come. Enough that it helped to lighten her spirits for the moment and ease her mind away from Mirage and war, if it ever came to that.

⁂

Amore was a little overwhelmed, if she could get any more overwhelmed than her life was. Staring at the beautiful ceiling, Amore could not sleep. To her dismay, by the time she started to grow tired the sunshine was starting to sprinkle into the room, stating a new day had started. As her maidens came calling to help her get ready for the day, Amore barely spoke a word to anyone even as she started down the hall. Her heart fluttered at the words of the horse trader. Yet she would keep her thoughts to herself. Xerxes was certain the man was trying to make the colt seem to be worth more than he was. Deep in her heart, Amore knew that the man was speaking truth. Still no news of Mirage or Leah reached her ears. It had been almost a week since returning to the palace.

"Amore, would you care to accompany me this morning?" A voice interrupted her catching her off guard as Braylin appeared next to her. Before Amore could answer, Braylin linked arms with her and began to lead her away. She kept her pace rather quick as they entered into the grand hall. Sun was streaking through the tall windows high above their heads. As the birds around the palace continued to sing.

"Braylin, where are we going?" Amore asked, glancing around at a company of at least twelve guards. Braylin's smile grew wider as they walked toward the doors.

"To see the market. This time of the morning the most wonderful bakers are out and they will make your mouth water. Then around ten in the morning the merchant's begin to show up and you should see what they make. There are a lot of beautiful jewels and decorations in the palace itself," she expressed, her brown gaze sparkling with a mischievous look to them. Her smile began to work its way upon Amore's face as she thought about seeing the market. She had heard some things about it from the maidens and servants, but had yet to experience it for herself. The warm breeze welcomed them as they walked over the river before entering the town. Braylin winked at her as they stepped onto the street and saw the looks that they received from those around the gate. This early in the morning, the street was quite empty, allowing them to move rather freely as the guards appeared more relaxed, unconcerned about those around them. A young girl stared at Amore before turning and dashing away behind some buildings. Her heart skipped with excitement as she glanced at the uncertain looks the maidens gave each other. The noise of the market place soon reached her ears as she soaked in the beauty of Roselyn.

⚜

The marketplace was already gathering quite the crowd when they arrived. The crowd bowed respectfully before moving like a rippling wave out of their way. Everyone was watching, listening, intrigued by their queen being within their own midst. Amore at first just listened to the murmuring of the crowd as they walked along. Braylin stopped at many of the booths and conversed with the baker before motioning for her to try a sample. By the fifth booth Amore could not eat any more and began to enjoy her time. The crowd grew friendly and many people greeted her with very kind words. One person caught her full attention. A young girl with curly brown hair slowly shuffled her way between people until she stood in front of Amore.

"Jenna."

Amore smiled as the young girl came forward and bowed real low. She almost did not seem like Jenna at the solemn look upon her face. Her eyes searched the crowd for her father Maverick. She was surprised that she appeared to be completely alone. In a large city like Roselyn, Amore would not think Maverick to allow his young daughter to travel by herself. So he had to be nearby somewhere.

"Your Majesty, it is so good to see you again. My father Maverick moved us to the city in hopes to expand his business," Jenna answered Amore's unasked question. Jenna continued to stay in the bowed position, causing Amore to glance at Braylin, who gave her a half smile and stood back, watching the whole display, waiting to see what Amore would do. Her statement did not fit the man she had met in Tylia. Nor could she imagine Jenna's father Maverick leaving the beautiful home that had been in his family for generations. Especially when he had been so passionate about trying to keep it within the family.

"Is everything all right, Jenna?" Amore asked, turning her attention back to the girl.

"If it pleases my queen, I wish to make a request of her," Jenna inquired making Amore frown. Jenna had been so carefree and lucky last time she had seen her when Mirage was brought back. The words she was speaking seemed beyond her age and sense of freedom. She glanced back at Braylin, who shook her head ever so slightly and gave the look, "She is facing you not me.".

"What is your request?" Amore inquired, her heart starting to pick up. She was not prepared for this type of thing and the crowd began to watch, waiting with anticipation and wonder.

"Would you and her highness Princess Braylin care to join my family and I for supper?" Jenna inquired, giving Amore the impression there was more but it was something that the young girl did not want to speak of in the open market.

"I would be honored, Jenna, as long as it is all right with Princess Braylin." Amore shifted the responsibility back onto Braylin who gave a smile.

"Of course."

With that Jenna's whole expression changed to a relieved look and she stood up before quickly turning and dashing off into the crowd. There was something different about the young girl's expression and her eyes. The look she had bothered Amore greatly.

"You handled that beautifully, Amore," Braylin praised quietly as the crowd began to disperse again and Amore barely heard her words as her eyes hit another pair of eyes. Her sister stood at a distance mixed in with the crowd but Amore could easily spot her. Aishlin suddenly turned mixing with the crowd in order to not draw attention as Braylin asked, "Are you all right?"

Blinking, Amore turned her attention back and smiled. Her mind was churning with questions and wanting desperately to talk to her sister. *What was she still doing in Avalon?* she wondered. She had not seen her at her wedding with Tyron and Lady Reni. She had not dared ask the governor and his wife anything during the celebration.

"I thought I saw something." It was the truth. She had seen something or someone. Braylin gave her a curious look before continuing on, making something dawn on Amore as she glanced around her. The twelve guards followed but were well mixed with the crowd and appeared to be completely relaxed within the city walls and people.

"Braylin, what does—"

It shocked Amore to see that Xerxes would even approve of so little guards outside the palace's walls. Before she could finish, Braylin flashed a grin before picking up a beautiful pair of diamond dropped earrings.

"He left early this morning with his general. Apparently they had some urgent business to attend to." Braylin brought the earrings up to Amore's ears and studied them.

"We shall take them," she said, handing them to one of her maidens. The merchant beamed and thanked Braylin until they moved to another table, causing those there to quickly come to attention. A necklace suddenly caught her eye, making her stop and walk up to the table. It had a large dewdrop red ruby with twisted diamond strands going around the neck.

"May I?" Amore asked, looking up at the older man. His expression filled with awe and excitement as he kept his gaze off to the side.

"Of course, Your Majesty, it would be an honor."

Carefully picking up the necklace, Amore smiled as it reminded her of the necklace her mother passed on to her.

"Her majesty likes the necklace?" the merchant asked, making Amore smile. She nodded her head and forced any tears down. Chills rang down her arms as one of the maidens took the necklace from her for later. Trying her best to be discrete, Amore scanned the crowd hoping to spot her sister once more. Would Aishlin dare try to speak with her? Allowing some distance between Braylin and herself, Amore kept an easy pace. The people kept any easy enough wide circle around her with at least one guard keeping close to her. No one else besides Jenna approached her further than the circle. Perhaps her sister would not dare.

"Make way for the king's horses," a cry rang out, causing the crowd to part and the guards rushed toward Amore and Braylin as a large herd of horses trotted down the city street. Their bodies were steaming as the soldiers kept them in line. The guards reformed around Amore making the people scatter out of their way. Amore felt something press into the back of her hand as her fingers closed around the parchment. A beautiful golden-colored horse quickly caught her eye, making Amore draw closer to the line of people to watch the animal prance next to one of the soldiers as he tried to keep the mare in control. The mare reared, practically pulling the soldier from his horse as his animal struggled to maintain a footing on the cobblestone road. Without thinking, Amore pushed past the guards and grabbed the rope as it slid from the soldier's hand.

"Eshea," she commanded, placing a hand on the mare's silky golden neck. The mare landed with a hard thud before giving a hard toss of the head. She turned her dark brown eyes on Amore watching her, her ears twitching in every direction. She was not a mean mare, just simply frightened, and the rough handling of the soldier wasn't helping. Smiling, Amore stroked the soft part of her forehead as the mare let out a long breath before turning her attention to the soldier. "She needs a soft hand, not a hard one," she instructed. The soldier looked displeased but hid it well as another cry rang out, "Make way for the king."

Stepping to the side with the mare in tow, Amore glanced at Braylin who turned a slight white color and her own heart sank. Xerxes was very protective and it was completely understandable. Everything that had happened to her outside the palace walls, and even in. No doubt the little she had gathered about his own mother, she had died tragically like her own. Upon reading some articles in the library, Amore learned more. Queen Clarice died upon being ambushed set up in advance. To this date, no one had been convicted of committing such a crime. No clues led to the further truth. It still remained a mystery, almost fifteen years later. Upon finding that out, Amore understood then why Xerxes rarely allowed her to leave the palace or on the rare occasion without a full company of soldiers.

Braylin came alongside her as Xerxes cantered closer upon a dark horse. His hooves made a beautiful noise on the stone. His expression quickly changed from pleased to a blank look that Amore knew well from being in the court of Emir, a well-placed shield guarding the true feelings of the person within.

"What is going on here?" Xerxes asked, looking at the soldier on the bay mare to the horse that Amore was now holding. The soldier seemed to shrink as his king's eyes turned upon him. His head bowed low as his horse shifted and shook its head.

"The mare was acting up and her majesty quieted the mare," the soldier briefly explained. Xerxes gave a motion with his hand for the soldier to take the golden-coated mare back, the mare alongside Amore locked up at first refusing to be returned to the soldier.

"It's okay, beautiful," Amore whispered, calming the mare back down before handing the rope to the soldier and watched as he led the mare away, her tail whipping back and forth.

Lowering her gaze, Amore turned back around to face Xerxes. He shifted in his saddle and his eyes quickly overlooked the crowd that still remained bowed low.

"Would you like to join us, my king?" Amore asked, seeing Xerxes was unsure of how to respond without showing his distrust of his people. To her surprise and obviously Braylin's also Xerxes swung his leg over the dark horse and got down. Handing the animal off to General Damon, he offered out his arm to Amore. The expression upon his face remained the same blank look as a smile was placed in its charge. Taking his arm, she smiled and turned back to walk down the merchants. He had surprised her greatly by joining them, causing Amore's mind to run away with herself. The people of Roselyn quickly cleared the path as their king walked among them. General Damon kept a few paces back, as more guards joined their ranks. Watching, protecting.

"You must try this wonderful bread, my brother king," Braylin explained, stopping suddenly and making the baker blush a deep red as Xerxes took a bite of it. Her heart flickered as she watched his expressions. She could not read anything upon his face.

"Very good," he expressed. Amore smiled as she flickered her gaze at Braylin, who seemed to be enjoying this very much. Her eyes sparkled as she walked. Easily conversing still with the few people who dared to approach. They continued on as Braylin made many stops admiring the merchants' items and every time, the merchants bowed low. Their expressions were beyond hopeful and the possibility of the king liking something upon their tables. They seemed to love Braylin as those who dared to venture closer offered out gifts to her. Amore enjoyed being surrounded by the people and their friendliness toward her. To her surprise, Xerxes just watched in amusement, or so that was the expression Amore figured.

"My king, Princess Braylin and I have been invited to a dinner this evening," Amore started to say as she caught a hesitant look from Braylin and quickly ended the subject. Xerxes's expression stayed the same as he quickly responded.

"Invite them to the palace. I'm sure the chefs can prepare an excellent meal. Now, my queen, Princess, would you be so kind to accompany me back to the palace?" The horses were brought forward. Braylin sighed softly and let out a smile that flashed beautiful as ever. No one would be able to see the resign in her eyes.

"Of course," Amore answered and smiled, trying to look pleased by the invitation. Trying to mask all emotion, Amore watched Xerxes mount his horse and was prepared to walk back to the palace with Princess Braylin when Xerxes offered out his hand. Before Amore could get any farther than nodding her head, he easily picked her up and sat her onto horse's neck.

"I will walk, if that is all right with you, Your Majesty." Braylin expressed.

Xerxes gave a nod of his head as General Damon quickly offered to walk with her. Nudging the horse into gear, the dark horse moved easily along as the crowd parted like a wave. His hooves made a beautiful sound as they hit the cobblestone path. The doors to the palace swung wide allowing Xerxes to ride the dark horse right into the grand hall. Swinging off first, he helped Amore. As he set her on the ground his true feelings emerged. His gaze filled with frustration and fear. Turning away Xerxes walked off, his shoulders showing his tension.

"Both of you should not have been outside of the palace so lightly guarded," Xerxes remarked, walking across the hall. Amore felt frustration rise up inside of her but quickly contained it. She knew what it was like to live in an already overprotective family. *Look where that got you.*

"Xerxes, the people need to know that we trust them. It is clear to see that they love Princess Braylin." Amore stopped in the middle of the grand hall. Xerxes turned around, his eyes narrowed with past hurts as his hand rested on the hilt of his sword.

"I have good reason to be cautious," he retorted. Sighing softly, Amore tried to pick her words carefully. It was clear to see at times that many of Avalon's subjects did not think that those in power truly cared for what was happening. Amore turned her softened gaze back on him.

"Yes, but perhaps at times being cautious may not look like it to others." How was she even to explain it? The words formed so easily in her mind but speaking them, it just did not match up. Taking a deep breath to calm herself once more, Amore slowly walked closer to him as his intense gaze watched her. Her gaze remained the same staring into his, hoping to find something to work from. "There are times we need to show the people of Avalon that we care about what is happening."

Xerxes turned away and shook his head his expression looked like he wanted to laugh.

"The people do not know half of what has happened. I do not have time to stop and console them for feeling like I haven't noticed." He turned to look at her once more. "I care deeply for the people of Avalon." His eyes grew strong. "Not everyone is good and kind, Amore."

His words startled her. Is that what he thought she felt? She knew that without a doubt. She knew there were people that where only bent on evil. Though maybe she pushed that thought deep down, thinking on the possibilities of everything.

"I know that," she insisted, smiling slightly as she looked down. Her mind thought back to the raiders and Zander. "I just prefer to think about the majority of the good in people," she said slowly as he smiled slightly.

"So did my mother, but that did not help her." His words sounded deeply pained as his eyes glazed over for a moment. Xerxes never mentioned anything about what happened to his mother to her before. She had learned little from Clarice, then at the library. Even a few things from Braylin, but Xerxes, he never opened up about the past. "They still turned on her the moment they could."

Sighing, Amore slowly walked closer until she stood directly in front of him as his eyes turned on her. She studied his face as her heart hurt for her own as well as his mother's death.

"You cannot blame that on everyone," she managed softly. His gaze did not change as he kept looking into her eyes. Slowly working her fingers into his, Amore looked down for a moment. "I had, and oftentimes still blame myself for my mother's death." Her heart began to hurt as she said those words. Her mind tried to flash back to that day but she forced herself to stay focused on the here and now. A sad smile worked its way upon his face as he studied her. "If it was not for me, she would still be alive today. From what I have heard, Xerxes, there are some people of Avalon who feel the same way. If it was not for them, she would still be alive." She felt like she lost him with the last statement as his smile faltered.

"You are good-hearted, Amore." He gently placed his hand on the nap of her neck and smiled faintly. "Do not let anyone change that." Kissing her softly on the cheek, he nodded his head to someone behind her before turning. Her heart slowly sank as she watched him walk up the steps and joined by General Damon as the doors shut behind them. The thud of the doors closing resounded in her mind loudly.

"Do not feel rejected by my brother," Braylin remarked softly behind her. Amore looked down and smiled slightly. She seemed to know a lot of how Amore felt at times. Braylin took a deep breath and stared toward the doors. "Xerxes has a bad habit of getting so focused on something important he oftentimes forgets about those who are dear to him." She smiled faintly. Her words were comforting but that still did not help the feeling that was trying to work its way into her heart. For now she could push it aside and perhaps focus on Jenna. The young girl seemed very out of place, alone in the large city. It just did not sit right inside her.

Burning

AMORE STARED OUT AT THE horizon. The birds sang a happy tune. Wrapping the shawl around herself a little tighter, Amore allowed the tears to roll freely down her tan skin.

"Atone Eloise Memoma." *Happy Birthday, Mother.* Amore sighed as her heart, heavy with cares, weighed her down. From her mother, her mind drifted to family. How were they taking this day? Typically her father would be busy, as was her brother. While Aishlin resorted to dragging Amore around the city of Varness, home to the palace of Emir.

"I beg your pardon, Your Majesty," Talia's young voice broke her thoughts as she bowed. "I thought you would want this." A small parchment sat in her hand, making Amore frown.

"Who did that come from?" she asked then remembered feeling it in the palm of her hand as Talia explained.

"You handed it to me when the beautiful mare acted up." Thanking the young maiden, Amore studied the parchment. It was still sealed firmly, so it must not have been opened. As she slowly broke the seal, Amore began to wonder what possibly lye inside.

Dear Amore,

As I am sure you have already been informed, Vainer has returned home to Father. I have decided to stay back a while longer with Governor Tyron and his family. I am certain that General Damon would have given the message that Governor Tyron sent. I had hoped to hear some news of you from him but he mentioned nothing concerning. I had wished to attend the wedding with the governor. I am sure you already know that it was mother's birthday today. I am sorry, I do not know why I even mentioned it. How I wish I could speak to you. To know how you are doing. I am not even sure how I shall get this letter to you. I pray that you are well and happy. I miss you terribly so. Tyson sends his regards. He had hoped to have someday serve in the palace regime but certain things have come up and he has decided to remain close to Valley of Fernon. Nothing else exciting has happened. Things are rather dull, I am sure, compared to palace life. Lady Reni has expanded her garden. She sends her regards as well.

Love,
Aishlin

Sighing, Amore slowly folded up the parchment. While growing up, Aishlin would always try her best to encourage Amore on this day. She never admitted to her family about her feelings of guilt with her mother's passing. Of course, no one ever spoke of her. Surprising Amore that Aishlin even mentioned her in the letter. Her sister's letter seemed uncertain. Aishlin's writing kept jumping topics. Very unlike her sister, who was an excellent writer. What could be going on with Aishlin that she was longing to speak with Amore? Could she possibly just be wondering how she was doing? Her mind began to run away with the possibilities when a stationed guard called from the bottom of the steps that led to the tower.

"Your Majesty, your guests have arrived."

Brushing aside her tear-stained eyes, Amore fixed her appearance before descending the steps of the tower. The guard kept his head low as Amore walked past and her maidens quickly joined her. The palace seemed terribly still until she was met by Braylin. The dark-skinned princess flashed a smile as Amore neared, her eyes looking benevolent as always.

"I am curious to know what these guests of your want," the princess expressed quietly.

Amore let out a soft smile and focused on the hallway. *As am I,* she silently added as they reached one of the banquet rooms. As they neared the sentries quickly pulled open the large doors and bowed their heads. The room was brightly lit and inviting. She was expecting to see Jenna and her father. Instead, the young girl sat alone with her hands in her lap and her head down. Hearing the doors open, the young girl's head shot up, eyes wide open with terror written on her face. As her brown eyes laid on Amore, she scrambled from her chair and raced over to them. Collapsing at Amore's feet, the young girl burst into tears. Surprised and worried, Amore crouched down at took the girl's chin in her hand lifting her face up toward her.

"What is the matter?" Amore brushed aside the tears that streaked down her face. Jenna tried to quiet her sobs as she loosened her grip of Amore and slowly sat up, still sitting on the floor. Her hair was long and loose but had lost a lot of its natural shine that it had before. Carefully taking a seat next to the girl, Amore gently wrapped her in a hug holding her close. Her heart melted with what could possibly be wrong, and where was her father? Glancing over at the princess, who looked equally concerned, Amore gently turned Jenna's young face up toward her own.

"You need to tell me, Jenna. Where is your father?"

Choking back her emotions, the young girl took a deep breath trying to contain herself. "They burned the village, my home. Everything it's gone." She started to choke up again. Amore whipped her gaze over to Braylin who moved closer. How could that have possibly happened?

"Who did?" the princess asked, her voice surprised.

Jenna's body shook as she rubbed her eyes, her small head shaking. "I don't know."

"Jenna, where is your father?" Amore asked again, voice soft.

The young girl's gaze filled with moister again as she burst into more sobs, tired of holding everything back. Holding her close, tears started to reform in her own eyes as her mind imagined the flames dancing toward the sky. "Try to remember Jenna," Amore encouraged, running her hand through the young girl's hair. Jenna rested her head on Amore's arm and took in a shaky breath.

"They were not like the normal raiders, this time. They wore the type of uniform that the palace wears, same with their horses. But the coloring and patterns were different," she managed through a shaky breath.

"Soldiers?" Braylin asked, startled. Jenna nodded, her eyes staring off into the distance of the dark room. Jenna gave them the best description she could and Amore felt her heart sink and hoped she was wrong but it sounded like an Emirian soldier's uniform. It couldn't possibly be. No one would come this deep into a country to simply burn down a town. Jenna grew silent as her eyes drifted close, exhausted. Calling for some maidens, they came and picked up the young girl and took her away to rest.

"If this happened more than a week ago, why have we not heard anything about it yet?" Braylin remarked, walking around the room. Amore stood and shook her head. Her heart began to pound against her chest. *She has to be wrong! No way would Emirian soldiers come this far into Avalon to burn down a town. It just does not sound right!* Amore racked her mind as she paced the room. The raiders had grown more and more predominant lately, but no one ever mentioned the uniform of Emir. Amore remembered her father talking about rogues. Soldiers who deserted. Could it possibly be the answer? Soldiers who still held onto the uniforms raiding towns and people. Amore faintly heard Braylin instruct for someone to find the general and asked where the king might be at. Once they were all gathered in the same room, Braylin and Amore told them what the young girl had said. General Damon confirmed her worst fear.

"The pattern she explained does sound like Emirian soldiers," General Damon confirmed, shaking his head as he pulled out a long map. Amore stood facing the wall as she thought.

"Explain to me though, General, in terms of military strategy. Would you as a soldier come this far into the country to burn down a small unimportant town?" Amore asked, turning around to face the man. General Damon looked thoughtful before shrugging. His expression gave away that he was hiding something. Amore shifted her gaze to Xerxes, who sat in a chair, chin rested on his fist, gaze distant.

"This is the first town to be burned," Xerxes admitted, shifting to sit up straight. Amore glanced over at Braylin. The princess was staring at the map as her finger ran along the line that was drawn.

"It leads directly toward a part of the border," she remarked, turning her gaze up at her brother. Her eyes filled with concern as she looked at Amore. She could feel her own fear begin to work its way through her.

"Yes. This is, however, not the first time we have heard of the Emirian uniforms on both horse and rider," Xerxes added, shaking his head as he stood up. Motioning with his hand for the map to be rolled back up, he clasped his hands behind his back. "We will ride out to inspect the town in the morning." The general nodded, already knowing what was to be done.

"I would like to come," Amore desperately wanted to prove it wrong. Emirians could not be possibly raiding Avalon's cities. Xerxes whipped around, his gaze flashing as he shook his head.

"Absolutely not!" His words were sharp.

Surprised, Amore felt dejected. Softening his voice, Xerxes continued as the others quickly left the room. "This is not something for my queen to have to see." He cupped her face with both hands but his expression was reserved, no warmth or love shown. Gently kissing her hand, he backed away and left. Amore felt rejected as she stood there blinking. They had not spent much time together lately, and it seemed like every time they even did it was filled with arguments and disagreements. Letting out a deep sigh, Amore found her way back to her favorite garden and stared out across the overlook. Her heart hurt both for the way Xerxes acted toward her and the thought of Emir. She could easily tell them that there was no way Emir would ever do such a thing. That would mean explaining how she would know and how she was even sure Emir wasn't behind it all along. She tried to recall anything she might have overheard from her father or any of her guards back home but all she could remember was the constant thought of doing what she wanted to do and getting away from those who watched her.

Flickering her gaze up toward the blue sky, her mind debated about praying. But to whom? Emir believed in one God only and only one. When her mother died her family rarely spoke of God. So how was she to know? No mention of God was ever heard within the palace walls, nor was she going to start asking those around her. Checking to make sure Jenna was comfortable, her heart hurt for the young girl. To have lost her home, and possibly her father. Amore only imagined what she must be thinking. She was resting peacefully in Amore's old chambers. Clarice happily took care of the young girl and reassured Amore that she would be well tended to. Sighing, she found a secluded place once more and allowed her thoughts to drift away with her, sinking her heart with it.

The palace grew quiet and very still upon the quick departure of the king and his officials. With the departure Amore felt incredibly useless. Frustration and fear began to build up on the inside of her until she felt ready to burst. At least here she was alone. So she hoped. Pacing along the garden wall, Amore took a sharp breath, it could not be so. It seemed ridiculous from all standpoints for Emirian soldiers to come this far into Avalon.

To reduce themselves to pillaging and burning? Turning away Amore wanted to disappear. Making her way to her favorite garden, she demanded to be left alone. Her maidens seemed greatly surprised but obliged and returned to the garden above. The animals scurried away as she sat down under a large shaded oak tree. The net above held in the birds and kept out the animals of prey. Her favorite pet, a female fox she had given the name Scarlet, batted at her hand before dashing across the garden and disappearing into the shadows.

"I thought I would find you here," the soft voice of Braylin remarked as she walked closer and took a seat next to her. Kissing to Scarlet, Braylin smiled as the fox came dashing toward them before freezing halfway and crouching down, her colorful tail whipping back and forth. "How are you?" she asked, even quieter this time. Amore smiled as she stared at the fox, feeling just as trapped as the small creature was. "Honestly, Amorita, nothing else." Braylin had never used her full name before. Sighing Amore shook her head.

"It does not make any sense to me," she sighed, keeping her voice low, so any ears listening would not hear. "Why would Emirian soldiers travel this far into Avalon to act like bandits? My father would hang any he heard harassing Emirian towns. I would not think him to stoop so low to approve this sort of behavior." Resting her head against the bark, Amore stared up at the cloudy sky. Braylin grew quiet as the sounds of birds chirped around them.

"What about King Haman? Would he approve, trying to start a war?" she inquired. Amore wanted to laugh harshly but kept herself in check. Never.

"No, King Haman would not."

"You know him well?" she offered.

Amore lowered her gaze and slowly looked at the princess. Braylin's gaze was distant. They had never spoken before of anything concerning her life before Avalon. After revealing everything to Braylin, then what the princess had decided, she had never asked anything further.

"Yes. I accompanied my father many times to the palace." Amore grew silent. She knew King Haman well enough to know he was not afraid to march to war. To defend his people, his land. But to provoke, burn, and torment others? Especially a powerful kingdom like Avalon? If so, then Amore would want someone to question the king's motives behind his actions. She hoped dearly that it was not so. "I do not think he would do something like this," she continued, hoping her voice sounded reassuring because she felt anything but reassured.

"What did you think of Avalon before you came here?" Braylin inquired softly, imploring into the world Amore never thought she would share here.

"To be honest, I never gave it much thought. Remember when I had asked you the reason Avalon and Emir hated each other?" The princess made a soft hmm sound. "I had inquired that same thing to my sister."

"What did she have to say?"

"That she was not sure, and to ask King Haman." It felt nice to talk about her life with someone for a change. As she shared, she kept getting an uneasy feeling inside of her. How was the princess receiving all of this? She had not at first taken very well to the knowledge Amore was General Divon's daughter. "Are you still unsure about my presence here?" The question came out before Amore could stop it. The princess stared at her in surprise.

"What do you mean?" She was obviously startled.

Smiling, Amore looked down at her hands. "I knew that you were greatly conflicted when I told you who I was." She stared out as the princess's eyes grew thoughtful. "Now talking about Emir, I did not know if..." How was she even to finish such a sentence?

"Your Majesty!" a voice called as one of Braylin's maidens dashed through the door and bowed low. "The king has returned." Her heart pounded as she hurried through the halls followed closely by Braylin. The sentries quickly pulled open for the doors as Xerxes and General Damon dismounted from the horses. She stopped short and bit her lip as she wanted to ask a thousand questions. As the mare was taken away, Amore slowly approached, a solemn look filled his eyes. Where was she to even start?

⁘

"What did you find?" she tried.

Xerxes shook his head and walked toward the front of the grand hall. General Damon avoided her gaze as a servant took away his horse. Lowering her eyes, Amore knew it was not good. "Jenna's father?" she inquired softly as the general started to pass.

"I am sorry, Your Majesty, but I do not have an answer for that," he sighed and gently squeezed her arm for a moment before continuing on. General Damon rarely showed any affection toward her. It made her heart sink even farther. Turning around she bit her tongue from desperately wanting to find out if it was really Emirians behind it all.

"Your Majesty, Mirage has returned!" a stable boy exclaimed, drawing her attention. Amore followed the boy through the palace until they reached the stable yard. Mirage stood in the center and let out a whinny to her, trotting closer he swung his head making part of his mane change sides of his neck.

"Where have you been!" she whispered, wrapping her arms around his neck. Leah soon appeared in the gates and cantered closer, her once dazzling white coat dirty and grass stained but the mare appeared content as she stopped short, allowing herself to be caught. Running her hand along Mirage's muscles, Amore anticipated the worst. As she ran her hands down his legs, relief flooded her as nothing seemed to be wrong. The small cuts on his coat would easily heal, his tangled windswept mane easily combed through.

"Claro yano," *Crazy boy,* she whispered, kissing him between the eyes. The colt walked up behind her and bumped her arm with his warm muzzle. Bringing the horses to a secluded area, Amore gently brushed the colts' shiny coast, sighing as she looked into his deep brown eyes. As the colt's health returned and his true beauty shone forth, she was glad she had spotted the colt. The colt resembled her father's stallion in every aspect. From the look in his eyes, to the willing attitude he was showing. Mirage grazed off in the distance, his tail swishing back and forth as he snorted suddenly shaking his head. In preparation for foaling, her father usually had the mares brought close to home to watch over them carefully. Her heart hurt at the thought of anything happening to those she cared for in Emir, as well as in Avalon. A few nobilities' wives walked past, their conversations hushed as their eyes shifted toward the horses inside the garden. Amore had requested for the colt and Mirage to be brought to a secluded garden that way if any news might reach her, she would not be hard to find. The colt perked his ears as he gently blew a breath on her arm. Back home, he would no doubt be starting some simple training. Learning the commands that Mirage knew. So at a mature age, he would be ready for anything. The colt stuck his lip up in the air, making her chuckle and smile, relieving her oppressed mood. Shaking his head, the colt turned and trotted off before finding a decent spot to roll in the grass, messing up the work Amore had just done. Glancing toward where the nobilities' wives had been, Amore turned her gaze toward where her maidens waited no doubt. Before looking back at the colt, letting out a quiet whistle, she waited. Mirage flickered his ears but did not move as the colt remained grazing as well. Trying again, Amore watched the colt's ears twitch before he picked up his head and turned to look at her. Swinging his head, he bolted galloping closer. Taking a step toward the colt, Amore threw her hands up as the colt slammed to a halt and reared. He stayed up in the air until Amore dropped her arms and clicked her tongue, smiling as he landed and stuck his noise out for a treat.

"Impressive," Xerxes's voice startled her, making her jump and the colt snorted. He looked impressed enough but something felt incredibly off. Smiling slightly, Amore could feel the tension radiating off of him. The colt pinned his ears back and picked his head up high as Xerxes reach out to touch him. Flicking his tail, the colt snorted and moved off, avoiding the king. "I do believe I underestimated him," he continued, trying to make conversation with her.

"He is handsome, no doubt," Amore remarked, turning her gaze at her husband for a moment before looking back at Mirage. "What news of Tylia?" she asked as the silence became too much to bear. Xerxes remained quiet as it began to eat away at her.

"Not good," he finally said, offering little information. Sighing, Amore shook her head as her heart began to hurt once more. "Do not worry yourself, my queen." He stood with his hands behind his back as his blue eyes watched her but even though his gaze was on her, it seemed like he was in another place completely. Turning her eyes away, Amore took a deep breath and dared herself to ask.

"What of Jenna's father?" She dreaded the answer and even dreaded asking about it. If the news was good, it would be a relief, but she did not want to hear the bad that could easily come along with it.

"I do not know." It both relieved her and made her worry as she thought of the once carefree young girl, dancing around the beautiful wood home. How friendly the townspeople had been toward her. The thought of losing everything in one night was unbearable to think about.

"How is Mirage?" The black stallion gently nipped the colt and twisted his head around to look at them.

"He is appearing to be fine. No damage has been done." Amore was not sure when Xerxes left her side. She was unaware of how long she stood there pondering her darkened thoughts before finally making her way to find Jenna. She was with Clarice, who was talking quite happily away as she brushed the girl's curly brown hair.

"Oh, I remember when my daughter Talia was your age," she was saying until she spotted Amore and stopped short, bowing her head low. Jenna turned her brown-eyed gaze upon her in anticipation as Amore smiled sadly. Her eyes slowly dimmed as she stared out once more at nothing.

"Have hope," she started but knew not how to finish as her own hope seemed to have diminished greatly. It hurt greatly to see the hopelessness in the once joy-filled eyes. Jenna had been so carefree and young. Life was only full of possibilities. Amore only hoped that her father was alive and searching for his daughter.

<hr />

Every attempt she made to try lighten Jenna's mood kept falling sort. Even the palace entertainers seemed to fail as well. Clarice seemed eager to attend to the young girl, treating Jenna like she was her own.

"How is she?" she offered one evening as Talia was showing Jenna the animals in Amore's favorite garden. Clarice took a deep breath as her gaze stayed upon the young girl, a sad smile filling across her face.

"In time, I believe she will come around. Any news on her father?" Amore shook her head and sighed. What little news she had been given, she had fished out of Braylin who no doubt got it from the general. Why was she not allowed to know anything further of what was going on? It bothered her greatly being so unaware of what was happening outside the palace walls, especially when those within seemed to know more. What could they possibly see as beneficial with keeping her in the dark, to find out information through rumors mixed amongst the palace servants.

For days Amore tried her best to inquire softly about anything tangible but failed. She was reminded again that she did not need to worry about it and to relax. She had so much relaxation, she was growing impatient and rather bored. Which did not help her mind from thinking about everything that was happening.

"Is there anything I can help you with, Your Majesty?" a maiden asked from behind Amore, reminding her that her maidens must have found her. Shaking her head, Amore flashed a forced smile.

"I do not need anything at the moment, thank you, Liana."

The maiden nodded and respectfully backed away. Amore watched her retreat and began to wonder what their stories were. How did they come to be here? Avalon, like Emir, did not allow their palace servants to leave. It was for security, the only times Amore ever saw any servants leave was for getting more food or supplies for the palace. The servants rarely went without a guard or two.

"Liana," Amore called the woman back as she quickly dashed forward her eyes expectant to be sent for whatever Amore needed. She turned to face the woman who had to be no more than a few years older than herself. "How did you come to be a maiden here at the palace?" she asked, growing curious to know more about the woman that tended to her every day. Could it be possible that one of them was hiding a deep secret like her own? She could tell she took the woman by surprise as she stood there unable to answer before snapping from her state of shock and blushed.

"My family could not pay the amount of taxes they owed on their farm." She looked down and quietly added, "I was the oldest girl in the family and was offered as payment."

Amore felt surprised but reminded herself that it was not uncommon. Still it must not have been easy for the girl to be brought here in such a way.

"When was the last time you saw your family?" she asked softly.

Liana smiled then and looked away toward the horizon. "Six years ago, my queen." Her faint sad smile filled her face. "I should have been able to go home once that payment was fulfilled but..." Liana stopped and looked away, blushing slightly at the amount of attention Amore was giving her. "I should not be bothering my queen with my problems." Amore laughed suddenly then felt bad for doing so.

"Please, Liana, tell me. It is nice to know things when I myself am in the dark about what is happening around here."

Liana smiled then and her eyes grew hopeful. "I do not mean to play any favorites, Your Majesty! I wish to have no such special attention but I would like to ask of you!" Liana fell to her knees then with her hands stretched toward her. "My queen, I know I am bonded to serve you but I must ask concerning that of a loved one. My family, you see, there was only three of us not including my parents. My parents died not too long ago along with my oldest brother. My sister…" She looked down as tears began to fill in her eyes. "My sister was pregnant and I have not heard anything about her since two months ago. I have asked and inquired of many people. I have heard that she is dead but no one knows what happened to the child." Liana paused to take in a sharp breath before continuing. "I have, however, heard about possibly where the child might be. In the city's orphanage." Amore had heard a little bit about that place but not very much at all.

"Have you gone to the palace officials about this?" Amore asked. The palace officials handled a lot of the petty matters that were not important enough to require the attention of the king or her. That was, if anyone would allow her to handle such matters. Liana's expression lost its hopeful glint as she shook her head.

"They would not even allow me to set up a meeting with them. They said it was not important enough for a servant to waste their time."

"How do you know when you even find the child?" Amore pondered.

"I have met the child once, and I would easily recognize the child again!" Her gaze filled once again with hope, eager that perhaps Amore would help her.

Children of Avalon

SHE HAD PROMISED LIANA SHE would speak to Lord Marcel about the matter. It was the least she could do, something she could handle. Be trusted with. Lord Marcel was an interesting man in that Amore had met him before and often felt unnerved by the proud man. He carried himself like a prince among many, only paying real respects when the king was present. Lord Marcel was going to be hard to deal with. As she entered the grand hall, the sentries bowed to her as Amore's eyes hit the man standing in the center speaking with another.

"Lord Marcel," Amore called as she walked closer. The man, around Amore's height, turned toward her. A somewhat pleasant smile flickered across his light-skinned face.

"What is it, Your Majesty my Queen?" His tone was light and filled with happiness. Amore was certain she had never seen him in such pleasant spirits before and it took her off her guard for a moment as he bowed to her when she stopped still a good distance from him.

"I have a request of you."

The man's smile grew wider as he nodded and asked for her to continue.

"I hear that you are in charge of many of Roselyn business. Like the orphanage." The smile slowly slid from his face and Amore knew she must have hit a nerve as his eyes grew serious.

"If this is about your maiden?"

"It does not matter whom it concerns, Lord Marcel. I wish to know more about the orphanage and those who are in it." Amore was not going to let this man back down and treat her with any disrespect. She could tell he was not happy with her inquiry.

Taking a sharp breath he narrowed his gaze. "No disrespect, my queen, but I have not the time to overlook that area at the moment." Bowing before she could answer, he turned and started to march off.

"Perhaps then I shall speak to the king about this upon his return," Amore remarked as a smile slid across her mouth. The man froze in his pace and slowly turned around as a placid smile took place.

"I shall see what I can find out, Your Majesty."

"Thank you." Turning from his presence, Amore walked off, very satisfied with herself. She reassured Liana that she had spoken with the lord, but it did not seem to raise the maiden's spirits.

The information Lord Marcel had provided was minimal at least. The orphanage was overseen by himself, under the direct supervision of a woman named Relix Manson. It housed fifty children at the moment ranging from ages zero to ten. Sometimes children a little older than that stayed at the orphanage but not normally. "Why is that?" Amore implored and the man took a sharp breath and forced out a smile.

"The law does not require us to hold children past the age of ten, so many disperse into areas unknown."

"That should not be so, Lord Marcel. How is a ten-year-old going to feed themselves?"

The man only smirked, frustrating Amore. "Bring it up with the king, Your Majesty," the man retorted. "That is all I can tell you and concerning your dear maiden. There is no child by that description in the orphanage. Excuse me, my queen."

Without waiting for a reply, the man bowed and hurried away. Clinching her fist, Amore let out a long breath and turned away. Liana was waiting for her outside the hall doors, her eyes

filled with hope and excitement. Smiling softly, Amore continued walking, forcing her frustration down before responding to
her maiden.

"What happened, Your Majesty?" Liana inquired, her
voice worried.

Stopping, Amore took a deep breath and turned toward her.
"I am sorry, Liana. Lord Marcel could not find anything on your
family member." *I would not be surprised he did not even check*,
Amore thought as she turned away once more and continued
walking, thinking. Stopping short again, she smiled slightly.
"Where is Talia?" she asked out loud.

"She's resting today, Your Majesty. She's feeling a little under
the weather," Namur answered. Making a frustrated sound,
Amore continued on. "Is there anything I could help with?"
Namur inquired and Amore motioned for her to walk closer.

"Do you know anything of protocols? More importantly
concerning the orphanage. That man bothers me," she admitted
then clamped her mouth shut. "I did not mean to say that last
part." She shifted her attention on the women she had come to
know fairly well. Namur and Liana did not look surprised but
smiled slightly.

"We shall speak nothing of it, my queen," the women said at
once and Amore smiled.

"I shall find out for you, Your Majesty. Talia has shown the
library to me a few times," Namur concluded and Amore nodded her head. The tall, beautiful woman hurried away and Liana
stepped closer, blushing slightly.

"I do not mean to be causing so much excitement," she apologized and Amore smiled.

"Please, do not apologize. It is more than your inquiry, Liana."
Amore squeezed the woman's arm and continued walking heading toward the servants' quarters.

"Your Majesty, you have a guest requesting to speak with
you," a servant called, stopping her short. No one ever inquired

on her before. It surprised her, and worried her greatly. As she entered into the grand hall, soldiers quickly neared her and followed. The room was empty save for a lone person standing in the center. As she neared she began to smile and her excitement grew. Turning to one of the guards beside her, she ordered, "Fetch Jenna." The man nodded his head and turned to quickly fulfill her instructions.

"Maverick, I am pleased to see you alive and well," she exclaimed as the man bowed low and Amore instructed for him to stand straight.

He kept his gaze low, respectfully, as he uttered, "Thank you, Your Majesty. I was very concerned about Jenna until I heard she had made it to the palace. Is she doing well?"

"Daddy!" an excited squeal rang out as the young girl dashed across the room and into the arms of her father. Maverick began to kiss the girl's cheeks in joy as a warm feeling hit Amore. Lowering her gaze she thought of her own father and what he must be going through at this time. Was he still convinced she was in Beliz? Setting his daughter on the ground, Maverick smiled brightly as he finally looked at Amore fully this time.

"Thank you for everything, my Queen." He beamed.

Smiling, Amore nodded her head. Fighting back the tears from coming to her eyes, until they were buried deep within her.

"Anything I can do for those who saved my life." Their home was burned, their town destroyed. "What are you going to do now?" she asked. Maverick simply smiled and looked at his daughter lovingly. His eyes filled with tears of joy.

"Start over, either in Tylia or in another place."

His gaze fell once more, as he kept his arm around Jenna's shoulder. Chills shot through her as Amore turned to see Xerxes had walked into the room as Maverick bowed low.

"It is good to see that you are alive, Maverick." His voice sounded pleasant, as Maverick slowly stood straight again. Uncertainty filled his gaze. "We wish to know more about what happened in Tylia." General Damon walked in then followed by a couple of officials. Amore began to feel rather out of place and it annoyed her. Maverick's gaze fell as his expressions grew solemn. Calling Jenna to her, after some encouraging from her father, Amore wanted to stay and hear what the men had to say. As she reached Braylin in the garden, she expressed her frustration to the princess.

"It is according to protocol mostly. It speaks nothing about the Queen not being able to be present. I feel that is more on my brother's part than anything else." She smiled as her gaze turned to Jenna, who sat impatiently in the chair waiting for when her father would call for her.

"Why is that?" Why did he not want her in the room, to hear what she already knew? Braylin shrugged slightly and smiled.

"He's been that way since my mother's passing. Perhaps he thinks that we would be better off not hearing the...unpleasant details." Amore had not thought of it that way before. She did not have a strong stomach to handle...unpleasant things. The most she was able to stand was watching the mare's give birth. Even then, it made her stomach churn.

"I suppose you are right."

"Am I?" she mused and looked over at Jenna as a servant hurried closer and bowed low.

"Her father calls for her." Jenna scrambled from her chair and started to rush away before turning and grabbing Amore's hand, making her heart warm as she walked alongside the girl. As soon as her father came in sight, she broke free and ran once more into his arms. The grand hall was empty, save for Maverick as he smiled and thanked her once more. Pulling her close, Maverick turned and left the palace as Jenna's eyes stayed upon Amore until the doors closed behind them. She truly hoped that whatever their future, they would thrive and make it. Amore felt like a part of her left with them as she slowly turned back into the safety of the palace. Finding her way to the library with Talia now returned to her side, Amore began to search through the chronicles. What was written within stated exactly what Lord Marcel had told her.

Nothing more was said concerning the welfare of the children. Nor the state of its housing for them. Why does this intrigue her so? she wondered. Perhaps it was finally feeling useful toward something.

"Go and search for the child," Amore permitted one day when it was just Liana, Namur, and herself. "I hope you can find her."

Liana grew excited as she nodded her head and bowed low. "Thank you Your Majesty!" Turning, she hurried from the room.

Her mind went back to the thought of raiders, and what else was Xerxes not telling her? Why did he seem so distant to her all of a sudden? She had felt it coming on slowly, with each passing moment it seemed like a divide had grown. The less she was inquired of, the less he seemed to notice her. No one in the palace would tell her what might be happening. Perhaps they themselves did not know. It was a couple of days before Liana returned to the palace in even lower spirits then before. She returned to her duties but she knew that the maiden had not been successful. She felt pity for the maiden and tried to inquire of the search.

"I had such hopes, Your Majesty, I searched everywhere in the streets. Inquired of anyone who would pay attention to me. I tried the home for the orphans but I might as well have thrown mud in her face." Sighing, Liana shook her head and rested back as her tired eyes flickered. "I feel that it is no use anymore." Amore felt useless all over again. She had hoped that Liana found what she was looking for but everything seemed fruitless. Lord Marcel was no help. The chronicles did not even carry the names of the children.

"Why do you say such a thing about the orphanage?" Amore inquired, probing into Liana's search once more. Sitting up, the maiden flickered her gaze up at Amore for a moment and smiled sadly.

"Because I am nothing more than a simple maiden, Your Majesty. I might as well have been a poor beggar."

"What if I went?" her words even surprising herself but she liked the idea. Clarice put a quick end to the idea. Surprising the three of them as she quietly walked into the room, overhearing their conversation.

"Your Majesty, you have no proper excuse to be inquiring into that place. It would seem rather odd in the eyes of the court." Sighing, Amore shook her head. What good was it to be queen if you never got to do anything worth meaning?

"Even though I am queen, I cannot simply inquire myself?"

"It would show favoritism, Your Majesty," Clarice insisted, making her nod her head and drop the subject. How was she not to become attached to the maidens around her? They were with her almost every day and night. Liana, Namur, Talia, and Clarice were her main maidens. At times others would serve her but only when they were not available. *Can I not be for one day simply no one, and walk amongst the people. Hear their true thoughts, know what they are concerned about?*

"I suppose you are right, Clarice. Though it does not make me feel any better," Amore remarked.

Clarice clapped her hands and the maidens quickly dispersed. As soon as they were alone. Clarice turned her full attention on Amore.

"What is bothering you, Your Majesty? For some time now you have been most miserable." Clarice kept her intense gaze upon Amore, making her slowly smile. Her maidens knew her well.

"I am feeling rather useless and unimportant," she admitted. Clarice seemed rather surprised as she raised an eyebrow. She started to object against Amore's statement but she quickly continued on, "What important things I have done? Have you seen anyone inquire of me on anything concerning the kingdom? In fact, Liana is the only one to really ask me for advice and help.

The king will not even confide in me." She had not meant to say the last part as the dawning look hit Clarice.

"So that is it? Your Majesty, you have to realize how busy the king has gotten lately."

I know, I know. Amore sighed. That was part of her whole problem, she was unable to help him. Comfort him in any way because, frankly, she had no idea what was going on and it irritated her greatly.

Clarice fell silent as she studied her hands briefly. "That is no excuse, is it?" she offered and Amore shook her head.

"I try to be understanding, Clarice, but when no one confides in me what is happening, how am I to know? I listen to rumors floating around the palace. I feel like what Liana said, a beggar, not a queen."

They grew silent with each other. Clarice had no help to give her and Amore really did not want any words of comfort. At least not from her. It was her life, something she was going to have to learn to live with each day.

"Have you inquired the king about it?" she asked softly and Amore chuckled.

"He does not have time for me. So how do I even ask? When I do ask, I am told that I do not need to concern myself with it."

"I suppose that is his way of protecting you. And injuring you at the same time," Clarice sighed, reminding Amore that she knew Xerxes as a child. Had she in some way helped to raise him?

"You were friends with his mother, the late Queen Clarice, were you not?"

The color in her face seemed to drain a little as she nodded her head. She could tell it was uncomfortable knowledge to be spoken and allowed the thought to dissipate. Just like her own mother, Amore was not allowed to know.

"Though I may not know how to comfort you, my queen, I wish I could comfort you, like you had me when my heart was feeling low." Amore had forgotten about Clarice's words, it seemed like such a long time ago. Clarice smiled at the curious look in her eyes as she slowly sat down. "I had come to realize my age, and it scared me greatly. To realize that one day, Talia would be left with no family to speak of. I feel rather ashamed that it sunk my spirits so low, but when you had given me your word, I felt relieved, that no matter what the future may bring for me, Talia would be taken care of." Amore attempted to smile and nodded her head. It was understandable for Clarice to have worried about Talia. The young girl had no family to speak of besides her mother. She would always have a home in the palace, as long as Amore could help it.

"Thank you, Clarice."

Her mind churned with the thought of Liana. She had an opportunity to know about her own distant family but was not able to because of her station in life. As the evening began to wane, Amore called Namur and Liana to her. "Liana, go back to the orphanage and search for the child. Take Namur with you, with my instructions to enter and observe the place. Bring words back to me what you are able to find. Take some money in case you locate the child."

Liana's face lightened as she nodded her head. Namur would surely help back the other maiden, she was tall and beautiful. She also knew how to command attention that would be needed concerning the caretaker of the home. As they bowed low, another thought came to her mind and she smiled. "In fact, I shall accompany you."

"My queen, I must surely protest this!" Namur exclaimed as she stood back up, her eyes wide with concern, making Amore smile.

"Not as queen, but perhaps another maiden," she concluded, standing up and nodding her head. She liked the idea already.

"Your Majesty, surely you cannot be found outside the palace walls at such a late hour. It is unbecoming, and most dangerous for yourself and us as well," Namur insisted.

She knew the dangers, the risks involved, but she really wanted to go. To see for herself. To be treated like a simple maiden. "If you truly insist, my queen. Let us take a guard. It is not usual for us to do so especially at this hour." Thunder rumbled above the palace, as Amore pondered the thought and nodded. Namur and Liana were not happy about her coming but arrangements were made between the four of them. Talia would make sure everyone thought she was resting for the evening. That she was not feeling well. As she pulled the cloak over her head, Amore felt her excitement begin to grow. Finally she would be able to know something for herself. Though to the maidens' dismay, no guard would accompany them tonight.

Thunder rumbled sending chills through her as Amore wrapped the cloak around herself tighter. She did not care to be caught outside during storms, it unnerved her greatly. The streets were empty for the most part, with luck they were able to get by the palace guards at the doors and gate. It seemed rather silly to her but she was enjoying herself. Amore's excitement grew as they neared the orphanage. She figured in her mind it would look beautiful. Well built, well kept. Tended to with care. What she got instead was the complete opposite. The rugged building looked ready to collapse. It was smashed between other buildings reaching desperately for the sky deprived from sunshine for far too long. It caused Amore to shudder at the thought of what the inside looked like, let alone the fifty children who were supposed to be housed here. Namur knocked on the tattered door, and shifted her gaze toward the darkened window until the door burst open suddenly startling them. An older, tired, skinny looking woman wrapped a shawl around herself tighter and eyed them with content.

"What?" she demanded, shifting her gaze at the three of them. Namur stood tall and looked the woman straight in the eye.

"We wish to see the orphanage, by request of Queen Amore," Namur proclaimed sounding very dignified.

The woman crossed her arms and looked unamused. "Really?" she remarked, shifting her gaze toward Namur. "All right, suit yourself," she muttered and stepped back. Amore kept the cloak over her head as she stepped past the woman. The tiny entryway held a stairway and a skinny hall that led toward the back of the building. Two open archways sat on each side of the hall at the beginning. The room felt damp and dark. Amore could feel her spirits already start to sink. She could tell by the look on Namur's face that she was not impressed. Disgusted was a better word.

The woman squeezed by them and muttered, "Follow me," and led them down the narrow hall. As they got to the back a few children scampered away hiding. At the end of the hall was a large eatery. Plates piled the sink and old food sat out upon the shelves. Amore held her breath and shifted her gaze at a horrified Liana. The woman's face showed no emotion as she brushed back a child's hair and eyed them suspiciously.

"Do you have anyone helping you with the children?" Namur asked, and the woman burst into a laugh before quieting.

"At times, a few of the townspeople help me, but for the most part...no." The woman's voice grew tired as she started to walk again, leading them back through the halls and up the rickety steps. A narrow hall held door after door, bedroom after bedroom. Ten at least, some were big but a majority were small. Guilt squeezed its way through her at the size of rooms Amore had lived in her entire life.

Before anyone could say anything, Liana burst out, "Chantal!" She dashed forward, scooping up a young girl sitting upon the floor. She began to rattle off in a language Amore had never heard before. Tears streamed down her cheeks. The young child burst into tears and wrapped her little arms around Liana's neck. Without any words to anyone else, Liana walked out of the room and down the hall. Her voice slowly drifting away into silence.

"What is the fee for the child?" Namur offered and the older woman's expression never changed.

"Ten serif."

Gasping at the amount, Amore was stunned. It would not surprise her if any of the children here did not get adopted. The commoners of Avalon would have to save for a few years to be able to take in a child at that price.

"That is preposterous," Amore exclaimed and the woman nodded her head.

"It takes a lot to feed and care for the children."

"If that is what you are demanding, how do you expect those of Avalon to take a child in?" Amore demanded and the woman narrowed her gaze slightly.

"Perhaps the royalty of this kingdom would live less demanding lives, those caring for the less fortunate would have better means," the woman snapped, glaring at Amore.

"Careful!" Namur scolded the woman as her fiery gaze turned toward Namur. "You forget whom we serve," Namur reprimanded, to not give away who Amore was.

"I have not forgotten!" she retorted boldly. "Even if I meet the queen herself, I shall be more than happy to repeat those words."

"I would be more careful with your words next time," Amore remarked and the woman shifted her angry gaze toward her until her eyes hit Amore's exposed face and fear filled her expression and she swallowed hard.

"I mean no disrespect, my queen," she exclaimed, bowing the best she could. "We just get so little funds as it is." She stayed bowed. Amore shifted her gaze at Namur who seemed to not buy her story.

"Does not funds come from the palace?" Amore asked, remembering what she read in the reports that Namur and herself had found. It showed every month sufficient funds were sent to Roselyn's Orphanage Asylum. The woman shook her head then stopped short.

"We do receive three serif every month, Your Majesty," she responded, still bowed. "Please forgive me of my temper, my queen," she apologized, sounding sincere.

"You are pardoned. I promise you that the ten serif shall be sent for the child Chantal. I shall also look into why the proper funds are not being sent forth as they should be."

"Thank you, my queen!" the woman exclaimed, her eyes lighting up for the first time since Amore had walked into the building. Pulling the cloak back over her head, she turned and felt relieved to escape the confines of the building but the looks of the children watching her stayed in her mind as she stepped into the evening air fresh with the smell of rain.

"My queen!" Namur whispered once everyone was out of the building and the woman Amore assumed to be Relix apologized again and said her ado. "My queen, I do not mean to scold, but I feel that you should not have revealed yourself or have been so generous with that woman," Namur remarked as they made their way back through the streets. It had grown significantly darker since their arrival. Liana coddled the child close and tried to wrap her in her cloak as best as she could.

"Allow me." Amore took the child from Liana and wrapped her large cloak around the small girl and continued on. "I feel there is more to the story, Namur, than what we are seeing. I feel that Relix must be doing the best she can, besides the look in her eyes when she sees the children speaks more to me than what the building may appear to be."

"You are more compassionate then I feel I ever could be, Your Majesty," Namur remarked apologetically.

Smiling slightly, Amore sighed. *If only you knew the true meaning behind it.* Amore felt her own personal life was like that of the orphanage. It may appear glamorous on the outside but she felt at any moment it could turn upside down on her, sending her into the slums.

It was taking them longer to get back to the palace than expected. The townspeople had gone home for the night and rain began to pound against their bodies but that was the least of her worries. They had to avoid the guards. Namur and Liana had permission to be outside the palace walls but Amore did not. She had gone along as a maiden. She had no escort, no protection, and no reassurance that behind any corner might lay something a lot worse than being caught by Roselyn's guards.

"Halt in the name of the king!" a voice called, making the women freeze in their tracks. Amore felt her heart almost stop as they slowly turned around and Namur quickly blurted as her eyes grew wide.

"Asher!" She hurried forward smiling slightly and the guard smirked but kept a firm look upon his face. "We are just on our way back to the palace now." Namur batted her long eyelashes at the guard as his reserved look slowly slipped from his face. Amore felt a smile creep upon hers. She had never seen any sides to her closest maidens beyond reserved and respectful, let alone flirtation. As Namur conversed with the guard, the slightest movement caught Amore's attention. A shadowed figure walked past the opening and stopped for a brief moment, their attention drawn toward them. They lingered there for a moment before moving on. Glancing at the maidens, Amore slowly made her way down the back street to the one the person had just been. They had stopped not far ahead and glanced back easily spotting Amore before drifting into another alleyway. Without really thinking, Amore followed suit. Something about the way the person moved reminded her of someone from her childhood. Before she could get too far she felt a hand on her arm pulling her to a stop.

Worried, Namur said quietly, "Please, my queen, let us be getting back." Glancing back the way the person had gone, Amore consented and followed Namur back. The guard bade them a quick return and went back to his post. The shadowed figure stayed on her mind as they made their way across the large city. The dark clouds above rumbled from time to time threatening to unleash its fury of rain. It took longer than normal to reach the palace walls, ducking the guards and the people of Roselyn that mingled out in the weather until rain began to fall scattering all into their homes. Except the unfortunate few. As they hurried along movement once more caught Amore's attention and she froze in the beginning of an alleyway. Close to the ground were three figures until they noticed Amore watching, standing quickly they dashed off into the streets appearing to be small people or children.

"Those are the children that the orphanage cannot take in or they no longer can be there because of their age," Namur explained, encouraging Amore to continue. She had never realized that the streets of Roselyn had even contained young children without a place to stay, or meals to eat. "I shall tell you more once we are back inside the palace." Namur smiled sadly and kept moving ahead.

The rain continued to pound against her back as she glanced toward the guards at the entrance of the bridge. Namur was still in the lead but froze at the last turn that Amore knew the palace gates sat beyond. They had to get through them to get over the bridge, then they could take a servant entrance. "Oh, no," Namur cried softly as she leaned back against the building, ready to give up.

"What is it?" Amore asked and her maiden shook her head.

"The two worst soldiers to pick to guard the palace gates, they had to be this night!" she exclaimed loud enough for only them to hear. Glancing around the corner, Amore spotted two men chattering to each other and even jeering some of the townspeople who hurried by in the rain. It would mean having to get by them without raising suspicion. She was not allowed outside the palace walls, let alone at night even. Namur went first, Liana behind, carrying the young child. *This is beyond crazy*, she thought suddenly. *Do you know what could happen if word spread?* She wrapped the cloak around herself tighter as she shivered from the rain. Though the weather was rather warm and the rain was a relief from the heat, chills ran through her body. Something drew the guards' attention away giving them a short opportunity to slip past without notice.

The tall trees protected them somewhat as they hurried through the courtyards. Thunder rumbled through the gray clouds as a bolt of lightning flashed. *Try not to panic*, she pleaded with herself as she picked up her pace. Her dress was clinging to her skin as they finally reached a small entrance, which would lead them away from prying eyes. Namur pulled firmly on the iron handle as the door refused to budge. Her heart pounded as the thunder boomed again, making the hairs on the back of her neck stand on end.

"What is it?" she asked as Namur tugged on the door but it refused to give. The taller woman spun around and hugged herself tightly.

"There is another entrance further down. If we run perhaps we shall get there sooner. Or the main doors." Namur looked down the length of the wall before it etched out into the courtyard and disappeared around the side.

"What do you suggest?" Amore asked as she glanced at Liana who was beginning to struggle carrying the child so long of a time. Namur hesitated as she looked toward the massive doors that led to the grand hall. No guards stood outside the gates because of the weather but no doubt they would be waiting inside them. Pulling her hood further down her face, taking a deep breath, Amore started toward the doors as the rain started to sting her cold skin. The doors moved easily inward as she pushed against them. To her great relief, the grand hall was empty as they walked ahead.

"Go on ahead of me." She motioned for them to proceed as she pushed the doors shut once more. The air was still and quiet as the water dripped from every part of her and onto the beautiful floor below. Keeping the soaking wet cloak around herself, she slowly made her way behind the tall pillars, watching to make sure no one noticed the maidens before her. *This is dangerous.* Not only for herself but for Liana if she was caught. Protocol was most certainly broken bringing the child within the palace. Not to mention Amore being outside the palace walls without protection. Relief started to ease away the fear as the grand hall continued to remain empty as she slowly relaxed her shoulders. There were many parts of the palace that were open, easy enough for her to explain her appearance.

"I find it most interesting, watching as three of the palace maidens slip into the grand hall late in the evening," a voice expressed, making her freeze in her steps. "Enjoy your little adventure?" His voice sounded familiar as she slowly turned around.

He was not meant to return so soon, she thought as her heart sank. Xerxes was back. He shifted and moved away from the pillars as she realized, she had been caught.

Prince Gabriel

How had she been caught? The king was not to return for another week. Yet as he drew closer Amore began to see his face more clearly, and she realized it was not King Xerxes. He just had the faint resemblance of the king. A smile slowly spread across his dark tan face.

"Hello," he sounded pleasant as he stopped in front of her. Hopefully Namur and Liana were well into the palace, deep enough to hide the child in the servants' quarters. She knew why the maidens had such a worried look in their eyes when they had quickly dashed back into the shadows. It was risky enough. Unsure of what to do, and if this man even knew who she was. Amore smiled slightly and bowed her head like a maiden before slowly moving toward the pillars and the man followed, blocking her path.

"Quite the day to be sneaking out of the palace," he remarked, stopping Amore in her tracks. *Just keep going, do not respond.* His smile grew, he knew he had caught Amore in the act, he just did not realize who he had caught for it almost seemed he was…was it even possible?

"I was not sneaking anywhere, if you please, I must be on my way," Amore conceded. A curious look passed over his eyes as he shook his head.

"To what was your business then?"

Amore narrowed her gaze. This man was acting like he had some authority in the palace and unless Amore had been mistaken, he was no official, nor any ruler of the towns nearby.

"It is none of your concern, sir," she expressed, moving into the hall between the pillars and the wall. The man quickly moved in front of her again.

"I must disagree with you. For I think it is my business if the servants are bringing things into the palace in secret," he remarked motioning with his hand as Liana and Namur were brought forth by a guard. However there was no child, and while the man's back was turned toward her, Amore gave the two women a quizzical look as Namur shifted her gaze down and off to the side. The child must have been hidden already. The guard did not recognize Amore from the hood that still covered her head and the faint lighting in the gloomy hall.

"Care to explain why three maidens came back to the palace empty-handed? If you were as one of you says out getting supplies, why is it that no one has anything to show for it?"

"The markets closed early today, sire," Liana expressed before quickly quieting down again and lowering her gaze nervously. Hearing a slight screech startling the group as a small child ran forward crying until she collided with Liana begging to be picked up as another guard walked forward, obviously having startled the child. The man remained quiet as he stared at Liana and the child while no one else spoke any words until Liana finally spoke.

"We went to fetch the child, sire."

The man stepped forward and took the young girl from Liana and turned her to face him as Liana's gaze fell. Frustration began to rise in her. They had tarried here long enough and someone was bound to find out that she was not in her room. The man had carried on long enough but it seemed like he was not yet finished as he suddenly turned and carried the child out into the middle of the grand hall. "You do know what the penalty is for fraternization of the royal maidens?"

Donna Rahkola

Liana swallowed as the two maidens glanced at each other. "Who would like to speak up that the child is truly theirs?" The air grew silent. The intention the man was searching for was clearly spoken.

"She is mine," Liana spoke softly. According to protocol, maidens were not allowed to take in relatives while working in the palace. If a maiden married under consent of the king, she could then continue her royal duties and raise her children inside the palace. Otherwise Chantal had no legal grounds to be admitted into the palace. Even if Amore had given consent. In the eyes of the officials it would look like favoritism and many of the servants would try the same. Sending the palace into chaos. What this man was leaning toward, Amore felt Liana would never do such a thing. Liana would be cast out of the palace in disgrace and most likely shunned from Roselyn and lot of respectable positions in Avalon.

"Who in the palace shall back this statement that this child truly is yours? You perhaps?" he asked looking at Namur, then Amore. "If this child is truly yours, it would have been found out by now unless you have not taken proper care of those you have been charged to care for."

Liana's expression grew terrified and she shifted her gaze at Amore before looking at the ground.

"Liana has done no such things that you are accusing her of," Amore defended her as much as she could. The guard's interest perked suddenly at the sound of Amore's voice. Making her clamp her mouth shut. Chantal looked just as equally terrified still being held in the man's arms. Nodding his head to one of the guards, as they took the now screaming child from his arms and walked away.

"Where are you taking her?" Liana pleaded, wanting to dash after her.

"Somewhere safe until we can handle this properly. For now you shall be detained and the queen informed of your activities. It shall then be decided your fate." Amore wanted to speak up now but held her tongue and waited it out. Liana nodded her head and was about to allow the guard to led her away.

A strong voice suddenly asked, "What is going on?"

Amore felt her heart sink even lower. He was not supposed to be back yet. The guards and maidens all quickly bowed low and Amore hesitated before doing the same, hoping to blend in.

The man, however, gave a quick bow before stating, "I found these maidens coming into the palace carrying a small child."

Xerxes flickered his gaze across all of them for a moment as the man continued, "Liana states the child is hers."

Liana seemed to grow smaller by the moment as her king turned his eyes upon her.

"I can without a doubt state that cannot be truth. Is it?" Xerxes asked still looking at the maiden. Liana broke then and cried.

"No, she's my family. My uncle shall be coming for her in a few days if I was able to find her. My queen said that I could go and look and we found her! Your Majesty, please forgive me."

"Return to your place, we shall discuss this later," Xerxes commanded and Liana nodded her head and slowly stood straight and dashed away, Namur following suit. Amore was about to follow when Xerxes quickly commanded, "Not you." She froze. "The rest of you are dismissed."

The guards hurried away while the man still remained and Amore did not expect the next words to be spoken. "Brother, I see you have met my wife." His voice sounded anything but pleasant. Turning around slowly, a thousand reasons came to her mind but she remained silent as her gaze caught his and a hurt look flashed over his eyes as his hand slowly pulled down the soaked hood from her head. Amore's mind faintly registered that he had called the man brother.

"Leave us for a moment," Xerxes asked, turning his attention to the man. The man nodded and quickly dispersed from the room. Amore tried to prepare herself. Sighing, Xerxes shook his head and walked away from her, taking a seat upon the stairs. Carefully walking closer Amore tried to read his guarded expression.

"Xerxes…" she started and he shot her a hard look and the explanation froze in her throat. "Please let me explain," she pleaded as his gaze drifted away from her. Taking the spot by his feet, Amore knelt down and kept her gaze upon him. She was terrified to think what he must be thinking. Taking a breath he turned his gaze back on her and waited. "My maiden Liana asked me to help find her niece, so I did. I wanted to do something important." A look of exhaustion quickly passed over his expressions as he leaned forward and studied her.

"The palace officials could have taken care of that," he remarked, shaking his head, and Amore wanted to laugh harshly but kept it inside.

"I tried that, I requested and I might as well have been laughed at. The information I received is nothing like it is in person. The orphanage, it is terrible," she pleaded, placing her hand upon his knee. Shaking his head in frustration, Xerxes stood and walked away. Amore felt like she had just been stabbed and gasped for a breath as she composed herself and turned to watch him.

"You are queen, perhaps it is time you start acting like one," he insisted softly. Amore started to object but was quickly cut off as he turned around and the look he gave her made her feel cold on the inside. "What would the people of Avalon say if they saw the queen, my wife, roaming the streets at night?" His eyes were growing flustered. Scrambling to her feet, Amore started to try and defend herself but quickly stopped as he exclaimed, "Enough!" He shook his head and turned away. "Leave me." His tone was strained and Amore felt torn. Keeping her eyes downcast, she quickly replaced the hood and hurried from the room. Thankfully the halls had no one in them and she made it to the room without any confrontation. Collapsing on the bed, sobs burst forth and every pressure and secret pressed forward until exhaustion claimed hold, sucking her into an uneasy rest.

Dreading morning, Amore slowly woke to dreary gray clouds that continued to cling to the earth, bringing with it gloom upon the palace. Amore sat on one of the cushions in her favorite garden and stared blankly across the empty space. Her heart still hurt from the events past. Liana slowly approached, eyes downcast, as she bowed low.

"I am so sorry, my queen," she started out, her voice strained, evidence of tears cried over a long period of time. "It was never my intention to bring you any distress."

Amore sighed and brushed off the maiden's words. "Do not apologize, Liana, you did not force me to go with you. I have brought this upon myself and shall take the responsibility for it." She smiled sadly and turned her gaze away for a moment. "What of Chantal?" she inquired and Liana turned her gaze away.

"She is being taken care of until my uncle can arrive to claim her, Your Majesty," Liana said softly. Turning her full attention on the woman, she studied her for a moment. Liana looked beyond distressed and overwhelmed.

"What of you?" she asked, even quieter so that no one would be able to hear. Those who sat not too far away. Liana hesitantly looked up at Amore, meeting her eyes for a moment.

"I do not know." With that she slowly stood straight and backed away until she took her place in the garden. Getting up, Amore walked across grounds pondering her life.

"My queen," a masculine voice called, startling her. The man from the night before stepped closer and placed his hand on his chest and bowed slightly, smiling. "I want to apologize for last night. I did not know that it was you," he remarked, holding a pleasant tone to his voice. Amore smiled, trying to lift her spirit but felt her attempt fall flat.

"Do not apologize, Your Highness. How were you to know?" The man grinned. "May I ask you a question?" Her mind at least shifted from its gloomy thoughts to curiosity. The prince grinned and nodded his head, his eyes sparkling.

"Anything for my queen."

"What is your name? For I have yet to hear anything about a prince." She did not mean it to sound the way it had come out. Blushing slightly, she smiled apologetically. "I am sorry, I did not mean for it to sound that way." The man continued to smile, reminding her of Braylin. The princess had been away for some time, and Amore was unsure of when she was supposed to return.

"No worries, I am not surprised that you have not heard anything about me. For the officials of Avalon have not been most pleased with me as of late. Though I thought they should have gotten over it by now." He continued, "I am called Gabriel." Curiosity began to grow on the inside of her. "I would tell you but I fear that our new friendship would be harmed, upon seeing that you have not heard of my stain against the family's name." He winked suddenly, seeming so carefree while yet stating the things he had.

"I fear that I have not done much better myself as of lately," Amore remarked, smiling softly before looking away. The man beside her chuckled suddenly, startling her.

"Do not take him so seriously. There are many things weighing my brother down, and I doubt that you are at the top of that list. Besides, I should probably not tell you the things we used to do as children, and the scolding we used to receive. I suppose myself was more of the reason rather than Xerxes. I must say though I was most surprised to hear that someone had actually captured the attention of my brother. I thought it was not even possible. I can see why."

Blushing slightly, Amore shook her head. "I do not deserve such high praise that you are giving me."

Prince Gabriel smiled. "Do not give up on him just yet. For you shall see he will come around." With that, the Prince bowed and continued on his way. He even walked the same way his brother did. Sighing, Amore slowly turned back to her seat, her heart heavy with cares as she leaned back. Part of her still wanted to explain everything to Xerxes, but what good would that do her when he would not even listen? The clouds loomed darkly above her, refusing to allow any sunshine to lift her spirits or those around her. Flustered, Amore made her way to the palace library in hopes to deter her darkened thoughts.

❧

The library was rather occupied until Amore stepped into the room and it quickly became deserted, leaving her in peace. Reading through some old scrolls she grew frustrated when she could not find what she was hoping to.

"My Queen," a startled voice said, making Amore jump as Talia blushed and bowed low. "I am surprised to see you in here, Your Majesty." Amore smiled slightly. "Is there anything I can help you with, my queen?"

"No, Talia, thank you." Amore sighed and shook her head. The scribes had written and Relix had signed the official papers stating the opposite from what she had told Amore. That she was receiving the full amount given for her to run the orphanage. The evening sun had set and Talia brought Amore a few candles to see with. Amore could see in her gaze the young woman was interested in what she was reading but did not want to intrude. Even with the money that was sent, with one woman providing for all of those children it was no doubt the place looked disheveled. Rolling up one of the scrolls, Amore set upon another and began to read the history on the building. She began to see why the young maiden enjoyed spending so much time in the libraries. It was fascinating reading about what had happened, who had founded it all. Amore began to wonder what was written about her in the palace scrolls. Watching the young maiden for a second, Amore was surprised when Talia bowed low and hurried from the room. Her heart flickered as he walked closer. They had yet to have spoken since that evening past. He remained silent as he got closer, before stopping at the edge of the table. His eyes glanced over the papers sprawled across the dark oak.

"I have come to a decision today," he remarked softly, not looking at her. Amore remained quiet as he stopped for a moment. "I have been looking into what you said and I believe you are correct." Amore began to smile then felt it slip from its place. The expression he still carried made her heart falter. She had gained something but felt like she had just lost something even greater. "If you can find the right place and materials, a new orphanage shall be built. Providing the funding does not take away from anything else." *What is he not telling me?* she wondered. He grew silent once more still not even looking at her.

"Thank you, Xerxes," she expressed as he started to turn away, making him stop. He finally looked at her but his expression was blank and he looked down.

"Can you promise me something?" he asked and Amore nodded eager to oblige. This time he caught her eyes and she felt her heart hurt even more. "Next time will you come to me?" Dropping her gaze, he turned and walked away, leaving her greatly ashamed of her own actions. She had not thought about talking to Xerxes about the orphanage. Over these past few weeks he had seemed to be so incredibly busy and with the rumors of war floating around, it had never crossed her mind to bother him with something so little as this. She should have handled it more dignified. She could see that now. Her mind had taken a step back and reverted to how she was before coming to Avalon. Childish and only thought of her own desires. Feeling completely defeated, Amore sank back into her chair and stared across the empty room.

It was well into the night before she left the library as she stepped past the large doors. Her heart sank once more at the sight of the empty room. She was starting to grow used to his absence and it did not make her feel any better. Morning came too early and Amore wished she could refuse to get up, but with the persistence of the maidens, she forced herself to rise and face another day. The fresh smell of rain did not help her as she started towards the library once more, at least there she could disturb no one.

"My queen," an excited voice called, drawing her from her stupor. Prince Gabriel flickered a wide smile as he neared and gave a playful bow, making her smile as he winked and stopped next to her.

"How is it, Prince Gabriel, that you and Princess Braylin always seem to have something to smile about?" she mused as the smile slid from his face.

"Not always," his voice suddenly becoming even, and he smiled sadly. "Partially I have not had to make the hard choices in life as others have. Being still a prince but living the way I do probably helps some as well. Princess Braylin, on the other hand, well, I cannot answer for her. She is more cunning than I am." The prince grew quiet. Her mind still grew with curiosity to why she had never heard of Prince Gabriel before. He let out a sigh as he leaned up against the wall. "How is your maiden?" he asked softly. Liana was pardoned, though she was still very low in spirits. Amore was not sure how to answer. She herself was caught up in her own dampened spirits.

"Good, I think she will overcome this." She took a deep breath and let it out as she started to walk. Trying to keep her mind busy. Prince Gabriel fell into an easy step alongside her.

"What about you?" he asked, even softer. Something about the prince reminded Amore greatly of a man she knew as a young girl. It helped to ease her mind off of Xerxes and her own foolishness.

"I shall be okay." The words sounded well enough though her heart did not agree with them. Hoping to avoid any more thoughts upon herself, Amore smiled. "I have been given permission to build a new orphanage," she said as Prince Gabriel studied her. His expression was compassionate and warm.

"That is wonderful." He looked forward and clasped his hands behind his back. Amore pondered the orphanage and the building around it. They all looked in desperate need of repairing. If placing the children somewhere else, could not more room be made within Roselyn to help those still living inside the city walls? "What are you thinking?" Prince Gabriel asked, making Amore smile faintly.

"The city of Roselyn, for the most part. The city seems to be prospering well. Though there are parts like the children in the streets, the orphanage. Though I do not think the Governor of Roselyn and I get along very well," Amore admitted. Prince Gabriel chuckled and nodded his head, an all too knowing look in his eyes.

"Yes, Lord Marcel. Am I correct?" Amore nodded and the prince shook his head. "He is a fascinating man. A good man, a little arrogant, but good," he reassured.

"Are you certain it is the same person we are speaking of?" she asked, making the handsome prince laugh as he nodded his head.

"I am afraid so." Lord Marcel is the one to discuss anything concerning Roselyn with. He was the city's governor, after all. Why could it not be anyone else but him? He had been less than cordial with her previous inquiry. How would he feel if Amore started poking around all of Roselyn? "Marcel is rather prideful as well. He does not take it well when something is found amiss under his care," Prince Gabriel continued as he let out a smile. "I am afraid you have wounded his pride greatly."

Sighing, Amore shook her head. "I did not mean to do so," she admitted.

"I am afraid oftentimes many of us do not mean the things we say. Then we are too stubborn to admit our faults." Xerxes happened to walk past as Prince Gabriel was speaking. Amore watched him as he barely seemed to even notice them. "Why do you not go and speak with him?"

Amore sighed, "Perhaps, I am too stubborn."

He chuckled as his eyes danced, "Perhaps but I think it would be best. He can be rather stubborn at times, unlike myself." He teased smiling fondly. "Xerxes just takes too much care upon himself, and often does not allow others to share it with him." The prince smiled then and nodded his head towards the way his brother had gone. Amore's mind tried to convince her self differently as she took his advice and began to look for him before finally inquiring of a guard.

⚜

Xerxes was resting in a quiet room. Calming her nerves she slowly walked closer as she pondered what she was going to say. Amore could easily learn the information she needed from the palace library, or the ever learning Talia. Yet she felt it was a meager attempt to bridge the ever-growing feeling inside her between Xerxes and herself. She had made plenty of mistakes in her lifetime but nothing felt as worse as the one most recent.

"You were asking to see me," Xerxes remarked even though he was still sprawled across the couch. Her heart skipped a couple of beats.

"I was hoping we could speak on a few things," she said as her mind began to muddle what she had planned to say. Pulling his arm away from resting over his eyes he studied her. For some time she had been unable to read his expressions. Today was no exception for her. *I am terribly sorry.* Stopping in the middle of the room, Amore took a sharp breath trying to calm her mind down.

"About what exactly?" he asked.

Why was it so hard to speak what was being said in her thoughts? Everything just needed to be said, spoken into words.

"A new place for the children." *Am I being too prideful to admit to him how terrible I feel?* she wondered. She continued on, remarking about different things, like what type of education would be provided to not only the children but the rest of Avalon's population. Anything to try and break the uneasy feeling settling upon her heart. Slowly sitting up, a heavy tired look passed over his eyes as he stared out at nothing in particular.

"What did my brother have to say on all of this?" he asked, his voice sounding flustered. Looking down, Amore struggled with the overwhelming feelings inside herself.

"I did not ask him his opinion concerning." She forced her voice to come out level and even. He kept his gaze away as the next remark felt like a knife into her heart.

"I figured you would have since you seem to be so closely acquainted with him." This time he did look at her, his gaze intense. Choking back the emotions that tried to blur her vision as Amore forced her hurt aside. "No matter, if this is what you desire, so be it then."

"At least it is one area I am not excluded from," she retorted, struggling to maintain herself as she glared at him. What had happened between them? How had they even gotten to this point, where it seemed they both were on different pages? Talking two different languages.

"What is it that you want then?" he exclaimed.

Amore wanted to laugh. How desperately she wanted to. She studied him for a moment. It was something she had always wanted. To be treated like she knew what she was doing, to be trusted. Her family always seemed to check her. That she only needed to concern herself with her studies. To always have someone watching over her. That somehow in Amore's world everything was perfect and she could not handle anything bad. To be treated like a child.

"To be trusted, that I can handle knowing what is going on." Her words were soft. Looking away, Amore sighed as she felt her shoulders slump. Amore slowly looked at him. He was quiet as he studied her. What was he even thinking? Feeling?

"Find your place then for the orphans." he stated, making her heart sink even further. She wanted to scream. It had nothing to do with the orphans. It had to do with feeling left out of his life.

312

She heard the rumors. She knew of the raids. So why then did he simply refuse to include her on anything else that seemed to be happening? Let her into what was bothering him so greatly.

"I made a mistake, to which I am most sorry for," she expressed, her eyes starting to blur. Before he could answer, and before the tears could flow, Amore hurried away. Burying herself deep within the library, she engulfed herself into reading on Avalon and its people. Anything to keep back the emotions, keep back the frustration and hurt that wanted to rise to the surface and overcome her being. As she searched through the chronicles her eyes hit an older looking parchment and she slowly pulled it out. The parchment was wrapped nicely in a beautiful ribbon.

> I make this record as of the fifteenth of Maron in the year of Ason.
>
> Overlooking the horizon of Miramar has helped to sooth my worries as I pray to God. Seeking His wisdom concerning the future. I have been at a great unease as of lately. Something has been bothering me. Perhaps it is the continuous tension between Emir and Avalon? I do not wish my children to continue on holding the long-lasting hatred between the two kingdoms. Why cannot one put aside the disagreements and realize that we are not so different? Throughout some time I have been looking back, trying to find where everything all started. Though my search has been in vain, I did find proof that at one time in Avalon's history, we lived quite peacefully with Emir. It appeared that the two nations were very close. What had happened?
>
> Signed,
> Clarice, Daughter of Eleanor, Crowned Queen of Avalon

> I make this record as of the twenty-ninth of Angros in the year of Ason.
>
> I wish that Miramar shall always be a place of worship to the Lord. That my firstborn son Xerxes shall follow in

the footsteps of the Lord God as well as his brother born shortly after him. Two sons, what an honor and blessing the Lord has given unto me. My father seems well pleased with my sons. Though at times they can be quite the handful and get into a lot of trouble. I can see within his eyes that he loves them dearly. To have such handsome sons is a sure blessing. If only those around me could see this as well.

Signed,
Clarice, Daughter of Eleanor, Queen of Avalon

I make this record in the oracles of the palace, in the year of Reina. My heart is growing weary of the hatred that fills these halls. To what means will it end? In war, a blood bath. I pray dearly that perhaps somehow we can look past the differences and realize both sides have something wonderful to offer. But no one will relent. As queen I can only go so far before protocol must be maintained. Protocol! I feel perhaps it would be best to just demand peace but that would not work as well. Even if one person wants peace, can you force others to abide by it as well? To what end? To what end... The death of all those who do not agree with what we have to say? Will that truly bring peace? Or even more unrest with those who edge the hatred on. To what end? Remien confides deeply in me concerning everything. How it is eating slowly away at him, I must do something to help. To lift the burden from his shoulders, to lift the burden from falling on Xerxes's shoulders. How he has grown these past few years. Such an intelligent young boy, already following closely in the shadow of his father.

Signed,
Clarice, Daughter of Eleanor, Queen of Avalon

It was late in the night before Amore returned to her private room. It felt like the world was placed upon her shoulders as she slid down into the chair to stare out into the empty night sky. The children remained in her mind as did the chronicles of Queen Clarice. No mention of God filled Avalon's palace. Back in Emir, frequent mention of a God filled the towns and palace though it was not mentioned in her own home. To why then was this knowledge escaped from her? She rarely thought about God, nor had she given much thought to why he was rarely spoken of.

"My queen," Talia called softly. Sitting up, Amore motioned for her to come closer.

"What is it?" she asked, studying the concerned young maiden. Talia was so mature for her age, so learned. Focused. The young girl could go far. Clarice's words flashed through her mind. *Promise me something, Your Highness! Make sure my daughter always has the best opportunities in life. Clarice shares the same name as the queen.* It had not really dawned on her before. She turned her attention back on Talia as the young maiden started talking.

"Are you well?"

Amore chuckled softly and nodded her head hoping to reassure the young girl. Even though she felt anything but.

"I just am not sure what to do about finding a place to put the children of Avalon," she admitted, smiling sadly. Talia's gaze grew thoughtful and it struck Amore then. Her expression in her eyes seemed so much like Braylin's in a way.

"What about outside the city?" she offered. It had not occurred to Amore before to look beyond the city walls.

"Thank you, Talia, I shall look into that option."

The young girl smiled, offering to help her change for the evening. Amore declined and dismissed the maidens for the night as her mind began anew with the possibilities. Keeping everything else at bay until later.

Fortress of Miramar

As SOON AS THE SUN rose the next morning, Amore was over-looking the map of Avalon and the possibilities of Talia's suggestion. Just a short distance from the palace was a small dot on the map. Gathering together those who had been helping her with the project as well as Lord Timothy, they all agreed that an outside location would suit perfectly. As soon as she could, Amore began to look, until she felt like she found what she was hoping for.

The town was perfect for the location of the new orphanage. It was not that far from Roselyn so it would be easy to protect. It surprised her greatly when she found out about the little town. Only a few subjects lived there but nothing was spoken of it. As they neared the guards around her grew uneasy until the carpenter asked, "My queen, this cannot be the city that you are thinking of?"

This surprised Amore. She studied the man for a moment and the uneasy look in his eye as she frowned.

"Why not? It is not that far from the city itself." As they neared, Amore's breath was taken away by the view. The land reached out for miles of rolling grass plains. The grass shimmered in the gentle breeze. The town itself was of a decent size, plenty of buildings that were not in too terrible shape. It looked like at one time, it would have been a favored place for the palace itself. The stone work and design of the town matched the palace. Mirage bobbed his head and snorted as his ears flickered around listening to the quietness of the freedom of the country.

"If you say so, Your Majesty," the carpenter remarked, shaking his head. As they rode into town, a middle-aged man hurried forward and bowed low.

"What an honor for her majesty to visit us!" he exclaimed, appearing very surprised at their arrival. As Amore dismounted, the guards complained and followed suit. Their reactions and opinions surprised her greatly but did not change her excitement over the opportunity that lay before her. "I am Nathaniel. What do we owe the pleasure of your visit to the Fortress of Miramar?" The man's eyes showed his uncertainty and excitement.

"How many live here?" she asked, looking around as she walked down the stone road that led through the heart of the city. It truly did look like a fortress at one time or another. The buildings were covered in dirt and age, but it appeared like the colt she had named Shytoc. That beneath lay beauty waiting to be revealed.

"Possibly thirty of us, my queen," the man remarked. "It has long since been left to return to the earth." Amore smiled as she looked at the beautiful old buildings. It must have been a wonderful place to see when it was built and tended to.

"I am thinking, sir, of rebuilding this fortress." Amore said, turning to him.

He looked greatly surprised as he stuttered, "Really? Are you certain!"

What was with everyone's reaction on this city? she wondered as she smiled. "Yes, you see. The king has given his consent to find a new place for the orphanage of Roselyn. This fortress is perfect, and looks like it would not take much work to rebuild. What do you think, Markus?" She turned to the main builder on her project. The carpenter eyed the town before nodding.

"It would not take a lot to rebuild, but I do feel Your Majesty, that this town might not be what you are looking for," he insisted, glancing at the guards who appeared rather tense.

"Why ever not?" Amore exclaimed, studying the carpenter as he avoided her gaze. The man named Nathaniel let out a long sigh. "It has been considered a cursed city because of the late Queen Clarice being ambushed and killed here." His words were quiet as he lowered his gaze. Looking around her mind tried to wrap itself around his words. No wonder they had reacted so!

"I wish I had known," Amore expressed, glancing at the guards. Someone could have explained it to her sooner. The man sighed and nodded his head.

"Since that day, everyone generally avoids Miramar. We have tried our best to keep the city from returning to the earth but it has not been easy when so little of people will come here. It was once the crown jewel of Queen Clarice's most favored retreat. She had the city built and established, Your Majesty." He sounded rather prideful about Miramar's heritage rather than the black stain against the city's name. It sparked her memory of the article she had read from the queen. Miramar. A place she would go to pray to her God. Amore continued on further into the town. Nathaniel rambled on about the fortress as Amore listened. Part of her wanted to ask him about it being a place of worship. Looking back at the frustrated and tense guards, she shifted her gaze to Nathaniel, who was still talking about the many fine qualities of the fortress. It already had many working and running wells. Many buildings only needed a little work to be used once more.

"I rather like Miramar. It would be considerably easier to use the fortress, once I speak to the king about it. I do hope to be able to start quite soon."

The man's eyes lit up as his smile grew widely. "Oh, thank you, my queen!"

Amore smiled faintly before turning her eyes on a house. The doors to the house were a smaller version of the tall doors on the gates to the grand hall. Except these doors had beautiful etched carvings in the wood. Patterns and swirls filled the wood.

Nathaniel had grown very quiet as Amore ran her fingers down the soft grain of wood. The doors looked well tended to.

"May I?" she asked, looking at him.

His gaze actually hesitated as the captain of the guard complained greatly, "My queen, I must protest! We have lingered here long enough. Let us return to the palace." She could hear the fear dripping off of his words. Sighing, Amore turned from the door, and nodded her head. The guards looked more than pleased. As they started back towards the horses, thunder suddenly rumbled in the sky above as lightening flashed through the clouds. The guards quickly hurried her into the nearest building that was large enough to house all of them as the rain began to pour.

⁂

The horses outside whinnied nervously. The guards were quite anxious. The storm had rolled in without warning, forcing them to remain in Miramar. Those who lived in the town had already taken shelter in their homes. Even as the thunder rumbled and the building shook from time to time, Amore could not help but admire the design of the home. Everything reminded her of the palace. The dark wood work mixed with carvings and stone. Amore had noticed that the town had once been well fortified. How had the queen been ambushed here? No doubt this place was once guarded closely. Watched carefully each time the queen returned. As the lightning flashed once more, the horses cried out as the sound of pounding hooves hammered the stone street. Through the window, one could see as the guards' horses and Mirage galloping away. The guards around her tensed as they all shifted closer to her, ready for a fight to break loose at any time. Taking a seat on the chair, she studied the room around her. Scrolls sat upon a shelf directly behind Nathaniel. His eyes were wide with fear as he studied the guards before turning his eyes back to scribble on a parchment. His mouth was moving quickly but no words escaped. A peace unexplainable to Amore remained inside her the whole time even with the high tension of the guards. A bright red wax caught her attention on one of the scrolls. From where she stood it looked like a symbol of the seal of the King. What would official scrolls be doing here, in a deserted town?

The storm did not last long as the rain came to an abrupt halt and the sun streaked through the clouds. Picking up the hem of her dress, Amore made her way to the main street. Grass grew in between the cobblestones. As she made her way to the main gate, where the walls surrounding had long since crumbled to the ground, Amore watched the horizon that remained empty as birds began to sing once more. The air smelled fresh and welcoming. Like new life. The dirt outside the gate was pounded with imprints of frightened horses.

"My queen, let us stay within the walls. Please, Your Majesty, I shall send another to return to the palace for more horses," the guard insisted as Amore smiled slightly.

"In due time," she responded as the guards glanced at each other. Letting out a long whistle that startled the guards, Amore smiled as she waited quietly. *Perhaps he kept running*, she thought as a few moments passed. Within seconds of the doubtful thought, she felt pride warm her heart as her black horse appeared on the hillside. His long strides at an easy trot before breaking into a canter. His reins broken from the scare. The others had yet to be seen. As Mirage stopped in front of her and lowered his head, his eyes looked fully concerned as he let out a long breath.

Where is Shytoc? The colt had bonded closely with Mirage and had rarely left his side. Her heart warmed once more as the bay colt appeared on the hill and let out a loud whinny in protest of being left behind. No sooner had he appeared did some of the guards' horses show up as well, cantering toward them. Not all had returned but enough that would satisfy the guards' uneasiness. As parts of the bridles were replaced with a few things from the town, the guards made sure Mirage's reins were the first things replaced. *I wonder what they would think if they knew he did not need them?* she pondered as she sat atop her horse and waited. Mirage was rather melancholy as his ears listened to her waiting. The ride back was short, as the horses kept an easy canter. The guards instantly relaxed as they entered the stable yard and the gates were closed behind them. Mirage pushed into her as she got down and he let out a long sigh before licking his lips as she pulled out an apple for him. Eagerly biting into the juicy fruit, his eyes looked toward Leah as he let a soft whinny. The mare responded anxiously as she placed her head on the rail and perked her ears forward. This made Amore smile. The mare usually ignored the stallion and cared nothing for him. She stroked her horse's neck one last time before a stable boy took him away. Amore felt the freedom of the countryside slip from her as she entered the halls of the palace once more.

Her muscles complained lightly from the short ride, reminding her how soft she had become. It made her smile as she gently brushed Mirage's fur from her dress. Amore wanted to ponder her words before speaking with Xerxes. How was she to explain the city she had found to be perfect would be the very city he probably distained? The Fortress of Miramar, it deserved a new chance at life, she would hate to see the beautiful fortress fall to any more ruin than it already had. Yet, she would understand why if the city was rejected. Taking a deep breath as she gathered her thoughts and headed to find Xerxes, she just hoped the Captain of the Guard had not already reported to him.

Her heart skipped a couple of beats. They had barely spoken more than a couple of words to each other. As she neared him in a large open room with a large map drawn into the floor, Amore feared that this was going to be no better than the other times.

"What is it?" he asked, his back still to her. At least this time he did not sound angry like he had before. Perhaps the Captain of the Guard had mentioned nothing to him yet.

"I found a beautiful place. I did not know the fortress even existed, nor did I know what it meant to the palace until we arrived."

"Any place except Miramar." His voice sounded hurt as he continued to stare at the map of the known world. So the Captain of the Guard had talked to him already.

"It is the perfect place for a fresh beginning, for the fortress and for the children."

"No."

"You cannot hang onto the past forever!" Slowly walking closer, Amore kept her eyes upon him as he continued to stay where he was. "You need to let her go, and look to the future."

"How can you speak such things when you yourself have not done the same?" he retorted, turning to face her this time, his gaze guarded. "Do not speak to me of looking to the future, when I know not what is to become of it." He stopped and looked down. "I know not of the present. Build your city, I want to know nothing concerning anything of it."

"You do not get it!" She wanted to scream but kept it under control as her heart felt like it was starting to crumble on the inside of her. He turned to face her again as she hoped that somewhere was the man she had desperately fallen in love with. That perhaps maybe somewhere he still cared for her as well. "It was never about the city."

"Then explain it to me. For I know not what to think anymore."

Her explanation fled her mind as she studied him. Sighing, Amore lowered her gaze. No words would come to her mind when she desperately wanted to speak what was in her heart but knew not how to speak them out loud. Turning away from her once more, he continued to study the map.

"I am leaving for three weeks. Perhaps by then you can explain it to me."

With a heavy heart, Amore turned, her heart caught for a brief second as Prince Gabriel stood within the room. He lowered his gaze as she walked past, determined to not look the prince in the eyes. She kept her pace quick, trying to escape her thoughts. *Could I have done such a terrible wrong?* Deep down she knew that it all started well before leaving the palace late in the evening with the maidens. Slowly the bridge had been built. Each caught up in their own reasoning. *I feel so...*

"My queen," the prince's voice pulled her to a stop as she watched him walk closer.

He surely cannot think there is anything between the prince and I? she thought suddenly. Prince Gabriel and Xerxes were brothers, Xerxes born only moments before Gabriel. What had caused such a rift between the brothers, to have Prince Gabriel's name never mentioned within the palace walls before? To only hear of him when he suddenly returned back to the palace after years of being away. As he caught up to her and stopped he smiled apologetically. "What can I say to comfort you?"

She smiled slightly and shook her head. "No words are needed, perhaps it is best if we speak not so frequently with each other." She really liked the prince but if it meant erasing any possibility in Xerxes's mind of something more between the prince and herself, she was willing to distance herself from anything. He looked surprised.

"Surely you cannot think him to be..." Smiling, he sighed and nodded his head. "If that be what you wish, then so be it." Bowing, the prince slowly turned and began to walk away.

"If I may, Prince Gabriel, ask of what you meant before—" Stopping, he turned to look at her and smiled before she could finish. The prince's smile faltered and he looked away for a moment. "I am sorry, I did not mean to cause you any hurt." Shaking his head, the prince sighed and took a step back in her direction as Amore began to feel guilty for speaking on such a personal matter.

"I fell in love not too long ago," he started, his voice soft. Amore smiled slightly. "To a beautiful woman. Smart, sort of like yourself." He grew quiet for a moment. "There were certain people within the palace that did not agree with her and thought it best to break all relations with her." Amore's mind began to spin with the new details, and her curiosity grew as her thoughts drifted toward herself. "So this woman fearing that she was threatening my life left late one night without saying good-bye. Against counsel that was against the idea, I went looking for her. I found where she went and we got married."

"That does not seem so terrible a thing," Amore remarked, and Prince Gabriel chuckled slightly and shrugged his shoulders as he appeared quite fond of the memory though it was frowned upon.

"Oh that is not the reason, that was easily forgiven but they requested I return to the palace without my new wife. When I declined and consented to give up my royal title and remain in the kingdom, she had gone to…well, that is another story. Good day, Amore."

If Prince Gabriel no longer lived within Avalon, to where could he have gone? Emir, perhaps? Though it teased the mind to think of Avalon's prince within her own kingdom and she within theirs. There was only Delmar and Cadaver. The mountain range was wide, and many had tried to cross it and were either never heard from again or came back barely alive. The ocean stretched for many distances before reaching other lands and other kingdoms. To which as far as she had read, Avalon has had to face before and remains a strong influence in those kingdoms. Surely Delmar could not have displeased anyone, even if it was some time back. It could not possibly be Emir? It seemed ridiculous with all the tension within the palace concerning her home. *Just as it is the daughter of Emir's commanding general married to the king of Avalon.*

From a distance, Amore could see Captain Ramses and she watched him as he made his way easily through the palace. Something about him unsettled her but since Crystal's departure from the palace she had no problems coming from him. He mostly seemed to keep to himself and many of Avalon's officials.

She watched him until he could no longer be seen before moving on herself.

Without warning, Prince Gabriel surprised her one evening as he explained about his imminent departure. Amore felt greatly responsible for his decision to leave early but dared not to ask it. Amore walked with him to the stables, she felt the guilt weigh upon her. Gabriel climbed upon his mount and smiled greatly at her, as his horse shifted.

"It was an honor to meet you, Queen Amore. May you live a long, healthy, joyful life," he remarked before his eyes shifted behind her. Turning her head, Amore caught Xerxes standing near the palace wall watching. Dipping his head to his brother, Prince Gabriel spun the mare around and waved before the animal cantered away. Uncertainty flickered in her as she watched the prince ride away. Watching Xerxes slowly turn and disperse back into the palace made her heart beat harder. Life was too complex. She wished she could go back to a simpler time when all she had been concerned about was avoiding her studies. Now she wished she could avoid her life. *Sometimes we are too stubborn to admit to our own follies.* She was just as guilty of it as anyone. No matter how sorry she felt, it was impossible to make Xerxes allow her into his own troubles. What was bothering him so much that he refused to share it with her? Mirage lifted his head off the rail and snorted as he watched her walk closer, his ears perked forward as his dark eyes watched her. Wrapping her arms around his neck as she entered his pen, she smiled as he stepped back and nudged her hands looking for an apple she had not brought him. *I wish the Princess was here, maybe she could relieve my sorrows.* The Princess had yet to return to the palace.

"Forgive me this one time for not bringing you something," she remarked, stroking his silky face as he kept his head low, soaking in her attention. Her eyes hit the colt dozing in the back of Mirage's pen and she sighed. Mirage helped to comfort her conflicted emotions until palace soldiers began to lead a large ground of saddled horses past, reminding her of Xerxes own imminent departure. She did not want to leave things between them the way they were. Pulling the hood up over her head, Amore made her way back to the palace to watch from a distance. No doubt, he would not want her there anyways. Xerxes soon emerged from the palace, at first he seemed solely focused on Leah in front of him but he paused suddenly and looked toward Mirage before swinging up onto his horse without looking around. Conflicted with her emotions, Amore watched Xerxes ride away. He would not be back for three weeks. During this time, Amore was left in charge of the palace and handling any matters that came to her. She wished they would be parting under different circumstances. Her heart still hurt greatly about the actions that had yet to resolve the wedge it had created between the two. Turning slowly, she made her way back into the palace and found the diagrams for the new orphanage. The Fortress of Miramar was already underway in preparation. She tried to force her mind to focus upon the drawings before rolling them up and sighing. She had wished someone had told her what Miramar meant to the king. Once she found out she understood the guards and carpenters' hesitation when they had arrived at the town. Amore buried herself into plans for Miramar. It helped to numb her mind and her heart as she put her own troubles in the back of her mind.

"My Queen," Clarice said late one evening as Amore blankly stared at the map. The only light she had was the moon and candles. "You should be resting."

Smiling faintly, she nodded her head but Clarice did not leave as she kept her eyes upon Amore. "I cannot sleep," she remarked softly as Clarice's persistent eyes never left her.

"Perhaps a hot bath would do best to relax you?" she offered, and Amore shook her head. She was in no mood for pleasantries.

"What do you think of Miramar, Clarice?" she asked softly as she stared at the map. Clarice drew closer and smiled gently as she glanced at the map for a moment.

"I think you are worrying too much over this. Quiet your mind and be at peace with it."

"Be at peace? That is all anyone will tell me. Not the truth, not what is really happening, just be at peace!" she snapped a little too hard and sighed, shaking her head. "I am sorry, Clarice."

"Do not apologize, Your Majesty." Clarice slowly sat down in the nearest chair to Amore, her gaze off to the side. "I know what it feels like to be in the dark from your family. It is not a pleasant thing." Growing quiet, Clarice studied the map before looking at Amore. "I think Miramar makes a wonderful city for your plans. It once was a beautiful place and I was saddened the day it was left to ruins. The late Queen Clarice would have been as well. She loved that city, had it built herself. She searched for months until she settled upon that place." She chuckled and shook her head. Amore could not imagine not knowing all this time who killed her mother. Perhaps she had been hasty to choose Miramar. Yet nothing in the records could be found about it.

What about the scrolls in the town? "Are all officials palace scrolls kept only in the palace library at the hands of the officials?" she asked. She knew it was the seal of the king on the scroll at Miramar.

"Yes, expect those that are sent out by the hand of the king to alert the kingdom concerning important issues. Carried by the couriers on horseback." *Those scrolls could mean nothing then.* "Please, my queen, get some rest. It will still be here tomorrow." Conceding, Amore gave in and instructed for Clarice to watch for her in the hall. Rolling up the map and the rest of the scrolls, Amore began to put them back. Hearing the door creak, Amore figured that it was just Clarice returning to see what might be taking so long but the hushed voices told her otherwise as she froze and blew out the candle nearest to her.

"What do you mean you cannot find them?" the first voice was unrecognizable to her as she slowly drifted back further into the library. "If anyone reads those, it will not only be your head on the line but mine as well. So I suggest you search! Hard!" The first person turned and the door creaked again as Amore's heart pounded as the second person drifted closer to her. Their shadow from the moon revealed how tall and big the person was. Taking a deep breath, she held it as they drew even closer. Her heart beat pounding in her own ears. The person stopped suddenly as he appeared in the aisle, but he was turned away from her. Amore could not see who it was, but she did not really wish for them to find her out. As the door opened and a light shone brightly in the room, Amore sucked in a breath as the man turned sharply and disappeared into the library further. The only glimpse she could see was a silver ring upon his right pinky finger. The symbol on the ring was not like any Amore had seen before. Taking her chances, she slipped through the library and out the door that Clarice would be waiting for her. The maiden looked at her quizzically but said nothing as Amore slowed to a walk and made her way back through the palace to the room. Her mind freshly awake as she pondered the man's words.

Councils of War

THE PALACE SEEMED ODDLY QUIET as Amore stared blankly at the plans for rebuilding the town. Miramar was still the perfect place for the children. It was close to the palace, barely a day's ride. Easy to rebuild and protect. Xerxes had not rejected the idea, but the impression Amore was given was that of great displeasure. Her mind shifted back to the event two nights before. Who where those men and what had they been looking for? Was there a scroll that would reveal who was behind the raids? Talks of war still lingered amongst the palace. War, the idea hurt every time she heard it. Yet it seemed inevitable. The certainty that Emir was behind it all was relentless. Everyone was ready to devour Emir at any time, all that needed to be done was for it to be declared by the king and Amore's worst nightmare's would come true.

"My queen," a voice called softly, drawing her attention away from the plans. Clarice slowly walked closer, her eyes heavy and tired. She bowed low waiting for Amore to call her any further.

"What is it, Clarice?" she offered, instructing for her to approach. Clarice smiled slightly as her eyes shifted toward the plans. "I feel like I have messed everything up," Amore admitted out loud and sat down in one of the chairs. Nothing seemed to be going right. Her plans came to a halt with the town of Miramar. Everything between Amore and Xerxes seemed to grow colder by the passing moment. War. At this point, could it even be prevented? Or was the demand for justice ringing too loudly, clouding the minds of the people to the truth. Someone else had to be behind the raids. Even though her father cared nothing for Avalon, she hoped that he would not stoop so low as the start of the raiding. Provoking Avalon's anger, it did not seem possible. It was not in her father's nature. Amore's heart began to pound as the room began to spin slowly at first. Resting her head in her hands, Amore took a deep breath to calm the nauseous feeling inside her. She had yet to eat this morning, that had to be the cause.

"That cannot be. Your Majesty, are you well?" Clarice's voice asked from somewhere. Until the feel of her hand was on Amore's arm. "Amore?" she asked as Amore finally looked up at her and tried to smile.

"I am fine, Clarice." Blinking a few times, Amore took a deep breath and straightened herself up. "I just need something to eat, is all." Without any more words spoken, Clarice had someone bringing Amore food and requested for her to relax. As Amore protested she could see the determination growing in Clarice. Obliging to the maiden, Amore had something to eat then rested for a while.

"Namur," Amore called as the maiden quickly showed in the doorway, her eyes bright as she awaited for instructions. "I wish to ask a favor of you." The maiden nodded as she walked closer and Amore began to tell her about the scrolls in Miramar. "It would probably be best if I was not the one to go get them. But I am most curious about them. Perhaps they shall shed some light upon the fortress for me. Find a couple of trustworthy guards to accompany you in your search."

Namur nodded and hurried away. Amore wished she could be the one to go to the town but knew it was best not to with everything that had been going on. As she continued throughout the rest of the day handling little things brought to her, Amore slowly began to feel useful and enjoyed it. Though she still felt guilty over the parting between herself and Xerxes. When he returned, she would make it right.

Namur returned late the next day. She looked exhausted as she found Amore and bowed low. A pouch was slung over her shoulder as Amore dismissed the others.

"What happened?" she asked as Namur sighed and set the pouch in front of her.

"The man Nathaniel was very helpful but we ran into some complications on the way." Namur slowly sat as Amore opened the pouch. At least seven scrolls sat inside but none of them bore any mark of the seal of the king and she sighed.

"What sort of complications?"

"A strange man was inside the town, he was very unsettling. He had been asking many things about Miramar's past, nothing that would seem unusual but I did not care for him. There was something about him that put me at great unease."

Nodding her head, Amore thanked Namur and allowed her to rest for the remaining part of the day. Without looking into the pouch, Amore had them tucked safely away. She would look at them later. For now she just wanted to walk and think.

"My queen!" a voice cried through the halls finally catching Amore's attention. Releasing the small animal, she stood as one of the servant girls came bursting through the archway, her eyes wide. Grabbing onto Amore's arm, the girl began to pull her. "My queen, you have to come see this!" Her voice was strained, causing worry to fill Amore as she raced after the servant girl and to the overlook that showed the court yard. Her eyes frantically searched until they landed on a rather large party parading itself. Her heart grew hard as her eyes narrowed at the man in front.

"What is he doing here?"The words sounded like venom coming out of her mouth as she glared at the hateful man. Racing to the grand hall just as they entered in like a conquering army, Amore kept her shoulders back as her gaze hardened. Lord Zander hopped casually off his horse and looked around with sheer glee in his eyes. Stepping to the front of the podium, the man boldly walked forward.

"Your Majesty, Queen Amore, such an honor to see you again." With the distasteful words spoken the man bowed low but every vibe that Amore got off of him was one of deceit and pride.

"I cannot say the same for you." Amore knew she dishonored him greatly but the man did not deserve honor. Zander smiled evilly, sending chills through Amore's veins.

"I would not say such a thing to Avalon's new regent, my queen." His words could not speak the truth! Amore let out a scuff and shook her head but quickly stopped when he raised his right hand and turned the back to her, revealing the king's seal placed on his finger. Amore felt her heart caught in her throat.

"We shall see." Her words were quiet but loud enough for just him to hear. Placing his hand on his chest he half bowed and grinned.

"Of course, my queen." Turning away sharply, Amore's heart pounded as she departed quickly from the room. Zander regent of Avalon? Who in their right minds would entrust that man with power. Any power, he should have been stripped of his title and kicked out of Avalon.

❧

To what madness had led King Xerxes to put Regent Zander in charge? He had often spoken of disliking the man. Something most definitely had to be wrong! If only the Princess was back. What was taking her soon long sense her departure weeks before. *Unless she found out!* The thought stopped Amore in her tracks. It quickly dissolved as the princess herself stepped out of the archway, her gaze soft as a small, sad smile spread across her lips. Amore poured out everything to Braylin, unsure of her mixed feelings.

"It cannot be true! Xerxes either had to have been tricked or Zander stole the ring!" she reasoned. Braylin sat down on the banister and sighed, her eyes low.

"I am sorry, Amore, but it is true. Xerxes will be leaving... him in charge of Avalon. He will be the second most powerful man." Braylin's spirits had to be very low. Amore took the spot next to the princess, a woman who had Amore's total respect and admiration.

"To what reason? Have I done something wrong?" Amore asked. Before the beautiful woman could answer a shadowy figure stepped through the archway furthest from them. Amore's heart was torn between joy that he had returned to pain, fear, and annoyance. Braylin gracefully bowed out, taking Amore with her. She could feel everything wanting to flee inside of her as he walked closer. His posture was exhausted but his expression held a strong reserve like Amore had never seen. Lowering her gaze, she shifted as he grew closer.

"Welcome back, my king." Her voice sounded not like her own as it responded unwillingly. Amore refused to look at him as he stopped in front of her. She desperately wanted him to state that Zander was mistaken. He could not have been placed in charge. He could not have power of the whole kingdom. Being the second most powerful man there was. His hand slowly lifted her chin but Amore kept her gaze downcast.

"Do not look like that," he expressed his voice quiet. Three long weeks felt like a lifetime. The parting they left upon each other seemed to still be there. Having not worked itself out in the absence of his presence.

"How would you like me to look?" she asked as her heart flickered, threatening to stop altogether. Her gaze slowly rose to look at him fully, as his hand still held onto her chin gently. The reserved look remained steady in his gaze, even as his expressions softened.

"Like perhaps you have missed me in some way."

Her heart sank as her shoulders fell forward. How desperately she had missed him. How she had wanted to make things right the moment upon his return, but everything was thrown asunder by Zander's prompt arrival.

"I have greatly missed you," she expressed, standing up and turning away from him. "More than you know." Chills shot through her arms as his fingertips brushed against her skin. The warmth of his breath heated her neck. Taking a sharp breath to keep her mind clear. "I must be going," she pulled away from him. The hurt in her heart fresh. Catching her hand, he pulled Amore to a stop, making her turn to face him. His expression confused and partly hurt at her rejection.

"Then why do you want to leave me so quickly?"

How could he even ask such a question? Her heart jumped as she wanted to cry. "I have greatly offended you," she expressed as the words slowly began to form in her mind. There was no other reason to why he would not leave her in charge of the kingdom. "There must be no other reason."

He frowned as he slowly pulled her closer. "What do you mean? You have not offended me in any way." He finally stopped when she stood directly before him. His gaze searching hers. "Because of how we parted last?" he asked. The tears threatened to blind her as her heart kept sinking lower.

"The Regent…Zander."

He sighed then and looked away, growing her confidence as she continued and the words started on their own. "To what am I then? If I have done nothing wrong to offend you yet I am so easily cast aside!" Amore's voice grew passionate. Lowering her gaze from his, Amore turned away. Was she nothing more than someone to wait upon him when he returned? Nothing more than an object of his affections? She knew deep down he was so filled with councils of war. Weighted down by making decisions that affected a kingdom, but her own feelings and hurts crowded her reasons. "Are you going to war?" she asked suddenly, her eyes staring out at the night sky and the land that stretched beyond what her eyes could see.

"We march on Emir in four days' time." His voice sounded hollow, empty. Her heart felt like it was shattering like a million raindrops falling at once. "Amore." His voice rose slightly as his hand clasped around her arm. Pulling away, Amore did not dare herself to look at him, fearing tears would overflow. Torn inside, Amore felt like it was eternity before her body moved pulling away from him and disappearing into the shadows of the night. Morning would be upon her sooner than she cared for. Returning to a private room, Amore spent the night alone as she struggled with the weight in her heart. As morning came, and the announcement declared, the palace seemed to light up with the chance to squander Emir and finally be rid of their neighbors. A feast was declared for the army commanders and their king. A victory celebration before the blood was shed. The pounding of her heart would not stop as the nauseous feeling grew.

Amore attempted to hide herself in the depths of the palace to drown out her thoughts. To condone her conscience to being oblivious to the world. Perhaps she was stuck in a terrible nightmare that was unending. A dream that refused to loosen its hold bringing her back to life. She felt empty and numb. At least she was slowly distracted by the world slowly spinning. Sliding down the palace wall, Amore stared blankly across the grounds until a soft nose wiggled against her fingertips. Scarlet, the beautiful fox. Her silky fur felt wonderful to her fingers as she brushed her hand across the animal's body.

"Amore." Her name was softly spoken. If she was not so nauseous she would have thought it had come from the fox itself. The princess slowly sat down beside her, her brown gaze concerned. "So what are we going to do about this?" she inquired, making Amore frown. What could she possibly be speaking about?

"About what exactly?" she implored as her world slowly stopped spinning as her mind focused on the princess before her. "Zander, perhaps?" she managed shaking her head. "To what excuse can we give for him?" *Tell Xerxes what he has done.*

"Have you told Xerxes about the afflictions he has committed?" Braylin expressed Amore's thoughts. Shaking her head, Amore laughed harshly.

"No doubt I shall be asked why I had not said anything the first time." Why had she not told when Zander attacked her while here with Princess Almeria? Would it not have spared the events following?

"Are you all right, Amore?" Braylin sounded worried as the look in her eyes slowly changed. Smiling, Amore took a deep breath and looked away.

"I shall be perfectly fine," she reassured, but deep down she felt her world slowly closing in around her as a heavy feeling began to squeeze her heart. If Avalon was marching to war, Emir would be ready. Her father, her brother, and her husband. The people most dear in her life. How long would they last? How long could she last? Would her heart give out in the weariness that ensued? The thoughts of war drowned her mind in despair. "When does the party subside?" she inquired, not really caring for the answer.

"Two days' time no doubt. The army is marching then. I am worried about you, Amore," Braylin remarked, making Amore smile as she shook her head and looked down at Scarlet.

"To what is there to worry about?"

Braylin allowed the subject to drop as they both fell into silence. *To what is there to worry about?* Amore returned to her private room, in attempts to sleep. Once more it fled from her, taunting her ever so often. Weary and exhausted, Amore rose slowly the next morning. The sun was shining but the world might as well have been painted in a deep, dark, despairing gray. She barely realized nor felt the maidens helping her dress as she stared out into the sky. *What is wrong with me?* she pondered as she struggled to focus past the heaviness upon her heart. Her emotions were torn apart, more than they had ever been before. She never felt this way before and it concerned her greatly. She faintly heard someone clap their hands and everyone around her disappeared.

"My queen," Clarice's voice rang in her ears, as she appeared in front of her. Her dark blue eyes focused strongly on Amore. Taking the chair, Amore kept to herself as Clarice started to brush Amore's long hair. "I wish greatly that you would be in better spirits, Your Majesty," Clarice remarked. *Perhaps if I had been able to sleep better these last few nights.* She credited this to her unending thoughts raging inside her and the ever-sinking sick feeling that was growing. "Perhaps tonight we shall get something for you to sip on to help you sleep better," she mentioned, making Amore smile slightly.

"Nothing escapes you, does it?" she asked.

The older woman shook her head. "No, especially when Namur reports to me of how badly you have been sleeping," she remarked. Of course, the maidens took turns sleeping in a small room off Amore's in case she needed anything. No doubt they reported to Clarice how badly Amore was doing. "Would you like to share anything with me?" Clarice asked softly. Amore's smile faltered as she shook her head before getting scolded from Clarice. Clarice slowly made her way around front and crouched down in front of Amore, her deep, thoughtful gaze never leaving her. "I care to think that perhaps women do not realize their full potential," she said, making Amore frown as the smile grew upon Clarice face. "Surely men think that perhaps we are not so important in the world of protocol and court life. But I would like you to show me a time where men did not need the woman. Even if they refuse to admit it." Standing up, Clarice went back to fixing Amore's hair before quietly adding, "Remember that today, you have a dinner with the officials' wives and the wives of the soldiers and other influential people."

Frowning, she searched her mind. "Concerning what?" she asked.

Clarice remained quiet before slowly answering, "The men are having a feast to march to war. So Lady Tamar asked for permission for the women to gather together in their own feast."

"It has been approved then?" she asked. Clarice nodded her head as Amore sighed. It was the last thing she wanted to do. Celebrating death in war. What part of celebrating could ever come from such an occasion?

"It would be unseemly for the queen to not attend such an occasion," Clarice remarked softly, making her heart sink a little further. *Wonderful*, she thought as she slowly stood.

"What time?"

"It starts at midmorning, Your Majesty."

Turning to face Clarice, Amore took a deep breath and nodded her head.

A wide smile slowly worked across Clarice's face, making Amore curious as the older maiden studied her. "What is it, Clarice?"

The maiden kept her gaze before quickly remarking, "Nothing, Your Majesty. Though I feel you shall find out soon enough." Her words confused Amore. So she pondered them as she walked through the palace. What could she have possible meant by that? The hallway was quiet as she walked along. The smell of the cooks preparing breakfast made her stomach complain as her mouth watered at the smell. Her pace slowed as Zander appeared in the distance. Everything within her cringed at the arrogance of that man. She did not even want to think of his name. His eyes studied her as a confident smile flashed across his face. Disgust filled her as she sharply turned away. Regent, regent. How had he been named Regent of Avalon? A person such as himself does not change that quickly, that easily. She knew. She knew when he left before, he left without a fight.

"My queen," his voice called after her. Amore desperately wanted to keep walking but her eyes could spot one of the officials in the distance as his attention turned toward her as well. He smiled as he gave a quick bow to her before straightening. "You must understand, Your Majesty, that I am most apologetic. I can understand the feelings you must have toward me. Be assured,

I would not be regent right now if the king was not so worried about your well being." His words were like a venomous snake sinking its fangs into her arm.

"I can assure you that my health is perfectly fine, Regent. Be confident of this, I do not care for you. Nor will I ever render that decision," she retorted, narrowing her gaze at him as his smile stayed firmly in place.

"Now, my queen, let us put the past behind us. Surely you cannot be angry with me for what happened with the Queen of Delmar?"

Amore wanted to hit him. Everything inside her desperately wanted to. She contained herself as his smile deepened.

"You will not get away with this," she remarked, her gaze narrowing, but the confident arrogant look stayed firmly upon his face as he moved on his last words ringing in her ears.

"I already have."

Amore stood motionless watching him until he disappeared from sight. Her heartbeat pounding inside her ears. She did not realize that she was shaking as she glared after him.

"Evil, disgusting. My queen, there are countless of ways to accidentally—" one of her maidens started.

"No," she expressed, shaking herself from the moment. Turning her eyes back on the maidens who had been with her since the beginning, she smiled sadly. "We will not stoop to his level." Attempting to calm herself, Amore focused on the open ground she had only been to on rare occasions. The days were slowly starting to loosen its hold on the heat of the summer. This part of the palace thankfully was void of people as she made her way down the large marble steps toward the gazebo located near the center of the open grounds. The curtains shuffled in the breeze as she paced the floor thinking. The maidens sat upon the gazebo steps and remained quiet. Namur, Liana, and Talia had come to know Amore quite well. She was quite pleased with how well they all got along. Servants of the palace began to show up.

Within moments the space was transformed into a beautiful area to gather and eat. The officials' wives gathered first as Clarice showed and stood at the steps of the gazebo watching. Taking a deep breath, Amore forced a smile upon her face and her eyes to lighten their gaze as she stepped slowly down the steps. The women bowed to her respectfully as she took her seat before taking theirs. Amore's maidens sat on each side of her. The food was soon brought forth and her stomach churned at the sight. The tray set in front of her was filled with all variety of fruits, meats, breads, and drinks. Slowly Amore ate the bread and listened to the women's conversations as Namur leaned closer.

"Is my queen not well?"

Amore flashed as smile as it drew the attention of the other women surrounding them. "I am perfectly fine, thank you, Namur."

"Perhaps her majesty is anxious about her husband going away to war, as no doubt many of us are," Lady Marcella spoke up. The women gathered ranged from the officials' wives to the wives of the soldiers marching to war with their king.

"No doubt, that perhaps a little disapproval of it as well?" Lady Gemini remarked bluntly. The women grew silent as their gazes turned toward Amore. It was just more than that. Yes, she greatly disapproved of war, especially between Avalon and Emir. Disapproved greatly of the regent being place in charge. "Perhaps it is the regent that has our queen so greatly unhappy," Lady Gemini continued, quite confidently.

Amore checked herself from showing her frustration and anger as she kept her gaze level.

"War can be a most wasteful thing, I will admit to that, Lady Gemini. As far as the regent is concerned, perhaps you shall focus upon your own affairs as I will mine."

Lady Gemini grew quiet as her gaze slowly lowered and silence fell over the group. Clarice quickly motioned in the entertainers to draw the attention away from the subject and distract those present. What was it their concern about the regent? No doubt he was still friends with majority of the officials. Her heartbeat started to pick up again, making her feel nauseous. So she tried to focus upon the entertainers. A woman a couple years younger than Amore who sat near to her slowly built up some bravery as the others were distracted.

"Your Majesty," she asked softly as Amore almost did not hear her but Liana gently nudged her. The woman kept her eyes downcast as the worried look stayed upon her face. "I am greatly concerned about the soldiers who are marching to war, and I feel terribly for feeling such." Her gaze slowly rose to look Amore in the eyes and she could see the fear written upon her face. "Am I wrong for feeling this way?"

Amore had never seen the woman before but her heart went out to her. "No." She smiled sadly as she looked down. "I am worried as well, and try not to put my mind toward it but it is hard not to."

The woman smiled slightly as she nodded her head. "I am afraid for my husband. From what I hear, Emir is a very powerful kingdom. Though no doubt, a grand victory would be in order when Avalon succeeds." Her words felt like a knife into Amore's heart as she struggled to keep the understanding smile upon her face.

"No doubt. Try not to worry, it does not help one very much." The woman flickered a smile and nodded her head as she turned her attention back to the entertainers as Amore's mind grew numb. Anticipation ate at her until it was late into the night and the fires burned from the basins to light up the world around them. Amore felt tempted to break up the gathering but kept silent until even the wives began to look wry and the gathering finally dispersed. Retreating once more, to clear, her mind Amore pondered her thoughts as she stared up at the stars.

Her thoughts suddenly shifted from complete despair to the chronicles written by Queen Clarice. Her prayers and beliefs in a

God who created everything. From the sky to the earth, the grass of the fields to the animals that relied upon it. The sea and every creature it contained, to every living thing upon the face of the earth. The queen's words sparked an interest in her but Amore had set aside the chronicles and was soon distracted once more by life. Her family rarely mentioned a creator God. With her mother's sudden and terrible passing, it seemed like a lot of things had changed in her family. Emir believed in a one true and only God. One that resembled the same in the chronicles of Queen Clarice. *If…If you are real.* She stopped and shook her head as she looked at her hands. Alone here in the garden with the animals in the midst of the night, Amore felt like the world was upon her shoulders. Falling to her knees, Amore finally let the tears spill down her cheeks. She could not do this anymore, handle the pressure placed upon her heart. The truths of her origin. Of her family ready to be destroyed. She could not handle the secrets that weighed her down. So she cried, with her forehead touching the ground. *Please, help me. Tell me what to do, show me why I am here. What is to become of me? I beg of you, to hear my cry. Do not let these kingdoms tear each other apart. Do not let blood be spilled that is innocent. If you are real, please show me.* As her tears slowly subsided, a peace swelled inside of her. Slowly Amore sat up. By this time the world was slowly growing lighter, as the birds began to chirp in the trees. No answer came to mind but the peace that lingered in her soul seemed to seep through her veins. She sat there in awe, unable to move. Unsure if perhaps she had simply fallen asleep. The gate to the garden squeaked as it opened. She could see the form of Talia until she drew closer to the large tree that covered the center of the enclosed garden of animals. Her expression was worried as her eyes finally hit Amore.

"My queen, I was worried when I did not find you in your room," Talia explained as her eyes studied Amore. "What troubles you?"

Amore sighed and motioned for her to sit. "I could not sleep, so I came down here...to pray," she explained.

Talia flashed a hesitant smile before looking down at her hands. "I have been praying as well, Your Majesty," she said, looking away. The young girl still amazed her greatly. So full of knowledge, wisdom, and understanding. She was so levelheaded and mature for her young age.

"You pray?" She did not mean to sound surprised but, well, she was surprised. For as long as she had been here, like her family, she had only read in the chronicles about a God. No one had spoken concerning. Talia nodded her head and tried to smile but looked weary.

"My family believes strongly in God. Because of the beliefs of the palace, we have kept quiet. Always praying for a hope, a redemption to be brought upon this kingdom. A returning to our beliefs."

"Whatever happened?" she asked, curious to know. Talia sighed as she kept her gaze turned away. "Please, I dearly wish to know more about God. I read some things in the chronicles of Queen Clarice but I cannot find any more."

Talia nodded her head and smiled hesitantly. "I know. I adore reading the chronicles both of her and the priests of Avalon. Though they had long since been cast aside. Not of the queen but the priests and the prophets. I sort of kept them to myself. I figured no one would miss them in the library." Taking a deep breath, Talia grew lost in thought. "I think a lot of the slow turn away from the Lord happened long ago. Not long after the hatred started between the kingdoms. It was slow at first until time slowly slipped and less and less chronicles were written by the prophets of God. Generation after generation passed and less people seemed to care about God and His Holy Word. It seemed like the kingdom would have been restored in Queen Clarice's time but with her tragic death it brought an end to any possibilities. After her death, any mention of God was very little spoken and very frowned upon." Talia smiled slightly. "From what my mother tells me, King Remien and his children were hurt greatly, and in that hurt they turned from Queen Clarice's strong beliefs." Shifting her eyes toward the gate, Talia blushed suddenly. "I should not be saying anything. I can get in trouble for doing so."

Amore's heart went out to the young girl. It explained the lack of mention of God in Avalon's palace. Nor anything to do with priests or prophets.

"Thank you, Talia. I greatly appreciate it. I promise I shall speak nothing of you mentioning anything to me. However, I have one question." Talia nodded her head as her eyes lightened up a bit. "What is His name?"

"He has many names. One of His names is Jehovah." Talia's words filled her mind as they continued to sit in the garden. Could it all be possible? If so why had he not done anything beforehand? Stopped the murder of Queen Clarice, who seemed to trust him so fully. The maidens tried to persuade her to eat but Amore had no appetite. The feast for the king and his men continued. Even the music from the grand hall pricked at her heart edging away the peace that had come upon her. The only thing she could be thankful for was not seeing the regent during this time. Rumors were spreading like a wildfire throughout the palace halls. They were empty words in her ears. Braylin, who had always been able to see the better side of things, seemed at a loss herself.

Can a heart feel this heavy and still allow a person to continue breathing? Torn between the growing feeling of complete despair and the peace that lingered in her heart. Even the soft evening breeze could not lift the mood off of her spirit. Her eyes gazed off deeply into the distance, wishing, hoping for an answer to her problems. Thankfully she was alone. Her maidens awaited her back at her room. Hugging the pillar next to her Amore felt a tear slip out and roll against her skin until it fell, landing on the stones below. She had to leave. There was no reason to stay. She had come to think about the possibility of what Queen Clarice had so wisely said before passing could have been her. But everything seemed to be stating otherwise. Hearing faint voices drew Amore out of her despairing thoughts. The hushed spoken words too soft for her to understand. She slowly took off her shoes to allow her bare feet to carry her across the stone flooring as she did not want to disturb the people whispering. Her heart picked up as she grew closer enough to catch the words.

"I have always loved you!" the first voice expressed, its deep tones giving away the masculine portal. Curiosity eased its way through her as she slowed her steps.

"Too much is happening and so little answers are being given."

They grew quiet and Amore's curiosity grew the best of her as she slowly leaned around the corner. Amore could not see very well so she stepped slowly out into the hall and her eyes recognized the back of Braylin kissing a man. The man saw her first and broke their kiss and quickly stepped away from the princess to which Amore could see him clearly now as General Damon. Braylin whirled around, her expression horrified.

"This is not what it seems to be," Braylin's voice shook as she tried convincing Amore otherwise. Braylin continued to rattle on until a sharp tone came out of General Damon that even surprised Amore.

"Braylin, enough, she knows now." His voice grew softer toward the end. Amore smiled as she studied the two. A sad sort of happiness filled her.

"To why should you two not enjoy some happiness? At least you can. Do not worry, your secret shall never part my lips. I am of no use anymore otherwise." The last sentence was not supposed to be spoken, yet it was out and could not be taken back.

"Amore, what could you mean? You are very important here," Braylin reassured, hurrying forward.

Stepping out of her reach Amore smiled and shook her head. "Do not play coy with me, Your Highness." Amore's voice shook slightly but she kept her gaze dry as she studied the two. The fact that General Damon had yet to speak verified her statement. "If I may, General, to what use am I? If the king has selected someone else to run his kingdom while he marches to war, if he no longer cares for me, am I nothing more than a slave? Is the palace my dungeon to where I am to sit and wait for my coming doom?" Amore asked, studying the man. They had never truly seen eye to eye with each other but Amore respected the man. He had a lot of dignity to him. General Damon's gazed locked with hers as he leaned up against the wall.

"Then do something about it, my queen." General Damon crossed his arms as he studied her. "I beg to disagree with you on several accounts. I have been the king's advisor for many years…" He paused for a moment and stood straight again. "I have not been able to do what you have done in these last few months. The people of Avalon love you, Amore. To which Zander has been able to play against you. You have wounded his pride and he does not care for it. For whatever reason the king has been blinded to him and has been listening to his corrupt council." She could tell the subject had been eating at the general as well. He stepped forward, his gaze intense. "Remind him who you are. Maybe it is time to tell him who you are." His statement made her heart almost stop. What could he possibly mean? What could she do? What did General Damon know of who she was? Her gaze flashed over at Braylin as she lowered her head, avoiding her gaze.

"I am sorry, Amorita." Her voice was soft, as Amore grew stiff, her breath catching in her lungs.

"I do not believe I know what you mean." It felt like a last attempt. A last plea for her sanity. The general let out a sharp laugh before smiling sadly and looking at the princess fondly.

"She did not mean to tell me, I tricked it out of her," he admitted rather bluntly.

Amore felt her heart flutter. When? Did that mean Braylin still did not trust her? "When?" her voice chocked. As her eyes danced between the two, she knew that someday this was going to happen. Her secret could not remain buried forever.

"A week after you revealed everything to me, I was conflicted upon what to do. After reading my mother's journal in the library, Damon found me there for other reasons." Braylin drifted off, avoiding Amore's gaze. It had been months since Amore had told the princess. General Damon knew all along? Her confused look must have showed because he quickly began to explain.

"I must say then respectfully state I will deny this. I do not believe we should be going to war with Emir. I think that there is something deeper behind this. Also if it had not been for you, my queen, I would not think this way. I will march with my king but if someone has any reasons to change his mind I will not stand in her way." Panic tried to fill her as she struggled to realize that General Damon knew. Yet he never said anything, even to her. Amore slowly walked to Xerxes's private room, her heart pounding as she stood outside the beautiful bridge and stared at flames dancing in the night air.

Why had she allowed them to convince her into this? Was she still in shock that General Damon, the commanding general of Avalon's army, knew? An army larger than the one Emir even had. Her heart hammered against her chest as her feet led her down the hall. She had almost convinced herself not to go along with it all but when the king had called for her, she took it as a sign this was meant to be. Her conversation with Talia in the garden lingered in her mind as she kept praying to God. The door slowly opened to the king's chambers and Amore froze. Her hands shook as she stood there. The guards waited patiently until she felt a gentle push from behind and glanced back at Braylin who quickly slipped back into the shadows of the night. With a thud that should not have rang in her mind as the doors closed behind her, Amore stepped closer.

You'll be meeting your mother soon. The thought floored through her brain. *You will never see your family again.* Proceeded shortly after. *I can do this, for my family. The one in Emir and the one in Avalon.* Feeling a deep strength surge through her body, Amore was sure she was dreaming as she walked boldly forward. King Xerxes sat on the railing surrounding his balcony. Amore stopped, still deep within the room, studying him for a moment. He looked fragile sitting there in the moonlight. Her courage started to falter. Thankfully, her voice saved her.

"You called for me, my king?" Who was speaking? It had to be someone beside herself. Xerxes spun around, startled by her. His expression softened slightly but did not hold the same look they had before, before they let everything grow between them. Amore felt faint for a moment so she dug her nails into the palm of her hand and straightened back up. She figured that the dizzy spell was from nerves.

"Of course, my queen. I feel we did not leave things very well the other night." He walked closer, smiling this time. *Do not make this hard on me,* she thought as he took a gentle hold of her arms. Amore studied his gaze for a moment, unable to read them so she turned her head away.

"To what might that have been?" she asked.

Xerxes let out a long sigh and sat on the bed in the middle of the vast room. She began to read the intentions for the reason she was here and it infuriated her.

"Amore, you are not easily replaced or cast aside. I just believe that a regent should be in place while we are at war. Zander knows a lot of Avalon's laws already…"

Amore felt her heartbeat begin to race as she stood frozen in her spot. Her mind was blank as her mouth began to speak separate from her own thoughts.

"Zander is blinding you. I recall a king who said that he could not be trusted!" Amore threw Xerxes's own words back at him as the pain of what Zander had done to her and others Xerxes cared for surged forward. How could he trust such a man?

"People change, Amore." He shook his head, his voice annoyed. Amore felt surprised General Damon was right. He was completely blinded by the man.

"Not that quickly. I thought you cared for me." Amore looked away, turning with the statement. Feeling his arms start to wrap around her, Amore pulled away before she could get trapped inside her love for him. "You are marching to war with Emir then?" she asked softly. Xerxes did not respond at first but it was enough of a clear answer for her. Turning around to face him Amore gaze grew strong as she look into the eyes that once showed her love. "Please do not go." His gaze closed as a loud sigh escaped and he stepped away from her turning his back to her as he placed his hands on the back of a chair.

"Do not do this!"

He grew hard but it only pushed Amore to finally make her secret known. If this meant the end at least she would be the first to die, she would not have to wait to know if the ones she cared for killed each other.

"You are going to war against my people."

He whipped around at her statement his eyes narrowing. "I am Emirian, Xerxes." Her strength grew even as he gaze grew confused and angry. Hurt.

"You are making this up to stop me from marching to war?" his voice grew louder and Amore suddenly felt small standing in front of him.

"I am not making this up! I am the daughter of General Alexander Divon, lady of the court of Emir, Queen of Avalon." Her eyes searched his darkened expression. A laugh suddenly escaped him as he sat back on the bed once more. He shook his head like she had just played a joke on him.

Donna Rahkola

"This is ridiculous. I knew you did not agree with war but going this far? Suddenly you are the daughter of the commanding general of Emir. Why have you not said this before?"

Shaking his head, Xerxes got up and walked back out to the balcony. The silence that followed began to eat at her as he leaned against the railing to look out over the garden below. "If this is true, why are you here?" His voice was oddly quiet. Amore felt like she had just been thrown from a horse.

"I never meant all of this. Why did you think I tried so hard to keep my distance from you? You made me fall in love with you. Then Princess Braylin got it in her head that I was meant to be here, convinced I would bring the kingdoms together. To keep us from war." Amore jumped as Xerxes whipped around.

"Braylin?" his voice astonished. Amore had not meant to bring his sister into this. She should have thought before speaking. Looking down Amore was lost for words. "What does Braylin know of this?" His tone was hard, his gaze flashed. Amore quickly looked away with no words to defend herself. Her heart was running wildly, as he brushed past her and paced the room. "Enough of this, I will discuss this more when I return." Amore's vision started to darken as her body swayed slightly. *Pull yourself together!*

"I…I…" That was all she could force out as the ground suddenly grew closer with each passing moment. Her world grew dark as arms caught her before she slammed in the ground below.

Everything around her felt strange, she felt such a weight upon her as she tried to look around but could see nothing. What was that smell? The stench of death and decay lingered in the air, it was so powerful. The land was covered in red as someone around her screamed. She tried to find the culprit but began to realize it was her own voice as her eyes found her father, brother, and Xerxes. Lying still, unmoving, not breathing, gazes empty beyond compare. *Settle her down!* a voice shouted in the distance as arms wrapped around her. Amore fought back, struggled with every-thing she could muster to return to the side of those she loved. *Get the physician.* They were dead, all of them! Her world began to fade into nothingness until a bright light flashed across her gaze forcing her to blink as the scene began to change. She could feel the soft cloth beneath her. As her eyes slowly opened her vision stayed blurry at first before slowly becoming clear. She was in Xerxes's chambers, her body felt heavier than normal as Amore rolled her head to the side to find Braylin sitting on the bed. Her head low as tears slid down her cheeks.

"Braylin?" her voice squeaked, causing the princess to startle before leaning across the bed to her and smiling.

"You are finally awake." Turning away from Amore for a moment, she hollered for one of the servants to find the king. Amore felt her head turn to look across the room as someone filled her vision shortly later. The bed beside her gave way as they took a seat. Their gazes locked for a moment before she felt her heart melt inside. He did love her. His eyes filled with utter worry and relief at the same time. She wanted to stay but her body demanded otherwise as it sucked her into a peaceful sleep.

As she slowly awakened, the sun felt wonderful against her skin as the nightmare still lingered in the back of her mind. The room was empty as the long drapes blew in the gentle breeze. Pushing herself up, she felt the weariness leave and she slowly slid her feet off of the bed. Her arms shook as she used the tall oak bed pillars to pull herself up.

"Amore, what do you think you are doing?" Braylin demanded, hurrying closer.

Taking a deep breath, she closed her eyes for a moment. "Where is Xerxes?" she asked softly. She wanted to see him, wanted des-perately to talk to him. Braylin grew quiet as Amore opened her eyes once more. The beautiful princess stared at the floor.

"He left this morning to head to war." She had to be mistaken, he could not have left. "I am truly sorry, Amore," she continued as she slowly walked closer, her shoulders sagging as her expression grew tired. "I thought with everything in me that…I am not sure anymore. Zander is regent, Xerxes still left with the truth known." Braylin slowly took the spot alongside her. "Can I be completely honest with you?" she asked, making Amore nod her head. Though her world felt like it was ending all together. Soon her nightmare would be true. "I did not have a high regard for Emirians. If war would have broken out before you had arrived, I would have thought no different. Since coming to know you, I feel very different about the whole thing. You have truly opened my eyes to everything my mother wrote about."

She grew quiet as she let out a long sigh and stared off into the distance. "It has only been a couple of hours but I already dread the coming days."

"You are not supposed to be the one with the bad tidings," she tried to tease. "Since I first saw you, you always seemed to have something to smile about." Sighing, Amore shook her head. What had happened to her? She had never experienced anything like that in her life. It scared her. "Did the physician have anything to say?" she inquired softly as Braylin stared off into the distance.

"He would not tell me. You scared me and Xerxes greatly. Has anything like that ever happened before?" Amore shook her head.

"I had been feeling ill for some time, but I counted to be the lack of sleep and distress from the rumors and everything that happened between Xerxes and I." She sighed. Turning her attention on Braylin, she tried to smile. "Your brother Prince Gabriel was here." Braylin had been absent when her brother was at the palace. She smiled slightly and nodded her head.

"I know. I had met him on his way to the palace. I had sent word concerning the councils of war. I thought perhaps he could speak with Xerxes and advise him against it. Then I decided to remain away for some time. I really did not want to know what might have happened between the two, so I thought it best to not be here." She slowly stood and squeezed Amore's arm. "Get some rest," she instructed softly before leaving.

The large empty room did not comfort her mind. Getting up Amore slowly made her way to the balcony and overlooked the land below. The time they had spent together upon Mirage seemed like lifetimes ago. The sun beating against her skin warmed her at least. The sky seemed unending as she stared up into the vast unknown. *I failed to stop the bloodshed. Failed to bring peace back into my own heart.* Turning away, Amore slid back onto the bed allowing the tears to sooth her. *Go to him.* The thought provoked her heart as she closed her eyes. She could not, it was impossible.

"Namur," she called out. The beautiful maiden hurried into the room, her eyes wide with surprise. "Help me get dressed, please." Namur tried to protest but fell quiet and began to help Amore. After she was finished, Amore ran her fingers down the beautiful dress and smiled faintly. "Thank you, that will be all. Please make sure I am not disturbed."

Namur froze, uncertainty filling her gaze. "My queen, you are not about to do what I think you are?" she asked. The peace that remained upon her told her she knew what had to be done. How it was all going to aspire, that she was uncertain about. "My queen!" she exclaimed as Amore remained silent. "You surely cannot do this! How do you expect to even reach the king in your condition? General Tiberus Damon has been sent to the palace to oversee the guards here. Oversee your protection. He is a most assured man," Namur insisted as she followed Amore down the steps leading to the king's private garden. "He is a well-respected man in Avalon. Please!" Namur gripped her forearm and pulled her to a stop, eyes pleading with her. "Do not throw your life away!"

Amore had no words to give her, so she gently wrapped her hand around her faithful maiden's hand and smiled. "Though you may not understand why I must do this, I ask of you to try not and stop me."

Namur slowly lowered her gaze as she let go of her arm and stepped back. "There is nothing that I can say to change your mind?" she asked softly.

She desperately needed to be going. Pulling the long cloak around herself and the hood over her head, she studied the maiden before her who had helped her so many times. "Thank you, Namur." Blinking, she looked up at her and frowned. "Speak of this to no one."

The maiden broke her gaze and nodded her head as she softly whispered, "As you wish, my queen." Turning away, Amore hurried through the garden. Wrapping a shawl around herself, she paused at the door and listened before gently pushing it open. To her surprise, no guards stood outside the doors, making her smile as she walked quietly down the stone hallway. Thankfully, the guarded path led almost directly to the stables. It took her longer than she cared for before being able to slip past the last guards before reaching the stable yard, which was only steps away. As the boys who cared for the horses mingled around the front conversing with each other and chuckling, Mirage's head could be seen just inside the stable. Perking his ears, he let out a soft snort and turned his head in her direction. She just had to get by the servants and guards then through the gate to the yard without being noticed.

"My queen," a deep voice called out behind her, making her jump. Whipping around with her eyes wide, she stared at the general whom she had only met once before. His fame was well known within the palace. Lucas Damon's father, Tiberius Damon. Both generals, he was once in the same position his son now occupied. His eyes were serious as he studied her before looking toward the building behind.

"Do not blame your maiden, Your Majesty. She is only concerned for your welfare. As I might add, she has every right to be."

Swallowing, Amore tried to calm her racing pulse. The man before her resembled everything his son stood for. The same dignity and certainty in wisdom written upon his face as it often was with General Damon. "I see little success of your venture with so much at stake."

Amore broke his gaze and looked away, his words trying hard to dissolve the peace within her heart. He grew quiet for a moment before adding sternly. "You are not just going before a king, you are wanting to go before his army, his kingdom. Even if you are successful, what do you think is going to happen to you? Is it that important to make your point assured in his mind—"

"General," Amore interrupted, turning her gaze up to meet him this time. "If you had a chance to stop something you knew was not right, would you not take it? Even if everything says that it will not work." He grew silent as he studied her. "I may not know how everything will turn out in the end, but if it can mean affecting someone like Queen Clarice has affected me through her writings."

"God? Is this where you are getting your motivations from? The writings of a God who the queen so strongly believed in but did not help her." His breathing came in quicker as he studied Amore and shook his head. "The king is bound by protocol of the land. How do you expect to stand against that? There is always another way, just be patient."

"By then it may be too late. Please, General, let my blood be upon my own head, and my beliefs in my heart. I must do this, you must understand."

He kept her gaze as they both fell silent with each other before he looked back at the stables once more. "Then I shall accompany you, even if it means to your end." Smiling faintly as Amore nodded consenting, he was not stopping her, so she could not turn him away, nor would he have taken no for an answer. The general appeared greatly displeased as he moved around her, the stable boys scrambled to their feet as he walked boldly across the grounds. Amore waited in the shadows, watching with interest. He spoke something to them and they nodded their heads before hurrying away. He waited until they were gone before motioning to her. Her heart leaped as she hurried across the yard and to her horse. He nickered in greeting. She saddled him quickly before wrapping a thick cloak from the stables around her. Mirage picked up on her excitement and began to dance in anticipation as the general led his saddled horse forward. Amore turned Mirage toward the stable gates that led out, but the general shook his head.

"This way, my queen." He muttered something else under his breath as he led his horse past the pens before turning sharply. Vines covered the wall as Amore frowned. No door stood before them. He began to peel away the vines to reveal an old door behind them, surprising her as he smiled slightly. The door was barely big enough for the horses to squeeze through, but they nevertheless did. Taking a deep breath, she mounted her stallion as he bobbed his head, eager to get going. As long as Namur remained silent to everyone else, she would be fine until reaching the Valley of Antigua. No doubt they would be there days before she reached them—if she was already not too late.

Her dream haunted her mind as they rode. Mirage kept the pace steady, sensing the urgency inside of her. He would stay with her to the very end, loyal and true. General Tiberius Damon's horse kept up well but could not match the stamina of Mirage.

The ride was taking more out of her than she expected. It seemed like it had taken them far longer to go as far as they did. She wanted to keep going, but she had already pushed herself and the horses to the limit; exhaustion filled her making the world spin. A small lone tent sat in the distance, making her feel like perhaps she was seeing things. Pulling Mirage up as they neared, she gripped the saddle to keep from melting off of her horse. General Tiberius Damon stopped alongside her and shook his head at the pitiful sight she was in.

"Not a word," she expressed, slowly pushing herself up. The hood stayed firmly upon her head, hiding her identity. The tent was rather large, but the pattern upon it was like none Amore had ever seen before. A man suddenly stepped through the flaps and stopped as he saw them. A smile flashed across his face.

"Hello," he called, stepping forward.

Spinning Mirage around to face the man, Amore stiffened. *Could he be a raider perhaps?* she pondered, looking around at the animals that surrounded him. Sheep, goats, and a couple of donkeys. He hardly seemed rather dangerous. "I am Joshua. I do not meant to frighten you at all," he reassured them, making her frown slightly. General Tiberius Damon appeared unconcerned at the appearance of the man. *How would he know?* Of course it could just be a lucky guess. "Please, rest yourself. Have something to eat," he requested, motioning her toward a cushion. Amore stayed upon Mirage, uncertain, until a young woman stepped out of the tent. Their clothing was rather different than Amore had seen in either country. Slowly sliding off her horse, Amore flung the reins over the saddle as Mirage lowered his head to the grass. "Good, good," the man remarked, motioning her toward the spot as another woman stepped out and smiled. "Peace be with you both," the man insisted, smiling as he motioned them toward the spots to sit.

Slowly sitting, Amore watched them both before the smell of soup reached her nose. Her stomach complained at how wonderful it smelled. "This is my wife, Hadassah, and our daughter, Rebecca. Our sons are tending to the flocks. Please rest, enjoy yourself."

"We cannot stay long," she informed, feeling bad for such wonderful hospitality. General Tiberius Damon remained quiet as he remained standing. "Where are you from?" she asked, studying them. The man smiled and glanced at his wife.

"We come from a land across the mountain ranges. We have been wandering for some time now looking for a place to reside, to where our Lord is bringing us."

Amore frowned as she kept watching the man. Something about him seemed quite different than anyone else. Besides the clothing and the tent they were staying in.

"I would be careful mentioning anything about God here. The people are not too friendly concerning the topic," General Tiberius remarked as the man turned his gaze upon the broad-shouldered man and let out a pleasant smile.

"I thank you for the warning, but I am not afraid. My God shall indeed protect me. As he has you."

This surprised her as he smiled. His wife Hadassah brought out the bowls filled with soup and took a seat. As they bowed their heads, Amore began to feel guilty and slowly pulled the hood from her head as she carefully watched them. Clear disapproval was written upon the general's face.

"We thank you, Lord, for getting us safely to this land, for protecting us, for your promised Word to have come to pass! Bless this young child of yours and the children that she shall surely bare! Amen." The man named Joshua seemed so at ease in their presence, so friendly and inviting.

"Have we met before?" Amore asked, frowning as he looked up at her and smiled.

"No, for we have never been to this part of the world before, nor doubt I that many of yours have been across the mountain ranges."

His words made her heart ponder as she thought about it. The young girl came running up and stared at Amore before slowly sitting down, quickly pulling the hood back up over her head and the diamond-laced band around her forehead she took a quick breath, breathing in the wonderful aromas. It was then General Tiberius decided to sit as the food was set before them.

"My queen," he whispered as she started to take a bite. "I feel that it would be best if I tried the food first." Obliging, Amore waited until he nodded his head and slowly began to eat the food set in front of her. She could see the curious looks in the woman's eyes as she looked down upon her daughter and smiled as the young girl continued to stare at Amore. The food tasted wonderful, and helped to calm the nerves inside her for the moment. It also made her desperately want to sleep but she could not risk it. It was taking long enough to reach the army.

"Are you a princess?" the young girl finally asked before being gently scolded by her mother.

Amore hesitated, before smiling. "Something like that."

"I am sorry, my daughter has a most curious mind," Hadassah apologized, making Amore feel a deep warmth in her heart.

"Do not concern yourself over it."

As the food helped to settle her insides, Amore began to ponder how far they were from the Valley of Antigua. It was enough for her to be going in front of King Xerxes, let alone tagging along was one of Avalon's most respected officers. Hadassah studied her with a curious look in her eyes. *If there was only some way, oh Lord, to make him stay.* She knew not of a way to withhold the general. A man tested in battle and wisdom. As Hadassah cleaned up the food, Amore pondered ways of how to stop the general from continuing as Joshua began to speak of their journey. General Tiberius Damon's horse was a war horse, trained to reliable, dedicated to remain with his rider. Mirage shuffled behind her and picked up his head, letting out a snort as did the other horse. Running around the tent in a start came Joshua's animals, all of them. His sons tried to corral them as the horses spooked and bolted. Amore barely caught Mirage's rein as he slammed to a halt and gave a little rear. Usually he was unconcerned about animals so his reaction surprised her. The general's horse galloped away with his reins blowing in the wind. *Go.* She felt terrible but in one smooth motion swung upon her horse, as Mirage tucked his hind legs and spun easily, bolting toward the south. Away from General Tiberius Damon and away from his horse. The animals of Joshua would never come close to catching Mirage and by the time it took for his horse to return, she would be close to the army.

Valley of Antigua

MIRAGE GALLOPED CLOSER. IT HAD taken her longer than she had wished to finally reach the army. Mirage's sweaty hide was evidence of his long journey. Shaking his head, the stallion slid to a stop on the hill overlooking the valley below. Both armies sat on each side, waiting as three horses from each direction cantered toward the middle of the peaceful valley. Their anticipation building in their cries, ready for battle. Her nightmares flooded back into her mind, making her heart hammer. It was the place that her nightmares had taken place in. Mirage danced beneath her, ready to charge into the fight. As the horses neared each other, she knew what had to be done. Bolting, Mirage propelled them down the steep hill and toward the men. The last of his strength eating up the ground as he barreled toward the middle of the valley. Pulling Mirage up, he slid to a stop, sending dirt and grass flying beneath his hooves. His neck arching as he slammed to a stop. Mirage's head lowered in exhaustion as Amore slid off her stallion. Her heart pounding hard against her chest as a light feeling tried hard to engulf her.

"What is the meaning of this?" King Xerxes's startled voice made her lower her eyes, refusing to look at him while she quickly gathered her thoughts.

How do I even start?

"I cannot be silent any longer." Her voice grew strong as she turned her gaze up. "You have been tricked my king. The palace has been taken over by the man who claims to be loyal when his heart is filled with deceit." Her voice rose as her eyes narrowed, staring into his wounded expression. His eyes pleaded with her to stop. Leah started to dance in place, causing their gazes to break as he settled his horse down. Feeling a warm breath against her shoulders, Amore turned around to find Sham, her father's stallion, nudging her. Her father's eyes looked exhausted and overjoyed at the same time. Her heart warmed at the sight of her father. A smile filled her face as she looked up at him.

"What in the world are you doing here, child?" he asked softly, his expression clearly confused as Amore cast a look at her brother, who quickly avoided her gaze as his horse shifted uneasily beneath him. Her father looked over at him as well before turning his attention back upon her and he began to explain. "Vainer gave me your letter. I have been so preoccupied; I should have realized something was wrong when I received no letters from either one of you." His gaze shifted upward with a distaste and annoyance. His words began to distract Amore away from her purpose as she shook her head. Having to put aside her own thoughts and focus once more upon what needed to be done.

"Please, Papa, listen to me. This is all a mistake. Our kingdoms have not been raiding each other."

She turned to look at Xerxes as she felt strength surge through her. "The raiders want you to go to war with each other, make both armies weak and easy to take over. Zander is behind everything." Amore stepped away from her father and back toward Xerxes. As she walked closer, horses began to whinny, catching everyone's attention. To her complete astonishment, Zander himself and his men galloped closer. Their horses oddly looking rather refreshed, as they neared.

"My king!" Zander called as he came to a stop and bowed low. "I apologize greatly! Her majesty is very ill and we were greatly concerned for her." Amore wanted desperately to retaliate but she kept her eyes focused on Xerxes, determined not to get sidetracked. Xerxes's gaze flickered back toward her as she kept his gaze. *Please, please, believe me and not him.* His expression was guarded as he continued to study her as his gaze flickered up, looking from her father to Vainer no doubt.

"I am telling the truth." She flickered her gaze at General Lucas Damon for a moment, but the look he had in his eyes made her confidence slip. Xerxes nudged Leah forward as Sham bumped into Amore.

"I would not advice coming any closer," her father, General Alexander Divon, snapped. Amore turned her head to look up at King Haman this time. His gaze was perplexed and conflicted. He had always looked greatly to her father for things concerning war. It had never been his strong suit.

"General," King Haman remarked, as Sham's warm breath blew against her skin. "Stand down." Amore let out a long breath as she turned her gaze back toward Xerxes who looked rather furious. It was then Amore noticed how calm her body was. Though she was shaking on the inside, she did not show it. Mirage flickered his ears and snorted as he stepped closer to her, once more returning to her side. His black coat covered in white foam. Sham reached over to sniff the other stallion before turning his head away once more.

"Perhaps it would be best to take into light the new circumstances and meet again," King Haman remarked, making Amore spin around. King Haman had always been a very wise man. Though he too had his own faults. He motioned for Alexander to step his horse back into line. Reluctantly, he obeyed as Sham easily backed up. "I also think it best if we all hear everything that Lady Amorita has to say."

"This is very interesting indeed," Zander remarked out loud before falling silent at the sharp look from Xerxes. Turning around, Amore studied Xerxes as he leaned closer to General Damon as the two quietly conversed. Amore had not thought past simply stopping them. She really had not even thought about how she was going to do it. Standing here between the two most important people in her life, she grew conflicted as she turned to look at her father once more, who she had not seen in months. Vainer had his gaze fixed straight ahead but Alexander studied her as he flashed a smile as she looked at him.

"It is agreed. Tomorrow when the sun reaches the middle of the sky, we shall gather. Be assured, any attempt made by Emir in any way shall be considered a declaration of war. Do I make myself clear?" Xerxes's voice was strong as it made her heart jump.

What now? she wondered.

King Haman remarked, "So shall it be."

The last rays of the sun sprinkled across the valley. It seemed to hold the world in a serene stillness. A warm breath blew across her neck, as she felt herself being lifted up. Leah's white neck arched, as she spun around easily and galloped back up the hill. Amore tried hard not to notice the looks of the soldiers, nor feel the tension in his arms as he rode Leah straight into his tent, no doubt. As he swung from Leah and helped her down, she tried not to wince at the tightness of his hands. His gaze was frustrated and angry as he turned sharply from her and walked to the other side of the tent, his shoulder's tense as he spun around to say something but froze and began to pace. Amore watched him as the words froze in her throat. What was she to say? What could she say? Nothing seemed fitting.

"If it was not for seeing your brother…" He stopped short and glared at her again before pacing the tent some more. "How am I to be sure that he is even your brother?" he asked, shaking his head as he stopped and looked up at her. The anger and hurt in his eyes stung deeply.

Breaking his gaze, Amore looked down. "What now?" she asked softly as she slowly looked up at him. Xerxes stared at her before turning sharply and walked out. She struggled to catch her breath as she squeezed her eyes shut hoping to block the tears. Sitting slowly on the bed, Amore closed her eyes and thought about the peace that had been in her heart. She had done the right thing, right? Opening her eyes once more, she refused to move from her spot before getting up to pace the tent. The camp fell to an eerie silence as night fell upon the valley. The air was crisp yet still warm. Fall would soon be upon them. Being so close to the sea, Avalon's weather year-round was mostly beautiful, while the nights could still get cold. Amore shivered as she sat at the edge of the bed. Her heart was heavy as she stared at her hands.

What did you think? They all would suddenly get along and be at peace with one another? The thoughts tormented her mind. She had not thought past simply making it to Antigua without her body giving out. Thankfully her adrenaline blocked out anything else. The quietness was eating at her. Why could not someone just come in? At least then she would know her own fate. The unknown was wearing her down as her adrenaline slowly subsided.

Shouts of exclamation filled the air as horses whinnied loudly. The night sky was filled with a brilliant orange and red glow. A blast of heat wafted through the tent walls. Stumbling to her feet, she reached for the tent's flap as everything around her slowed down. The feeling of a hand covering her mouth felt greatly out of place as she was pulled backward suddenly. It took her a moment before attempting to strike back as their grip tightened around her and her screams never left. *This is your fate.* The thought flashed through her mind. This is it. She had failed. How greatly she had failed. The thought of her life soon ending seemed to fuel her as she slammed her elbow into the attacker. Twisting out of his grip she kicked him in the knee as she scrambled toward the edge of the tent. A sickening feeling slammed over her head as she sank slowly to the ground. Her heart pounding, the world slowly blackened out and the man above her made her heart hurt greatly. A silver ring upon his hand was the only thing she could see.

CPSIA information can be obtained
at www.ICGtesting.com
Printed in the USA
FFOW01n1601211016
28687FF